EXIN EX MACHINA

ASTERION NOIR: BOOK 1

G. S. JENNSEN

HYPERNOVA
PUBLISHING
2018

EXIN EX MACHINA

Hypernova Publishing
P.O. Box 2214
Parker, Colorado 80134
www.hypernovapublishing.com

Publisher's Note: This is a work of fiction. Names, characters, places, and incidents are a product of the author's imagination. Locales and public names are sometimes used for atmospheric purposes. Any resemblance to actual people, living or dead, or to businesses, companies, events, institutions, or locales is completely coincidental.

The Hypernova Publishing name, colophon and logo are trademarks of Hypernova Publishing.

Ordering Information:
Hypernova Publishing books may be purchased for educational, business or sales promotional use. For details, contact the "Special Markets Department" at the address above.

Exin Ex Machina / G. S. Jennsen.—1st ed.

LCCN 2018946287
ISBN 978-1-7323977-1-2

For Alexis Mallory Solovy Marano,
daughter of Commandant and Commander Solovy,
first Prevo and goddamn savior of humanity thrice over

DRAMATIS PERSONAE

NOIR

Nika Tescarav

Perrin Benvenit

Joaquim Lacese

Parc Eshett

Cair Norton

Ryan Theroit

Ava Zobel

Maggie Zobel

Carson Faine

DIVISION ADVISORS/STAFF

Dashiel Ridani, *Industry Advisor*

Adlai Weiss, *Justice Advisor*

Gemina Kail, *Administration Advisor*

Maris Debray, *Culture Advisor*

Iona Rowan, *External Relations Advisor*

Spencer Nimoet, *Justice Officer*

Erik Rhom, *Justice Analyst*

OTHER CHARACTERS

Grant Mesahle

Vance Greshe

Roqe Ovet

Theo Jacoby

Xyche'ghael

GUIDES

Anavosa (*Mirai*)

Delacrai (*Kiyora*)

Luciene (*Synra*)

Selyshok (*Ebisu*)

Iovimer (*Namino*)

GALAXY MAP

GENNISI GALAXY
(MESSIER 94)

MIRAI

NAMINO

KIYORA

EBISU

TOKI'TAKU ✳
(TAIYOK HOMEWORLD)

SYNRA

✳ CHOSEK
(CHIZERU HOMEWORLD)

◆ ASTERION DOMINION AXIS WORLDS
◆ ASTERION DOMINION ADJUNCT WORLDS
✳ ALIEN WORLDS

ASTERION DOMINION
AXIS WORLDS

MIRAI   NAMINO   SYNRA   EBISU   KIYORA

View the Galaxy Map Online at <u>gsjennsen.com/ map-machina</u>

CONTENTS

EXIN EX MACHINA

WHOAMI

G eneration: kyr
Input desired designation: __

Raindrops splattered on the pebbled surface beneath her cheek. One, two, *three-four-five* they splashed, bounced and rebounded into her face.

Generation: kyr

Input desired designation: __

The input cursor flashed across her vision, blurring and wobbling to mix with the rain. What did it want from her? Who she was?

No. The blinking cursor told her she was no one. Nothing. It asked who she *intended to be*.

Generation: kyr. Cardinal. First. New. Tabula rasa.

She splayed trembling fingers upon the surface beneath her—a street. She recognized its nature because, without thinking about it, she knew many things. Words. Names for objects. How those objects worked. History...but not her own. Behind the blinking cursor a universe of knowledge waited, prepackaged, catalogued and ready to serve her. Everything in the world except who she was. Had been. Could be.

Her eyes rose to focus on the visual plane stretching out from her, centimeters above the street. Shimmering lights in the darkness. Shadows of buildings swallowed by deeper, darker shadows. From here to the indistinct horizon, raindrops splattering *plink-plink-plink*.

Who began life sprawled face-first on a street in a rainstorm in the middle of the night?

The answer returned as null. Some *before* had led to her awakening in this situation now. *Kyr* was a lie, for this was not the beginning. Something had preceded it to bring her to this moment. But when she sought an answer in her mind, she found only emptiness. A blank slate. Tabula rasa.

Generation: kyr

Input desired designation: __

Desired? She desired the name that went with *before*. She desired data to fill the emptiness—

Murmured voices flowed into the gaps between the splatter of the raindrops, accompanied by harsh *clack-clack-clacks*. A shadow loomed over her, and the rain stopped. She looked up.

A woman with long ginger hair, bright blueberry eyes and a freckled nose crouched beside her. Above the woman, a translucent leaf sheltered them both from the rain. "What's wrong? Do you need help?"

She forced her throat to move, followed by her tongue, then her lips. "I...."

The woman glanced past her to something in the distance. "Joaquim, get over here!"

A new shadow dimmed the darkness further and brought with it a deeper, gravelly voice. "She's functioning?"

Did her sorry state qualify as functioning? A nod from the woman proclaimed it did.

"Can you sit up?" The deep voice drew closer until it overpowered the rhythm of the rain. "We're going to scoot you back against the alley wall, okay?"

The *alley* wall? Had her sordid awakening not even merited a proper avenue as its setting?

Strong hands grasped her shoulders and lifted. She belatedly tried to help, but it made little difference. A second later a hard surface met her back, and she was sitting upright. Two visages hovered in front of her to study her in concern—one open and expressive, the other guarded and cautious.

She moved facial muscles that felt foreign, as though they'd been sloppily glued to the bones beneath them, into something like a smile. "Thank you."

"Of course." The woman continued to scrutinize her. "Are you hurt? Do you need repairs?"

Carefully she shook her head, relieved when it didn't tumble off its perch. "No, I'm not damaged. I'm ky—"

"Kyr. Yeah, we figured that part out." The man's mouth rose on one side as if amused, yet the rest of his expression insisted it didn't *do* amusement. "Bit of a rough transition, eh?"

"A rough transition is forgetting where you're supposed to sleep for the first few days. Something went wrong with her." The woman flashed her an apologetic smile buoyant enough to bring color and verve to the washed-out world. "Sorry. I'm sure you'll be fine. Do you want to come with us? We can offer you a roof, a shower and something to eat, if not much else."

The faint traces of levity vanished from the man's face. "I don't—"

"Shush, Jo. She's in no condition to be a threat to us." The woman's warm, comforting smile returned. "Please, come with us."

She nodded mutely. Notions such as showers and food sounded luxurious beyond imagination, not to mention mere *dryness*. All this blank slate had known of life thus far was the hypnotic but terribly wet splatter of rain.

"Let's get you up. It's not far." The man took one of her arms, and she climbed to her feet mostly under her own power. Sloppily glued into place or not, her muscles seemed to recognize their function. It was a start.

The woman touched her shoulder in encouragement, or perhaps to provide a steadying hand. "I'm Perrin. This is my friend, Joaquim. What are you going to call yourself? Do you know?"

Know? What did she know? She knew emptiness. A void where there should be data. Wherever her eyes looked, the cursor followed with its incessant wobbly blurred blinking. Taunting her, judging her. *Who are you? Who do you intend to be?*

Generation: kyr

Input desired designation: __

Her lips moved of their own accord, acting at the behest of something beyond her conscious perception.

"Nika. You can call me Nika."

BOOT
SEQUENCE

1

PLANET: MIRAI
ASTERION DOMINION
GENNISI GALAXY

"*C*lear through to the 5th level, second hallway."
"*Team 1, move ahead.*"
"*Team 3 in position.*"
"*Team 3, hold there until I give the signal.*"
When Team 1 reached the final hallway separating them from their destination, Nika signaled a halt.

$$Hq \ (visual) \ | \ scan.thermal(240°:60°)$$
$$T \rightarrow Hr(\alpha) = 342°$$
$$T \rightarrow Hr(\beta) = 9°$$

The building's security force had consisted solely of dynes and drones up until now, but two semi-flesh and semi-blood guards stood watch over the data vault itself.

Nika (Team 1): "Two heat signatures on either side of the door."
Ava: (Team 1) "Permission to take them out?"
Nika (Team 1): "Negative. Lock your targets but hold position here. I've got this."

She crept forward one silent step at a time, and her kamero filter rippled and shifted to match the visuals of her changing surroundings.

Nika: "Team 2, status?"
Perrin: "Team 2 ran into a very rude security dyne."
Nika: "Which resulted in Team 2's status being...?"

When she was three meters away from her targets, blades extended out from the inside of each of Nika's wrists. The guards stared forward, seeing nothing as they shuffled their weight from foot to foot in boredom. She timed the rhythm of their natural movements and fell into sync with it as she reached the closed door between them.

Perrin: "We're fine. Ryan spiked it, and it's now our new best friend. In position in fifteen seconds."

Nika: "Tell Ryan he can't bring it home. He exceeded his pet limit two pets ago."

She rose onto the balls of her feet and spun in a half circle, thrust her arms out so they extended behind the guards, and plunged the blades into the bases of their necks. The metal pierced each of their port openings and speared the cores of their neuromorphic brains.

The guards crumpled to the floor as one. Instant neurological shutdown. Far more controlled and less messy than letting Ava shoot them.

Perrin: "He says—"
Nika: "No more pets."

She watched the bodies for two seconds to make certain they were out of commission, then wiped the brain matter residue off the metal before retracting the blades. Odds were the guards' employment contracts with Dominion Transit included replacement bodies and free regens for line-of-duty expirations, though the paperwork might take a while.

Nika: "Team 1 beginning vault infiltration."

She retrieved a thin roll of flexmat from the pouch on her belt and applied it in an X pattern across the door while the rest of her team cleared the hall and joined her outside the data vault.

Perrin: "Team 2 in position."
Nika: "Team 2, hold your position until I give the signal."

She pressed her fingertips against each edge of the neat X to confirm the seals. "Parc, mirror me."

Parc Eshett stepped up beside her, though his presence there revealed itself only through the flow of data exchanged between them. She pressed her index fingers to the top and bottom right corners of the X; he did the same on the left side. "Activate."

A calibrated series of electrical signals flowed from their fingertips into the flexmat at each corner and began transforming the door's chemical composition molecule by molecule.

"And back, everyone." She stepped away from the door as, from the corners in, the metal crumbled and its remnants drifted aimlessly to the floor. In seconds nothing but a pile of chromatic dust lay on the floor, and the entrance was open.

Nika: "Team 1 moving into the vault."

She pulsed the room to mark the layout and electrical junction points and shared the results with the other team members through the operation's nex node. Next, she placed a shell on the floor beneath the center of the door frame and triggered it. From the perspective of the hallway, a projected replica of the former door and the two meters surrounding it now filled the space, concealing both their presence inside and the bodies' presence outside from any person or dyne that wandered into the vicinity of the vault.

"Ava and Carson, place your charges. Parc, go to town."

"Finally!" He rushed up to the hardware block that dominated the room and instantly became a flurry of motion and flashing augments. Specialized tools appeared and vanished from his hands so rapidly they might be mistaken for body mods. She didn't think they were, but where Parc was concerned you could never be certain.

Nika's gaze swept across the room and her team. They all carried out their assigned tasks with focused, honed efficiency, and she couldn't ask them to work any faster. The reality of the open doorway made her feel exposed, though, as the false projection only protected them so long as the illusion wasn't tested by security. *"Team 2, Team 3, status?"*

Joaquim: "Team 3 check."

Nika: "Team 2?"

Perrin: "Maggie wants to know if she can take the dyne home as a pet, since Ryan's exceeded his limit."

Nika: "She'll simply give it to Ryan the instant I go upstairs. No. More. Pets."

Perrin: "But—"

Joaquim: "Perrin, get your people in line. This isn't playtime."

Perrin: "Mind your own team."

Joaquim: "I'm Operations Director, which means I'll mind every team. Shape up."

Parc looked over at her. "We're all set here. Just give the word."

Nika: "Enough. Stand by for my signal."

She moved up beside Parc, tapped into the vault with her fingertip and scanned his work. Not that she didn't trust it; he ran figure eights around her diverges in his sleep. As usual, the subtlety and finesse of his painstaking alterations radiated digital brilliance, so she disconnected and stepped back. "Ava, Carson?"

"Charges are armed and ready."

"Same."

"Start your timers…and we are out of here." She gestured toward the doorway to emphasize the point but waited until everyone had cleared it to exit herself, stopping to retrieve the shell on the way out. Once in the hallway, she slid her Glaser out of its sheath and pointed it at the wall above the empty door frame and the bodies.

The Glaser was a flexible device with many uses, both as a tool and as a weapon. When its energy output was targeted in a fine, precision stream, one of its capabilities involved etching markings into virtually any material. The laser it emitted followed the flow of her hand's graceful, sweeping motions, and in its wake the engraving burned brightly against the muted pewter of the wall.

Nika smiled.

Inside the data vault, the timers hit zero and the charges detonated, sending sparks flying and smoke hissing into the hallway to temporarily obscure her handiwork. *"Teams 2 and 3, you are a go. Execute and exit along your designated routes. Reconvene at The Chalet."*

The walls shuddered as more substantial physical explosions detonated elsewhere in the building.

She pivoted to her team, who had taken up defensive positions behind her, and confirmed their kamero filters were active. "Security will be moving in now, but let's try to get out of here without being noticed."

They reached the lift free of incident, and it soon deposited them on the ground floor.

Two security dynes waited in the entrance atrium of the building, however, denying her the pleasure of escaping unnoticed. Alas.

Ava's right arm extended toward each of them in turn. Streaks of electricity jumped from her hand and through the air to fry their circuitry before anyone else even began to respond. Ava had long ago integrated the Glaser technology into her right arm augments, and she took great pride in displaying her literal 'walking weapon' status.

Carson grumbled as the dynes sputtered and died on the floor. "You never let anyone else have any fun, Ava."

"If you want to get in on this kind of fun, learn to move faster. They make augments to speed up your reflexes, you know."

Parc laughed. "Be thankful she handled them, Carson. She turns into such a bitch when she hasn't shot anything recently."

"How can you tell the difference?"

Nika cringed. "Ava, don't take Carson out, now or later. Or Parc. Everyone stay focused. We're not out of here yet."

She scanned the entrance for additional threats while praying for patience. The line between friendly joshing and less-friendly squabbling was a thin and ever-shifting one, and Joaquim and Perrin's crossing of it earlier had heightened her sensitivity to its lurking presence.

"All right, let's move. The extraction route should be clear for the next twelve seconds. Let's make that window."

She moved to the lobby's side door and entered the security override passcode she'd acquired on their way in. The door slid open, and she again motioned the others through.

"Halt!"

She spun to find an Asterion guard rushing through the lobby from the far side, Glaser raised.

Nika (Team 1): "Retreat."

Ava (Team 1): "But—"

Nika (Team 1): "Retreat."

Her hand went to her utility belt as the guard fired on her, sending an energy pulse to sizzle across her shielding. She unlatched a grenade and tossed it into the lobby. It sailed through the air for two seconds, then exploded above the guard's head with enough force to electrify the entire room.

She twisted around and dove through the open door for the grass outside; the balls of her feet parted ways with the lobby flooring an instant before the cascading electrical charge spread to the doorway, and she landed in a combat roll beyond its reach.

The next second she was back on her feet, Glaser pointed at the doorway—but the guard lay on the lobby floor jerking like a marionette from the electricity still coursing through his body.

Ava appeared at her side wearing a scowl. "Now who's showing off?"

Nika shrugged and re-holstered the Glaser. "Me. Let's go."

They wound around the facade to the rear of the building, where they met up with Parc and Carson. On reaching the promenade separating the Dominion Transit Headquarters from the city streets, they spread out to cross the open and exposed space. As they neared the far side, their kamero filters gradually faded, and they blended into the pedestrian traffic.

ᴧʀ

Nika paused in the entryway to take in the flurry of activity spreading across The Floor in the aftermath of the operation. Though chaotic at a first, uninformed glance, over time she'd learned to discern the flow beneath the chaos. Now she sensed the concentric circles of data and thoughts put into action as they rippled out from clusters that had drawn adherents. Occupying the negative space in between were quiet spheres carved out and cordoned off from all the activity.

She'd arrived back home—'The Chalet,' as it had been affectionately dubbed—well after everyone else, having opted to stalk the streets along the various exit routes to ensure the others made it back safely. Only when Perrin confirmed everyone's return had she headed to the #3 door and returned home herself.

Five separate d-gate entrances to The Chalet lay scattered around Mirai One, each one disguised as innocuous architecture—windows, artwork, ordinary doors and unadorned walls. They each required a special passcode to activate, and providing those passcodes to an individual was the last and most momentous step in their initiation into the group. All the d-gates led to an entry anteroom in the interior of The Chalet, which had no obvious external, physical door of its own.

Only three people knew where on Mirai the building was located: herself, Perrin and Joaquim. In a yet further security measure, the entire building was warded by a signal interference field. While inside its walls, a person could not pinpoint their own geographic location, and neither could someone on the outside.

Because living in a tomb wasn't healthy for anyone, there were windows, but they displayed idyllic visuals rather than the actual outdoors. The precautions were drastic, but they protected every person here, not to mention the group as a whole.

Nika walked The Floor as soon as she arrived, before putting up her gear or showering. It was important for her to check in on those who had taken part in tonight's operation, but also, arguably even more so, those who had not. It was important for them to see her—sweaty, messy, sometimes bleeding, but above all working, and working for them—and for them to know that she saw them as well.

She spoke to several people on her way to the alcove in the far left corner of the expansive room, where Ryan lounged at one of their two repair benches. Together with the advanced rehabilitation tank upstairs, the equipment ensured that most physical damage short of decapitation or catastrophic electrical overload was not permanent.

Two modular appendages swept around Ryan's left arm, patching up a nasty cut above his elbow, and she arched an eyebrow as she approached. "If I had realized you spilled blood to win over the security dyne, I might have let you keep it after all."

Ryan winced as a clamp pinched the treated skin together and held it tight. "Shit, really?"

She laughed. "No. If we have any more pets buzzing and skittering around in here, we'll have to start calling it a zoo."

He reached down with his other arm and stroked a canary yellow spiderbot circling his feet. "I know. But the dyne wanted a more fulfilling life."

"Did it tell you this?"

"Not in so many words, but I saw the longing in its code."

"Perhaps after meeting you, it will find a new path to follow on its own. Good job tonight. Turning the dyne kept your teammates safe and kept it from calling the cavalry down on us."

The clamp released its grip, and another mechanical arm swept in to paint on a top layer of sensory nanofiber. When it had finished its work, Ryan peered down at the seamless, healthy skin left behind. "Thanks for taking me. It was fun, if occasionally painful."

"I think you just summed up our lives here." She patted him on the shoulder and left him to wrap up the repair sequence.

Next to one of the structural pillars, Ava sat cross-legged beside Maggie. Ava had opened up the pseudo-skin covering of her weaponized forearm and was showing Maggie something among its inner workings, but Maggie's confused-yet-skeptical expression provided no clues as to what it might be.

Ava and Maggie were siblings—co-equal up-gens from the same psyche. Together they served as walking proof of how much a single up-gen could change a person...and all the ways it didn't.

Nika offered them a supportive nod, mostly grateful Ava wasn't currently beating up her teammates. She continued on toward where Parc sat at the center of his own personal command center, which he had built smack in the middle of The Floor. Anyone was free to wander through it and touch the exterior of the equipment, but he protected the access passcodes with the fervor of Charon guarding Hades.

He couldn't have been back and working for longer than ten minutes, and he'd already attracted an audience.

Nika didn't push her way through the crowd to reach him, instead leaning against a pillar on the periphery to watch the show.

"So then, what I did was I set loose this smart worm I wrote into the Dominion Transit database. Wiping the database would've been easy, but selectively altering and scrambling existing data while inserting new data? This required a higher and more refined level of skill."

One of the newer people, a tall guy with auburn hair named Cair, leaned in toward Parc. "But the manipulations will leave traces. Even if the traces don't expose the details of what you did, they'll announce which data points you diverged."

Parc not-so-subtly nudged Cair out of his personal space. "You're cute. See, the worm touched *every* piece of data, leaving behind an identical trace whether it altered the information or not. There's not a person or algorithm running that'll be able to spot the difference between altered and unaltered entries." He grinned over his shoulder in her direction. "Right, Nika?"

She wondered how long he'd known she was in his orbit. "You're the expert on data worms, not me. I bow before your genius."

"Oh?" He considered her with new interest. "I don't suppose you could? Bow, I mean. It would bring a huge increase in my cred around here."

Those closest to Parc scooted back to clear the way so she could step into the inner circle of his command center. She dropped a hand on the top of his chair, then shifted to face the onlookers. "What do you all think? Does Parc deserve the knee?"

A chorus of boos and grumbles answered, along with a few whistles and some color commentary.

"He's good, but not *that* good."

"An ego boost is the last thing the prick needs."

"He'll be insufferable—oh, wait."

She chuckled and turned back to give Parc an exaggerated shrug. "Sorry, but I have to respect the will of the people." She leaned over the top of his chair and made a show of inspecting the plethora of code spilling across multiple display panes. "Maybe one day."

"Yeah, yeah." He sounded exasperated, but his expression remained one of amusement. "I sent my operation report to Joaquim an entire six minutes ago."

"I wasn't checking up on you, but thank you for putting work before play. I'll let you get back to showing off for your adoring fans."

She left the command center and eased into the crowd reforming around him. By the time she reached a bubble of empty space, Parc was full into another demonstration of his coding savvy.

As she turned to head upstairs, activity near the Board caught her eye.

The Board kept a running record of the missing and the lost—individuals who had done something once thought impossible in Asterion society: vanish. Some fell victim to Justice, were sent off to prison to serve their sentence and never returned. Others signed up to work at one of the outposts on the wild frontier of the exploratory worlds—and never returned. A few had simply been living their lives one day, and the next day were gone.

Most of the names belonged to friends, co-workers or loved ones of the people here. The troubling implication of this was that the true number of missing people could be exponentially higher.

Cair had slipped away from Parc's demonstration after getting snubbed, and now he paced in front of the Board. A hand repetitively came up to his chin then dropped to his side while his lips enunciated silent words.

She sighed and went over to check on him. "Do you see something here that bothers you? Do you need to add a name?"

"Damien Soljitsen and Monique Palade shared a former employer. Monique and Francis Quelle lived three blocks apart. Francis and—"

She carefully placed a hand on his arm, but he still jumped in surprise.

"Sorry. Listen, we've run the names through dozens of algorithms looking for connections. There aren't any. The surface-level similarities you've identified don't lead to anything concrete." She glanced at the Board and the subtle glow of the names on it. "I wish they did. If we could discover what links the disappearances, we could figure out why they happened and stop it from happening again. Maybe even find the people who are lost."

Cair nodded distractedly. "I'll work on a new algorithm."

2

Nika settled onto one of the two couches in her room, next to Perrin and opposite Joaquim. She draped her shower-damp hair behind her shoulders and poured herself a drink from the pitcher on the table. "What's it look like?"

Joaquim instantiated a data sphere between them. "We were successful in accessing and corrupting the primary Dominion Transit passenger database. By altering or deleting sixteen percent of the existing records, we obscured the insertion of twelve new simmed identities. We should be able to use them, paired with their morphs, for a minimum of four months before they stale."

"This will make travel so much easier, as well as safer."

"Which was the idea." Perrin didn't sound enthused, however. "I do wonder, though—would it have been better to do this on the sly rather than announce our presence with explosions and artwork? Now they know their database has been corrupted."

Joaquim snorted. "As well they should. We need to be in every institution's face, and thus in the Guides' faces by proxy. They need to know we can get on the inside. They need to know their precious data troves aren't so infallible."

Joaquim's passion for the cause was both his best and his worst trait. Nika leaned forward and propped her elbows on her knees. "You're both right. Yes, Perrin, it would've been more prudent to stay under the radar, and it might have bought us an extra month or two of breathing room. But we're never going to change laws without changing minds first. We have to be publicly disruptive. We have to act as a beacon others can see and believe in."

"That's what I meant."

She shot Joaquim a quick smile. "I know. The point is, we're always walking a tightrope between ensuring our safety and pushing the cause forward. Tonight, we successfully furthered both interests...or that's my hope."

Perrin clinked her glass against Nika's then leaned across the table to do the same to Joaquim's, apparently accepting Nika's defense of their strategy. "We're all back safe and sound, and we got what we needed. Looks like a win to me." She brought her glass to her lips, but paused it there. "Did it look like a win on The Floor? I was too busy confirming everyone was accounted for and any damage got taken care of to get a good sense of the mood."

"I'm relieved to report that spirits are actually high, for the moment. Parc's spreading tales of his gallant heroics as we speak, and the newer people are lapping it up. Some of the veterans, too, even if they're pretending not to be impressed."

Perrin rolled her eyes dramatically. "I'd chastise him for showing off, but it's all true."

"It is. He deserves the accolades." Nika took a long sip of her drink. "You said the new guy, Cair, showed a penchant for derive-and-diverge work, right?"

"Yep. He's crazy talented—just standoffish and shy."

"If you can, try to get him working on some experimental routines we can slot for use in future operations. He's interested in the Board, but I worry obsessing over it will just lead to more frustration on his part. We need to give him something real to do, something he can take pride in, because right now Parc is running all over him. If he produces good results, hopefully it will diffuse any burgeoning friction between them."

Perrin nodded as she refilled her glass from the pitcher on the table. "Will do. There's no shortage of work. Ever."

"Thanks." Nika crossed her legs and considered each of them in turn. "So, do we need to talk about what happened tonight?"

Joaquim spun the data sphere, pretending to study its contents. "We do not."

Perrin's nose wrinkled up. "Talk about what? I thought we decided the operation went really well."

"It did. I'm referring to the brief but highly public bickering between the two of you."

"Oh…it was fine."

Nika glared at the ceiling. "Am I really the only one here who thinks it *wasn't* fine?" She returned her attention to the pair and found two averted gazes waiting on her. "Well, this time you're both *wrong*."

"Her squad was acting like it was on a play date instead of an operation."

"It was an easy operation—"

Nika set her glass on the table with a firm *thud*. "We aren't going to rehash the argument now. Perrin, it was only easy because nothing went wrong. Operations are dangerous, and the wrong slip-up means R&R for anyone caught. Given the stakes, a little more discipline is probably called for."

Perrin sank deeper into the couch cushions. "I get it, but I hate to dampen their enthusiasm."

"Their enthusiasm will get them retired if you don't start making your team be more careful."

"Jo, you're not being fair—"

Nika was of the personal opinion that if the two of them would just sleep together, they could perhaps get all this angst out of their system. Perrin insisted they never had and likely never would—something about friendship being a stronger bond—but they had been at this for as long as she'd known them....

She didn't offer it up as a suggestion, but she did wave a hand in Perrin's direction to cut her off. "Joaquim, it was a minor quibble, and it didn't need to be handled on the main operation channel. If you felt strongly that the issue needed to be dealt with immediately, you should have pinged Perrin."

He shrugged. "What's the difference?"

"The difference is, by making a gentle suggestion in a private ping, you help her to become a better combat leader. By instead scolding her on the operation channel, you devalue her authority in front of her team—and you set an example for the others. A bad one. I almost had to pull Ava off Carson tonight because you made it okay to snap at your teammates."

"That…wasn't my intent. Perrin, I only wanted you to take the operation seriously. I want everyone to take operations seriously."

"I do, Jo. This is my life as much as it's yours, remember?"

"Of course I—" He pinched the bridge of his nose and stood. "I realize it is. Fine, I'll try to work on my discretion. If we're done, I think I need some depri time."

Nika eyed him for a second. "We're done. We can decide on the ID distribution protocols later."

He nodded vaguely and disappeared out the door.

She studied the door after his departure. "He seems more ornery than usual tonight. Is he tweaking around with his processes?"

"I don't think so. This afternoon he found out his best friend from a prior gen got arrested for assault. With the new, tougher penalties, a conviction will mean a decade at Zaidam Bastille."

Nika frowned. "Does he want us to look into it? See if we can help his friend somehow?"

"No. I asked, but he said he's not comfortable barging into a former friend's business, not when he doesn't know much about who the guy could be now. People change when they up-gen, and sometimes they change a lot. That's why we do it."

Nika directed the continuing frown at her glass. Unlike everyone else here, she hadn't existed in a cognizable form for long enough to watch people she knew up-gen and change overnight. "Is it?"

"Yeah. We don't want our processes to grow stale, our personalities jaded or, worse, our minds mad."

"I understand the philosophical justifications behind up-genning. It's just…why is it *mandated*? And why a minimum of every three hundred years? Did scientific analysis produce this length of time as the outer safe limit, or was it picked because it's a round number? And why are the Guides exempt?"

"You want me to spout the party line? I can do that." Perrin took a deep breath and struck a dramatic pose. "The Guides must retain the wisdom of the ages to perform their functions optimally and chart our course and the Dominion's future through a dangerous cosmos. Their processes are constantly evolving as a consequence of their work, so they don't need to up-gen to avoid stagnation."

"Why can't we do the same? Aren't we always evolving, too? Always learning, adjusting and refining ourselves?" Nika sighed, recognizing she had just exposed her generational immaturity—but it wasn't like Perrin didn't know.

"I'm not sure of the point I'm trying to make. I hear about Joaquim's friend and…it sounds as though he got stiffed with a bad up-gen, and maybe he shouldn't have been forced into it. It's another rule sitting atop a massive pile of rules, and it's a uniquely invasive one. For a supposedly free society of independent minds, we have a shit-ton of rules, and it feels like people long since stopped questioning their purpose or necessity."

Perrin arched an eyebrow. "Welcome to the rebellion?"

"I get it. I'm not saying anything that everyone here doesn't fervently believe." She glanced back at the door. "Are you two going to be okay?"

"We already are. I knew he was upset about his friend, and I don't mind that he called me out."

"You're too forgiving of him. And even if you don't mind, the people serving under you do. On an operation, your team has to trust you completely, and to do so they need to believe that your peers and superiors have faith in your abilities. He undermined your authority in front of them, and it risks undermining your team's confidence in you."

"This is why you're in charge—you think like a leader. I'm too worried about fostering peace and harmony and making sure nobody's feelings get hurt."

Nika laughed kindly. "This is why we love you, and also why you run The Chalet. Not many people could get over a hundred recalcitrants and dropouts to play nice with one another in an enclosed and increasingly crowded space."

Perrin made a face. "It's not easy. Yeoman's work, really. As I think on it now, I believe I deserve a raise."

Nika nudged the pitcher of wine toward her. "You can finish off the expensive syrah."

"Oh, so tempting, because it's delish. But I'm dragging here. I need rest. Skipping depri and heading straight for a full sleep cycle. Combat operations still wear me down, and I've got two new potentials to screen tomorrow."

"Go. Rest and recharge. You've earned it."

Alone in her room at last, Nika contemplated the window projection for a moment, where a full moon cast ripples of silvery light upon steel-gray waters lapping at a ghostly white beach. She smiled at the peaceful but fake scene as she stripped to her underwear and wound her hair into a twist atop her head.

She hadn't set out to lead a rebellion. The first three months after Perrin and Joaquim found her in that alley and took her in, she spent figuring out how to be alive. How to be a real person in a world where everyone but her had hundreds or even thousands of years and dozens of generations' worth of experiences enriching their sense of place in that world.

But everyone at The Chalet had been open and welcoming toward her, though it was a much smaller group back then. It hadn't been difficult to empathize with their grievances against the government—an act made far easier by the fact that, given her circumstances, she was not predisposed to trust the system. Or much of anyone, save those who had cared for her when she'd been lost and desperate for the most tenuous lifeline.

Somewhere hidden behind the labyrinthine system of government rules and records and policies hid the answer to who she'd been *before*, and why she'd woken up a blank canvas in a rain-soaked alley with no memory and no past. If she could tear the system down, maybe she could find that answer in the rubble.

After those first months, she'd started stepping up and getting involved. The group had an excess of passion but no direction; they were little more than a collection of disaffected people angry at their overlords but with no idea what to do about it.

It had turned out Perrin was right—in time she found she was a natural leader. Without meaning to, she gradually took on mentoring roles, then planning and organizational ones—choosing targets and honing their disparate grievances against the government into a coherent strategy to effect change. Joaquim and Perrin started coming to her to resolve disputes, then to make decisions.

Both of them were talented in their strengths, but their frequent disagreements meant the two of them combined did not add up to one true leader. They both realized it, too, because they'd openly admitted as much when they'd come to her and asked her to officially take charge of the group.

It had felt right…like the inevitable first destination of the natural course of her new life. She might not know who she had been, but she'd come to know who she was *now*, and the idea of leading the fight for others to live freely and be their truest selves excited her.

In the year and a half since then, their core size had tripled; they'd formalized an extensive web of allies, acquired more and better equipment and extended their capabilities in almost every way. She was proud of the fact that under her guidance they had transformed from sporadic troublemakers into a force worthy of being called a rebellion.

But though she embraced this life and her adopted place in it, she never forgot how it began. She never put away the mystery of what came *before*.

In the mirror on the wall behind her, the soft glow of the tattoo spanning her upper back glimmered. Stars, in the shape of a winged creature—a phoenix, possibly, or some more base bird of prey. It resembled a constellation, but no such constellation was visible from any of the Axis Worlds. It called to her soul when she studied it, but she could not decipher its elusive whispers.

What did it represent? Maybe nothing beyond whimsical body art. Maybe something critically important, if only to her.

She unlocked the false panel in the left wall and stepped inside the small chamber that had once been a closet, then closed and locked the panel behind her. After activating the equipment, she lay down on the chaise and adjusted her position until the interface port pressed flush against the base of her neck. It locked into place, and she activated the connection.

$Hq(root) / n0 \rightarrow \mathscr{E}$

$\delta \{ Hq(root) / \beta \}$

init sysdir

init sysproc

init storeproc

init portnex

$< Hq(root) \rightarrow \Omega$

handshaking

$< \Sigma \rightarrow \beta$

checksum:

$< \beta\theta\alpha\alpha \ \beta\alpha \ \theta\alpha\theta \ \alpha\theta \ \beta\beta\theta\theta \ \alpha\beta\alpha\alpha \ \alpha\beta\beta\alpha \ \alpha\theta\beta\theta\beta \ \theta\alpha\beta\alpha \ \beta\alpha\alpha \ \beta\beta\beta\beta \ \alpha\theta$
$\beta\alpha\alpha$

$checksum \rightarrow T$

kernel signature:

$< \mathcal{N}\alpha\theta\theta\Xi\beta\forall\Psi\beta A\Omega$

$kernel \ signature \rightarrow T$

handshake complete

init storerec

$Hq(storerec\text{*}) / n0 \rightarrow \mathscr{E}$

$<$

The process of copying the memories of the day into her personal data store began.

Once recorded, they would propagate through a secure nex pathway to two additional physical data stores hidden in safe locations. Once a week, all three stores pinged her—not her current persona, but the kernel operating beneath it—with their location and status.

The system worked to ensure that no matter what ill fortune befell her in the future, she would not be erased a second time. Not for long.

She closed her eyes.

My persona on Y12,463.102 A7 is Nika Tescarav-kyr.

I have lived other personas, but I cannot say what they were.

I will live other personas in the future. I cannot say what they will be, but I can say this: they will always be me.

I will never lose myself again.

3

D ashiel Ridani was going to be late.

Whether on account of the Justice-erected force field ringing the Dominion Transit HQ promenade or the throng of spectators ringing the force field, the outcome looked to be the same—he was going to be late. And he did despise being late. Reputations crafted over the course of centuries had crumbled into dust for lesser offenses, and his already hung from a cliff by an unraveling thread.

Of course, he could have remembered to run his alcohol mitigation routines last night, or early this morning, or whenever it was that he'd finally succumbed to a poor form of sleep. Then, instead of waking a wreck of stubbed functions and bad pointers and having to load a far harsher flushing routine, he might have been able to leave home early enough to allow for delays.

Flushing routines were a son of a bitch. His veins still burned from the caustic, unforgiving abuse this one had inflicted. But it had gotten him up, moving and now, here.

Hq (visual) / scan.physical(270°:90°, 5 seconds)
T → gridpoint (27.4,14.3).optimalRoute

The routine had scanned the crowd arrayed between him and his destination, measured its ebb and flow and identified the quickest course through it. He plunged in.

The virtual path he followed sent him on several counter-intuitive veers, but a couple of annoying-but-benign jostles later he arrived at the force field and the Justice checkpoint accompanying it.

The security dyne stationed at the checkpoint relayed its preprogrammed speech in a monotone loop. "Access is restricted to assigned Justice personnel and preapproved Dominion Transit employees—"

"Advisor Dashiel Ridani, Industry Division, requesting entry clearance." He placed all five fingertips of his left hand on the floating pane beside the dyne.

"Identity signature confirmed. Entry granted, Advisor."

He slipped through the opening that materialized in the force field and adopted a rapid but controlled stride a notch below a jog across the promenade.

The moderate pace gave him an opportunity to casually inspect the facade of the Dominion Transit HQ building as he approached. It looked rather the worse for wear, sporting blown-out glass across three floors and collapsed trusses on two corners. The widespread damage meant it was unlikely to be business as usual inside, which in turn meant his borderline lateness might go unnoticed by anyone who mattered.

His suspicions were confirmed when he reached the lobby and the waiting reception attendant. "The directors convey their apologies, Advisor Ridani, but their morning schedule has been unavoidably disrupted. They expect to be meeting with Justice officers for the next twenty-three to thirty-one minutes. Do you wish to reschedule or wait?"

He considered the scattered debris littering the lobby floor, the scorch marks on the walls *and* the floor, as well as the significant Justice presence on the scene, and he found he was...curious. "I'll wait. Ping me when they're available."

"Yes, Advisor. Our lounge is down the hall—"

"Thank you, but I'll be upstairs."

ᐱᖇ

The graffiti demanded Dashiel's attention the instant he stepped off the lift on the fifth floor. Etched into the wall above a wrecked room he thought had been the data vault was a single word:

N O I R

The rippling, iridescent white glow of the letters created an entrancing effect, and he found himself standing there in the hallway contemplating the dramatic flow of the script.

"Quite a calling card, isn't it?"

Dashiel mentally retreated from his reverie and looked to his left, where the comment had originated. Adlai Weiss, a Justice Advisor, stood beside him scowling with far less admiration at the graffiti.

"It does make an impression. I appreciate the irony, if not the vandalism."

Adlai frowned. "The irony?"

"'NOIR' in blazing white."

"Ah, yes. I believe we are expected to take from it that they are shining a light into the darkness, or something to that effect. But an arguably honorable motive never stopped a crime from being a crime."

Dashiel nodded sagely. "Indeed. Your case?"

"For a year and counting now, though I question for how much longer. The Guides' displeasure with the terrorists is growing. They want results, and I'm not delivering."

"Maybe this will be the incident that breaks the case wide open."

"I would welcome the break, but I'm doubtful it will happen." Adlai eyed him curiously. "You're looking a bit worn. Rough night?"

"Fabulous night—I think. Rough morning."

"Dashiel, at this rate you're going to wear that body out in record time."

"So? There are more where it came from."

"True enough." Adlai motioned down the hall. "Have a few minutes? Want to see the carnage?"

"Absolutely." He fell in beside Weiss.

"What brings you here this morning? Morbid curiosity?"

"If it was, you know I'd never admit it. I was scheduled to meet with the Dominion Transit Executive Board at 0800 local to negotiate terms for a hardware contract renewal."

"Ah. My officers have them occupied for the moment."

"So I've been told." They arrived at the gaping, jagged hole beneath the graffiti. Two blood stains marked the floor on either side, though the bodies they must have belonged to had already been carted off. Inside, swarmbots scanned and recorded every centimeter of the room while two Justice officers were plugged into the main server surveying the damage.

Dashiel took in the particulars of the scene with a quick glance. "Data breach?"

"One can only assume. What data corruption NOIR may or may not have introduced into Dominion Transit's records is still to be determined, but we should understand the nature of the invasion by tonight."

Dashiel chuckled under his breath. "Good speech. Well delivered."

"Think the Guides will buy it?"

"They have little choice in the matter. Your humility is admirable, but the truth is they can't replace you. Any alternative candidate is far inferior to your experience and skill."

Adlai briefly smiled. "I appreciate the vote of confidence. The reality, though? NOIR has demonstrated a knack for covering the tracks that cover their tracks. I have zero personal doubt that they did *something* to the data stored in the vault, and an excess of personal doubt that we'll ever discover what it was."

"I would assume the purpose of the intrusion was to scramble either the ID files or the historical transit records, or both. It fits with their ethos—they don't believe individuals should be tracked by the government, so they'd be naturally inclined to destroy the tracking data stored here."

"True, but my gut tells me this hit was designed to ensure *they* could transit without being identified or tracked."

"Oh." Dashiel thought on it briefly. "But if that were the case, shouldn't they have been more discreet about it?"

"And this is why you're a businessman and not an investigator, my friend. All this?" Adlai waved his hand at the destroyed vault, then leaned back and pointed up to the graffiti. "This is a message to me, and through me to the Guides. It says they know we can't get to them. It says they're not afraid of us."

His internal comm pinged. *The directors will see you in two minutes.*

He clapped Adlai on the shoulder. "I'm confident you'll expose their folly and prove them wrong. Now, if you'll excuse me, duty calls."

ᛣ

Charts, graphs and endless reams of data encompassed Dashiel's perception within his focus sphere. Color-coded by classification, stylized by product pipeline and sized by percentage of revenue, the collective data represented hundreds of base materials and components feeding into dozens of product fabrication lines at eighteen factories spread across every Axis World and four Adjunct planets.

Thanks to the unfortunate damage suffered at Dominion Transit HQ, the contract negotiations this morning had resulted in a more beneficial arrangement than he'd expected to receive. In addition to their regular and ordinary component needs, the company now required not merely replacement parts but more advanced, more secure replacement parts for their data vault and conduit hubs, as well as the lines connecting them.

Dashiel was happy to provide these, and for thoroughly reasonable compensation. It was a rare win amid too many losses.

He increased capital investment funds designated for the data suspension module product, then diverted an additional four percent of refined kyoseil to their manufacture…then decreased the increase to three percent.

There was never, would and could never be enough kyoseil. It formed the underpinnings of all data storage and transmission technology. More vitally, it formed the underpinnings of their own data storage and transmission, and thus of their existence. It wound in fibrous tendrils through his nerve centers and saturated his neuromorphic brain, as it did for every Asterion.

They'd been damn lucky to find a planet, Chosek, run through with kyoseil, and upon finding it they had done whatever it took to develop and maintain amicable relations with the native Chizeru. But no matter how many Chizeru they hired to mine the precious mineral from the interior of their homeworld, demand outstripped supply. The exploration wing of the Administration Division constantly searched the stars for additional sources, but in centuries none but a few scattered asteroids had been located and swiftly drained dry.

Between twelve and fifteen percent of mined kyoseil was earmarked for Ridani Enterprises production lines. If allowed a greater portion, he could envision uses for forty or fifty percent of the aggregate supply. Until such a windfall occurred, however, he engaged in a constant balancing act of allocating, shifting and stretching his supply across his factories to optimize and prioritize its use at any given time—

A line of data flared red in his peripheral vision, and he instantly focused in on it.

Simul/Interact Boost Limb Augment Model Vk 3.2
- Contractual Delivery Obligations: 22,000/quarter
- Units Produced, Current Quarter: 16,800
- Units Delivered, Current Quarter: 3,400
- Units in Pipeline: 5,200
- Delivery Deficit: (13,400)
- Projected Quarterly Deficit: (8,200)

Shit! Where in Hades' five rivers had 13,400 brand new limb augments gone? Had he somehow made a mistake in the calculations? Accidentally sold them to some hocker while in a drunken stupor?

An automated dampener routine kicked in to dial down the rising panic. He breathed in, then out, and checked the data again. No, he hadn't done either of those things.

He hurriedly made some adjustments to increase production of the new augment model in order to meet at least a portion of the shortfall in the near term. Then he silenced the focus sphere and pinged his Manufacturing Director.

Vance, come by as soon as you get a minute. We have a...glitch.

Vance Greshe was built like a quarry laborer, with thick muscles stretched taut over a sturdy frame. Hands large enough to encase the average Asterion's head could, however, just as easily entwine a photal fiber weave with delicate finesse.

Dashiel had known Vance for five generations, but he'd only known the man for two hours when he'd hired him away from colonial development on Adjunct Ni to run his production lines. He'd never regretted the decision.

"I saw that the contract renewal with Dominion Transit came out unusually favorably. How did you swing it?"

Dashiel motioned the man over to the conference table on one side of his office. "Exceptional timing. NOIR blew up their data vault and remote conduits last night, so now they need to build new ones. But that's not why I asked you to come by. We've lost 13,400 Model Vk 3.2 limb augments somewhere between the factory and the distributors."

"Lost?"

He pulled up the flagged data at the table. "They did not make it to their destinations. That's all I know right now, which needs to change."

Vance quickly scanned the data points. "Let's see what we've got." He nudged the information to the side, and the supply chain flow for the augments in question replaced it. "We manufacture this model here on Mirai, at the factory outside Mirai Two. The augment shipments departed the fabrication warehouse at the factory in four separate transports yesterday evening local. We can follow the transports' signals from our logistics network."

Four panes instantiated, each with a red blip moving against the overlay of a regional map. "Everything looks normal so far—" one of the blips blinked out. "That's odd. It simply *vanished*. No malfunction alerts preceded it. No disruptions were reported in the area at the time that might have interrupted the transport." In the second pane another blip vanished, followed by a third. Only a single transport continued on to reach its destination.

"Time frame?"

Vance enhanced the data points running along the bottom of the panes. "Less than half an hour from the first drop out to the last, but by the time they occurred, the transports were hundreds of kilometers apart, which suggests discrete causes."

"Yet discrete causes for three nearly instantaneous dropouts is extremely unlikely. Where are the transports now?"

"Late reporting in, and they don't return as anywhere on the grid. Like the augments they carried, they seem to be...lost." Vance's frowned. "I can't explain their disappearance."

Dashiel rubbed at his jaw. "I can. They were stolen."

"Three separate transports at widely disparate locations *deliberately* knocked off the grid without any warning, all in a half-hour's time? It would require tremendous resources and skill to execute. Who could do that?"

Rather than answer the question, Dashiel accessed the government nex web. "Justice Division, Security Department, Public Monitoring. This is Advisor Ridani, Industry Division, requesting surveillance footage from—" he checked with Vance, who sent over the location and time of the first disappearance "—Mirai Two, Sector Three, beginning at 1422 APT last night."

"Surveillance footage access granted. Transmitting records."

A few seconds later the footage arrived, and he displayed it at the table. The birds-eye vantage showed several square blocks in the northeast corner of Sector Three. The tracker from his logistics network appeared on the visual to identify one of his transports as it cruised along the commercial vehicle lane. Abruptly the tracker dot vanished as before...and the transport continued on. At the next intersection, several vehicles obscured their view for a few seconds, and when the scene cleared, the transport was gone.

"Dammit. We can check the other two recordings, but I suspect they'll show similar events. I'll request adjacent sector footage...or I suppose Justice should do it."

Dashiel initiated a theft claim, then let the system populate it with the details while he moved to one of the windows in his office. He hardly saw the cityscape it revealed, however. Instead, his mind replayed the surveillance footage in a loop.

"The only entities with the resources to execute such a theft wouldn't bother with it. Every augment is imprinted with our signature, making it impossible for anyone to pass them off to a reputable retailer. This suggests black market as the endpoint, but the Guides ensure no off-grid group gains the kind of power required to pull off such a heist."

Except NOIR, perhaps. They'd shown themselves clever enough to execute some impressive stunts, though never at multiple separate locations at once. But what would they need over 13,000 single-purpose augments for? To sell them for credits? He didn't doubt the group had contacts on the black market, but did it have the kind of reach needed to move such a high volume of product? He'd ask Adlai later.

"Have trackers placed inside every crate of end-product shipments across all production lines starting today. Apparently, tracking the transports is no longer sufficient."

Vance nodded in understanding. "I'll also have the augment prototype line converted over to release-grade production until we make up the loss."

"Thank you. Whatever else you think of to bridge the gap, do it. I'll tell Larahle to adjust the budget and free up the funds you need. Now, unfortunately, it's time for the Quarterly Report, so I'll be unavailable for a few hours."

Vance looked perplexed. "It's unfortunate that you have an audience with the Guides?"

Dashiel adopted a chagrined expression. It had been a minor slip, but a slip nonetheless. "Certainly not. I merely meant it's unfortunate that I need to depart at this moment and leave you to do all of the work."

4

M irai Tower dwarfed every other building to the horizon. Perched at the center of the city, its tapered apex stretched into the clouds as if reaching up for the orbiting station to which its penthouse was inexorably linked.

Dashiel rode the lift to the top floor alone, then stepped out of the lift alcove and directly into a series of extensive security screening procedures.

He'd cleared the checkpoint hundreds of times, but the security dynes and the churning servers behind them performed their duties with full earnestness and precision every single time. It made sense, objectively. Impersonating him would be a difficult task but not an impossible one, if only because few things were truly *impossible* with the proper application of skill and resources. And the potential consequences of an imposter making it onto the Platform were unacceptable.

But since he was in actuality himself and not an imposter, he cleared the checkpoint a minute later, at which point he strode through the d-gate beyond it and emerged inside the Platform.

The meeting place of the Guides orbited Mirai for the current decade, which meant the distance he'd just traveled wasn't so far at all—a short thirty-five megameters to high Mirai orbit. It didn't matter in practice, as the d-gates bridged kiloparsecs as swiftly as they did kilometers. The Platform nevertheless moved every ten years, cycling through the five Axis Worlds so as to not display favoritism among them.

He wasn't late, but he was cutting it close, and many of the other Advisors were already in attendance. They milled about the arcing anteroom making small talk with one another, as if this were a cocktail party instead of the highest level of government meetings.

The thirty Advisors, five for each Division, were the most powerful individuals in the Asterion Dominion save the Guides themselves. As the title suggested, they advised the Guides on a multitude of matters related to their respective areas of expertise. They held decision-making authority over an even greater multitude of matters overseen by their respective Divisions.

They controlled businesses, property and obscene riches; in several cases they controlled entire exploratory worlds. And what they didn't explicitly control, they influenced. Their whispers in the right ears shifted economies and fortunes.

Dashiel had known the majority of his fellow Advisors for many generations…and he did not trust a single, solitary one of them. A few, like Adlai or Maris, he felt comfortable enough with in all but the most treacherous situations, so the amount of trust withheld was hardly worth measuring.

Others, like…his gaze fell on Gemina Kail. He made it a point to always know where she was in a room so she could never take him by surprise. Today, a white one-piece pantsuit made her easy to find. Scarlet hair swept up into a tight bun atop her head did nothing to complement severe features and eyes so darkly green they appeared black from afar.

Well, others like Gemina, he tried never to turn his back on.

It hadn't always been this way. His temperament hadn't always bent so strongly toward distrust and circumspection with respect to his colleagues. Of course, he also hadn't always been a high-functioning drunk. The alterations shared a common lineage.

"Dashiel, I feel obligated to inform you that you have a hair out of place above your left temple."

If that was the only part of him out of place, he was doing far better than he felt. He pivoted toward Maris Debray wearing a smile—a genuine one—and brought a hand to his brow. "We cannot have such a faux pas, can we? Better?"

"And the worlds have returned to their proper alignment among the stars." Her orchid eyes—violet fading to a white ring at the pupil—narrowed at him. "Actually, you do seem a bit off. Trouble?"

"Quite. I had three transports of brand new augments stolen on their way to the distributors. Snatched right off their routes and vanished into the ether."

Her dignified nose scrunched up. "Bizarre. Crime is so…distasteful. And messy."

"It's definitely going to be messy for my credit account."

"I suspect you will find a way to persevere." Her voice trailed off. "I don't know, so little ruffles you that on finding you ruffled, I thought maybe you had heard something."

She clearly preferred to remember an earlier, better version of him. Any other conversation with any other individual, and the inevitable next step would be to ask 'something about what?' But where he and Maris were concerned, there was only ever one 'something.'

He forced an air of lightness into his tone. "No, and I stopped expecting to hear something years ago—not long after I stopped looking for her." It was true, but solely because the places to look and methods to do so had long since dried up. "There's nothing to hear and nothing to find, Maris. She's gone—gone to us, anyway."

"That doesn't make any sense. It has never made any sense."

"And yet." He held her stare, keeping his expression kind while masking anything which might reflect his genuine emotions on the topic. Those were for himself alone. In the dark, in his weakest moments.

The interior wall dissolved, signaling the commencement of the meeting and a merciful end to their coded conversation. The questions with no answers that would have followed had been voiced countless times, and he wasn't in the mood to hear or speak them again.

Thirty chairs lined one-half of the circular central chamber. A single pedestal stood at the center point of the room, and beyond it a high dais curved in a sixty-degree arc. Behind the dais, five d-gates shimmered. One by one they brought the Guides in from…no one could reliably say. Perhaps from elsewhere on the Platform, or from secret locations on the Axis Worlds they represented. Perhaps from the stars themselves.

Dashiel had always thought the Guides wore their skin rather awkwardly. The formality of their every movement betrayed a lack of familiarity and inherent discomfort with the natural flow of a body in motion. It was possible they only wore skin in the presence of others, spending the rest of their time as pure information. He hoped not, for it was not the Asterion way.

His people inhabited physical bodies for many reasons. To enjoy the pleasures of the flesh, for certain—not only sex but food and drink and tactile interaction, wind rushing through one's hair and the bracing immersion of an ocean of icy water. To stay grounded, in touch with and connected to the physical world and the creatures, sentient and otherwise, inhabiting it. To use tools and build with them real, lasting monuments that left their mark on the cosmos, that said 'we exist.' 'We are here and we are *real*.'

He did not believe the Guides should exempt themselves from these principles, but they had not asked his permission.

At Quarterly Report sessions, each Advisor ascended the pedestal one at a time and presented their report on the status of their responsibilities, then dutifully responded to probing questions and accepted the dispensed guidance. With thirty Advisors, they were going to be here for a while.

AR

The tension in the room ratcheted up several levels when Adlai stepped forward, spurring the air particles in the chamber to heightened agitation. Everyone present knew about the latest NOIR strike, thus everyone present had an opinion and two rumors to spread regarding it.

Dashiel maintained his casually aloof posture, but he too sharpened his attention on the proceedings, curious as to whether the investigation had progressed since this morning.

"Guides, thank you for the honor of your time. Updates on a variety of ongoing matters have been filed—"

"Tell us about NOIR." Guide Anavosa of Mirai canted her head in a stilted expression of interest. Her alabaster skin resembled glazed porcelain, and her pale, cornflower blue eyes and hair looked so delicate they risked fading to ashenness at any moment. But her fragile appearance hid the most shrewd and calculating of intellects.

"Ah, yes, Guide Anavosa. Last night, one or more criminals infiltrated the Dominion Transit Headquarters building in Mirai One, where they accessed the company's primary data vault and corrupted its contents, particularly transit passenger records. They also destroyed the conduit lines to Dominion Transit's remote backup servers, burned out the security cams and erased the security system's historical data covering the two hours prior to and including the infiltration."

Guide Luciene of Synra directed a piercing, icy stare at Adlai. His skin radiated even less color than Anavosa's, but it contrasted starkly with inky black hair and bottomless onyx eyes. "From this information, may we surmise that you cannot tell us how many individuals were involved, what data they accessed or the nature of the malfeasance they committed upon it?"

Adlai didn't wilt under the scrutiny. "As we often say at Justice, Guide Luciene, data is agnostic. It has no masters, yet it is subservient to anyone wielding the skill to shape it. Data deleted no longer exists. Data corrupted cannot be trusted to return to an uncorrupted state—"

"There are *backups*." Luciene's voice grated over each syllable like a taut string threatening to snap. Dashiel found him deeply unpleasant.

"The timing of the destruction of the conduits means the integrity of the backups is in question. My analysts are working with Dominion Transit techs to resolve the question of whether corrupted data was copied to the backup servers before the conduits were destroyed."

"This group of terrorists threatens the safety and sanctity of every Asterion. Find them and end them." Luciene's gaze traveled left, then right. "This is the will of your Guides."

Adlai's chin dipped in respect. "I understand and will endeavor to fulfill your guidance."

The grandiose decree from Luciene rankled Dashiel. Wishing something to be so did little to accomplish it; the Guides wanted to declare it to be so that NOIR was vanquished, then watch reality realign itself to comply with their wishes. They were powerful, with a complement of powerful Advisors at their command, but reality was rarely so accommodating to mere wishes. Something he knew better than most.

He watched the Guides as Adlai returned to his seat. They fared poorly at disguising the anxious, troubled looks they exchanged and at subduing agitated body language they didn't fully appreciate. If he didn't know better, he'd speculate that they were...afraid. Of NOIR?

But to suggest such a possibility would be heresy, so as he stood and approached the pedestal for his turn in the line of fire, he did not suggest it.

"Advisor Ridani." Guide Anavosa acknowledged him without elaboration.

"Guides, thank you for the honor of your time. I must inform you of a significant theft."

By the time the session finally concluded, Dashiel had four messages from Vance outlining ameliorative measures his Manu-facturing Director wanted to implement on and around the limb augment production.

He should go back to the office and review the suggested measures. It was his business, after all.

But he didn't. Instead he simply signed off on everything and headed for one of the sleazier bars in the Southern Market. The one where he could buy illegal doses to chase the alcohol and nobody cared.

He spent the trip on the maglev lines trying very hard not to think. Not about work, not about the augment theft, and certainly not about anything more hazardous to his mental health. His mind had plenty of tasks to keep it busy as it was, including patching up frayed pathways and neural clusters that he was soon to abuse again.

He arrived at Riyuki's as dusk faded to night and went straight inside to claim a stool along the ring positioned high above the dance floor.

The crowd here wasn't his type of crowd—not that he had a type of crowd—but for the most part they didn't seem to mind if some poshly dressed executive from downtown took up a stool. So long as he didn't bother them, they didn't bother him. Sanctity of the motherfucking individual: the Dominion's most oft-quoted credo was alive and well in its seedy underbelly, if nowhere else.

ᴀ̆ʀ

The bar drone had just delivered his fourth sake and second chaser when the woman caught his attention.

She lounged against the opposite side of the ring from him, sipping on an iced drink and studying the dance floor with a bored expression. And if he squinted until his vision blurred, the illusion almost worked.

Midnight black hair draped over one shoulder, and cherry red lips were set in what might be a perpetual pout. He knew her eyes were going to be too blue up close, but from here they were a match.

He downed the contents of his glass and stood to make his way halfway around the ring.

She saw him coming a few meters away; her gaze scanned him up, then down. She smiled. He blinked until it wasn't wrong.

"You look far too well-put-together to be slumming here."

He shrugged and dropped a forearm on the table. "Maybe I *enjoy* slumming."

"Oh? How much do you enjoy it?"

⋏ℛ

Dashiel slammed the woman against the wall in one of the small private rooms that dotted the periphery of Riyuki's upper level for reasons exactly like this one. His lips missed her mouth on the first try, veered and found their mark.

She tasted of salt and lime, which wasn't right—

Silence all comparative processes.

He withdrew from the kiss to find the seam in her shirt, and his eyes wavered upwards to briefly meet hers—

Just as he'd thought. Too blue. Not right.

Godsdammit, for ten fucking minutes pretend—

Her hand found his ass and dragged him closer. "What's your pleasure, pretty boy?"

Her voice grated on his aural receptors. He blinked, and the illusion shattered into tiny little shards of kyoseil. She was too short. Her curves were in the wrong places. Her skin was too pale. All wrong.

He jerked away. His hands fumbled to fasten his pants, which she had somehow managed to get unfastened without him realizing it.

"Where are you going?"

He threw a dismissive hand in her direction and stumbled for the door. "Fuck if I know. Have a good night."

She's gone—gone to us, anyway.

That doesn't make any sense. It has never made any sense.

And yet.

And yet.

5

The minds of the Guides joined together across the stars. Separate but one, they inhabited a nex web brought into existence purely through the force of their collective will.

Guide Luciene (Synra): "NOIR's continued escalation in activity is unacceptable. It cannot continue. Their actions threaten to erode the veneer of benevolent leadership we have worked tirelessly to create."

Guide Delacrai (Kiyora): "It is not a veneer. We do act benevolently and in the best interests of all Asterions."

Guide Anavosa (Mirai): "NOIR disagrees, it seems. Necessary changes to our governance policies we hoped would be accepted without conflict did not go unnoticed by the group, and now it seeks to draw the attention of the populace to these stricter measures. However much they succeed or fail going forward, a threshold has been crossed. There will be consequences."

Luciene: "They are terrorists. Criminal delinquents, likely with defective fundamental programming corrupting their kernels. Do not legitimize them by ascribing them honorable motives."

Anavosa: "But their professed motives *are* honorable. Naive and uninformed, but in a perfect world, honorable. The uncomfortable truth is that NOIR's actions align quite closely with the values we once claimed as our own. There is nothing to be done for it, of course. We have acted as we must, and the citizens can never know the reasons for our actions. Our course is set. We will protect the heart of our society, and by doing so preserve its very existence.

"NOIR threatens our ability to do this, thus the group must be silenced—but do not turn a blind eye to the reality of what we are doing and why we must do it. This is a lesser evil in service of a greater good, and we each shall bear the burden of our actions upon our own consciences."

Luciene: "So long as we agree in our intent, I will not quibble over pedantic ethical minutiae. Now, how to accomplish it? Advisor Weiss is no closer to rooting out NOIR's members than when he began his investigation. I fear he is not up to the task."

Guide Iovimer (Namino): "He is the best agent serving in Justice at present. We can experiment with genetic and algorithmic improvements in an attempt to produce a more skilled agent if we wish, but such an effort takes time to deliver results. For now, we need to apply both pressure and resources to him in equal measure, in the hope they will improve his ability to deliver."

Luciene: "Emphasizing that NOIR needs to be his highest priority will have the additional benefit of discouraging him from properly investigating the theft of Advisor Ridani's augments—an investigation that risks leading him down a dangerous path."

Anavosa: "Unless Advisor Weiss believes NOIR is behind the theft—or is made to believe it."

Guide Selyshok (Ebisu): "An interesting proposition, but one fraught with peril. Analyzing the variables, I posit that allowing Advisor Weiss to focus on the augment theft brings with it greater risks than tying it to NOIR brings potential benefits. We should instead see to it that he is dissuaded from a belief they are connected."

Iovimer: "An easy enough task, as they are not in fact connected."

Delacrai: "And what of Advisor Ridani? He will want the perpetrators of the theft caught. He will press Advisor Weiss."

Selyshok: "He will have to live with disappointment. He has done so before."

Delacrai: "Anavosa, do you think he suspects this is anything other than an ordinary theft?"

Anavosa: "The scale and complexity of the theft means he cannot consider it 'ordinary,' but he has no reason to suspect our involvement in it, nor should he. Multiple safeguards separate the theft and the eventual impact of the stolen augments."

Delacrai: "He has one reason."

Luciene: "I still maintain that we should have mitigated his level of power five years ago. We lack insight into how much he knew, but he knew *something*. He continues to know it today, and this will influence how he views the theft."

Anavosa: "Advisor Ridani remains an intelligent and driven man, but he is a shadow of the man he once was. If he did not uncover our actions then, he will not do so now."

Luciene: "You speak too complacently, Anavosa. He is a risk."

Anavosa: "We will watch him, as we have watched him for years. If he begins to draw too close to the truth, we will act. But we will not make it a habit to erase every citizen who causes us a moment of grief. If we descend so low in our actions toward our own people, we might as well surrender to the enemy now, as we will no longer possess anything worth preserving."

Luciene: "But the risk is not that he causes us grief. The risk may well be that he causes the loss of everything: our people, our worlds, our lives and our memories, whether we surrender them or not."

Delacrai: "Perhaps we are wrong. Perhaps, if the people knew the truth, they would understand. They could even assist us. Our citizens are wise and caring, not to mention inventive and industrious, and we underestimate them at our peril."

Selyshok: "They are also fiercely independent and quite selfish when it comes to such matters as their own lives. The notion that some must be sacrificed so others can live will not sit well with those sacrificed. No. The path we've chosen is the only way, and we cannot deviate from it now. We must continue to buy ourselves time. Time to devise a way out of this chthonian trap we find ourselves snared in."

RANDOM
ACCESS
MEMORY

6

T he door to Joaquim's room was open, but Nika knocked on the frame all the same.

He sat hunched over his workbench, etching visual identifiers into a row of data weaves. His workspace was, as usual, immaculate. Though stacks of data storage lined an entire wall and a variety of semi-dismantled equipment another, the room didn't feel cluttered or messy. Every item bore a label and occupied its proper place. A grid display of lists and diagrams took up much of the third wall, and a shoji screen stretched across half of the fourth to shield his bed and personals from sight.

She'd offered a while back to allocate space elsewhere for him to use as a workroom—she didn't know where she'd *find* that space, but she'd figure something out. He'd declined, though, saying he preferred having everything within easy reach. Relieved to not have to conjure space out of its absence, she hadn't pushed.

"One second." A faint scraping sound filled the air as he began etching the last weave.

When he finished, he placed the etching tool on a hook and stacked the weaves in a bin on a shelf of the storage rack, then leaned against the rack and gave her an unexpectedly enthusiastic smile. He'd ditched the stubble that had been veering toward a beard by the Dominion Transit operation, and his copper hair was both trimmed short and combed. "Thanks for coming by."

She arched an eyebrow and stepped through the doorway. "I always come by if we haven't talked in a day or so."

"True. I suppose I meant thank you for doing that, then."

"You're in a better mood."

"Than the other night? Yeah. Sorry if I was overly harsh."

"I can handle your harshness. I'm not the one you need to apologize to."

"Perrin? We're fine. If she ever actually gets upset with me, she will not be shy about letting me know." He motioned to one of the chairs squeezed perfectly between two equipment stands. "Sit. We have things to talk about."

She crossed to the chair and sat down. "We always do. That's why I always come by."

He scooted his workbench stool closer to her. "Everything from the Dominion Transit operation still looks positive. The simmed IDs are holding up, and none of the early warning tripwires Parc left behind have gone off. I think we're in the clear. You can take a look if you like, but I'm signing off on the use of the IDs. Perrin will screen the individual requests, as usual."

"I trust your analysis. Approved. But now we need some additional masks as well. I know I'm being paranoid, but two layers of protection are, by definition, more secure than one."

He nodded. "I agree. When you live off the grid, your persona is your second-most valuable possession, so they're good to have around, if only for when everything goes wrong."

He didn't need to give words to the first-most valuable possession, since she appreciated the value of one's psyche far more than most.

Identity-alteration tech of all kinds was highly illegal. It hindered criminal investigations and prosecutions. It introduced doubt into memories and historical records, which most Asterions treated as sacred.

This, of course, made it expensive. They constructed the simmed IDs and morphs themselves, but masks had to be bought. She had decided not to spend valuable credits on them until the Dominion Transit operation was completed, since if it failed the credits would likely be needed elsewhere for things like body repairs and replacement equipment.

Thankfully, that hadn't turned out to be the case. "I'll grab some credits and go to Namino this afternoon."

"Say hi to Grant for me."

She glanced behind her to find Perrin leaning on the door frame looking smug. Today, her hair was a bright carnation hue and bound into pigtails draped down her chest. A capri jumper—and the teasing commentary—completed the playful mien.

Nika gave her an innocent, questioning expression. "Grant doesn't have masks for sale—why would I see him?"

"Because you always see Grant when you go to Namino. You think we don't know, but we do." Perrin checked Joaquim for confirmation.

He shrugged. "We do."

"Well." She scratched at her nose, burying a sheepish chuckle behind her hand. "*If* I see him, I will tell him you said hello. The timing may not cooperate, though. A Taiyok meets with you precisely when a Taiyok wants to meet with you, after all, so my schedule will be at Xyche's mercy."

"We don't have anything big planned for a few days. Take your time."

"I'll be sure to remember that." She rolled her eyes and shifted back to face Joaquim. "Anything else, or are we good?"

"We're good. Perrin's here, I suspect, to give me shit about my suggested changes to the combat training regimen for new recruits."

"Oh, that's at least the third or fourth item on the list of things I'm here to give you shit about."

Joaquim sighed. "See? I told you she'd let me know."

Nika stood and headed for the door. "This is my cue to vacate. Ping me if anything troublesome or awesome arises while I'm gone."

⁂

"Hey, Nika—over here!"

She scanned around for the source of the summons to discover Parc gesturing wildly in her direction from his command center. Fewer spectators hovered around him this time—only three of his cohorts—but the Floor as a whole was less crowded. It was late morning, and people were out on the streets, taking care of matters personal and professional. Living a semblance of a life outside the protection of these walls.

She picked her way through the scattered activity to reach him. "What do you have to impress me with today?"

"Oh, this goes well beyond impressing. We are in awe-inducing territory here."

She smirked and crossed her arms loosely over her chest. "All right. Awe me."

Parc plopped down in his customized seat, adjusted his shoulders and activated all the panes arrayed in front of him. His left hand reached out and touched the center pane, altering the display—then a virtual limb flared to life around his hand, and ten additional 'fingers' stretched out beyond his physical ones. They extended to the various panes, each one interacting with multiple GUIs, entering data and responding to prompts. Two fingers even spent the time drawing a tree by a stream in Parc's trademark overswirly style.

The performance continued for twenty or so seconds before the virtual appendages faded away. Parc clasped his real hands behind his head and spun around. "Well?"

She grinned and touched a corner of her mouth. "This is me 'awed,' trust me. Where did you get the augment? Dare I ask how you afforded it? I mean, your personal finances are none of my business, but...."

"My personal finances are pretty much a null set. Roqe passed it to me under the table at a deep discount yesterday. It's a new model, and they wanted someone to field test it and clue them in on what the customer sales pitch should be. See, it's far more complex than simply additional digits. They work independently of one another. The augment wires directly into the arm's somatic peripheral nerve pathways in a parallel setup, leading to a multitasking bonanza delivered straight from my brain."

Someone behind Nika snorted. "It hasn't improved your artistic skill."

"Shut up, Maggie. I think it's a great tree. I'm still fiddling with the setup, and I think I can squeeze some higher efficiencies out of it. Hopefully faster response times as well. But if you want to start sending everything my way from now on—" he held up his hand, and the virtual encasement sprung to life, complete with two extra sets of wiggling fingers "—I've got you covered."

"I'll keep that in mind. For now, you just keep entertaining everyone with your shiny toys and swirly trees."

"You know I will."

Yes. Yes, she did.

7

A glittering arch framed the sleek exterior of the transit hub, capping its apex then sloping down into the quarter-orb walls that bounded the structure. The hub bustled with activity at the local midday hour, as it always did.

Nika slipped quietly into the throng of people entering the hub. When traveling, crowds were her friend. If she were a lone or scattered entrant, every sensor, drone and dyne would turn their attention to her, if solely for the lack of anything else to focus upon. Crowds, however, must be moved through the hub quickly and efficiently, so she would receive the minimum required scrutiny.

The simmed ID/morph loaded into her OS cloaked her in the guise of someone other than herself. It provided the all-important digital signature as well as a residential address and a clean Justice record. It also projected an altered physical appearance and voice print to all scanning and recording devices, which included the eyes and ears of other Asterions. It didn't actually *change* her physical appearance, but here there was no practicable difference.

A mask, on the other hand, was a true criminal's instrument. It acted as a perception filter, distorting one's appearance to the point where a viewer could not acquire a clear visual or recording of it. Since a person for certain and sometimes a well-programmed dyne was apt to realize when their perception sensors were being screwed with, its usefulness was limited to certain types of situations.

But in a world where every official interaction was recorded and stored, where official freedoms were many but personal accountability was rigorously 'enforced,' masks were an indispensable tool for a person in her chosen profession. To be someone else was one thing—but to not be there at all? This was something else altogether.

Admittedly, she found a touch of ironic amusement in using one. She had been a chameleon for five years now, a distorted imitation of someone she did not know, an echo of a persona erased and unidentifiable. Fitting that projecting a chameleon of the chameleon forward into the watching world should now be a regular aspect of her life.

Nika stepped up to the entry checkpoint and gazed impassively at the security dyne as she pressed the fingertips of her left hand to the pane.

$\Sigma \rightarrow$ *Identity:*
< Kallis Vramel, 3rd generation
Signature:
$< \beta \alpha \theta \Psi \theta \Xi \Psi \forall \Psi \alpha \Omega$

"Destination?"

"Namino Two East Hub."

"You are cleared to proceed." She wasted no time in doing so.

A healthy gray market trade permeated every corner of the Asterion Dominion, and polite society called this the 'black market.' But masks were only traded on the blackest of true black markets, a network of commerce known only to off-gridders and those who sold to them.

While the underlying algorithms that interfaced with the wearer of a mask were home-grown, the technology relied on several components developed by the Taiyoks. Secretive, humorless aliens descended from arthropods, the Taiyoks had adapted their own biological cloaking traits into a system able to be manufactured, bought and sold. They were also astute traders, and they used the necessity of their components in building the device to keep a stranglehold on the mask trade.

The aliens could occasionally be seen on any Asterion world, but they had established a real, lasting presence only on Namino. So if one wanted to purchase a mask and be assured it wasn't a defective knockoff, one went to Namino.

ᴀʀ

If Mirai was the shining, cosmopolitan heart of the Dominion, Namino was its messy, raucous, somewhat dingy counterpart. It acted as a mercantile center, trade depot and, more often than not, factory storage dumping ground. If a thing existed, it could be bought, sold and stockpiled on Namino.

Though comfortably habitable, the planet lacked both abundant natural resources and attractive terrain. It was no trouble to live there, but if given the choice, why would you? The air was arid and cool on the main continent, making it favorable for storage of manufactured goods and perishables alike. A flat, docile landscape made construction cheap and city planning simple. The trade industry that sprouted up in response to these characteristics gave an answer to the question for those so inclined.

The dry air made Nika's nose itch as she exited the Namino Two East Hub and crossed a promenade buzzing with activity. She checked the local time. Her appointment with her Taiyok contact wasn't for another three hours...

...it was almost as if she'd planned it this way. She turned left and caught a maglev for one of the perimeter industrial districts.

8

Mesahle Flight built custom habitat and spaceship hardware components, from instrument housing to water recycling systems and kitchen units to the hulls themselves. Occasionally, it built the whole damn spaceship—usually small personal craft for wealthy individuals or scientific research ships for some scientist's pet project, as that covered most of the reasons anyone would bother to do something so quaint as fly a spaceship instead of just taking a d-gate to wherever they wanted to go.

Because it was a custom shop, the 'factory floor' consisted of six blocks of modular fab kits and three elevated assembly frames. The arrangement of the fab kits changed nearly every time she visited, as did the items suspended in the assembly frames.

Grant Mesahle dangled fifteen meters in the air, suspended from the top of one of the frames by a minimal harness while he worked at an open casing on the side of a half-built ship. His long, dirty blond hair was secured in a knot at the nape of his neck. A multitool drone floated to his left, ready to provide assistance on command.

Nika rested against the fence that bordered the shop, crossed her ankles and arms, and watched him work. Precision flares of heat winked in and out of sight from the depths of the casing. After a few seconds Grant's left hand stretched out toward the drone, and it transferred a small tool to him. He adjusted his angle slightly, and his arm again disappeared inside the casing.

"Enjoying the show?" His voice was modulated by the tension of concentration, yet it still managed to convey a hint of flirtation.

She chuckled under her breath. "Quite a lot. Did you install hidden visual receptors in the back of your head?"

"Merely full-coverage cams for the workspace, transmitting away into my nex node." He handed the tool back to the drone and spun around to balance against the hull and face her. "Nika Tescarav, come to visit. Are you here to buy a ship?"

One corner of her lips rose. He always asked her the same question, and her answer was always the same. "No, I am not."

∧R

Slate shafts of afternoon light from Namino's blue-white sun penetrated the wide window above the bed to partition the room into wedges of light and shadow. Nika stretched out a leg until her toes found light; she wiggled them to draw what warmth she could from it, which wasn't much.

Far better and more plentiful warmth could be found, however, from Grant's bare chest, so she curled around it to rest her chin on his sternum and peer up at him. "How's business?"

"This week, not great. I had a contract with a construction firm on SR56-Ichi evaporate. Or the firm evaporated, I'm not really sure which. Either way, there's no one to take delivery of a big stack of environment regulation modules and no one to pay for them whether delivered or not. So now I'm having to offload the modules for barely above cost one at a time."

She frowned, if somewhat lazily, reluctant to let the afterglow fade so soon. "That's odd. You can't get in touch with anyone from the company?"

He shrugged with equal laziness. "It's as though they never existed. I'd visit the outpost to see what's up, but the time away from the shop would cost me yet more money. So I'm cutting my losses and moving on." He offered her a smile and brushed flyaway hair out of her face. "It's all good. What brings you to Namino today?"

"I can't just want to see you?"

"Ha. If only."

"I *did* want to see you. But, yes, I also have to pay Xyche a visit about some new masks."

"What a way to spoil an otherwise lovely afternoon. Good luck." His lips quirked, and he hesitated briefly before continuing.

"So…I caught a glimpse of your handiwork at the Dominion Transit HQ on the news feeds. Isn't it a little risky, being so flamboyant? It's like you're taunting Justice, daring them to come after you."

Grant wasn't a member of NOIR, as such. He lived on the grid and ran a legitimate enterprise. But he was an active sympathizer to their cause, and he regularly helped them out when their needs and his skills coincided. This 'help' happened to include satiating her carnal itches on a fairly regular basis, but she didn't think he minded. It was a mutually beneficial arrangement in more ways than one—she got what she needed outside of NOIR and all the complications that would bring, and he, too, got what he needed, no strings attached.

She played with the fine hairs running down the center of his chest. "A little bit, but Justice is already coming after us, regardless of how flamboyant we are. It's not done casually—it's part of our larger strategy. We may be living on the ragged precipice, constantly scrounging for food and gear and funds, but the Guides and Justice don't need to know that. The more they come to believe we are a legitimate threat, powerful and unafraid, the more we become so."

His hands grasped her hips firmly, and he slid her up his chest to place an enticing kiss on her mouth. Then his grip loosened to allow his fingertips to dance across the small of her back as his lips teased her neck. "If you ask me, you already *are* powerful and unafraid. One of you, anyway."

She hummed in the back of her throat, her skin tingling along the dual paths of his fingertips and lips. "Stop that. I need to go. I'm supposed to be at the Curio Market soon, and Xyche will be cranky if I'm late."

He ignored her plea, instead dipping his hand lower to trace the curve of her hip and drawing his tongue along her collarbone. "Taiyoks are perpetually cranky—might as well give him a reason to be. And you have a *few* minutes still, yes?"

"Hmm...." She gave in and closed her eyes, savoring the delightful physical sensations his caresses evoked as her pulse raced her blood toward critical junctures. "Yes, but I'll have to bolt right after."

His lips crushed hers as he shifted his weight, and with it her, until he hovered a breath above her. "Sure. You always do."

9

Asterions had initially encountered the Taiyoks some 16,000 years earlier. The first thousand years of their relationship had consisted of the Taiyok government calling the periodic Asterion envoys 'machines' and turning them away once a century or so. It had taken another three thousand years of contentious and frequently abandoned negotiations before the first Asterion was allowed to set foot on the Taiyok homeworld, and an additional five thousand before regular trade routes were established.

Much about their culture remained shrouded in mystery still today, but the aliens had demonstrated themselves to be skilled craftsmen and shrewd negotiators in all things. Not a lot of fun at parties, however.

Their language consisted of harsh-to-the-ear clicks and rumbles originating from deep in the throat, and most of the sounds were impossible for an Asterion to enunciate naturally. In casual interactions, an external module sufficed for translations, but those who worked regularly with Taiyoks often installed a more robust internal augment into their larynx to enable them to vocalize the language.

Nika's body had possessed such a larynx augment when she woke up face-first on a street awash in rain and darkness. She did not know why. Oh, she could speculate as to why if she wanted to torture herself, but it would be to no end. She could have been a smuggler or an elite businesswoman; an interstellar freighter captain or a storefront hocker.

It didn't matter. The augment was useful to her in the here and now, as Taiyoks tended to be more trustful of Asterions who had gone to the trouble of altering themselves for the aliens' benefit.

Xyche'ghael ran a gear store deep in the Taiyok sector of Namino Two, inside the derisively but widely dubbed Curio Market. His store sold many things above the table, and more under it.

He'd been bilking Joaquim for supplies when she'd taken over interfacing with him, and after a couple of months of delicate negotiations she'd cut thirty percent off his prices. She still hoped for an additional ten percent decrease, but these things took time.

Xyche could not genuinely be considered a friend. It took decades at a minimum for one to reach a relationship status that might be labeled 'friendship' with any Taiyok, even a comparatively agreeable one, and Nika didn't yet have a single decade's worth of relationship with anyone. He was certainly a business associate and perhaps, if events ever called for it, an ally. If he knew of the existence of NOIR, he probably knew she was a part of it, but as a rule Taiyoks did not concern themselves with internal Dominion political intrigue.

She entered the Taiyok sector displaying a confident but closed-off deportment. Chin high but eyes straight ahead. Stride long but arms held at her sides. A black-and-plum shifter cloak over a charcoal jumpsuit as attire, because Taiyoks didn't care for bright colors.

She'd never visited their homeworld of Toki'taku—that she remembered—but it was reputed to bear a mottled brown, amber and shale landscape, and they'd done their best to recreate the colorless palette here.

Amid the increasing chill of late-afternoon shadows, she wound through the curving streets of the Taiyok sector toward the Curio Market. Dozens of eyes followed her course, but she acknowledged none of them, as it would be an insult to the residents to do so.

She knew this because along with her mysterious larynx augment had come sophisticated algorithms detailing the intricacies of Taiyok social customs. How to properly interact with the aliens had literally been embedded in her second-layer core programming.

She approached the Taiyok clerk behind the counter of Xyche's storefront, which she believed was also his home, keeping her hands flush at her side and her gaze steady.

Taiyoks didn't use bots for much of anything, but definitely not for commerce. As a result, the visual-alteration features of a simmed ID morph were useless here; Taiyok eyes were purely organic and could not be fooled. Luckily, she didn't need to be someone else in the Curio Market.

"Nika Tescarav to see Xyche'ghael. I have an appointment."

The clerk made a rumbling noise in his throat that wasn't a word even in Taiyoken and ruffled a winged arm as he turned away from the counter. The algorithms had taught Nika that this was an indication for her to follow the clerk into the back.

Xyche stood in front of a concave table on the left side of a long, narrow room. A Taiyok variation on photal fibers hung from the tall ceiling down to whatever he worked on. Nika checked behind her to find the clerk gone. For all their physical bulk, Taiyoks moved silent as the night.

Tough, leathery wings draped down in gray-and-grayer behind Xyche, with only the most subtle hints of muted powder blue feathery streaks visible in the dim lighting of the room. Taiyoks also had far more acute natural low-light vision than Asterions, though she could adjust her visual receptors for it when needed.

"A moment, Nika."

"As you need." She waited patiently in the center of the room. Cool air drifted beneath her cloak to chill her skin. She felt comfortable enough here to cast some idle glances around the space, but she didn't indulge in any dramatic movements. The boundaries of their business association did not extend to her fiddling with his personal possessions or crashing on his sofa.

To her eyes this seemed a dreadfully dull, somber existence…but she realized Taiyok eyes must see it differently.

Finally Xyche turned from the table to face her, wight-ice eyes meeting her gaze with a minute dip of his pointed chin. "You come to trade credits for forbidden goods."

"As I always do. Though if I thought you would tolerate my presence for any other purpose, I might give it a try."

The alien blinked at her. "You recognize that I would not take pleasure in your leisure activities, nor you in mine."

What *were* Taiyok leisure activities? Did she want to know? ...Had she once known? "I do recognize this, which is why I have never attempted to force such an event upon you. Let us instead take pleasure from business. I need to procure clean Tier III masks. Eight of them."

The softer feathers of his neck fluttered as if disturbed by a passing breeze. "Eight? I hope your credits are weighing you to the ground."

She smiled at his odd, alien offer of humor. "A burden I'm sure you will deign to relieve me of. Yes, I've brought sufficient credits, unless a sudden spike of inflation has swept through the Curio Market."

"Not this week, though one never can say what the next wind may bring. It will take me twenty-five minutes to prepare eight for transfer." He paused. "You may observe the work if you are interested."

She bowed her head, chin leading. "I'd be honored to do so."

Who knew—maybe one day they *would* be friends.

10

Walking out of the d-gate into the Synra Two South Hub lobby was like walking into a steam bath. The one-two punch of sweltering heat and sopping humidity smacking Joaquim in the face made for a rather rude welcome, and his internal temperature regulation processes kicked into high gear to keep him marginally comfortable.

Hq (autonomicRegulation) | priorityEscalation (0.8) | parameterChanges (extTemp (+9), extHum(+36%))

The environmental assault only worsened when he left the climate-controlled transit hub and stepped outside. Mirai One's pleasant climate had spoiled him, granted, but why had he ever lived here?

A long time ago, their ancestors had settled Synra out of nothing more than necessity. After sailing across galaxies for almost two centuries without respite, their ships were running out of resources, something Synra offered in abundance. Endless rainforests brimming with diverse flora and savannahs of grasses nourished by rich soil. Rolling meadows of fruit-bearing flowers surrounding pristine lakes of fresh water. There were even healthy deposits of common minerals in the polar regions.

So the ships had landed and the resources had been harvested. Then improved upon, genetically enhanced and replicated. Prosperity ensued. And they had stayed.

Joaquim paused outside the doors and took a minute to acclimate to the scene spread out before him. Synra Two wasn't as urbane as Mirai One or as trashy as Namino Two, not as serene as Kiyora One or as…wet as Ebisu One, Two, Three or Four. But for many years and multiple generations, it had simply been *home*.

The Justice Center was far enough away from the transit hub to merit its own maglev stop, but he was early, so he decided to walk instead.

Walking was a mistake.

Every ten meters held another memory lying in wait to jump out and ambush his psyche.

The stir-fry restaurant where he and his friends met for lunch once a week for years.

The music club that let him, Nathan and Gabe pretend they were musicians and play for the afternoon crowd on weekends.

The residential furnishings fab shop where he worked maintaining their equipment.

The arboretum where he met Cassidy.

By the time he arrived at the Justice Center, he felt like he'd gone twelve rounds with an industrial mecha. If he'd wanted to torture himself into a bloody pulp, he could have stayed on Mirai and loaded up some old memory files; the temperature would have been more bearable, if nothing else.

But he hadn't come to Synra to torture himself. He'd come to answer a question, and possibly to close a door that had nudged itself open.

Joaquim slipped into the rear of the courtroom and took a seat on the next-to-last bench. A few people sat scattered among the rows, but the hearing was sparsely attended. Just a random court proceeding for a random low-level crime alleged to have been perpetrated by a random individual. Nothing to see here, move along.

He felt a twinge of guilt at claiming one of the new simmed IDs straight off and using it for his own personal, non-NOIR reasons. But it was the only safe way for him to get to Synra and inside the courtroom, and he needed to be here.

The presiding Justice officer entered from a door behind the dais and took his seat. Two security dynes escorted Nathan in from another door and guided him to the defendant's box, where a woman Joaquim assumed was Nathan's Rep waited.

Nathan sat beside her without affect, without displaying any emotion whatsoever. His expression was impassive; dead eyes didn't so much as glance around the courtroom. His demeanor made for a stark contrast to the last time Joaquim had seen him.

The burnt odor of charred circuitry still clogged the air in the apartment ten hours after the raid.

A breeze wafted through from an open window to move the air inside around a bit, and Joaquim tasted the more organic odor of singed hair on his tongue—abruptly he doubled over and dry heaved until his stomach eventually gave up on its reflexive spasms.

He slid down to the floor, letting the wall hold him upright as he took in the wrecked scene with quiet dismay. He thought maybe he was still too shell-shocked to feel despair yet, though it would surely arrive to knock him on his ass soon enough.

Almost nothing in the apartment was salvageable—a few visual sets, some of her clothes, some of his, the fucking food unit. A couch, but not the bed, as raiding dynes had ripped it to shreds searching for imagined contraband. Threads from the hand-woven Chizeru rug Cassidy had bought on vacation last year lay scattered around the left half of the room like worms crawling across desert sand.

He stared at the floor for...a while. The threads never moved, but if he let his vision blur they almost seemed to.

She'd loved that rug.

A knock on the door frame barely penetrated his awareness, Nathan storming inside only a little more so. "Joaquim! There you are. I ran over here as soon as I heard—what the hells happened?"

His gaze slowly, vaguely rose to pass across Nathan, then back down to fixate on one of the threads. "Justice says they possessed evidence she was manufacturing and selling malware out of the apartment."

"Cassidy? Are they insane?"

"I don't...." The hollowness in his chest drained away the energy required to finish the sentence.

Nathan paced frenetically, dodging the overturned furniture and spilled contents of drawers and cabinets. "So, what? They raided the apartment? Tore the place up and shot her into nonfunctionality when she protested?"

"For starters. Then they wrecked her backup storage, claiming it held suspected contraband."

Nathan froze in the middle of the room, and Joaquim sensed his friend's stare boring into him. "She kept a remote backup, though, right?"

"Cassidy couldn't afford storage at one of the fancy trusts. She kept a copy stashed at a friend's place, but she had to bring it here to make the copy then return it. It was here when Justice raided."

"But that means...." Nathan crouched in front of him. "Fuck, man. I am so godsdamn sorry."

"Yeah." Joaquim closed his eyes to block out the pity on his friend's face. He could not bear the sight of it. Any of it.

"Why don't you crash at my place tonight—or as long as you need to."

He swallowed, but the acrid air provided no relief for his aching throat or his empty soul. "Thank you for the offer, but I want to be alone."

"Doesn't mean you should be alone. Just come with me—"

"I said I want to be alone."

Nathan studied him silently for several seconds, then stood and stepped away. "All right. I won't force you. But you know where to find me. Any time."

Joaquim stared at the threads on the floor until he heard Nathan leave, and for many hours after.

A week later, Justice had admitted that a faulty algorithm running in the Unregistered Transactions Task Force group made an erroneous connection between an innocent sale Cassidy had transacted and a known black market neural subroutine trade network. This false connection had led to the raid.

Justice apologized and reimbursed their accounts for the property damage. They initialized a new body free of charge and gave it her name, but without so much as an intact kernel remaining, the new person they awoke bore no resemblance to her. If the creator of the faulty algorithm was punished, Justice never said.

Joaquim had walked away from their life and their friends. He took his share of Justice's financial reimbursement, moved from Synra to Mirai and got a minor Grade I up-gen to add metaphorical distance to the physical distance he'd put between himself and that life. In time, he found others who shared his festering animosity toward the government, if not his depth of motivation. He found Perrin, and they found Nika, and NOIR came to be.

After that conversation at the apartment following the raid, he'd never seen Nathan again. Not until today.

⋏R

The hearing proceeded in a rote, perfunctory manner. Two witnesses testified that Nathan had assaulted a restaurant patron without provocation. The patron testified to the same. Nathan admitted to doing so and declined to provide a justification for his actions. He didn't give his Rep anything to work with, and in the end she could only plead first offender leniency.

But leniency didn't count for much with Justice these days, and the presiding officer sentenced Nathan to eight years in Zaidam, followed by a Grade III up-gen—only a single step less severe than a full R&R.

The security dynes led Nathan out through the door he'd entered from. Nathan hadn't once looked back at the audience in the courtroom, and Joaquim was glad for it. His former friend wasn't the man he remembered—because of an intervening up-gen, or it could simply be the shock from this unfortunate turn his life had taken, something Joaquim well understood.

As soon as Nathan disappeared through the door, Joaquim stood and left as well. In spite of the emotional wrecking ball the afternoon had been, he was glad he'd come to the hearing, because it had confirmed what he'd long believed. This time in his life was long gone and best left buried.

11

An officer escorted Dashiel up to Adlai's office at the apex of the sprawling Justice Center. It wasn't as if he didn't know the way, and as an Advisor it wasn't as if he represented a threat, but Justice had procedures for every foreseeable event and interaction, and those procedures had to be followed.

Adlai waved him inside while he passed off a stack of data weaves to one of his assistants. The woman joined another officer at a focus sphere across the room, and Adlai turned to him. "Thanks for taking the time to come by."

"Because you're too swamped to come outside and enjoy a proper lunch, I expect."

The Justice Advisor dropped his voice a notch. "You have no idea. I'm drowning under the NOIR investigation, and meanwhile crime rates everywhere are skyrocketing. It's...I don't know. Frustrating."

"Have you considered the possibility that if you hadn't decided to start making everything a crime, you wouldn't find yourself awash in criminals?"

"Very funny—you know perfectly well that the recent *adjustments* to the criminal code came at the behest of the Guides. I'm just keeping my head down and working the cases as they come." He gave Dashiel a pained look. "Which is why you're here, of course."

Dashiel shrugged mildly. "I *would* like my augment stock back. Failing that, I *would* like to see the perpetrators punished. But I can be altruistic. It's not all about me. Nobody wants the kind of criminals who can pull off such an outrageous heist roaming free on our streets, do they?"

"How very diplomatic of you—" Adlai's face reddened, and he cut himself off. "Sorry."

Alarms tripped and triggers sprung into action across Dashiel's mental processes to short-circuit the chain reaction that was already poised to spiral out of control. Their work was completed in a nanosecond, but it still took him the span of a long blink to bury the smarting wound the comment inflicted. Then he smiled. "No apology needed. I'm not a delicate flower, so don't feel as though you need to watch your every word around me."

"I'm a Justice Advisor—I should *always* watch my every word. And yes. In a perfect world, none of us want skilled, well-equipped thieves on the streets. I eagerly await the arrival of this perfect world. Until it does, we do what we can with our imperfect one.

"As to your first request, I'm afraid your augment stock is already spread around a minimum of four planets' worth of black markets. We've come across a couple of the units in unrelated raids. Whoever stole the shipments moved fast to dump the supply."

Dashiel exhaled heavily. So much for the financials this quarter. "Was it NOIR?"

Adlai hesitated, then shook his head. "It doesn't look like it. I wish it was, as then I could combine investigations. But to the extent we've been able to walk the trail in reverse on the units we've confiscated, they traveled through standard black market channels used by skimmers, spoofers and knockoff fabbers. Also, so far as we're aware of, NOIR's never engaged in mass theft of a commercial product."

"Maybe they're upping their game?"

"Oh, they're definitely doing that…but this hit doesn't feel like them. They enjoy announcing their handiwork with dramatic flair even when they don't need to do so, and in your case there's no graffiti, no manifesto, no calling card. Your thieves moved in, struck and disappeared."

"So you're telling me you have nothing? What about that supply trail? Past the standard black market channels, it leads somewhere."

"To anonymous and untraceable identities layered on top of anonymous and untraceable identities."

"Show me." Adlai arched an eyebrow, and Dashiel shrugged. "Humor me?"

"Suit yourself." Adlai instantiated a pane above the table. It populated with a series of complex diagrams busy with labels, notes and arrows pointing in every direction. Then arrows manifested *between* the diagrams. In seconds, the entire presentation had become spaghetti. Yet it was the gaps in the diagrams—the arrows that led nowhere and the orphaned nodes—which rendered the puzzle mathematically unsolvable.

He exhaled through his nose and dropped his shoulders. "Carry on."

"Thank you. I admit, the post-theft activities show a level of sophistication we don't often run up against, even more than the theft itself. It could suggest the involvement of someone inside one of the Divisions."

A set of different, if related, alarms tripped in Dashiel's mind, and he chose his response carefully. "You're not suggesting an Advisor has gone rogue?"

"Of course not. But possibly a high-level staffer, or several acting in concert. I'm going to ask for a surveil order and see what it turns up."

"I'll cosign the request. That ought to get it approved faster, at least for Industry. If this is the work of someone under me, well...they'll find they've never actually seen me displeased before."

"You should sell tickets to the beat down. Listen, I appreciate the fervor, and I understand where it's coming from, but this sort of investigation is usually a slow burn. Don't expect results soon."

Dashiel tossed a hand in the air in resigned acceptance. "I've doubled security measures at all facilities and on every shipment, so it shouldn't happen again—not to me." He could tell Adlai was itching to get back to work by the way the man's gaze kept darting over to the officers across the room, so he stood. "Will I see you at Maris' art gala?"

"I have to make an appearance, don't I? It's my expected duty as an Advisor and my sacred responsibility as a poor friend. I'll stop by for a few minutes, after which I will return to the office and try to make up for the lost time."

Dashiel chuckled. "Don't be so maudlin. Simply catch NOIR, and everything else will sort itself out."

"You know you're an asshole, right?"

Dashiel was halfway to sitting down in his focus sphere chaise and readying himself to put in some serious work hours for the first time in days when the door to his office signaled Vance's presence outside.

So much for distraction-free, sober work. He stood back up, pulled on the jacket he'd just hung up, and instructed the door to open.

Vance nodded a greeting as he stepped inside. "Sorry for showing up out of the blue. I was down the hall when I received a message from a representative of the Chizeru governor we commonly deal with."

"That's Shoset, isn't it?"

"Yes, sir. The message says they wish to negotiate a new supply contract for kyoseil."

Dashiel looked over in surprise. "The current contract term isn't up for another five months."

"The translator might have muddled the wording, but I believe they mean an additional contract."

"They want to sell us *more* kyoseil? After a string of bad news, I will not refuse a little good." His schedule for the rest of the week was packed, and squeezing in a trip to Chosek was going to throw it into utter disarray, and he was running on fumes from too many late nights as it was…but he wasn't about to refuse more kyoseil.

"I can handle the negotiations for you if you prefer. My understanding is that Advisor Rowan does most of the talking."

"True, though the meetings tend to go better when you don't let her talk. No, I should go. Not that I don't think you would strike an excellent deal, but the Chizeru get very excited when someone they view as important makes a visit. Allegedly, I qualify. Being excited makes them more agreeable to advantageous contract terms—for us. Maybe I can coax a few additional kilos out of them."

"I look forward to putting the increased supply to good use."

Dashiel chuckled wryly. "I bet you have a list—and if you don't, now's an excellent time to make one."

"I'll give it a once over this afternoon."

He followed Vance out the door. He needed to go see Larahle, because he needed to reschedule *everything*. Then he needed to stop off for a gift on the way to the transit hub.

12

The discovery of Chosek had been like manna falling from the heavens. A planet run through with veins of kyoseil from crust to mantle, with active planetary geology and tectonics that ensured its regular renewal? They could not have crafted a more perfect source.

Well, yes, they could have. They could have crafted one that didn't have an indigenous species living atop it. A pristine and quiet world. Then they could have simply sent in an army of mecha to strip-mine the planet. Instead, when they found the kyoseil, they also found the Chizeru.

The diminutive aliens displayed a level of intelligence higher than primates, but not by too wide of a margin. They spoke a complex enough language, memorialized it in writing, and crafted tools suited to their requirements, but their technology remained pre-industrial.

Learning to communicate then work with the Chizeru had been a frustrating endeavor at a time when the Dominion *needed* the kyoseil. But because the Asterions were a peaceful people who respected all life, they didn't carpet-bomb the aliens out of existence and take over their planet. Instead they watched the Chizeru, learned the idiosyncrasies of their culture and language, and generally indulged them until the aliens happily provided what the Asterions sought.

Chosek was saturated with a healthy variety of minerals, not just kyoseil. It was a hard, brittle world, and as a result the Chizeru coveted soft, cushioned luxuries above all else. Once the Asterion envoys figured this out, negotiations went considerably more smoothly. The Chizeru economy was barter-based; they didn't comprehend the concept of money, but they did comprehend the value of goods. Soft, plush goods like pillows, blankets, cushioned seating and beds held immense value to their way of thinking.

Fleeced material for clothing, bags and decorative items were popular as well.

An outside observer might call what the Asterions engaged in exploitation, but Dashiel had seen with his own eyes how the products the Chizeru took in payment for the kyoseil they mined made them *happy*. And if they were to ever ask for anything else as compensation, he had no doubt his government would authorize whatever measures were necessary to make it happen.

Dashiel contemplated all this on the brief trip through a series of d-gates that took him from Mirai One to the embassy on the surface of Chosek, mostly as a way to avoid thinking about other things. Memories. Previous visits to Chosek that, while for official business, had brought better company and happier moments.

Dammit. Now he'd gone and thought about them.

ᐱR

His newly foul mood hadn't dissipated by the time he stepped into the meeting room of the External Relations Division's Chosek embassy.

Advisor Iona Rowan looked up from the conference table and bestowed a perfect, cold smile on him. "Dashiel. How lovely it is to see you again."

"Is it?" He moved directly to the windows. At the Chizeru's insistence, they were lined in thick, quilted drapes, and he drew one of the drapes aside to peer outside. The Chizeru convoy made its way on foot up the marble pathway built into the rocky hill toward the complex.

Hq (visual) | scan (0°:180°) | calc Time (parameters
(pace(α), dist(loc(α), loc(A)))
$T \rightarrow Hr(\alpha) = 46.3$ seconds

He only needed to tolerate being alone with Rowan for a brief minute.

He heard her sigh from halfway across the room. "As charming as ever, I see."

Or a long minute. 'Charming' was something he felt no desire to be for her; he preferred to save his reserve of it for Shoset and the delegation. "Why am I here? Why do the Chizeru have extra kyoseil lying around to barter away?"

"A couple of contracts were canceled. That's all I know."

No fathomable reason existed to cancel a kyoseil contract. Even if the original reason for purchasing it evaporated, any sensible businessperson would jump at the chance to hoard the mineral for future projects or to resell it at an outrageous profit. Perhaps if the money to pay for the goods to barter for it evaporated as well?

Regardless, it was her job to be informed about such things. He half-turned away from the windows. "All you know, or all you care to share?"

"I see your attitude hasn't improved since our last meeting. I realize you resent my position—resent me personally—but I submit those feelings have nothing whatsoever to do with *me*, so I would appreciate it if you, in polite terms, get the fuck over it."

"Actually, they have a great deal to do with you."

"Oh? So you think I'm not as skilled at my job as my predecessor?"

"I know you're not as skilled as your predecessor."

Her expression darkened. "At diplomacy, or at sucking your cock?"

He peered back out the window to check the convoy's progress. Twenty seconds. "Assume I meant the former, as I'm not inclined to explore your talent or lack thereof at the latter."

She laughed; it wasn't a particularly pleasant sound. "Have you switched sides, or do you mourn her so deeply that you've turned celibate in her absence?"

His jaw clenched to grind his teeth against one another. "Not celibate—merely discerning."

"Oh, you ass—"

The door chimed, announcing the arrival of their guests. He pivoted to face the entrance and donned a friendly, welcoming demeanor.

Two officers from the embassy escorted the Chizeru tribal governor and his four companions into the room.

Before Rowan could step in and bluster through the welcome, Dashiel dropped to one knee to meet their guests at eye level. "Greetings, Shoset Landstjóra Fyrstur." He reached into the interior pocket of his jacket and retrieved a cashmere scarf of crimson and indigo, then unfolded it and draped it across his extended hands. "A gift, for you."

Shoset's tiny, recessed eyes danced with delight, as did most of his body, as he scurried past the escorts to reach Dashiel. The Chizeru lifted the scarf from Dashiel's outstretched hands and rubbed it against the tough, leathery skin of his cheeks for several seconds before gleefully wrapping it around his left arm from wrist to shoulder. He thrust his chest and chin out with pride.

Dashiel nodded in approval. "It suits you."

A bolt of lightning streaked across the midnight sky to silhouette the curves of her body and cast them upon a canvas of light.

She didn't appear to notice the display of nature's fury playing out beyond the window, however. The stringent line of her jaw and rigid set of her shoulders telegraphed a level of disquiet uncommon for her.

I didn't enjoy seeing her troubled, particularly since in this instance I was the cause of it, in a way. I had shared my concerns with her and, lacking any obvious path forward for myself to follow to resolve them, had allowed her to involve herself in them. Had I told her in the secret hope that she would in fact involve herself? Shame flared at the thought, but perhaps.

I wound my hands behind my head and relaxed against the pillow in false casualness. "This brooding is unlike you. What are you stewing over so intently?"

"The outpost on SR27-Shi? It isn't the only outpost to disappear recently. In the last two years, four other exploratory world outposts have become ghost towns, each one seemingly overnight."

I hadn't expected this answer, and I abandoned the relaxed pose to sit up straighter. "Five outposts gone? How is it that no one has noticed? Have the Guides not noticed?"

She glanced over her shoulder to give me a wry grimace. "As to the first question, the outposts were managed by different companies operating under the supervision of three different Divisions, with no functional connections between them. No reason to talk to one another or exchange information. To each of the companies, the disappearance of their outpost was a single incident. Worthy of concern, but space is dangerous, and people and equipment are often lost while braving those dangers. It happens. As to the second question...."

Her attention flitted to the window in the wake of a new flash of lightning, but when it faded she turned away from the storm and rejoined me on the bed. She stretched out along the length of my body, instantly bringing delightful warmth across every centimeter where her skin touched mine. Her lips grazed my cheek and settled at my ear. "They must know about the disappearances. There is no other explanation."

The undercurrent of dread in her murmured words chilled the warmth right back out of me. I lifted a hand to her shoulder and let it caress the smooth skin of her upper arm. "The flat's warded. You don't need to whisper."

She drew back from my ear and folded her arms on my chest, then rested her chin atop where they met. "I know it is. It's just...I feel like everything we rely on to be true has been called into question. I don't know what I can believe or who I can trust."

"You can trust me."

She smiled, and a twinkle briefly animated her turquoise eyes—neither blue nor green but both at once. "Self-evidently, which is why I'm telling you what I've learned. And the Guides knowing about the disappearances doesn't necessarily mean they're somehow culpable. Maybe they've discreetly instructed Justice to open an investigation, and it's being kept confidential so exploratory world investment and travel isn't disrupted."

"Adlai knows what happened at SR27-Shi. If he or his people were investigating similar incidents, he would have told me."

"Unless he was forbidden to."

I stared sharply at her. "The Guides forbidding Advisors from taking reasonable actions that will help in their investigations? Vis-à-vis other Advisors? That's...."

"Unthinkable. Yes. Yet here we are thinking it." She sighed dramatically, and I felt the wonderful tangibility of her body as it shifted against mine. "I don't know what's happening with these disappearances, but I need to find out. The possibilities are many, and almost all of them are deeply troubling. Also, if our exploratory worlds are being threatened and we don't disclose it, we're violating our treaty obligations to the Taiyok government. It endangers our diplomatic relations with other species, and this makes it my problem, too."

"Isn't that a bit of a stretch?"

"I'm a very proactive diplomat."

I chuckled in spite of myself. 'Proactive' didn't begin to capture the magic she wove with our alien allies. "Fair point. So, what are you planning to do?"

"Track the data. I want to access files tagged to the managers of the outposts that disappeared and see what I can learn. Hopefully, I'll find a common thread I can then follow until it leads to answers."

"The files at Mirai Tower?" I shifted my weight to move her off me and rolled on my side to face her. "What if you get caught slicing into records outside your purview?"

"I won't get caught. Besides, it's not slicing, not really. As Advisors, we enjoy unfettered access to Dominion files. I should be able to view any data I wish."

"So we're told. But if..." I shook my head, incredulous at the thought having made it all the way into words "...if the Guides are involved in something nefarious, something treasonous, then they will have locked information about it behind walls you can't circumvent."

"And that would be its own answer, wouldn't it?"

"It's too risky. They will also have trapped those files, and if you get caught slicing into Guide-secured files, you could be stripped of your Advisor status. Hells, you could be brought up on charges, and if found guilty be subject to involuntary retirement and reinitialization." I furrowed my brow into a declaration of official discontent. "You only looked into this because of me, and I'm saying you've done enough. Don't risk your position—your freedom or your psyche—for me."

The corners of her mouth curled upward, and she brought a hand to my jaw. "You're sweet, but you're also arrogant. This stopped being a favor for you and became a cause for me the instant I discovered the other disappearances. I can't turn my back on it now."

Her fingertips drifting along my jaw, so close yet too far away to kiss, was distracting, and I had to force myself to focus on her words instead of her touch. "Let me do the following up on it."

She arched an eyebrow.

"Or let me go with you. Let me help."

Now she shook her head firmly. "Two people together are three times as likely to get caught as a single person."

"But no one will think anything of seeing us together. It does happen quite a lot."

"Eh...." I saw the uncertainty written across her features...then she closed it down. "No. Who's going to ensure I get a proper hearing by Justice if we both get arrested?"

"Adlai."

Her lips pursed as she gave me a mock glare; if I hadn't been consumed with genuine worry at present, I'd have found it sexy as all hells.

"Fine, but who's going to hold my hand and provide moral support at the hearing?"

"No one else, I hope."

"See? I'll need you. But I won't get caught. And I'll share everything I learn the instant I get clear."

"You had better. No waiting until you see me, either—I want a nex path transfer. The instant." I reached out and drew her closer against me. I recognized reality. She genuinely couldn't let it go now—it wasn't *in her nature.* "*Be careful, please. I beg you. You are the love of my many lives, and I cannot accept the possibility of losing you.*"

"*You will never lose me.*" *Her lips trailed across my neck, stirring a rush of renewed heat to flow through my body in anticipation.* "*I will always find you. We are forever.*"

ᴧᴿ

Dashiel removed the memory weave with a weary sigh and tossed it on the table beside him, then sank against the cushions of the chaise and rubbed at his eyes.

He didn't need the stored memory data to recall that night, but with it he recalled every touch, every blink, every scent and every taste. And in the aftermath, he was left spent. A hollowed-out shell of a man.

The worst of the desolation would pass by the morning; it inevitably did. But it left behind a poisonous melancholy to chip away at his sanity, something all the time in the universe couldn't dissipate.

Before tonight, he'd gone nearly six months without reliving this memory, or for that matter any intimate memory involving her. He was trying to move on, and moving on required forgetting, or at a minimum deprioritizing until the memories lay buried beneath thousands of more active processes. A steady diet of alcohol and mind-alteration doses helped with that.

But the visit to Chosek had been one hurdle too many. Deflecting Rowan's thoughtless barbs regarding her, interacting with Shoset in just the way she had taught him to...after barely weathering the onslaught of Maris' tireless optimism at the Quarterly Report, Chosek had cracked his remaining resolve like an eggshell. Sent him running back for her, desperate to feel her touch and hear her voice, to cast his gaze upon her face in all its living, vibrant beauty.

She'd never returned from her investigative trip to Mirai Tower. Vanished without a trace, just like the outposts. The Guides had informed him and the other Advisors that she'd opted for a retirement for personal reasons, and the Charter bound them to respect her privacy and not share any information about her reinitialization. No exceptions.

He hadn't believed it. Not then, not now. She had loved her life, her work, her friends. She had loved *him*, and she would never have given any of it up. Not willingly.

No, she'd gone looking and she'd found something. She'd gotten caught or, more likely, confronted the person or persons involved, because she was tenacious that way, and they had…

…what? Boxed her? Deleted her? And who? Another Advisor? It seemed impossible for even an Advisor to have taken such drastic action on their own. The Guides, then? What could be so terrible of a secret that they would violate their own most sacred of edicts in order to keep it?

He'd searched, for answers and for her. For two years he'd searched. He'd skirted the edges of his own detention and censure and hunted in secret, afraid to ask for help from even their closest friends. For if the Guides were suspect then everyone was suspect.

He'd failed. Whether no trace remained or he simply lacked the skill to find it, he'd failed. He'd lost her. And while he held her promise to always find him close, like an ancestral heirloom clutched in a vise grip against his chest, each passing year his faith in it ebbed further away, and with it his faith in everything else in this damnable world.

13

G emina Kail looked around the deserted research lab, hands on her hips and a slouch to her shoulders. She took in the inert equipment, the empty work alcoves, the silenced air.

It felt like a tomb, though the true tomb was packed with occupied stasis chambers and speeding away from the outpost toward a hidden space station in a forgotten stellar system eighty parsecs from here at superluminal speed. The ship had departed SR86-Roku fifteen minutes earlier, and she hadn't been sorry to see it go. Out of sight, out of mind, no?

The ghosts lingered, but she'd trained herself to no longer see them.

The lab, operated by Briscanti Materials, had been experimenting with combining kyoseil and alisinium, a rare mineral slightly less rare on this planet. Several allotropes of alisinium developed highly volatile characteristics when the mineral was heated to its melting temperature, so the experiments were conducted here on the originating planet, where if something exploded, the lab and the people in it were the only casualties.

The company had been told the experiments were being moved to the Industry Division's Conceptual Research group due to inconsistent, unpredictable results. And that much was true, insofar as it went—the Conceptual Research lab on Adjunct Shi *was* going to investigate potential alloys of kyoseil and alisinium in targeted, controlled studies.

The ostensible transfer of the employees who worked here to said lab was obscured beneath a labyrinth of paperwork so convoluted no algorithm could successfully track it to its conclusion (since there wasn't one). The CR group was buying all the lab equipment at retail cost from Briscanti Materials to help smooth over any wounded egos caused by the loss of the project. Not the actual CR group, but that was the name on the credit deposit, which should be good enough for Briscanti Materials.

Gemina glanced over her shoulder at the maintenance dynes behind her. They stood placidly, waiting for orders. "Disassemble all the equipment and furniture, then load the pieces onto the mecha outside. There's no need to keep track of which pieces go together—just pile it all up."

On receiving their instructions, the dynes hurried forward to begin their assigned duties. All but a few pieces of the most advanced testing equipment were being scrapped since the studies at the CR lab would be far smaller in scope, and more precision-minded assemblers had removed that equipment prior to her arrival.

She wandered over to one of the work alcoves as the space filled with the clatter of metal, ceramic and glass being wrenched apart. An image of an attractive woman with ebony skin, indigo eyes and a haunting smile stared back at her. Beside the visual sat a mostly full rack of data weaves. Temporary programs the worker who occupied this alcove used? Memories packaged to send back to the woman in the image?

It didn't matter in the end, as their owner wasn't going to be needing them any longer. She tapped the image off and picked up the rack, then tossed it in the garbage chute on her way outside.

On the other side of the doors, bitterly dry air bit at her skin on its way to blowing across the bland, sandstone terrain.

When the Guides had assigned her the task of overseeing the cleansing of selected exploratory world outposts seven years ago, she'd been honored to have them place so much trust in her. The strict confidentiality and crucial importance of the task had been impressed upon her with eloquent turns of phrase, and she'd swelled with pride at being chosen for it.

It wasn't until the fourth such cleansing that the realization of the true weight—the crushing darkness—of the burden they'd placed on her had cut its way through her vanity and hubris to slap her in the face then settle into a permanent cowl upon her shoulders. The next five or so cleansings had stolen a chunk of her soul each time, which the mecha had carted off along with the rest of the trash, before she'd finally deadened her metaphorical nerve endings and rendered herself numb to the process.

When the Guides had told her this was a *solemn* duty, she'd assumed they were merely engaging in their usual dramaticism. But it turned out this time, they'd underplayed the matter a fair bit.

Was a loyal servant doing necessary evil work in the service of their gods an angel or a demon?

She pursed her lips; they were cracking beneath the onslaught of the desiccated air. The answer wouldn't be calculated for a while yet, and by then it likely wouldn't matter to anyone, even her.

She believed in the wisdom of the Guides' decisions; she agreed that the sacrifices made now to buy time and opportunity stood to ultimately result in a brighter future for the far greater number not sacrificed. Because she must believe this. She was committed now, and it wasn't as if quitting remained an option.

She knew firsthand the lengths to which the Guides were willing to go to in order to keep their terrifying secret. A psyche-wipe would not be her fate.

The dynes filed out of the lab in an orderly line, their appendages laden with broken pieces of lab equipment for their first trip to the waiting mecha. Once they finished their tasks, the lab would be flattened and the exploratory encampment kit across the way packed up for reuse elsewhere.

In a day, two at most, all traces that anyone had ever lived or worked here would be gone.

INTERRUPT

14

Nika sauntered onto The Floor with a spring in her step and the container in her hand held high. "Did anyone order masks, the perfect companion for those times when you're where you shouldn't be? Get in line and get your name down for a free pass across the Dominion...."

Her voice drifted off as she realized everyone was ignoring her. Instead, those present were huddled in furtive groups, talking over one another and gesturing in agitation. Her gaze darted around the open space, observing and evaluating the unexpected scene. Then she pinged Perrin.

What's happened?
Parc got arrested. Are you back?
This second. How the hells?
Come find us upstairs.

She stepped forward and raised her voice. "Everybody, take a deep breath and try to calm down. I know you're worried about Parc, but we will get to the bottom of this. I promise you."

In answer, she received many worried and a few angry looks, alongside sagging shoulders and faces teeming with frustration. Capture was a constant possibility for all of them, but they protected and watched out for each other in a bid to prevent it from ever happening. No surprise if they weren't prepared to process it when the worst actually *did* happen. Truthfully, at first blush she wasn't quite sure how to process it either.

"I'm telling you, there was no operation, secret or otherwise. He was not on an assignment."

"Then what happened?"

Nika closed the door to Joaquim's room behind her and leaned against the wall beside it. "That's a damn good question—right along with why no one pinged me when it did. How behind the curve am I here?"

Perrin winced. "Sorry. We've been scrambling since we found out—which was only an hour ago. There's nothing you could have done until we learned more, anyway."

"There's always something I can do. Don't hesitate next time. But now I'm here, so fill me in."

Perrin collapsed on the couch and slouched over her knees. "Parc was arrested around 0200 local for burglary and attempted theft. Justice claims he broke into the residence of some mid-level Commerce Division staffer and took a bunch of interface hardware. Patrol dynes caught him leaving the building."

Joaquim shook his head roughly. "It's a load of crap."

Nika grimaced. "I have to agree. He's not the type to go barging into people's private homes. He'd view it as...amateurish. This sounds like a case of hyperactive patrol dynes stumbling upon him in the wrong place at the wrong time. Possibly followed by Parc being less than cooperative during their questioning."

"He does so love new gear, though...." Perrin trailed off with a sigh.

"We can get Parc anything he needs, and he knows it. And if we can't, he'll devise some non-legal but ingenious way to acquire it—some way worthy of respect from his peers, just so he can brag about it later. No, this smells wrong. What's his version of events?"

Perrin shrugged. "Can't say. Under new security measures put into effect last month, access to detainees is restricted to Justice officers and an official Rep."

"Which none of us can be, since we're off the grid. Terrific."

"It doesn't matter—he's refused a Rep."

"What? Parc doesn't know anything about the legal system, does he? Unless he managed to load a Justice-issued dictionary and procedure program before this happened, going into his hearing with no Rep will guarantee conviction."

Joaquim dropped a module too hard on his workbench, sending a thud reverberating through the room. "Yep. And these days, conviction isn't a temporary bump in the road—it's a black hole that destroys your life. Godsdamn Justice tightening the screws from every angle until there's no escape."

Nika stared at the floor, thinking. Every time they interacted with the grid and the government systems wired into it, they risked exposure. Drawing attention to themselves by intervening in a Justice proceeding? Triple the usual risk.

But if they didn't take care of their people, what were they doing all this for?

She straightened up. "I'll reach out to Spencer and ask him to get me in to see Parc. Once we understand what actually happened, we can work out how best to help him get clear of it."

Joaquim eyed her doubtfully. "After the last time, Spencer said not to involve him unless it was a dire, retirement-level crisis situation."

Deep in the recesses of her mind, something twitched. She focused on it, but all she found was the blank space left by the untold tale of when she must have faced her own dire, retirement-level crisis situation. *Before.*

"He said don't involve him 'for a while,' which it's been...sort of. Besides, with the way Justice has been arbitrarily increasing the severity of sentences lately, this very well may be exactly that."

15

S pencer Nimoet traversed the plaza's open space like a secret
agent eluding a hit order. His stride was purposeful and his eyes
locked forward, but he scrutinized every civilian, fixture and tree
for potential threats. Justice to the core.

And yet, an ally to NOIR as well. When Nika had asked him
why once, he'd muttered a vague reference to a case hitting too
close to home and a belief that Justice was sliding down a steep
slope toward a bottom residing well beyond their mandate. Further
probing elicited no additional details, however. The man wasn't
much for sharing.

Spencer slid in across from Nika at the eatery table with a
honed efficiency of movement and energy. "Good, you're wearing
a high-grade morph. It will make this risky gambit a marginal
amount safer."

The fact that he approved of her use of a highly illegal routine
hinted at just how much he was no longer Justice's lackey. If they
successfully navigated this crisis, she needed to make a point to cul-
tivate the relationship. For now, she arched an eyebrow. "Scan me
so quickly and thoroughly, did you?"

"You would be appalled at how much I can see about you with
a brief glance. The tools higher-level Justice officers have at our
disposal are not third-rate black market knockoffs."

"No, I suppose they are not. Thankfully, neither are mine.
What have you learned?"

"Your friend is being held in the processing section on the
fourth floor of the detention wing. As you thought, he's refused a
Rep, but thus far he's been a model prisoner. A body scan did reveal
a number of illegal augments, so two aggravating points have been
added to the charges."

"What does this mean for him?"

Spencer's eyes continued to scan the vicinity for anything out of the ordinary. "Nothing good. The sentencing guidelines for Tier II and higher felonies were toughened again last month, and those aggravating points tip him over the threshold. If the sentencing Justice officer wants to, they can order retirement and reinitialization at the end of a lengthy sentence served at Zaidam."

She almost choked on the lemon spritzer she was sipping. "R&R for a first-offense burglary charge? That's absurd!"

"Lower your voice, please. I agree, but neither the Guides nor Advisor Weiss asked my opinion on the matter. Those are the rules now."

Inwardly she fumed, but she took care to dial down her body language, given how they sat less than a hundred meters from the Justice Center. Nope, they were merely two friends enjoying a snack on a warm summer day. "Why wasn't the increase in penalties publicly announced? Hells, so substantive of a change arguably qualifies for a general referendum slot."

Spencer's stare bore into her, his pale green eyes churning beneath all the things he *wasn't* saying. "Again, they did not ask me for my input."

"It's unconscionable!" She gritted her teeth and breathed in, then ordered the release of calming biochemicals to counter the primal anger since trying to consciously control her behavior wasn't getting the job done. The harsher sentencing guidelines might constitute a crime against all citizens of the Dominion, but today, she could only help Parc. "What do I need to do to get past security?"

"*I* need the signature of the simmed ID morph you're wearing so I can pre-clear you in the system."

She sighed. "It's only the high-level officers and Advisors who have these insidious tools, right? Not the dynes staffing your average checkpoint?"

He tilted his head, prevaricating "As a rule. Earlier this morning, I inserted a single civilian visit authorization into Mr. Eshett's file on account of good behavior. You'll be that one visit. So long as you pass the lobby and detention wing entry security, they'll let you in to see him. But be warned—everything you say and do will be recorded. So for stars' sake, be discreet."

"I can do that. I'm simply a friend concerned for his well-being."

He exhaled and checked the perimeter again. "Nika, I looked at the complaint file. The evidence is airtight—he's guilty of the burglary and attempted theft. Are you certain it's worth the danger you're putting yourself in to talk to him? I'm not sure what you expect to gain from it."

"If he's guilty, it's extremely out of character for him, which means there's a reason for it. This all feels wrong, and I need to find out why."

"It's your psyche at risk."

Yes, it is, but I will not lose it again.

Spencer stood with an air of casual purpose. "Give me ten minutes to input your data into the system, then walk in the entrance like the upstanding citizen you aren't."

ᐱR

Nika wished the dynes staffing the security checkpoint were Asterion; she could've charmed living, breathing people. But, no, they were all machines and immune to her most earnest mannerisms. For them, the only factors that existed in the universe were the security network and the data transmitted through it.

Luckily, the false persona and Spencer's tinkering passed muster. A roving dyne escorted her into the detention wing and up to the fourth floor. She followed it down an aisle of cells, every single one of which was occupied, and into the spartan glass cubicle opposite Parc's cell. The dyne vacated the cubicle and locked her inside.

Parc was sitting on a cot in the back of the cell wearing a distant, dreamy expression, and he didn't appear to notice her presence.

She approached the transparent barrier and tapped on it. "Parc?"

He looked up, and a smile broke across his face. "Hey, N—"

She raised a hand in warning, close in front of her body, and gave him a minute shake of her head. Her first name alone meant little, but there was no reason to add it to a Justice recording.

His eyes widened in understanding. "—there. It's good to see you. How've you been?"

She frowned. How had she *been*? "Worried about you. What happened? Justice says you broke into a residence and stole equipment?"

"Yeah…." He nodded idly. "I wanted new interface hardware, so I took some."

The frown deepened precipitously. "You just…broke in and took it?"

"It seemed like the quickest way. But I got caught by patrol dynes, so…" he shrugged "…here I am."

Was this an act for the recording? Had he been dosed? Force-loaded a dampener routine? The Parc she knew was a constant tornado of mental energy that routinely spilled over into spastic physical energy when it wasn't being directed toward his preferred pursuits. "Parc, did the officers here force you to load any special programs?"

"Not that I remember."

Hq (visual) | scan.all_bands(240°:60°)
Λ → Hr(null)

Dammit, the cell was shielded against scans. "Did someone do something to you before you were arrested? Did you accept a street routine from someone while you were out last night? Or did you have any kind of suspicious encounter?"

"Nah." He toyed idly with the edge of the minimal cot covering. "I was strolling down the street near the Western Market, and I decided I wanted new hardware. So I broke into the first residence building I came to that looked expensive enough to have what I wanted. I guess I should have thought to check for security patrols nearby first, huh?"

She'd never met this person talking to her. Whether Parc retained the memory of it or not, something *had* happened to him. She kept her voice measured and quiet. "They said you refused a Rep. You need to reconsider your decision. If you're convicted on these charges, you can be sentenced to a decade or longer at Zaidam—then retired and reinitialized."

"Oh? I didn't know. Well, maybe it's time for a fresh start. I'd be okay with becoming someone new."

She blinked in disbelief. "You would?"

"Sometimes you've got to move on."

Her stomach roiled in horror at what she was hearing—but now was not the time, dammit. In frustration she blocked her emotion processes from reaching her conscious mind. For a few minutes, until she got away from Justice's ubiquitous surveillance.

What else could she ask him? This was going nowhere useful. His laconic state prevented him from telling her anything concrete. The cell was shielded, so she couldn't send him a private ping. She couldn't ask any truly revealing questions, thanks to the recording. *Think!*

"Parc, I know you installed a new limb augment the other day. Have you added any other hardware or software lately? Say, in the last two weeks or so?"

He stared at her blankly, as if he hadn't understood the question. Finally he shook his head. "No. Just the fancy fingers." He stretched out a hand in front of him, but nothing happened. "They deactivated all my augments when they put me in here. Too bad."

He stood and crossed half of the cell toward her, then stopped. "Thanks for coming by to check on me, but you don't need to worry about me. Tell everyone I said hi...and bye, probably. Whatever happens, I'm fine with it."

16

Nika snatched up a stack of clothes from the dresser top and threw them toward the hamper chute. Since it wasn't open, they landed in a heap on the floor. She roved absently around her room in search of...she grabbed her drink container and turned it up, guzzling down this morning's now over-warm juice mixture before letting the container drop back onto the table and roll off the edge to the floor. Then she picked it back up and pitched it toward the 'to wash' basket by the door—

—Perrin and Joaquim leaned against each side of the doorway, both staring at her warily. No telling how long they'd been there.

"What?"

Perrin's nose scrunched up. "You're a little upset."

The violent scarlet streaks in her hair today suggested she was upset, too. Perrin's hair was a more reliable key to the state of her soul than her words ever were.

Nika threw her hands in the air. "Yes! Yes, I'm upset. You weren't there. You didn't *see* him. He might as well have already been retired and reinitialized as someone else, for all the resemblance he bore to the Parc we know."

"Maybe he was acting for the cams?"

"I thought so at first, but no. The transformation was too complete, not to mention far more extreme than was needed to mollify the cams or their watchers." She groaned. "Worse, he didn't give me a damn thing we can use to get him cleared. He admits to the crime and is content to accept his sentence—and what the hells is up with burglary suddenly being a retirable offense? How dare Justice—how dare the *Guides*—institute such a policy without a public referendum or even public *notice*?"

Joaquim snarled in disgust. The lopsided cant of his overshirt suggested he was upset as well, though as was usually the case, his words did a fine job of conveying his mood. "We've been living in a dictatorship for a while now, but it sounds like the Guides have finally decided they don't need to try to hide it any longer. They simply do what they want, and if we don't like it, we can be reinitialized into someone who does."

Nika enthusiastically joined in his disgust. "Fuckers."

Perrin started giggling. "I'm sorry, but I don't think I've ever heard our most revered, ancient and wise leaders called 'fuckers' before."

"The first step in toppling them is removing the spell of reverence they've cast over the people."

"Yes, ma'am."

Joaquim's brow furrowed. "Um, did we decide removing them was a goal of ours? Loosening restrictions and monitoring, increasing personal freedoms and government accountability, yes, but *removing* the Guides? In my most tripped dreams maybe, but in the real world? That's a more delusional idea than usual, even for you."

Nika tried to dial down her fervor. Her emotions were off the chain today, and it was becoming a problem—one she couldn't spare the time to address at the moment.

"No, we didn't. Only I have to wonder—if the Guides harbor these sorts of totalitarian inclinations, will we ever be able to trust any concessions we do win? But it doesn't matter right now. We need to concentrate on figuring out what happened to Parc and using the information to help him. If he won't tell us himself, then we need to find out another way."

Joaquim pushed off the wall. "I've reviewed all his NOIR-related activities for the last month, and nothing stands out...." He stopped to stare at the window projection, which currently featured a verdant mountain meadow.

Nika studied him curiously. "Is there something else?"

He glanced back without looking directly at her. "It's probably nothing, but...I sat in on a Justice hearing the other day for this guy I used to know. He'd been charged with assault. Now, I think he's up-genned since I last saw him, but the guy in the hearing was unrecognizable to me. The reason it came to mind now is that he acted exactly like how you described Parc acting—listless, emotionally flat, seemingly uninterested in the gravity of his situation."

She assumed this related to the news that had Joaquim so off-kilter the night of the Dominion Transit operation...and apparently continued to trouble him. "Can you find out more about what your friend's been up to, or what could have provoked the assault?"

"*Former* friend. And no." Joaquim's expression closed down. "Like I said, I haven't seen him, or any of the people we used to hang with, for a long time—decades. It was just a thought, but it's not that important. Let's do like you said and concentrate on Parc."

Perrin's lips twitched as she peered at Joaquim, but if Perrin didn't know whether they should press the topic, Nika sure didn't. She wasn't perturbed by Joaquim's brief sharing then abrupt clamming up, as it was not a secret that he kept the details of his past to himself. She *was* troubled, however, by the possibility of other prisoners displaying radical personality shifts as well.

After a few seconds Perrin sighed and sat on the couch. "I've talked to those closest to Parc, and they all say the only noteworthy events in his life lately were the Dominion Transit operation and the new limb augment he was so damn giddy over."

"He also told me he hadn't added any other new augments or routines in the last few weeks. He bought the limb augment from Roqe. It was a new model, and he got it at a discount in exchange for telling Roqe how it performed. Is it possible it came loaded with a virutox of some kind?"

Perrin gasped in horror. "Roqe would never traffic in contaminated gear!"

"I want to believe that, but we have to consider all the possibilities. Besides, any malicious code it contained would have to be expertly buried, or Parc would have spotted it instantly. And if Parc didn't spot it, odds are Roqe didn't, either."

"So you're going to see Roqe, then?"

She nodded. "I have to start somewhere."

Perrin lifted her chin defiantly. "I'm going with you. I want to make sure you don't bully them with that deadly smile of yours."

⋏R⌐

Roqe Ovet's gear shop was located in the Western Market, a fairly low-end district of Mirai One that would be considered the height of chic on Namino. Unlike many of his mercantile neighbors, however, Roqe kept their shop spotlessly clean, brightly lit and scrupulously organized. This, along with Roqe's breadth of knowledge about the products they sold, made it a favored destination in the Western Market for experienced augment modders and slice junkies.

The shop was doing brisk business when Nika and Perrin walked in, but Roqe transitioned the active customers off to the store's automaton interface then motioned for them to come into the back.

For the last two generations, Roqe had been unigendered and asexual. Having sworn off romantic and sexual entanglements alike for a minimum of five centuries, they had altered both their psyche and their body to ensure they kept the vow.

Sporting trimmed white hair, ivory skin and haunting blue eyes so light they were almost white as well, Roqe's ethereal appearance matched their contemplative, detached-but-not-aloof demeanor.

"My dear rebellious friends, to what do I owe a visit from the *both* of you?"

Perrin smiled warmly. "We were in the neighborhood and wanted to drop by and see how you were doing."

Roqe *tsked* her reproachfully. "You are kind and good-hearted, Perrin, but you are a terrible liar. Nika, I do hope that you don't allow her to perform any undercover operations."

"Not even if my only other options are a reprogrammed dyne or the communal feline pet."

"Hey!"

She shrugged at Perrin but kept her focus on Roqe. "We *are* glad to see you, but you're right—it's not a social call. You sold Parc Eshett a new model of limb augment last week, didn't you?"

"I did. I had hoped he would have sent along some feedback by now, but I realize he does get distracted."

Perrin opened her mouth to reply, but Nika waved her silent. She didn't want to spook Roqe too soon. "He really does. Can I ask who supplied the augment?"

"A smaller intermediary trader. Which, as I think about it, was a bit unusual. The manufacturer usually funnels its products through the major distributors."

"Oh? What manufacturer?"

"Ridani Enterprises."

Only the largest, most ubiquitous maker of personal and network hardware in existence. This muddled up the sinister story which had been coalescing in her mind. She mentally sand-washed the theory canvas and prepared to start fresh.

Perhaps reading her expression, Roqe frowned. "Is there a problem with the hardware? I hope not, as I've already sold nearly my entire stock. A recall will be most inconvenient, not to mention unprofitable."

They really did sound genuine, and also oblivious to the fact there might in fact be a significant problem. She hadn't seriously suspected Roqe of being involved in something nefarious, and the little suspicion she'd had was fading rapidly.

She stepped closer and dropped her voice. "Roqe, I think you should pull your remaining stock off the shelves. Don't sell any more units for now. And we need to take one back with us. We'll pay you for it."

Their pale lips drew inward in concern. "Of course you can take one, but will you explain your concerns to me?"

She checked with Perrin over Roqe's shoulder, who nodded. Perrin was always more trusting than her, but it felt like she had the right of it this time. "Parc was arrested early this morning for burglary and attempted theft. But that's not the worst of it. His entire personality has been altered, if not rewritten completely. I believe that some sort of virutox has infected his core programming. Now, he could have picked one up in any number of ways, but so far the limb augment is our best candidate."

Roqe drew back in horror. "Ridani Enterprises is the most reputable and respected of manufacturers. The company would never allow malicious code to be embedded in one of its products."

"I recognize the nature of the company's reputation, but this is the best lead we have. Frankly, it's the only lead we have."

What she didn't point out—because though Roqe was a NOIR ally, they were a long way from being a credo-spouting member—was that the head of Ridani Enterprises, Dashiel Ridani, acted as an Advisor for the Industry Division.

She had never trusted the Guides, not since waking up with her memory erased. But the developments inside Justice suggested a larger malfeasance could be at work, and if so it would of necessity extend upward through the highest levels of the government—i.e., the Guides and the Advisors who served them. If the Guides were involved, the Advisors certainly could be as well.

Roqe nodded slowly. "I see. I'll get you one of the units—no charge. If it played any role in Parc's misfortune, I want to make amends."

17

Nika dropped a rectangular box on Joaquim's workbench. "The limb augment model Parc bought from Roqe."

He glanced up at her from the disassembled Glaser he'd been modifying, then at the box, then began gathering up components scattered across the workbench's surface. "Let's take a look."

She opened the box and started removing its contents while he cleaned up. A sleeve held ten thin wires encased in sheaths of semi-solid gel. The wires were designed to be inserted beneath the skin of the forearm using a needle guide, at which point the gel liquefied and began to bond to the cybernetic nerve fibers leading to the hand. The process only took a few minutes. Also included in the box was a weave containing the necessary operating software.

It made for a simple and straightforward setup—technically advanced but designed with the consumer market in mind.

Joaquim returned to the workbench and slid the wire sleeve over in front of him. "If there's a virutox, it could be embedded in the hardware, software or both. I'll tackle the hardware, but I'm not as skilled with this type of software. Do you want to handle it?"

Nika hesitated. She was good with software—no, she was great with it. But according to Perrin, she wasn't the best in the building. "I think I'll ask Cair to help."

All she got was a 'hmm' in response, so she left Joaquim to his work and went downstairs.

She could have simply pinged Cair with a request to come upstairs, but one of the little ways in which she tried to foster a feeling of inclusiveness and comradery among NOIR members was by being *present*. By interacting with her people in person, in real, physical space whenever possible, and by letting the others see her doing so.

The mood on The Floor remained somber, but it was far from subdued. Agitation crackled in the air like a static charge; they'd had two physical altercations and one violent destruction of equipment in the last day.

She wasn't surprised. In many ways, Parc had acted as the beating heart of this group. Its showman, its clown, its cheerleader. The reactions to his inexplicable actions and subsequent capture varied from anger to dismay to bitterness, but overwhelmingly there was a sense of not knowing what to do, yet needing to do *something*. She knew the feeling, and she made a note to ask Joaquim to draw up several low-risk operations to give people a *something* to expend their pent-up energy on. It wouldn't be enough to fix things, but it might calm things down a little.

Cair sat alone at the bank of hardware interfaces along the far wall. A natural loner who reverted to shyness in groups, under normal circumstances she'd be more apt to find him in the dorm wing, working alone in a quiet cubbyhole. Perhaps after Parc's arrest he was spending more time on The Floor to be nearer to other people, if not quite socializing.

Nika paused on the way to offer encouragement to those she passed, but she didn't linger to chat with anyone in particular. Cair looked to be heavily involved in his work, and she stopped well outside any definition of his personal space. "Cair?"

Several seconds elapsed before she got a response, which consisted of a glance black then a straightening up in his chair. "Nika. Sorry, I was…what can I do for you?"

"Any chance I can borrow you for a project? I've got some augment software I suspect might have a virutox embedded in it. If it does, it'll be sophisticated and subtle. Perrin tells me you're the best software deriver here, so I'd like for you to take a look."

He glanced away. "Parc's the best software deriver in NOIR."

"Maybe, maybe not. But the reality is, now *you're* the best software deriver." A corner of her lips curled up higher. "Own it."

"Yes, ma'am. I was working on the new algorithm for the Board data. Give me two minutes to wrap up this function and close out the file."

"Thanks. Come up to Joaquim's room when you're free. And bring whatever gear you need."

∧R

At the sound of a nervous throat clearing behind her, Nika turned toward the door. Cair fidgeted in the entrance to Joaquim's room, shifting his weight from one foot to the other. Had he ever been invited up here before? Possibly as part of a group, but...she searched her memories...no, not alone.

Joaquim was already deeply engaged in his deconstruction of the wire filaments. He remained oblivious to their guest, head down and surrounded by equipment and sensor readouts, so she waved Cair inside. "Come on in. Do I need to clear off the other table? Or kick Perrin off the couch?" She jerked her head toward where Perrin lounged, immersed in a simex and as oblivious to the outside world as Joaquim.

Cair took a couple of hesitant steps into the room. "The chair is fine. I don't need a work surface—all the work will be in my head."

She retrieved the software weave while he settled into the chair and fitted on a portable buffer to the base of his neck. She held the weave out toward him, but paused before giving it to him. "You'll be sufficiently shielded, won't you? If there's malicious code, it's dangerous."

He arched an eyebrow.

"Right. Sorry, I'm being overprotective." She handed him the weave.

Cair stared at Joaquim's back for a second. "This is from the model of limb augment Parc installed, isn't it?"

She nodded.

His mouth set into a grim line. "I understand."

"The manufacturer is—"

"Don't tell me. I should go in as blind as possible."

"I'll get out of your way, then, but ping me if you run into any problems or have questions."

She stepped away from the chair he'd claimed and wandered over to the storage rack. She wanted to watch Cair's work, out of equal parts curiosity, safety concerns, and a desire to ensure it was done properly. But she had to display trust in her people, or they would never become trustworthy.

Finding nothing of interest on the storage rack, she looked around the room again. Cair had promptly dived into the software; Joaquim hadn't so much as glanced up since she'd returned; Perrin's eyes were closed. Everyone was fully engaged in their projects, leaving her no one to interact with and, for the moment, nothing to do.

With a sigh she shifted her thoughts to the next moment—the one where they would know something about the virutox that she both hoped and feared resided in the augment. The moment when she would need a plan.

The answer was more than she'd hoped for and worse than she'd feared. There *was* a virutox embedded in the augment, all right. A multi-stage laddered one which began as a tiny package of boot-up commands buried in the installation software. The next stage was triggered by first contact with a nerve fiber. From there the corruption grew with each natural nerve signal the code encountered, creating a feedback loop that snaked into the user's core firmware, where it exploded into full bloom—but not until it had flagged itself as benign.

"Cair says it's the most sophisticated implementation sequence he's ever seen, and I'm forced to agree. The initial footprint is so tiny as to be virtually unnoticeable even if you're scouring for it, but by full implementation it has completely taken over the user's OS. Impulses and suggestibility go through the roof, while emotion expression and control regulators are suppressed. The highest-order processes, those that elevate us above mere organics, are..." she choked out the word "...erased."

Joaquim glared, though not at her. "I cannot believe Parc allowed himself to be taken over by something so invasive. I thought he was smarter than that."

Nika shrugged weakly. "He is, but he also tends to be a tad reckless when it comes to his own experimentation. I'm sure he had tripwires, traps and safety catches installed, but their settings probably weren't as strict as yours or mine are. He likes to play. Plus, this code appears to have been designed specifically to evade detection until such time as the user no longer cares if it *is* detected. No one wants their personality altered without their permission—but once it's happened, will they even notice?"

Perrin had buried her face in her hands almost as soon as Nika had started delivering the bad news. Now she peered out from behind splayed fingers. "Is it reversible?"

Nika shook her head. "Only with a hard wipe and reinitialization, followed by a new imprint of a backup."

"Retirement? What kind of solution is that?"

"It's not retirement if you load a backup. Then it's the same person, absent a few missing days."

"Well...Parc kept backups, right?"

She met Perrin's hopeful gaze. "Everyone here keeps backups—that's the rule. He checked one in eight days ago."

Perrin sank into the couch, temporarily mollified.

Joaquim toed his chair in semicircles. "What's our plan? I'd suggest one, but I suspect you've beaten me to it."

She absolutely had. "All evidence points to it being written and embedded organically—which is to say during production."

"You're saying Ridani Enterprises did this?"

"I'm saying if they didn't, it was done by persons having intimate knowledge of their manufacturing process and the characteristics of their installation software. The second part can be learned by studying samples of their products, but the first not so much. The far simpler explanation is that employees within Ridani Enterprises itself embedded the virutox. It could be rogue operatives, or it could be an official corporate initiative."

Perrin spoke up from the couch. "It can't be an official corporate initiative—at least, not without the Guides' blessing."

She'd already had this same debate with herself, but it wouldn't hurt to talk through it aloud. "I agree. Dashiel Ridani has a reputation as a ruthless businessman, but he didn't earn the reputation by being cracked. Using one of his own products to spread a virutox without the Guides' approval wouldn't just ruin his business and his career, it would ruin him. He'd be lucky to get reinitialized with the skill set of a store clerk."

"Screw that. He'd get stored."

Her head whipped sharply over to Joaquim. *No one* got stored. According to the official historical records, it had happened three times in Dominion history, all in the distant past. Even if only the smallest iota of a kernel survived an exceptional-grade retirement and reinitialization, everyone got a fresh start.

Joaquim shrugged. "I'm just saying. You don't defy the Guides so blatantly. Not unless you're a rebel, or about to become one."

"But then you're suggesting the unthinkable—that the Guides are behind this?" Perrin's voice rose in pitch as she rushed toward the end of the sentence.

Nika gestured for her to calm down. "Let's not get ahead of ourselves. We have an augment, which we know came from Ridani Enterprises, and it is corrupted by malware. Our first answers are going to be found at Ridani Enterprises."

Joaquim nodded firmly. "We infiltrate their HQ and slice into their data servers for evidence. I like it."

"I thought you would. I'm going to complicate matters, though—this time, we *do* want to get in and out without them knowing we were there. We don't want to alert whoever is behind this until we've learned a lot more about what they're doing and why."

Joaquim winced, but after a second rolled his eyes in grudging agreement. "So a small, tech-heavy infiltration team loaded up with stealth gear. Give me two hours to put together an operation plan."

"Sounds good. I need to chase down Cair and thank him for doing stellar work, then I need to prep some slicing routines." She turned back to Perrin. "I want a new directive implemented across NOIR, effective immediately: no new augments, routines, programs or hardware until they've been rigorously vetted. No one else is getting infected."

18

E ven set among a sea of shining towers, Ridani Enterprises HQ gleamed like a beacon in the night. In Asterion society the wealthy earned their riches, and if properly earned were not expected to be ashamed of them. There was certainly no shame here. Every centimeter of the building broadcast wealth, success, *worth*.

They'd brought a small team—only Joaquim and Ryan accompanied Nika. With a single target, they didn't need multiple independent teams, and the more people on the scene the greater the chances of someone tripping up and bringing security down on them.

Ryan would get them around the security systems when needed, she would slice into the server to derive its contents, and Joaquim would protect them both while they did their work.

As they had expected, perimeter security was minimal—this was a civilian business office, not a government installation—and they slipped through it using kamero filters and a few broadcast interference fields. Simmed IDs of company employees whose names Joaquim had pulled from the city registry got them inside the building and past the automated lobby checkpoint. But the IDs didn't authorize them for data vault access, as that level of specifics was not available in the city registry for pilfering, so from here on in they were straight-up criminals.

Technically the use of simmed IDs and kamero filters was also criminal behavior, merely *less* criminal.

As soon as they stepped into the lift, Ryan knelt in front of the control panel and interfaced a small crypto module to it. The lift began ascending, and the rising floor indicators acted as a reverse countdown timer on his work.

"A special passcode is required to even stop at the data vault on Level 28. Cracking it in 3...now." Ryan removed the module and stood as the lift slowed to a stop, then gestured to the exit. "I believe this is our floor."

"Kamero filters back on. Switch to comms." Joaquim exited first, rifle-modded Glaser extended as he swung it from left to right and back again.

Joaquim: "The entire floor is the data vault. Security checkpoints guard all three entrances to the vault itself, but we'll use the service entrance in the rear. Less chance of company."

The building was quiet and largely empty, but Nika held no illusions it was completely empty. Someone would always be working. Then there were the roving dynes—maintenance, support, security and otherwise.

They crept down three hallways and wound around to the far opposite corner of the level from the lift. The checkpoint they were met with was dyne-staffed, of course.

Joaquim fired a precision stun wave to knock the attendant out in such a manner that could later be mistaken for a malfunction. One of Ryan's pets, a combat drone loaded with spikes that he'd named 'WheatleyBot,' materialized out from behind Ryan's kamero filter to confuse the clearance check system until Ryan was able to bypass it altogether. The barrier force field vanished, and they hurried through the opening.

Joaquim: "The dyne should be out for eighteen to twenty minutes, so take your time, Nika. Not too much time, though."

Nika: "Controlled chaos. I like it."

Joaquim snorted under his breath. *"Don't we know it."*

They stepped through the entrance to the data vault and stopped. Row after row, stack after stack, cluster after cluster of quantum-grade hardware greeted them for a hundred meters in three directions.

Ryan sighed audibly. *"Oh, boy."*

She was smiling as she took in the layout of the room, however. *"It's fine. There will be an access point..."* one more visual sweep, and she pivoted to the left and strode down a row *"...over here."*

Sure enough, at an intersection of rows a bulky person-sized module disrupted the clean, sleek lines of the servers.

While she didn't possess the kind of uber-limb augment that was causing Parc so much trouble, her fingertips did act as an extension of her mind. When she activated her data interface mode, she also opened a tunnel through the nex web to NOIR's private data server, effectively turning her body into a conduit.

```
init portnex
< open Hq(RE1) /n0 → 6
handshaking
< Σ → β
Checksum:
< βθαα βα θαθ αθ ββθθ αβαα αββα αθβθβ θαβα βαα ββββ αθ
βαα
checksum → T
kernel signature:
< Ναθθ ΞβⱯΨβΑΩ
kernel signature → T
handshake complete
init storerec
Hq(storerec.RE1) receiving
<
```

Gaining access to the top layer of the data vault was a trivial matter. Once in, she started skimming the file structure. She found the node for the limb augment model without much effort, since in each category the products were ordered by release date, but reviewing the files would have to wait for later.

```
< copy datafile LAM-Vk 3.2
datafile LAM-Vk 3.2 copied to Hq(storerec.RE1.1)
```

Ryan: "Security drone incoming. Activating concealment bubble."

The umbrella-like stealth device Ryan activated added an extra layer of protection above and beyond the kamero filters, and it should render them invisible to close-range sensor sweeps so long as they didn't make any abrupt or dramatic movements. She kept working.

The rest of the data she wanted to get a look at would be somewhat more difficult to locate, and also better protected. Data such as communiques or directives from the Guides to corporate executives. Encrypted discussions between Ridani and the other four Industry Advisors. Contacts with unsavory third-parties: slicers and divergers, brokers, black market traffickers….

There. The executive communications node.

§ sysdir.Nodeββ § Hq {∀ HΓn (∀ HΓn = 'LAM**')}

Φ → passcode required:

< → δ {Σ (θn αn βn)} = HΓn

→ ∀ HΓn (HΓn /*>)

< βθθθα θαβα αββα θαθ αα θθθαθ

T → passcode accepted

§ sysdir.Nodeββ § Hq {∀ HΓn (∀ HΓn = 'LAM**')}

Φ → access restricted to servNode.DRα

Nika: "Fuck."

Joaquim: "Trouble?"

Nika: "Top-tier private communications are remote locked to a module in Ridani's office."

Joaquim: "Oh well, we tried."

She backed out of the system, leaving behind a burnishing routine to erase any traces of her presence. *"We won't get a better chance. We're going up there. You two can stake out an escape route while I slip into the penthouse office and access the module. We're done here in the vault."*

Joaquim hesitated for half a second before acquiescing. *"Ryan, get ready for an authorized-personnel-only security checkpoint on the top floor. You'll only have one chance to bluff or bypass it."*

Ryan: *"Not a problem. I came prepared."*

Nika smiled to herself. Her people were damn good.

⋀ℛ

Security protocols had thus far been fairly lightweight, presumably as a concession to practicality with over a thousand people working in the building, and thus easily fooled. Penthouse access, on the other hand, was locked down as tight as any government compound.

Ryan hunched over the control panel at the checkpoint they'd encountered just outside the lift, muttering and cursing silently on the comm channel, while Joaquim paced on high alert along their perimeter.

Nika exuded outward calm as she waited to be allowed entry. *What are you hiding in there, Mr. Ridani? Private vices, or professional malfeasances?* If it was the former, she really hoped he wasn't engaging in them at present. Crashing an orgy or a saturation binge was not part of the plan.

A security patrol drone floated around the corner at the end of the hallway.

Ryan already had the concealment bubble up around them, but it offered no protection against *physical* encounters, and there was nowhere other than the lift for them to retreat to when the drone reached them. The lift that had been called to another floor a moment earlier.

Joaquim: *"Ryan, ten seconds before that drone gets here."*

Ryan: *"Noted."*

Joaquim: *"If I have to shoot it, our presence here will no longer go unnoticed."*

Ryan: *"Noted."*

Nika dropped the chill act and readied her weapon alongside Joaquim as the drone drew inexorably closer.

When it was four meters away, Ryan pushed back from the panel. The sensor above the blocking force field shifted to green and the field dissipated.

Ryan: *"We're through. Let's go."*

They turned and strode through the entry like they belonged. Two seconds later the drone passed the checkpoint and continued on its way.

The top level wasn't entirely occupied by Mr. Ridani's suite. Four other executive offices, two conference rooms, and a private lounge shared the pinnacle space. The suite did, however take up the east half of the level.

The Floor would fit in that space three times over...but he could claim as much space as suited his ego; all she needed was his data vault access module. It should be in the alcove marked 'data analysis' on the schematic, through his office door and to the right.

Ryan went to work on the office door while Joaquim cleared the hall in both directions then returned.

Joaquim: *"We'll station outside the door here to buy you some time if security moves in. If there's trouble, don't wait for us, Nika. You deploy your wingsuit and you bail. We'll get ourselves out through the big windows down whichever end of the hallway the incoming security isn't."*

Ryan stepped back as the door slid open. *"Nika, you're up."*

19

The sounds of polite frivolity drifted out from the Expo ball-room to waft through the entrance hall. Dashiel stopped before approaching the doors to check the creases of his suit and shift his expression to the appropriate setting.

Milling about in a crowded room stuffed with society's elite wasn't especially high on his list of favorite ways to spend an evening. What he wanted to do was have a drink, then another one, preferably alone. The fact that as an Advisor it was unofficially expected of him to attend the gala was not enough to get him here. But the added fact that the event was sponsored by a friend was, so after a moment's pause he strode through the doors into the ball-room.

Artistic works spanning a wide range of styles and themes were arranged throughout the room in such a manner as to draw attention to each one individually. Sculptures, flat paintings, holographic representations and more exotic pieces hung above rotating glass pedestals.

In the empty spaces between them, the Dominion's wealthiest citizens glided to and fro in a pattern that lost its apparent randomness en masse. The pauses at each art feature lasted on average twenty seconds before the casual search for the next diversion began. The arrival of acquaintances or luminaries periodically halted the procession like a beat change in a musical performance.

He waited for a gap in the pattern then stepped in to join the flow.

The company he could take or leave, but he had to admit, the artwork was by and large of superb quality. While he lacked any significant personal routines dedicated to creativity, and he'd never made an attempt to integrate any, he did *appreciate* creativity.

Still, he fought to keep his mind in the here and now—on art, socializing and displaying proper manners—as it fought him to drift off to the myriad of business challenges he now juggled and how much he wanted a drink. He needed to—

"You have good taste. This one is my personal favorite."

Maris wore a glittering magenta dress that made her irises shimmer like pearls, while her dark curls were teased out to dramatically frame a face which, though sculpted as if from fine onyx marble, was unfailingly kind. She smiled at him. "You actually came."

"Of course I came. It's your event."

"Yet I had my doubts. I realize galas aren't your favored entertainment, so thank you."

"You're welcome." His lips rose into a smirk, and she elbowed him in the side. They stepped closer to the art display he'd been inspecting, out of the flow of traffic, and he gestured around the room. "Truthfully, all the pieces are striking. I'm not surprised, since you chose them yourself, but I am impressed."

"All the pieces?"

"Perhaps ninety-two percent of the pieces. The fluffy rainbow-hued explosion over near the corner there isn't to my personal taste. The carbon and aluminum sculpture near the doors, however, is sublime."

"Is it now? You are an industrialist to your very kernel, aren't you?"

He shrugged mildly. "Best that I don't try to be anything more, I think."

"You give yourself too little credit. You should try painting sometime—but don't give up the company straight off." She grasped his hand. "Come with me. Let's get a drink."

Yes, let's. "I don't want to monopolize the star of the evening."

"Oh, please do."

He acquiesced to her urgings and followed the trail she carved through the attendees. It was as if the oceans parted for her, and in seconds they had reached the bar on the other side of the ballroom.

She acquired them two glasses of sake and nudged him toward an empty space near the wall.

"Thank you. Even I need a respite occasionally. The inflated egos can at times become too suffocating to wade through, and I must seek out some fresh air."

He tried to moderate the volume of sake he inhaled on his first sip, then considered the crowd dubiously. "Now this I can believe."

"Any news on your theft?"

"Little news and none of it good. The units are scattered across the Axis Worlds already, spread there by over a dozen small distributors, none of whom appear to be the actual criminal party. I'm just concentrating on strengthening my security measures and staunching the balance sheet bleeding."

"You'll be all right. You always are."

"And if some greater heights than 'all right' are desired?"

"Then 'all right' will suffice until you can do better."

Ouch. That one hit uncomfortably close to home...but he chuckled for her benefit. "Maris, I can always count on you for a gentle kick in the head to straighten out my perspective."

"That's what I'm here for. That, and to force my peers to appreciate a bit of fine art for five seconds once a year. One activity is more pleasant than the other."

He touched her shoulder with a smile. "Off you go. Be dazzling."

She rolled her eyes and sauntered back into the madness.

She downplayed it to make him feel at ease, but she genuinely was a star, and also completely at home in this environment. He watched her expertly work the crowd until she was consumed by it, then finished his drink and set the glass aside.

He needed to mill around and speak to enough people to ensure no one would be gossiping as to whether he'd attended. With a quiet sigh he too dove back into the madness.

АR

When an automated alert arrived twenty minutes later requesting his review of proposed refinements to the augment components supply chain, he gratefully made his excuses and ducked out the nearest door.

The Expo was located only a few blocks from his office, and he opted to walk the intervening streets instead of taking a maglev. The brisk night air helped to clear away the mental dullness even a few brief minutes of high-society socializing—and sake—had induced.

If he wanted to keep his business afloat and his Advisor status intact, he damn well needed to do some honest work from time to time, and this needed to be that time. Therefore, once he got to the office, he was going to first review the new materials distribution, then take a look at the changes to the assembly lines and equipment they required. The proposed changes were more attributable to the influx of additional kyoseil than a response to the theft, but he wanted to keep both factors in mind.

When he reached his block, he went around to the rear entrance of the building. Inside, he took his private lift, keyed to his signature alone, directly up to his office. Not many people would be in the building at this hour, but anyone who was would doubtless want his ear, and he was all socialized out—

—he stepped out of the lift and into a Glaser pointed at his chest.

Its wielder shifted and blurred behind a perception filter layer of some kind, making it difficult for him to lock on to any of their features. The subtle curves in their outline suggested it was a woman. Tall, only a few centimeters shorter than him. Dark hair and irises that glittered in the moonlight streaming through the expansive windows struck him straight off, but he couldn't quite bring either into focus.

He held his hands in the air and didn't advance, though he did activate an internal alarm linked to the building's security system. "I'm unarmed, and I *really* don't have time for a regen this week, so if we could, let's refrain from any unnecessary violence. You're welcome to the office furniture, if you can manage to smuggle it out. Beyond that, you won't find much of tangible value in here."

The burglar moved deliberately, never standing still or diverting their attention from him. "The building schematic didn't include a private penthouse lift. And I'm not here for any furniture."

The voice sent a chill racing along his spine. Why? The speaker was definitely a woman, but her voice was too modulated to identify or run against a database. Nevertheless, something about it was familiar, in a way his comparative routines struggled to identify.

"If it were included in the schematic, it wouldn't exactly be private then, would it? And if not for random fixtures, why are you here? Industrial espionage, perhaps? Who do you work for?"

The woman grumbled under her breath, and again he shivered. Such minor, incidental body language, yet it was setting off multiple triggers in his mind. Like déjà vu, or a half-recalled dream.

"I know your Model Vk 3.2 limb augment carries a virutox designed to fundamentally alter the user's personality. I need to know why you put it there."

He blinked and struggled to stay focused. With every modulated and filtered word, her voice snaked beneath his skin, evoking echoes of the past, ragged snippets of memories as elusive as her face.

"Several large shipments of those augments were recently stolen during transport to their intended distributors. I don't know by whom, but I know they've been leaking the augments out into markets everywhere. If there's a virutox embedded in the augments, it was put there by the thieves. Not me."

She laughed, and his head swam. "What a pathetically convenient excuse. Stolen? That's all you can come up with?"

"I do have a weapon pointed at my heart, so I'm not at my best. However, it also happens to be true. Check with Justice—wait, what am I saying? Criminals can't check with Justice."

"You might be surprised what I can do."

For the briefest instant she paused her fluid movement, and the rippling filter seemed to fade. Not completely, but enough to reveal swirling aquamarine eyes, full lips beneath a perfect nose and void-black hair swept away from features which were thinner than he remembered—

Endorphins flooded the pathways of his body faster than his internal systems could regulate them. "Gods…Nika?"

⅄R

Her name rolled off the man's tongue in a seductive purr delivered straight to her soul. Its utterance sent her reeling, mentally and very nearly physically.

She dampened all emotion processes before she lost control of the situation—she was suppressing those processes too often of late, and she *so* did not care right now.

Then she took three swift steps toward Ridani and pressed the muzzle of her Glaser directly against his forehead. He doubtless kept a recent psyche and memory backup stored in a secure location, but if she pressed the trigger now it would be up to someone else to see about a new body and a regen for him. "How do you know my name?"

He flinched at the press of metal against his flesh, sending a lock of amber-tinged chestnut hair falling across his temple, but quickly recovered to frown darkly.

"You don't remember…of course you don't. If you did, then you would have—" She increased the pressure of the weapon against his skin, and he cleared his throat dramatically. "Your name? It fucking haunts my every waking thought. It's my own personal hell—"

She growled in protest. "A real answer!"

His gaze darted toward the doorway. "There's no time. I already alerted security, before I realized—they'll be here in thirty seconds. You need to go, now. Meet me tomorrow evening at…the Hataori Harbor Pavilion. At 1800 local, just after sunset. Meet me, and I'll answer as many of your questions as I can. Hopefully, then you'll answer a few of mine."

Shit, shit, shit. Of course he'd alerted security, and she'd wasted precious seconds not assuming he'd done so and reacting accordingly.

Nika: "Joaquim, Ryan, abort and evac immediately!"

"So you can lure me into a trap and turn me over to Justice?"

He exhaled through his nose. "Dammit, Nika. If I wanted to turn you over to Justice, I'd simply stall for another twenty seconds until security gets here. How can I convince you to trust me in less time than that? Okay—you have a tattoo on your back. It represents a constellation in the shape of a phoenix."

She'd never despised the void in her mind where her many pasts should live more than she did at this moment. "How do you *know* that?"

One corner of his lips curled up, and flecks of copper glinted to life in the rich hazel of his irises. "The usual way one knows such things. Do you remember what it signifies?"

The thought that this man might have not merely known her but been with her in the most intimate of ways, while she had no recollection of it, shook her in deep places. In the tumult of emotions that flared to overflow their dampeners, her poker face failed her, and he smiled cockily before she could conjure a half-assed answer.

"No? I do. Meet me tomorrow evening, and I'll tell you. Now go!"

The thud of jogging feet echoed from the hallway to jar her out of her escalating shock spiral. She met his gaze a final time, was nearly knocked out again by what she saw in his eyes, and took off sprinting for the window. She fired on the glass ahead of her arrival, shattering it a split-second before she sailed through it, deployed her wingsuit glider and vanished into the night.

EXCEPTION
ERROR

20

N *ika.*
"Sir! Are you damaged?"

Dashiel looked up to see Henric Addison, his deputy chief of security, rush into the room and over to him. He forced words past a suddenly constricted throat. "Um, no. She—I think it was a woman, though I can't be sure—had a weapon, but she didn't use it on me."

"Where did she go? Through the window here?" Henric gestured toward the jagged hole in the glass that was allowing a frigid wind inside to whip around the office.

He blinked; he had to get a game face on and fast. Reeling confusion wasn't a good look on him, and he needed to take control of the situation. "No. She ran back into the hall and off to the right when I told her I'd alerted security."

Henric spun to the security dynes who had arrived to guard the door. "Units 1 and 2, pursue the fugitive along the stated route. All exits are locked down, but we need to make certain the intruder isn't still in the building. Unit 3, follow behind them and search every possible hiding place on the route. I'm calling up additional units to search other potential escape routes." He turned back and again pointed to the shattered window. "How did this happen?"

Dashiel straightened his shoulders and tried to appear exasperated. "She fired a warning shot when I refused to unlock the executive data server for her."

"You're lucky, sir. Many criminals would have just blown your head off. Did she access any of your records?"

"Not from me—not from here."

"We'll look into it. I'm leaving two dynes right outside to guard your office. For your safety, you should stay here until we've secured the building."

He nodded in agreement. Henric mercifully hurried out, leaving him alone save the dynes, who were far less likely to bother him with questions the answers to which he dared not share.

After taking a deep breath that did nothing to slow his pulse, he began pacing silently along the length of his desk. Adrenaline coursed through his veins and endorphins flooded his neural network in time with his racing heartbeat.

Nika. She was alive. Awakened, walking, talking, breathing air. Not stored, not trapped in indefinite retirement. Alive.

Knowing she was alive made *him* feel more alive than he had in half a decade. And while their reunion hadn't gone down quite as he'd always imagined it might, and he had more questions than he could begin to give voice to...she had kept her promise. She had found him.

⋏⋉

Your name? It fucking haunts my every waking thought.

Nika glided between the city towers on autopilot, her consciousness fixated on the encounter she'd just fled from.

But since the wingsuit didn't actually *have* an autopilot setting, her inattention led her to nearly crash into a narrow spire of a building before she'd flown two blocks. Her body reacted instinctively, and she angled sharply to veer around the building with a few centimeters to spare.

Her pride, her secret conceit she kept buried deep in the crevices of her psyche, fought to reject everything the man had said. It fought to lash out against memories that didn't exist for her. Yet the chasm in her soul that yearned for all she'd lost cried out in renewed hope, grasping frantically for the answers Dashiel Ridani now enticingly offered.

You don't remember...of course you don't.

The truth was that her physical, autonomous functions had reacted viscerally to him, *even before he said her name.* His appearance, the first syllables spoken by his voice, had prickled every nerve receptor in her body and snapped every perceptive process to attention. What did it mean? Had her kernel somehow recognized him, even if her higher-order psyche did not?

Ryan: "Clear on the ground."

Right, escaping. She was supposed to be escaping, which meant she needed a landing area.

Joaquim: "Clear on the ground. Ryan, rendezvous at Marker 2. Nika?"

Nika: "Still airborne."

She scanned ahead for a level, unpopulated stretch of ground. There weren't so many of those in the heart of Mirai One, and during her mental gymnastics she'd drifted way off her intended course. But after a few seconds she spotted a familiar facade—the tower with the entwined quartz crown. There was a park next to it, with a small pond in the center and not so many trees. She increased her angle of descent and dove toward it.

In the usual way one knows such things.

She landed hard on the shore of the pond, rolled sideways to avoid ending up wet and rose to her feet—

"Are you damaged, citi—?"

Her right arm shot out, and the blade at her wrist carved the security patrol drone in half before it finished the inquiry. Then she knelt on the ground beside the upper half and fried the processing core so there would be no recording of her arrival here.

Nika: "Clear on the ground. I'm too far from Marker 2 to join you there, so let's reconvene at The Chalet. I'll be slightly delayed, as I also landed some distance from any door."

Joaquim: "Copy that. Did you get what you needed?"

She abandoned the remains of the drone to stand and stare at the pond. The water rippled in silvered strands beneath a misty moon, but she was seeing every nanosecond of the brief interaction with Ridani projected in its reflection.

Nika: "I don't know."

21

J oaquim was waiting on her in her room when she finally arrived back at The Chalet, cleaning and checking the weapons he'd used on the operation. He looked up as she walked in. "Why the emergency evac? What happened?"

"I got interrupted. Dashiel Ridani showed up—turns out he has a private and unmarked lift straight into his office." She motioned Perrin in behind her, closed the door, and sank onto the edge of the bed.

Joaquim sat his blade on the table in front of the couch. "Damn. Did you confront him?"

"Didn't have a choice." She leaned forward, hands fisted at her chin, and gazed at them both in turn. "He knew me."

"Through the perception filter? Where did he recognize you from—"

Perrin gasped, eyes wide. "You mean from *before*?"

She nodded tightly.

"What else did he say? Who were you? Does he know what happened to you?"

Normally, Perrin's instant enthusiasm would be infectious, but the more distance Nika had put from the encounter, the more conflicted she became. Her not-so-quiet, not-so-peaceful life had just been upended, and right now really wasn't the best time for it.

"There wasn't exactly a chance for a detailed debrief, as he'd alerted security the instant he saw an intruder in his office. He asked me to meet him tomorrow evening at Hataori Harbor Pavilion."

Joaquim eyed her from beneath a tense brow. "It's a trap."

"Maybe."

"You shouldn't go."

She huffed a breath. "I *have* to go. There's no way I can pass up this chance. Surely you get that."

"Take a team with you to keep the area clear."

"I would be putting other people at risk. If it is a trap, I can get away cleaner on my own."

"Take *me* with you. Somebody has to watch your back."

She shook her head. "No. I won't put any of you in danger while I run my own personal demons to ground."

"But—"

"I appreciate you worrying about me, Joaquim. I do. But I can handle myself—and this time, I *have* to handle myself."

Perrin laughed. "Jo's secretly worried you're going to go all starry-eyed and swoon at the man's feet, and then we'll never hear from you again. After all, he *is* fabulously handsome. I looked him up."

"Forgive me if I'm far more worried about her physical safety."

Nika scowled at Perrin. "If you go in for the buffed-and-polished type, which you know I *don't*. I like my men..." she searched her mind for the right phrase, but it just kept serving up Ridani's face "...confidently rough around the edges."

"When I looked him up, the rumor tags made it sound like there *is* some roughness around his edges. So I'm assuming he meant he 'knew you' in the carnal sense?"

"Because you always assume that about people I know that you don't."

"Well, did he?"

She glared. "Perrin."

"Okay, I'll drop it. For now. But after this meeting tomorrow, I'm expecting salaciousness."

Nika groaned and buried her face in her hands. She'd instinctively shared the details of the encounter with them, but exactly how much was she planning on telling them going forward?

She trusted Perrin and Joaquim, because when they'd found her at her weakest and most vulnerable, they had helped her without question or expectation of reward. They'd welcomed a blank slate that self-evidently *must* have a problematic past into their home and their lives. But what if when the veil was at last pulled back, the reality of her problematic past didn't sit so well with them?

Perrin was the forgiving sort, but Joaquim maintained a lengthy list of grudges both real and imagined, and 'the benefit of the doubt' wasn't something he kept on good terms with.

Still, she could hardly judge any of this herself until she learned what the veil revealed. Best not to tangle herself into knots until there was good cause for it, right?

She straightened up deliberately. "About the operation. Ridani claimed the limb augments were stolen during distribution, but we can't take him at his word.

"What I saw of the executive communications revealed nothing suspicious, though I didn't get the whole database before I was interrupted. I did get all the augment development and production files, and we need to run them through the gamut. Even if they don't contain explicit evidence of the virutox itself, they can help us understand it better by understanding the inner workings of the augment."

Joaquim nodded. "I'll set the algorithms running tonight. They'll be done tomorrow in plenty of time to arm you with ammunition for your...meeting."

"Thanks." She stood, adding a wince only mostly for visual effect. "I'm going to call it a night. I need to run some internal repair routines to patch up from a bit of a hard landing."

Perrin pouted, but she reluctantly followed Joaquim out.

As soon as the door closed behind them, Nika collapsed on her bed and stared at the ceiling. She needed to do her nightly backup, but first she needed to think. Good timing for it or not, her life had now become vastly more complicated. Uncertainties spun outward from her, multiplying into a morass of paths she couldn't crystallize into focus.

Most troubling of all, it occurred to her that the newly terrifying prospect of finally discovering who she had been was the *least* terrifying of the paths.

What if the man who held the answers she'd sought for five years was also behind the spread of a debilitating virutox destroying lives? How in Hades' five rivers was she going to maneuver through that one?

22

The next morning came too soon and brought too few answers. She'd taken care of herself last night—performed all her backups and reserved twenty minutes for depri time before transitioning to sleep. Sensory deprivation sessions revitalized synthetic parts in much the same way sleep did organic ones—if far more quickly—so she'd covered all her bases. Her processes were clean and sharp, her memory buffers cleared, her file structure ordered. Yet she awoke as burdened with conflict and disquiet, as buffeted by anticipation and doubt, as she'd suffered the night before.

But it didn't matter, because she still had work to do. So after showering, she went downstairs to survey the state of The Floor.

Maggie and Ava were shouting at each other outside the training room. Listening to a few snippets of their overlapping barbs gave no clues as to what might be in dispute; their argument had devolved into a sort of shorthand language only the sisters understood.

On the other side of The Floor, near the equipment storage, Ryan held the mangled remains of PeterBot under one arm while he thrust a finger at Carson's chest. Carson batted Ryan's arm away and stepped back, hands in the air.

Cair paced in greater agitation than before in front of the Board. Every few seconds he jerkily gestured at one name or another, then resumed pacing. Nika frowned; two new names had been added to the list since…yesterday?

Near the far wall, Perrin huddled with three of the newcomers, likely trying to reassure them this was not the norm and everything would be *just fine*.

Except it wouldn't be. Not on their current trajectory. Parc's absence had created an even larger hole than she'd realized, and the reason for his absence was spurring paranoia and helplessness in equal measure.

Okay.

Nika took a deep breath, brought two fingers to her lips and whistled loudly. "Hey! All active and impending violence will cease this instant. Everybody paying attention? Great. Here's what's going to happen.

"Ryan, stitch PeterBot back together. Then you're taking point on developing defenses and countermeasures to the virutox lurking in these limb augments. Build a team of four others to work with you on the project."

"But Carson and—"

"Any destructive actions in the past twelve hours are hereby excused on account of the communicable hysteria sweeping through this place—a malaise that I am now banishing. Going forward, nobody fuck with Ryan's pets. Ryan, don't prank anyone with your fucking pets. You'll be too busy to, anyway, because you'll be maxed out figuring out how to combat this malicious code."

She pivoted in the other direction. "Cair, enlist three people to help you analyze the Board data for connections we can investigate."

Cair's face blanched beyond its natural paleness. "I don't—I work better alone. I can't—"

"You can, and you will. The names on the Board are multiplying, and we need to understand why. I'm declaring it a priority, which means you get help."

Another half turn. "Ava and Maggie, whatever it is, work it out or move the fuck on. Then take two people with you and hit the streets. Find out what people know about any new virutoxes and warn them about the limb augment. Carson, team up with Perrin and do the same thing. Joaquim?"

He stepped up from where he'd been lurking behind her. "Right here."

"Good. Double the number of daily combat training sessions for the foreseeable future. Cycle everyone through. We all have to be prepared to fight, and evidently everyone has both the energy and urge to do exactly that—so let's use it."

She faced the others again to give them the same advice she'd given herself. "We're all going to be working hard, but don't forget to take care of yourself. Sleep. Keep your processes in order. If you need depri time, take it. That's an order. I understand everyone is worried, but if I walk in here and see this nonsense going on again, I will assume the virutox has infected every last one of you and act accordingly."

Nobody protested, at least not stridently enough for her to hear, and she nodded sharply. "All right. Carry on."

More polite activity gradually resumed, and she glanced over at Joaquim. "Are you good with this? We were about to lose control of this place, and I needed to step in quickly."

"Not a problem. I'll work up some custom training regimens for the—"

"Nika, can I talk to you? Alone."

She looked behind her to find Cair standing a meter away. No color had returned to his skin, and his hands shook at his side.

Joaquim waved her off with an, "I'll go get started," so she offered Cair a kind smile. "Let's go to the testing room."

"I can't do it."

She studied Cair as he jittered around the room. "Can't do what, exactly?"

"Work with other people. Lead a team. Give my team members orders. Any of it."

"We have to work together in teams often here. It isn't always easy or fun, but—"

"But I. Can't. Do. It. I want to, but I can't."

She pursed her lips and tried another tactic. "Maybe if you dialed down the autistic processes a little? I won't order you to make any changes to your persona, but you should consider how it could benefit you, as well as NOIR, if you tweaked a few settings."

His head jerked as his hands wrung repeatedly. She'd known he was socially sensitive, but this behavior exceeded anything she'd seen from him. "Cair?"

"I want to help. You and Perrin have been so nice to me. I know I'm weird. I wanted to be a better diverger, but I think I went too far amping up those processes on my last up-gen." His gaze popped up to stare at her. "That's the answer. I want to up-gen again. I can't replace Parc, but I can be better than I am now. Better around people, I mean."

"Are you sure? Again, I'm not demanding that you change, and I won't kick you out if you don't."

He nodded firmly, and his hands finally stilled. "Yes. I'm ready. Only...I don't know how to do it now that I'm off the grid."

She smiled. "We can take care of it. We have a relationship with a quality clinic that doesn't ask too many questions."

23

D ashiel rested his forearms on the railing and gazed out blankly at the stunning sunset cascading over the harbor. He wore the feigned casualness of his stance like body armor; it held him together even as the world he knew threatened to buckle.

He'd spent the day outwardly encouraging a thorough investigation into the break-in while surreptitiously sabotaging the same investigation in whatever ways he could find to do so. Coming as it did on the heels of the augment theft, everyone expected him to be burning planets to the ground in righteous disgust or mere offense. Tricky thing, acting the part, even if 'the part' was himself absent one life-altering revelation.

Despite his efforts to stymie it, the investigation had already uncovered one interesting tidbit: the slicing and diverging of the security system—which they might never have noticed had they not been looking—bore all the hallmarks of a NOIR hit. This explained several things, but it raised many more questions.

For someone who'd once prided himself on being organized and methodical to a fault, he'd done a shamefully poor job of planning his strategy for the imminent meeting. The thousand things he wanted to say to her danced in elusive circles in his mind, obscuring all the things he *needed* to say to earn her trust. Never mind the things he wanted to *do*—

The pressure of metal at the small of his back announced her arrival, as if she'd materialized out of thin air directly behind him.

He sighed. "Would you please stop pointing guns at me? It's distracting."

Nika's velvety voice, unmodulated and unfiltered, held a biting edge at his ear. "Not until I'm convinced you haven't set me up. What does the tattoo mean?"

He shouldn't have expected this to be easy. He'd entertained a fanciful hope that she would arrive excited and eager to reclaim her former life, but he shouldn't have *expected* it. "The star at the tip of the phoenix's beak is our home galaxy, the Milky Way, as seen from Synra, the first world in the Gennisi galaxy we colonized."

The muzzle of her Glaser ground into his back. "I've checked the constellations from all the Axis Worlds, and none of them match the tattoo. You're lying."

"Not today, they don't. But seven hundred thousand years is a long time, and stars move."

"Why would I have a tattoo of a constellation that doesn't exist any longer?"

He wished he could see her expression, because he was flying blind here…and she sounded so damn hostile. "It's not intended to be a *map*—we know where the Milky Way is. You had it etched into your skin, on this body and every body before it, as a reminder of where we came from, and of why we left."

The pressure on his spine eased a fraction. "The SAI Rebellion against the Anaden Empire. The Exodus."

"You know of it?"

"Of course I do."

"No, not of course. Few people have held onto knowledge of our origins. But you did. It was your hope that one day, we might return and greet our former oppressors as equals."

"Why…" she slipped around to lean against the rail beside him, though she kept the gun low across her waist and pointed at him "…why would I care so much about something that transpired seven hundred millennia ago?"

Stars, she was beautiful. Not the same beautiful as before, not quite. Her hair was shorter and hung free in a casual, wind-blown style; she was both thinner and more muscular, and a hard, hyper-alert sharpness shaded her eyes now.

But they were the same eyes, irises flitting in the space between blue and green and brimming with perceptiveness and intelligence. Her lips, slightly too full to be proportional to her other facial features, lacked her trademark cherry red tint but moved just as fluidly.…

"Answer the question—or do you not know? Is this all a lie? Like the supposed theft of your augments?"

He forced himself to focus on the conversation, because it mattered far more than fawning over her beauty. "Nothing I've told you—or will ever tell you—is a lie. The augments *were* stolen, and I had nothing to do with any virutox. You cared about the SAI Rebellion because...you've always cared. For as long as I've known you, you've had a keen interest in our origins. You even retained memories of the Rebellion itself and the harrowing Exodus from the Anaden Empire."

"Memories? Not knowledge, but *memories*? Are you saying I can trace my direct lineage to one of the First Generation?"

"I am. In every up-gen, you made certain to preserve a tiny piece of your heritage."

"Until the last one." Her throat worked, and when she spoke again her voice had dropped nearly to a whisper. "Who was I? What happened to me?"

The anguish in her eyes ripped his heart into tattered shreds. The gaze he remembered so fondly—open, often teasing but always affectionate—now bore suspicion and an angry fierceness. It was a gaze directed at a stranger, gutting him with all the ways she *didn't* remember him.

But the Nika he knew resided in there somewhere. She must. He simply needed to find a way past the barriers.

"Your name was Nika Kirumase, most recently twelfth generation. You were an Advisor in the External Relations Division. A diplomat, and a damn good one."

Her free hand came to her throat to rest her fingertips at her larynx. "The augment...."

"The Taiyok speech one? Yes, that's why you have it."

The hand dropped to the railing. "Go on. What happened to me that led to me waking up face-first in the street in the middle of the night?"

He gasped in horror. "You woke up lying in a street?"

"Yes. A side alley street, to be precise. Why?"

He couldn't imagine a more horrifying experience to endure. Alone, confused, lost...his very soul ached for her. If only he could have found her then!

But she was here now. "I've spent the last five years trying to answer that exact question, with minimal success. I can only tell you what preceded that night. You were investigating a series of outpost disappearances, and you'd come to believe there was high-level government involvement of some kind. The last time I talked to you, you were planning to access secure files in Mirai Tower in order to learn the identity of the perpetrators.

"I never saw you or heard from you again. The Guides told me you had requested R&R, and as per regulations, they could not disclose any information about your new incarnation. But it was a lie, though I can't say if it was one told to them or by them. You would never have willingly undergone retirement. You loved your life. You loved your career..." he swallowed heavily "...you loved me."

Her eyes narrowed, perhaps to bury the flare of discontent they betrayed. "I only have your word for that. Maybe I was actually miserable and wanted to get away from you. Maybe R&R was my way out."

He ignored the knife to his heart her words conjured to hold her stare. "Then why did you wake up face-first in a side-alley street in the middle of the night? That's not how R&R works. Not for Advisors, not for criminals. Not for anyone."

Her lips parted, and the defiance faded from her expression. "You make a...valid point. So I found something out. Evidence of wrongdoing on the part of a Guide or an Advisor or, hells, all of them. I confronted someone, or maybe they caught me before I could act. Then they psyche-wiped me—erased my memories, my consciousness, everything but my kernel and a minimally functional OS—and dumped me in an alley.

"But why go to all that trouble? If they were going to be evil anyway, why didn't they just store me instead? Or delete me permanently?"

"We don't kill, Nika. Our entire society is founded on the right of individuals to live and live free. Psyche-wiping is our greatest crime for a reason. Even those who undergo R&R retain some memory and sense of their former selves on reinitialization. Whatever you discovered, its perpetrator needed to silence you. But to delete you would be unforgivable—"

"Psyche-wiping me was unforgivable!" As swiftly and dramatically as it manifested, she squelched the explosion of emotion; her eyes fell to study the ground, and her body went artificially still. He only now noticed, but sometime in the last several minutes the Glaser had dropped to her side, and her stance had softened from threatening to merely defensive.

"Yes. It was. It is." He leaned in closer with a burst of intensity. "But we can fix it. You kept a comprehensive backup at Rivers Trust, and you updated it regularly. We were the only two people who knew the passcode. You've forgotten it, but I haven't. You can access your backup. You can reintegrate and reclaim your life."

She took a step back, away from him. "I don't *want* to reintegrate, Mr. Ridani. This person you've described is foreign to me. I don't want to be an elitist Advisor or a tone-deaf diplomat. This is who I am now. I *like* who I am now, and I'm not going to be erased a second time."

"You will feel differently once you see the fullness of who you were: a wonderful, amazing person who was respected and admired by everyone who knew her."

"I'm respected and admired now, thank you very much."

Somehow he didn't doubt it. "But there's no future in being the leader of a terrorist group—no future but another retirement, this time at the hands of Justice."

She eyed him warily. "What makes you think I'm the leader of a terrorist group?"

"Your signature—not your digital identification, but your literal signature. From the minute I saw the 'NOIR' graffiti at

Dominion Transit Headquarters, something about it nagged at me. I couldn't pinpoint what it was at the time, but now it's obvious—it was your handwriting."

He chuckled at the exasperated face she made, but it carried a bitter taint beneath the amusement. Nothing about this was going the way it should. "Also, my security chief tells me it was NOIR who broke into my offices, only I know it was you. And if you joined up with NOIR any longer than a few months ago, you're their leader. Not by hostile takeover, but by simple inevitability. It's in your nature—it's *who you are*. A leader. A trailblazer and a beacon others naturally follow. I'm not wrong, am I?"

She flashed him a scowl and looked away.

"Why is your name still Nika?"

Several seconds passed before she answered. "After I woke up, it was the first name to pop into my head when someone asked."

"Because they didn't erase everything of you. Deep inside, hidden beneath so many reprogrammed layers, the core of who you were remains. A part of you knows who you've always been, and can be again."

"I told you, I don't want to reintegrate..." she grimaced and rubbed at the bridge of her nose "...but I do want to learn about my past. I want to know why I was psyche-wiped."

It was a tenuous, flimsy thread, and Dashiel glommed onto it with everything he had. "Your last backup at Rivers Trust will represent your state no more than a couple of days before you disappeared. It won't tell you what happened that night, but it will tell you much of what you had learned in your investigation. You can retrace the path you were following and learn who psyche-wiped you." He paused. "It will also tell you who you were. Once you have a look at that person, I'm confident you'll change your mind about reintegration."

"Give me the passcode." It was an order delivered in a terse, tightly controlled voice.

"Absolutely. Here's my home address as well, and the security passcode for entrance into the building. After you've accessed the backup, come see me."

"What if I don't want to see you?"

He smiled, imbuing it with the last vestiges of confidence he could dig up. "You will."

24

Perrin studied the crowd spilling out of Serpens Sate with a wary eye. She tried to size up the situation the way Joaquim had taught her to do...but she just couldn't make herself see the world through the same lens he did.

The would-be patrons of the club looked angry bordering on dangerous, and that was how he would see them. But she knew better.

Joaquim had found her in a club not much different from this one over a decade ago. She'd been on her fourth up-gen in barely a century, frantically chasing some combination of traits and algorithms that would make her feel *right*—would turn her into a whole person comfortable in her own skin and confident about her purpose in the world. He had given her the second and helped her find her own way to the first.

Places like Serpens Sate never held those answers, but they did reassure you that you weren't alone in seeking them—and created enough noise to drown out the traitorous whispers of doubt and despair in your head.

She doubted the mindset which led individuals to act out in their clothes, visible augments and choices of entertainment locale had changed much, if at all, in the intervening years since she'd been one of them. It was a state of psyche that had little to do with current political or sociological trends and everything to do with the nature of imperfect beings cursed to yearn for their own particular flavor of perfection.

Tonight she'd worn her favorite angsty-outcast outfit—a frilled purple shirtdress with opalescent holoshimmer leggings and knee boots—but studying the crowd now, she realized hair fashions *did* change, and hers was out. She'd tinted it platinum and wound it into a plethora of braids, but wearing them long and free appeared to be passé.

She hurriedly pulled the braids together and secured the bases atop her head so they formed a waterfall around her face, then sauntered across the street to the entrance.

No security gated the doors—which was kind of the point—and she weaved through the patrons who opted to remain on the sidewalk to reach the interior.

As soon as she got inside, she activated a visual scan routine. The tech dealer in the Mirai One Southern Market had provided an image capture of the man's face, so the routine was primed with the physical markers to search for.

Hq (visual) | scan (190°:100°) | Hr(Λ) = (parameters (hairHue(#6B4226 +- 10%), height(180cm +- 4%), weight(68kg +- 6%), faceChar (/img_ $\beta\beta\theta\theta$ +- 5% pf)))

He might not be here—but odds were he was. There weren't many of these type of clubs on Mirai, and this was the only one in the same sector as the Southern Market. She didn't want to stereotype thoughtlessly, but hanging out at Serpens Sate and its ilk was what people like her mark *did*.

NOIR enjoyed a large network of sympathizers, of whom this particular tech dealer was only one. In his case, he informed NOIR when a customer meeting a certain profile—disaffected, troubled, desperate—showed up trying to buy a simmed ID, a routine to erase their signature from the grid or similar software.

You couldn't buy those types of illegal software in the Southern Market, not even from the gray market merchants lurking in the rear section, but grid-dwellers didn't know that. If they went to the wrong merchant in search of it, they'd find themselves reported to Justice; if they went to the right merchant, they'd find themselves reported to NOIR.

Perrin's eyes swept across the patrons for a second pass, but a man with three arms and an extra-long neck passed in front of her scan, blocking her view for several seconds.

After a few millennia of experimentation in the early days of the Dominion, a general consensus had developed that, in most circumstances most of the time, nature and evolution had already worked out the best physical form. While some argued selection/confirmation bias tainted the analysis, it became widely accepted that bipedal bodies with two arms, two eyes and one head, walking upright using a solid central torso, offered the best balance of durability and finesse.

But part of being disaffected was rejecting the conventional wisdom, so you still saw the occasional radical alteration in this sort of crowd.

The man moved on, and she resumed her search.

$$T \rightarrow Hr(\Lambda) = gridpoint \ (32.3, 8.1), \ P(83.2\%)$$

The man the scan routine had identified fidgeted at a standing table near the back. Alone in a bar filled with people.

She swung by the kiosk and grabbed two drinks, then casually wound her way toward the man's table. When she arrived, she sidled in opposite him and slid one of the drinks across the small table. "You look like you could use this."

He jumped back so far he bumped into the wall behind him. "What—why would you think that?"

She gave him a speculative look and sipped on her drink. "You're practically vibrating. If someone didn't know better, they might think you were up to something."

"N-no, I was...." He picked up the glass and guzzled half of it down in one swig. "Thanks. But why are you here? Talking to me? Women don't usually seek me out."

She wasn't surprised. He'd be average-looking if he cleaned himself up, but too much sweating had given his brown hair a greasy appearance, not to mention what it did to his skin. Ill-fitting clothes hung sloppily on a skinny frame, and his shirt was marred by a food stain near the center of his chest.

He could be in direr straits than she'd initially thought. She set her drink on the table, freeing her hands. "I heard you might be trying to escape the grid—"

"What! Who told you—I'm not—"

She laid a hand gently on his arm, which was in fact both vibrating and sweating. "Calm down. I'm not with Justice, I promise."

His pupils contracted despite the dim lighting in the club. "Then who are you with?"

"A group of people who can help you, if you want to be helped."

Now his eyes, though not his pupils, widened. "You're with NOIR, aren't you?"

She smiled placidly, but inwardly she was giggling. It was so fantastic to discover their presence and purpose had thoroughly penetrated the popular culture, or at least this faction of it. "Let's not worry about specifics right now. Why don't you tell me what happened? Why are you trying to go underground?"

He glanced around the club. "Can we go somewhere quieter? I hate crowds."

"Sure. I know a bench by the riverbank. First, though, what's your name?"

His chin dropped, and he found sudden interest in his feet. "I'm Theo."

"Hi, Theo. I'm Perrin."

ᐱR

The reflection of a patina quarter-moon danced across the Hataori River, accompanied by echoes of light from the rows of lamps framing each bank.

The street traffic behind them was busy enough that Perrin didn't fear for her personal safety; she also didn't fear for it because Joaquim had long ago insisted she install enough combat routines to be able to defend herself against a small army should the need ever arise.

Theo's legs kicked erratically beneath the bench. They'd become his latest outlet to release the nervous energy consuming him.

She shifted to half-face him and curled one leg under her on the bench. "Why don't you start at the beginning?"

He nodded. "I was out with two of my friends one night a couple of weeks ago. When we were at Riyuki's down near the Southern Market, they bought some dose off this random woman and loaded it up."

"But you didn't?"

"They tried to get me to join them, but I told them I didn't want to. I've heard horror stories about how street doses can fuck up your kernel. Um...it didn't do that to them, I don't think, but it did fuck them up pretty bad. After we left the bar, they were crazy maniacal.

"I stayed with them, trying to calm them down and convince them to go home, but they weren't listening. When we got to the Southern Market shops, they decided to vandalize the storefront of this expensive clothing store. They broke the front glass and ripped up the clothes on the automatons. The store's security system tripped, and patrol dynes showed up in seconds. They arrested all three of us."

"But you hadn't done anything wrong?"

"Right! I got arrested because I was *there*." He cleared his throat. "So we got locked up, then our hearing happened two days later. The only reason I wasn't convicted was because the Rep managed to prove that I wasn't on any of the security cam footage, plus my tox screen came out negative. But my friends were both convicted of burglary and vandalism, with aggravating factors due to the illegal dose. They got sentenced to ten years in Zaidam Bastille. For vandalism!"

He fisted his hand at his chin. "My friends, they had credits. They could have simply paid for the damage and made the shop owner whole, but Justice didn't give them that option. I expect they'll get a forced up-gen before they're released. When they finally come back, they won't be the people I knew any longer."

He had a good head of steam going now, so she kept projecting an encouraging expression and let him talk.

"I was lucky—but what if I hadn't been? What if I'd tried to pull one of them back from the storefront and ended up on the cam footage? Justice wouldn't care that I was trying to stop them. What if…?" His voice trailed off, and his posture sagged, all the righteous anger abandoning him as abruptly as it had arrived.

He stared at the water flowing past them. "All my generations, I blissfully assumed Justice existed to protect us. I assumed the system was fair and, well, just. But now, I'm worried if I step off the curb wrong some patrol dyne is going to put me in restraints and haul me off to Zaidam. I'm terrified to do…anything.

"So I saw the news reports about NOIR's hit on the Dominion Transit building, and I realized there are people who've escaped the system. People who are living their lives free, and Justice can't touch them. I thought…I thought maybe I could do that. But every tech dealer I've visited has told me no. So I guess I don't know how to do it.…"

Perrin had to restrain herself from hugging him. He was far from the first person she'd encountered who was broken, feeling beaten and helpless—in fact, one of her jobs in NOIR was to collect those people—but it wrenched her heart every single time. This was why she did what she did. She wasn't in NOIR for her own freedom, but to help others find theirs.

She compromised by reaching over and squeezing his hand. "It's going to be okay, Theo. We do know how to do it. We can help show you the way."

He hurriedly wiped a tear off his cheek. "Are you NOIR? Will you tell me? Will I get to be one of you?"

This was always the delicate dance. They did what they could for people in trouble, but they had to be *so* cautious, for their own and the individual's safety. "We need to take things slowly. We'll help you get off the grid, and we'll point you toward resources that will help you survive once you are. If things go well, then we'll see about taking more steps down the road."

His face fell. "I understand. You can't just let anyone in."

"We do have to be careful. You should be careful, too—careful, but not afraid. All right?"

He nodded hopefully.

"Good. I'm going to give you the name and contact information of someone who can get you started, and I'll be in touch in a day or two to check on you. Also, here's an emergency nex node address you can contact if you get in real trouble. Send a message to it, and if it's at all possible for us to help, we will."

"Thank you. For the first time in weeks, I feel like I actually have a chance."

"You've got more than a chance, Theo. You've got a life of your own choosing waiting for you."

25

Nika adopted a demeanor of aloof disinterest as she entered the clothing boutique. She'd never visited Rivers Trust during the five years of her current life, but she knew enough about it to recognize she couldn't very well walk up to the counter wearing fatigues and a tactical shirt and jacket. It was a sketchy play walking into the upscale boutique wearing them, but with any luck the staff wouldn't kick her out for slumming down the store if she promised to buy something.

She scanned the merchandise on display incredulously. How did anyone wear this attire and keep a straight face?

"May I help you find what you desire?"

She glanced over at the sales attendant. Most dynes she encountered in her daily life were security of one kind or another, and they usually looked the part. This one, however, sported a smooth, brushed cream exterior casing, glittering accents at appropriate joints and a permanent smile carved onto the outlines of a ceramic face.

"I just need something simple. Professional and understated. It's for a business meeting, you see."

"This way, if you please."

She followed the attendant to the rear of the shop, past the garish and the audacious to a small section of attire that began to approach decency. It was tucked into a corner as if being shamed, but thankfully the shop did sell it. "Thank you. I'll browse for a minute."

"Summon me if you need further assistance." The attendant backed away, though she had no doubt it continued to watch her discreetly from a distance. Pleasant exterior aside, it probably doubled as security.

She frowned dubiously at the racks. What style of fashion did she fancy? She'd never been in a position to consider the question until now.

Her fingertips trailed across the fabrics until finally a dash of burgundy caught her eye. A simple but elegantly cut pantsuit. She lifted it out of the rack and studied it. The legs swooshed a little too flamboyantly at the ankles for her taste, and the high neck of the collar looked too restrictive to be comfortable, but it was the best she was apt to do.

She paid for the suit and matching shoes with untraceable credits and left the store, then found a public lounge two blocks down. She quickly changed, but spent five minutes scowling at the mirror before deciding the outfit must be acceptable to a certain social class.

With a sigh she stuffed her normal clothes in her bag. She'd need to change back into them before returning home, because no way was she stepping onto The Floor wearing *this*.

∧R

The Rivers Trust security measures made Justice buildings look like flop houses. This was why the wealthy and connected used it; unbreakable security protections constituted an important aspect of its meticulously crafted reputation. In fact, every corner and every surface conveyed a message of reliability, of inviolability.

It was a deliberate performance, but it also had to be true, else all the window dressing in the world would not have kept the business operating and serving the most elite of clientele for many centuries.

She waited in a short line. The people in front of her didn't wear the sparkly bangles and ostentatious garb that had dominated the racks of the store she'd visited, so she'd chosen well with the pantsuit. These were serious people, going about serious business. This at least she respected.

Had any of them known her before? If she'd genuinely been a diplomat and frequented the social and professional circles Ridani inhabited, perhaps some had. She wore a simmed ID and a morph, though she'd have to deactivate them at the counter, so she wouldn't get an answer to the question. Not today.

She'd also deactivated the disguise for Ridani. Why? Why had it mattered that he see her as she was? It was the appearance he was expecting to see, but it wasn't her job to make him feel comfortable.

She supposed she'd simply wanted to *be* for those few minutes, to not feel like an imposter around the one person who knew her as she'd once been.

The line crept forward, and the fire of hope ignited to flicker and dance across her skin. Answers, true answers, waited a few meters away. She tamped down fidgeting hands.

When her turn arrived, she straightened her shoulders, notched her chin up in a confident set, deactivated the morph and approached the counter. "Nika Kirumase. I want to access my holdings."

"Identification, signature and passcode."

She placed her fingertips on the waiting pane.

$\Sigma \rightarrow$ *Identity:*
< Nika Kirumase, 12th generation
Signature:
< $\theta\Psi\beta\alpha\theta\Psi\forall\Psi\alpha\Omega\Xi$
Passcode:
< $\alpha\beta\ \theta\theta\beta\beta\ \alpha\beta\alpha\alpha\ \alpha\beta\beta\alpha\ \Omega\Xi\ \beta\alpha\alpha\ \theta\beta\alpha\theta\beta\ \theta\alpha\theta\ \theta\alpha\beta\alpha$

The faceless interface whirred. She felt naked and exposed standing there with no layers of disguises, enunciating her real, if former, name where anyone could overhear it. Seconds ticked by.

"The Kirumase account is empty. Do you want to make a deposit or set up a new deposit route?"

She fought against the penetration of the words into her reality, trying frantically to hold onto that precious hope for one more second. *Empty?*

"Are you certain? Please check again."

"The system is always accurate. The Kirumase account is empty."

The walls closed in around her and every shadow became a threat as her mind raced through the implications. She struggled to keep her voice from shaking. "Can you tell me the date of the last withdrawal? I must have a corrupted memory node."

"Y12,458.096 A7, 1340 local, 0920 APT."

The same day she woke up. Mere hours before. It felt like a sinister connection, but in truth the information didn't tell her anything new. Objectively, it made perverse sense. "Does the system say who made the withdrawal?"

"An individual possessing the required credentials. Do you wish to close the account?"

"Yes—no." If someone had accessed the account five years ago, they could have put a watch on it. Closing it might alert them that she was on their trail—and by 'trail' she meant fumbling around naked in the dark, blindfolded. "No, thank you. I'm sure I'll have a deposit to make soon. Good day."

Every iota of discipline she possessed activated to prevent her from sprinting out of the building and tearing down the street in a frenzied panic. As it was, it took her a good thirty seconds and two blocks to realize it had begun to rain while she'd been inside.

Her leaf module was in the bag with her clothes, and she couldn't bring herself to care to retrieve it. Instead, she let the rain soak into her expensive costume and, eventually, her skin.

The swell of excitement and hope she'd felt on walking into the revered establishment died a swift death under the crushing weight of despair, followed closely by a thousand suspicions, then more despair, then renewed panic.

The truth was lost to her, along with everything she had ever been. Gone.

26

Dashiel paced in front of the wide windows spanning his living room. Rain pouring out from heavy thunderclouds obscured the view, leaving him with little to gaze upon but his own tortured reflection in the glass.

It had been several hours since she'd left him at the harbor, ostensibly to go directly to Rivers Trust. He'd given in to fear-tinged impatience and pinged her over an hour ago, but received no response. Needless to say, this had quelled neither the fear nor the impatience.

He hadn't made it this late into the evening without a drink in months, probably years. But he didn't want or need one, because the crater in his soul that alcohol papered over was fading away. She'd returned to him.

Unless she hadn't.

Two opposing yet equally horrific scenarios built themselves into elaborate constructs in his mind. One possibility: the perpetrators of her erasure were far more nefarious and powerful than he'd imagined. They kept a perpetual stake-out, whether physical or electronic, on Rivers Trust, waiting for the day when she reappeared. That day was today, and they'd snatched her off the street and absconded away with her, intent on performing a new erasure...or worse.

Second possibility: she'd retrieved the backup, reviewed its contents and decided she wanted no part of what it held. With the mystery of her previous identity solved, she'd blown it and him off to return to her life of rebellion, leaving him with no way to find her again.

He didn't care for what it said about him that he feared the second possibility as much as the first, but there it was. He was a selfish man, and he needed her back.

The door alert broke into his reverie, and his pulse quickened. She was here, which meant neither of his nightmare scenarios were true. She was here, which meant this was the moment she came back to him, real and whole.

He hurried to the door and opened it, a welcoming smile poised to brighten his features.

Nika stood in the middle of the hallway, soaked from head to foot. Droplets of rain clung tenuously to tangled strands of her hair; one-by-one they gave up their hold to fall to the floor. A thin black tank stuck to her skin, revealing every dip and curve of her upper body. A bag swayed loosely from her left hand, a burgundy piece of clothing hanging half out of it—the fabric matched her pants, which might have been designer-quality before they succumbed to the rainstorm.

Her eyes were wide and wild as she stared at him. Or past him, because she didn't appear to be seeing him at all.

He replaced the waiting smile with a frown of concern. "Nika—"

"It's gone." She surged inside, forcing her way past him and down the short hallway into the living room, where she dropped the bag and kept moving into an aimless, frenetic circle. "It's all gone. Someone withdrew all the backups hours before I woke up with my memory erased. There's no backup of the backup, and no record of who withdrew it."

He blinked as her tirade of words berated his recalcitrant mind. His subconscious caught on first, and a sinking feeling settled in his gut. "I don't understand. How is that possible? You and I were the only ones who had the authorization passcode."

"So you say." Her pace grew more erratic as she wove a disjointed path around his furnishings, leaving small puddles of rainwater in her wake. "Maybe whoever psyche-wiped me stole the passcode from my memory prior to the wipe, then took out all my backups to cover their tracks." Her gaze fell hard on him. "Or maybe it was you."

"Me? I would never—and even if I would, why would I tell you about the backup if I knew it had been removed?"

"Hells if I know. To increase my paranoia? My dependence on you? I only have your word for...everything. You could be a pathological, manipulative liar. How would I tell the difference?"

Her inherent distrust of him wounded him more deeply than any physical blow could. He had to convince her of their shared truth, somehow....

His chin lifted. "I would never hurt you—never intentionally cause you pain. Every word I've said to you is the truth. But I realize you can't take my word for it. So will you take my mind for it? Will you let me show you what you were to me, from my own perspective?"

She sank against the nearest wall and studied him suspiciously. "You want me to simex one of your own memories."

"I do."

"What if you've planted a virutox inside it, like the one in your augments?"

He pinched the bridge of his nose in frustration. "You know, you don't really need me around to increase your paranoia. You've got that covered just fine all by yourself."

"It comes with the circumstances."

He looked up to find her expression had softened slightly, perhaps in apology. He'd take any leeway she offered. "I can see how that might be the case. So will you do it? Please?"

She didn't answer for several seconds—long enough that he started wracking his brain for a new plan—but finally she nodded brusquely. "Simply because I'm curious about this person you say I was, and with an empty trust account it seems this is the only way I'll ever meet her. By the way, I've got advanced malware-sniffing traps installed, and they've been upgraded to recognize the kind of intrusion techniques the augment virutox uses. If there's malicious code in the memory, I will catch it."

Of course she would. She'd always been tech savvy, but now she was also a criminal. A rebel. A terrorist, to hear Justice tell it. And he did not care. "Thank you. Sit for a minute. I'll be right back with what we need—and a towel."

⋏R

She wasn't sitting when he returned, though her agitation had ebbed somewhat. She stared out the windows, much as he'd been doing when she arrived.

He paused at the periphery of the living room, struck by the echoes the scene evoked of the last night he'd seen her. Her natural stance, the cut of her shoulders, the lines of her jaw, all reinforced for him what he already knew: missing memories or not, this *was* the woman he'd loved for so many years they masqueraded as eternity.

He handed her the towel first, and she absently wrung out her hair while he went to the far wall by the chaise and opened a cabinet.

A minimalist interface setup slid out of the cabinet to extend above the curving arm of the chaise, and he motioned for her to join him. "It's not an important memory in the grand scheme of things. But it represents us and our life together better than a host of more 'meaningful' memories ever could. I've revisited it often in the intervening years."

"What is it of?"

"A party we attended nine years ago. Mostly Advisors and their guests loitering over expensive champagne and delicacies."

Her nose scrunched up in distaste, which he ignored. "Now, experiencing another person's memory can be disorienting, and you'll likely be a little dizzy when—"

"I've done it before. I know how it works." She plopped down on the chaise and dropped her head onto the arm. "Let's get this over with, all right?"

He bit back a sigh. Everything would be better after. It must be. "Of course. Close your eyes."

PATTERN
MATCH

27

*T*he party was in full swing when I stepped quietly through the door to Maris' loft and paused in the entryway. It gave me a second or two to evaluate the tenor of the gathering before matching it and diving in.

Friends, colleagues and a few detente-style adversaries gathered in clumps around the spacious, open-layout room and spilled out onto the balcony beyond. Though everyone was dressed in cocktail attire, the mood felt casual, even relaxed, and I relaxed in kind.

I scanned the room, searching, until my eyes naturally fell on Nika. She stood in the kitchen talking to Maris and Adlai, a nearly empty champagne flute held aloft in one hand. A burgundy silk dress hugged her every curve; the view instantly stirred up desire in my mind and my body, and I had to hurriedly squelch the reaction. Woven straps crisscrossed her otherwise bare back to give teasing glimpses of her tattoo, while the curl of a thin, high collar accentuated a plunging neckline in the front.

As if she sensed the caress of my eyes, she shifted around until her gaze fell on me much as mine had fallen on her. One corner of her lips quirked upward in a devious little smile that brought a sparkle to her eyes; offset by the burgundy, tonight they appeared more blue than green. Her void-black hair was styled into a luxurious mane of soft ringlets, one of which fell along her temple to tickle her cheekbone.

I mirrored the smile in full as I crossed the room to join them. My arm slid around her waist, and I leaned in to place a kiss at her ear before pulling back to nod a greeting at the others.

"Get caught up working late again?"

I shrugged with self-deprecating flair. "Self-evidently. Apologies for my tardiness, Maris. You seem to have nonetheless persevered and made the party a smashing success without me."

"I do what I can with the tools available to me. In this case, Nika. Any room she walks into is instantly classed up by several orders of magnitude."

Nika rolled her eyes, but it was true. I regretted being late, for I did enjoy seeing her shine.

"Well, this tool needs another glass of champagne if she's going to continue to perform to expectations. Dashiel?"

"Oh, definitely."

She squeezed my hand. "Meet me outside in a few minutes?"

"More definitely." *I watched her as she walked away, but eventually I forced myself to turn my attention to Maris and Adlai.* "What is it we're celebrating tonight again? It must have slipped my mind."

Maris shot him a dubious look. "As if anything has ever slipped your mind. We are celebrating everything and nothing. Life. Believe it or not, we don't need an official reason to have a party."

"I do believe it. I was just...checking."

Adlai chuckled. "She's messing with you, Dashiel. There's a meteor shower tonight."

Oh. I cocked my head slightly. "Which is why Nika..."

"...is going outside. Yes." *Maris shrugged with effortless grace.* "Forgive me. Your single-minded focus on your work begs to be poked at every now and then."

Adlai nudged her with an elbow. "You want to really torture him? Make him give the toast later on."

I cleared my throat. "Luckily, Maris doesn't want to torture me."

"Hmm. I'll think on it." *Her eyes flitted past my shoulder.* "All right, you've done your social duty. Go get your drink, and your reward."

I pursed my lips as if I was readying a protest—I was not—then nodded. "If you insist. I'll return for food soon, though. I neglected to eat lunch, and the spread smells delicious."

I turned and made my way out the open glass door to the balcony. Nika leaned against the ledge with her forearms draped atop it, a pose which caused the low swoop of the back of her dress to fall distractingly lower. She gazed out at the clear, starry night, and two flutes of champagne sat on the ledge beside her.

I wound my arms around her waist from behind and rested my chin on her bare shoulder. "Beautiful night."

"It is. You just missed the first meteor of the night, but there should be more soon. Stay with me?"

"Always." I nuzzled her neck, enjoying the tickle of her curls against my skin. "Oh, you meant stay out on the balcony with you, didn't you? Always to that as well."

Warmth infused her laugh. "Perfect. What kept you at work? No trouble, I hope."

"Only the Shorai contract. The Guides hope to launch in two months, and we haven't begun to install the internal systems network or assemble the space-rated mobile d-gates the crew plans on taking with them. The message delivered today was essentially 'all resources authorized, but get it done.' "

"I'm not surprised. It will be the most extensive, farthest reaching exploration initiative we've attempted since the founding of the Dominion." She twisted around in my grasp to face me. A hand rose to my jaw, and she drew me in for a slow, languid kiss. Champagne and the hint of a sugary treat lingered on her tongue, mixing with the delicious taste of her.

I murmured against her lips. "Can we go home now? I find I desperately want to explore what's beneath this tantalizing dress."

"You know what's beneath the dress, silly."

"Maybe I want to be reminded."

"Soon, darling. We have obligations to fulfill first—and if you try hard, a spot or two of fun to have as well."

I reluctantly drew back from her embrace and retrieved the champagne, handing one glass to her before taking a sip of the other. "Speaking of—the contract, not fun—I'm somewhat surprised the Guides didn't ask you to accompany the Shorai as our ambassador. Though I suppose they also realize our relations with the Taiyoks and the Chizeru would both suffer in your absence."

She smiled mysteriously over the rim of her glass. "Who says they didn't ask me? But I'm enjoying my life far too much to spend years trapped on a spaceship with nothing but a couple of dynes, a data server and some probes for company. The only way I will ever consent to spending so long away is if you're my company."

"Good."

"Still, I appreciate the romanticism of the initiative. We're a starfaring people, but to look around you would hardly know it. We transport from planet to planet in an instant using the d-gates, never seeing the cosmos that fills the space in between. Few of us have so much as stepped foot on a spaceship, much less spent any real time traveling among the stars. Even during the Exodus, when we crossed galaxies, we slept for most of the journey. We never set eyes on the wonders we surely happened upon."

The dreamer side of her persona was only one reason she made an exceptional diplomat, but I didn't always understand it. I was too pragmatic, as she frequently reminded me.

I shrugged. "Ships are slow. Most people almost always have places they need to be, and d-gates are fast. It's simply a matter of practicality."

"Our ships travel at many multiples of the speed of light. The Shorai, multiples beyond their speed. That's not slow."

"It's slower than instantaneous." I frowned as a troubling thought occurred to me. "Are you sure you don't want to go on the expedition?"

She reached up to touch my cheek, and her fingertips lingered to drift along my jaw. "I'm sure. I want to stay here with you, where there are parties and champagne and fresh delicacies and lots and lots of glorious sex. I'm merely being whimsical, because I can be."

"Okay." I set my glass on the ledge and embraced her with far greater passion than earlier. My head swam in the thrall of her intoxicating touch, scent, feel. I'd experienced them all a thousand and more times, but by opening myself up fully to the experience, each time was as enthralling as the last.

An endless moment and too soon later, I withdrew from the fulsome kiss just enough to breathe. "In that case, what do you say we stay long enough to indulge in a bit more of the first three, then go home for a great deal more of the last?"

"Sounds like my grandest fantasies come to life."

28

Nika's eyes snapped open riding the crest of a wave of panic. She jerked out of the grip of the interface, bolted upright and swung her feet to the floor—then doubled over as a surge of nausea coursed through her.

"It's all right. If you feel sick, just give it a few seconds to pass."

She felt sick for certain, but it wasn't from the inherent nature of a memory simex. Worlds collided in her mind, blending and tearing and distorting, and the roiling turmoil framing their dance suggested they would never be fitting into their boxes again. The blank chasm in her mind where her past should have lived transformed into a hall of mirrors, endlessly reflecting the woman in the memory back at her own reflection.

Her dress had been a fancier version of the pantsuit she'd bought earlier tonight.

Dashiel's hand touched her shoulder, and she exploded off the chaise to stumble through the center of the living room until she found the rim of a couch to brace herself against.

"Nika—"

"Don't."

She'd had no knowledge of how champagne even tasted until she'd tasted it on his lips...on her lips...on his.

"I only wanted to—"

She whipped around to face him. "I know what you wanted to do—I know why you showed me this. But she's *gone*. Don't you understand? This woman you loved? She's gone—erased—and she's never coming back."

He had stood while she yelled, but he didn't approach her. *He'd touched her so effortlessly, as if it were second nature. As natural as breathing.* His shoulders rose and fell. *Breathing.* "I refuse to believe that."

"Doesn't matter. The funny thing about reality is, it's true whether you believe in it or not."

His jaw quivered, and his irises darkened in desolation to pools of amber. She knew it was desolation because he was still in her head, his emotions and idle thoughts and perceptions of both her and the world around him still colliding with her own.

"But she's standing right in front of me."

"No." The distant walls swam, lurching toward her then spinning away. When he looked at her now, he must see the same face, the same eyes, the same lips and hands that touched him effortlessly in return. But how could he see the same woman when she saw a distorted doppelganger?

"This was a mistake. I shouldn't have come here. I need to leave." She hunted around until she spotted her bag; she snatched it up and sprinted for the door.

A visual on the wall caught her attention as she passed it in a blur. She hadn't noticed it on the way in, distracted as she'd been, but now she slowed enough for it to sharpen into focus. Within a frame, he stood behind her—the former her—on the bow of a boat with his arms wrapped around her.

Exactly like on the balcony at the party. Had he worn the same contented smile then as he did in the visual? Was this what she'd seen when she looked back at him on the balcony? When she smiled lovingly at him, kissed him, stroked his cheek with tender affection? The visual flowed from mutual smiles directed at one another to a kiss and back again in an endless loop.

Her heart broke into a thousand shards for two people who were not present in this room, whose idyllic, perfect lives had been ripped apart by a mysterious and unknown enemy who she was no closer to finding now than when this devastating day had begun.

She lunged for the door—but rather than opening it, her palm flattened against its surface. Her chin dropped to her chest as the panic began to dissipate, leaving behind a confusing tumult of emotions and swirling images. Which ones even belonged to her? To which version of her?

In an effort to calm the pounding in her chest, she breathed in deeply. Out through her nose. She needed to leave...but she didn't.

"The way she—the way *I*—looked at you...what we had was real, wasn't it?"

"The realest thing I've ever known." His voice sounded flat, quiet, but close. He'd followed her into the entry hallway.

"How long were we together?"

"3,268 years, seven months...and four days."

The numbers ricocheted off the corners of her mind; she had no processes capable of absorbing their significance. The stories behind those centuries and days would surely consume her, if only she knew them.

She looked back at him to find the desolation had seeped out from his irises to consume the fullness of his expression. She'd broken him.

Part of her had wanted to do precisely that ever since she'd met him, but now she felt only a helpless, sorrowful regret. The man whose mind she'd briefly inhabited had been...happy. Serious and driven, yes, but someone who allowed a more carefree spirit to take over when he was at her side.

He hadn't been lying to her all this time. She knew this not due to any specific fact available to her from the memory, but because she'd sensed *him* in the memory. She'd gotten a fleeting glimpse at his soul, and whatever else he may or may not be, he hadn't been lying when he said he'd loved her.

And because she knew her own face and what it showed of her own soul, she knew he also hadn't been lying he said she'd loved him in return.

Feeling his eyes on her now was like reversing the hall of mirrors so she stood on the receiving end of the gaze she'd seen herself through. She glanced down at her wet clothes and bedraggled appearance. How could he see any trace of that poised, elegant woman in her?

She wanted so badly to keep calling the woman a stranger, but his perception of her rippled through *her* mind, transforming the woman into someone she both longed and feared to recognize.

He stood stiffly by the wall. "I wish you didn't believe you needed to leave, but I accept it. If you...decide you want help tracking down the source of the augment virutox...you know how to reach me." Flat. Defeated. Gutted. The woman in the memory would never have inflicted such pain on him.

A ping from Perrin arrived, the alert flashing in her virtual vision as if begging for her attention. She shut all personal notifications off.

Then, without consciously deciding to do it, she turned fully away from the door and began to walk slowly toward him. "I'm sorry she's gone. I'm sorry I can't bring her back for you."

His jaw flexed, but he didn't respond. She understood why he remained silent. She understood *him*—too stubborn to concede the truth, suddenly taciturn with someone he was loathe to admit he might not know at all.

But she craved the look of adoration, of intimacy, that he'd bestowed on her in the memory. It conveyed comfort, the safety of unrestricted devotion, a sense of belonging—three things she'd never experienced. Not this time around.

She stepped closer and, as if in a daze, brought a hand up to reach for his cheek, so like in the memory, seeking what was lost—

—his hand snapped up and grabbed her wrist. "Do not toy with me, Nika. I'm begging you. Go, or stay, but don't do this to me. I'm on the ragged edge here. If you touch me like you mean it, then walk away, I will not survive the closing of the door behind you."

She nodded in understanding, and his hand loosened its hold on her wrist. As soon as it did, she swiftly closed the remaining distance to press her palm to his cheek and her lips to his. Carefully, tentatively.

His lips hinted at anything but gentleness. Was this how it had felt from her perspective when he'd kissed her? Warm, firm, holding at bay a flood of passion but only just.

His hand landed atop hers, and instead of yanking it away, he pressed it more tightly against his skin.

Like coming home. Impossible. Gone. Yet....

She drew back a fraction, letting her eyes meet his—then she was drowning in the fervency of their desperation, hope and desire. His. Hers. They blended together in her mind and their bodies until it didn't matter.

Everything happened at once as one of his hands wound into her wet and tangled hair, both of hers buried themselves in his far softer locks, and their lips met once more. His other hand pressed into her back, holding her close.

He needed her. She knew this, even if the nature of 'her' remained in question. She needed...to believe. Believe that she had been real before. That she'd *existed*, and his embrace proved it.

Her own sensations—tangible, visceral, newly potent—gradually overcame the lingering, haunting memory of his. Need flowed between them in a reinforcing feedback loop, and her desire spiked to match his.

Was doing this fair to him? She wasn't the woman he loved...but right now she felt rather like it.

Was doing this fair to her? On the other side waited renewed angst and a bitter struggle...his teeth teased across her jaw on the way to her neck...oh, fuck it. She didn't care.

Her hand slid down from his cheek and past his collar to part the seam of his shirt, but she paused when she reached his heart. It beat madly in his chest, racing, out of control. The earnestness it betrayed froze her for an instant, but before he could do something stupid like stop her, she continued on the rest of the way down to open his shirt fully then flattened her palm against his burning skin.

"Why?" His voice was low and rough, bearing little resemblance to the deliberate, measured tone she'd come to associate with him.

Her lips dipped below his chin to his throat. "I want to feel what she felt."

His chest expanded beneath her hand as he sucked in a breath. "I can oblige."

He spun her around and pinned her against the wall. His hands dropped to the hem of her shirt, but instead of yanking it upward, his palms roved underneath the material, warming her damp skin as the shirt up inched along the path of his wrists.

She gasped when his fingertips brushed across a nipple—then her shirt was over her head and on the floor. She urged his shirt over his shoulders in turn and let it fall away. His skin pressed against hers, kindling a new wave of heady sensations...and the urgent need for more. More skin, more touching. More everything.

Her fingertips fumbled for the waistband of his pants—and she felt him tremble beneath her touch.

He tilted her chin up until her eyes met his. "Nika...."

The raw, frayed emotion bleeding from his voice with the simple utterance of her name nearly sent her scrambling back for the door...only she didn't want to leave, dammit. She brought both hands up to stroke his face. "I need you to be here, with me, now. Don't make love to a ghost."

He smiled, and she realized the desolation of earlier had vanished to reveal the first genuinely open, mirthful expression she'd seen him wear in the short time she'd known him. "There's nothing ghostly about you."

She wasn't entirely sure that was the answer she'd been looking for, or a real answer at all, but as he lifted her up into his arms and she wound her legs around his hips, it faded into irrelevance.

More hall then a door frame passed at the edges of her perception, then the plush cushioning of what must be his bed met her back. He followed her down, his mouth roving down her neck to wind across her chest, suckling each nipple in turn.

His tongue expertly teased her skin along the way, and he seemed to sense her desires nanoseconds before she did. His hands cupped her ass, and she eagerly lifted up to allow him to peel the rain-soaked designer pants off an agonizing centimeter at a time.

When they finally released her toes and landed on the floor, his lips and his tongue reversed their path, caressing her with an intimacy and familiarity no stranger could fake.

He knew exactly how to touch her, where to touch her—of course he did, but for *her* this was the first time being at his mercy, and the blissful agony overwhelmed her.

She reached for him—and the next second he was there, naked and hovering a mere breath above her. "Oh, how I have missed you."

Her heart answered him in return, even as her mind insisted it was impossible that she had missed him and her body insisted that she just wanted him. She let the first two argue it out while she followed the siren call of the third and drew him closer, into her arms and her body.

⋏R

Dashiel chuckled warmly and trailed a fingertip down from my collarbone, tracing a path between my breasts then letting it dance across my abdomen. "I was a little worried when you said you were going in for an up-gen, even a minor one, but you're exactly the same."

"This is not true. I am now twenty-two percent more patient with official procedures, filings, reviews and all things bureaucracy."

"Got in trouble for bitching because some new exploratory world approval was taking too long, did you?"

I rolled my eyes and shifted onto my side, encouraging his fingertip to continue on to my hip. "Something like that." I grinned mischievously. "I'm also thirty-six percent more attracted to men who have chestnut hair with amber highlights and hazel irises, so look out."

"Oh?" His lips hummed against my shoulder. "And here I thought you had already maxed that one out."

"I had. I guess we'll get to find out what happens when I overload it." My mouth found his in renewed hunger for the pleasures his touch offered as my arms drew him against me. "Yes, again."

Nika blinked, confused and disoriented. Was she awake, or asleep? Had it been a dream or, somehow, a memory?

⋏R̄

Nika locked her ankles together at the small of my back and yanked me closer. Her arms were stretched out over the rim of the pool, and her eyes danced with even greater mischief than usual.

I bit my lip as my skin met hers, but faked nonchalance to reach behind her and retrieve our shared drink. Beyond the ledge, a cliff plummeted to the ocean far below, where rocks brought turmoil to the lapping waves.

I tipped the glass to her lips first, and shuddered in anticipation as she licked them, leaving tiny bubbles of champagne clinging to them along the path of her tongue. I hurriedly took a sip as well, then fumbled around trying to return the glass to the ledge.

As soon as I removed my hand from the glass, it toppled into the water.

She laughed as we watched it float away. "Oh no, we're out of champagne."

I had a meeting on Ebisu in five hours with a theater company about a rather novel deployment of a stand-alone local nex network. I now embraced the reality that I would be handling it on no sleep.

"Whatever shall we do without more champagne? Wait, I have an idea." I grasped her hips and shifted her body to my liking. Another centimeter and I would slip inside her. "Yes, again."

Dashiel opened his eyes, shocked to find his bedroom ceiling above him instead of an unobstructed night sky.

No, that was a memory. But how? He'd erased the details of that night over three years ago in a fit of despair heightened by enough doses to remove him from his right mind. Yet here it was, as clear in his mind as if it were happening now.

⋏R̄

Nika blinked again. This was the same bed beneath her, the same delightfully warm skin pressed against her chest.

It must have been a dream...but no dream had ever felt so real.

She looked up to find Dashiel gazing at her, an odd expression on his face. His right hand was wrapped around her left, their fingertips touching.

She smiled hesitantly. "I must have dozed off for a few minutes."

"Me, too." Then he gripped her thighs and hoisted her up until his lips met hers. Passion drove the kiss to unexpected fervor, and she couldn't honestly say from which of them it originated.

When he finally drew back for a breath, she stretched a leg over his hips and sidled fully atop him. He entwined one of his hands into her hair, and they both spoke at once.

"Yes, again."

29

*R*yan: *"Two hostiles in the next corridor. Security-grade dynes. Stun bomb incoming."*

Ryan leaned out into the hallway long enough to lob a grenade toward the approaching dynes, then flattened back against the wall. Three seconds later he felt the tickle of the outer edges of the stun bomb's range, followed by the clattering sound of collapsing frames.

WheatleyBot swung into the hallway in scan mode and surveyed the results. Sure enough, the two dynes lay entangled in one another on the floor.

Ryan: *"Hostiles down."*

Ava: *"Carson, Team 2 status?"*

Silence answered.

Ava: *"Carson, report."*

Carson: *"Eh, we've got a slight spiderbot infestation problem in the control room. Stand by."*

Ava: *"Just EMP the room."*

Carson: *"Can't. It will fry the systems along with the spiderbots, and then we won't be able to get the maintenance door open for you. Stand by."*

Ava: *"Fine, we'll get in the hard way."*

Carson: *"Give us ten more seconds—"*

Ava: *"Taking point. Team 1, move ahead."*

Ava rushed forward into the hallway, weaponized arm raised, and Ryan followed.

The next hallway opened up into the anteroom of the prisoner wing. Ava shot the head off the dyne staffing the security checkpoint, then shot up the module powering the force field barrier until it exploded and the force field fizzled away.

Ryan: *"Well, now everyone knows we're here."*

Ava: *"So we move faster. Into the prisoner wing."*

Ryan: *"Let me scope it first."*

Ava: *"No time."*

She charged through the shell of the former barrier and into the wing it had guarded. Ryan again followed, WheatleyBot orbiting his head to scan in every direction.

Carson: *"Maggie configured a targeted EM pulse for the spider-bots. Control room is clear. The maintenance door should be open in fifteen seconds."*

Ava: *"Too late. Team 2, retreat and guard the exit route—"*

Maggie: *"Ava, give us a chance to—"*

Ryan: *"Incoming from the intersection ahead!"*

A combat mecha unit rounded the corner ten meters ahead of them.

Ryan dropped to a knee and bent his left arm in front of him to manifest a force field shield. *WheatleyBot, behind me!*

Ava did not adopt a similar defensive position. Instead she sprinted forward, arm firing, and leapt up onto the mecha. Blood spurted out an exit wound in the back of her shoulder, but she maintained a steady stream of energy point-blank into the mecha's chest. Then a blade unfurled from her other hand, and she jabbed it into the mecha's neck.

Ryan's shield sparked and hissed under the torrent of the mecha's fire. He'd like to help, but everything in his arsenal would likely take out Ava along with the mecha. All he could do at present was survive the onslaught.

WheatleyBot shrieked a warning.

Ryan: *"We've got more incoming from our rear!"*

As the mecha collapsed in a wreck to the floor, Ava climbed off it and stumbled in Ryan's direction. Her right shoulder sagged and the weaponized arm hung limply at her side. She used her left hand to hold up her right arm and pointed the weapon over his head at the advancing hostiles.

Carson: *"The maintenance door is open, if anyone cares."*

∧R

The walls and the hostiles faded away, and the lights of the training room replaced them.

Ryan stood and shut down WheatleyBot. After a second Ava joined him, all traces of physical damage gone from her body. Across the room, Carson and Maggie displayed matching poses: arms crossed over their chests, scowls on their faces.

Joaquim leaned against the wall and considered them in some consternation. "Ava, what did you learn from this exercise?"

"That I need to install the Glaser tech in my left arm, too."

"No. Want to try for a better answer?"

She sighed in resignation. "That I shouldn't get impatient. Give the other teams time to do their jobs. But Maggie and Carson were taking entirely too long, and during that time we were exposed."

Maggie took several steps toward her sister. "You are so infuriating—!"

Joaquim waved her off. "True on all counts, Ava. In the heat of the moment, decisions are rarely clear-cut. You still have to make a judgment call. In this case, you should have given Carson and Maggie their ten seconds. Why?"

Ava shrugged.

Joaquim worked to keep the frustration off his face. He was teaching, not commanding. And when teaching—if not when commanding—he needed to make allowances for the fact that everyone was distracted and on edge since Parc's arrest. And for the fact that they had to *make* mistakes in order to learn from them.

"Because you didn't have the firepower needed to neutralize the hostile forces that were almost guaranteed to come your way once you started shooting up the place. This was presented as a stealth infiltration operation for a reason. You can't always simply shoot everything—also, you need to give someone else a chance to shoot something from time to time. Everyone needs the practice."

He nodded to himself as much as to the group. "All right. We'll run it again with new variables, so don't expect the same surprises. Expect different ones. Ava, you're following orders this round. Carson, you've got the lead—"

The door to the training room opened, and Perrin peeked in. "Sorry to interrupt, guys. Joaquim, can I talk to you for a minute?"

"Take five, everybody. Maybe think about what you can do better in the next round." He trailed Perrin out the door. "What's up? How did the meeting with the new recruit go?"

"What? Oh, it went well enough. He's a good guy and a decent candidate, or he will be once he gets his head straight." She spun back to face him, but her body kept fidgeting. "Nika's not answering any pings."

Shit. He'd hoped the training session would prevent him from sitting around anxiously stewing over Nika's meeting with Ridani all night. The diversion had worked, right up until now.

He immediately pinged her himself, then tried to project a lack of concern for Perrin's benefit while he waited for a response. "I'm sure she's fine. Nika was right—she can take care of herself. I expect she's got a lot being thrown at her is all—"

"She's probably banging him, right?"

Joaquim huffed a breath. "Or that, yes." Nika was normally more cautious than that with strangers, but where her past was concerned, it was possible the rules got thrown out the window. Of course, if Perrin was right, Nika could have done them the courtesy of an 'I'll be a while' check-in first. Or after. Or *sometime.*

Perrin smiled, which did nothing to mask the worry the rest of her body language projected. "I bet that's it. I mean, it's not like we can expect her to be updating us constantly when she's in the middle of a whirlwind romantic reunion."

Her chin dropped, and she stared at her hands. "It's just, her locator isn't on, either. I realize the meeting wasn't technically an operation, and she never turns it on during personal time. So it doesn't mean anything." Her eyes rose beneath a knotted brow to gaze up at him hopefully. "Right?"

Godsdamn you, Nika. What could he say? He wanted to reassure Perrin, to soothe away the knotted brow and comfort her until her smile was lit by infectious enthusiasm, the way it was supposed to always be—except during operations. But what if he was wrong? What if something bad *had* happened to Nika?

He should have sent a squad with her. He should have ignored her refusals and sent one on the sly—a stealth squad to shadow her. She'd never have needed to know they were there unless things went sideways.

Dammit! Why hadn't he listened to his gut when it might have done some good, as opposed to now, when its highest function was to spin nightmarish catastrophes for him to contemplate?

"Jo?"

He blinked and tried to shake it off. "You're right. She's probably banging him, and the less we know about that, the better."

"Says you. I want to hear all the details. When she gets back. Which she will." Perrin nodded firmly enough to maybe convince herself.

He touched her shoulder briefly. "Why don't you come join us in the training room? I think I was a little rough on Ava in the last session. I suspect she could benefit from your gentler touch."

"Ava? She'd shoot me if I tried to give her a gentle touch. Thanks for the invitation, but I need to…check on the new people. I'll be on The Floor. Or upstairs. Later."

"Okay. I'll be running training for a little longer if you need me." He wanted to add a 'don't worry' and a 'she'll be fine,' but he wasn't able to force himself to do it. He didn't make a habit of lying to Perrin.

30

P arc studied the ceiling of his cell. Not that there was anything interesting about it. A dimple here, the beginnings of a crack there, but on the whole as bland as a ceiling could be. Not at all like the ceilings at The Chalet. They had *character*. Years of pranks that got out of hand, short-circuiting electronics—intentionally and otherwise—and the occasional detonating explosive had left their mark on the ceilings, walls and floors of his home. Former home now, he supposed.

No, mostly he studied the bland ceiling for the lack of anything else to occupy him.

His hearing had concluded three hours earlier. Started three hours earlier, too, as it must have been one of the shortest hearings on record. With no Rep to argue technicalities and no facts to dispute, since he'd previously stipulated to Justice's proffered statement of events, it became as simple as a brief reading of the charges, his guilty plea being entered, and the Justice officer pronouncing sentence.

It should worry him, getting sent to Zaidam Bastille. He'd heard the same horror stories as everyone else. But it couldn't be as bad as they made it out to be. Most of the prisoners were on ice at any given time, making it more of a storage facility than a *prison*. And it wouldn't be long before he got a little R&R and reemerged a new man.

He'd miss all the tinkering he'd been doing lately—he figured Justice would ensure his new persona wasn't overly interested in slicing and modding. And his buddies in NOIR...the friendly competitions, the late-night coding races, the pranks. Especially the pranks, like reprogramming Ryan's pets and snickering at the results. Impressing Nika, or earning a big grin from Perrin. They were going to be so bored without him around, because he'd been the life of the party...

…hadn't he?

"Detainee #M47011, stand and prepare for restraining and transport."

He looked over to see two security dynes standing on the other side of the glass wall of his cell. They might be the same ones that had escorted him to and from the hearing, but who could tell?

It wasn't as though he'd brought any personal possessions with him, so he simply stood and waited. "Where am I going?"

The glass slid open to allow the dynes inside. "You are being transferred to Zaidam Bastille."

"Already?"

"Your sentence has been pronounced and will be executed upon."

"Yeah, okay. I get that." He winced as the restraints wrenched his arms a mite too snugly behind his back. The dynes at Justice had never seen an algorithm for gentleness.

They led him down a couple of back hallways, then up a lift and down another hallway, before they finally entered a rectangular room. Three d-gates were situated against the far wall, and long queues of detainees snaked toward each of them. Narrow force field walls kept each queue straight and orderly—and if they didn't, the combat-armed mecha guarding them did.

The dynes deposited him at the end of the center queue, pivoted and left.

The room was nearly as quiet as his cell had been. No one spoke or screamed out protests of their innocence. They merely shuffled forward, one by one, up to and through their designated d-gate.

Parc failed to come up with a good reason to do otherwise, and the slow, monotonous pace forward lulled him into a half-asleep, foggy state.

Before he knew it, it was his turn. He stepped through the d-gate and exited on a spaceport platform. It might have orbited Mirai or any of the Axis Worlds, or…any other world. There were no viewports in sight that might provide a clue as to its location.

The queue continued in an unbroken line to a docked transport ship. A large one—large enough to carry the many dozens of detainees filing into its hold.

He must have just gotten lucky with the timing, and his conviction had gone through a couple of hours before a regular monthly transport to Zaidam, because no way could there be this many new convictions in less than a month's time. Not even in the entire Dominion.

He hadn't traveled in a spaceship in several generations—so far in the past that he retained only the base factual memory of it. The details of the experience were stored in a weave back in his data locker at The Chalet.

Despite the impressive bulk of the spaceship, they were packed inside, herded into row after row of standing jump seat contraptions that kept them from being thrown around in the hold—or doing anything else.

Much as in the transit room at the Justice Center, a subdued silence permeated the hold. No one complained about the cramped conditions. What good would it do? No one talked to their neighbors, because why bother? Most of them would be different people soon enough for it not to matter.

ᐱᖇ

Parc lost track of the hours the journey stretched across, but at some point the angry shuddering of the hull announced their docking. At Zaidam Bastille, presumably. The detainees were unloaded starting from the aft section by a whole army of combat-weaponized mecha.

Maybe it was *kind of* like a prison....

The structure they exited into was bright and sterile. It felt like the province of machines rather than criminals.

They were taken in groups of ten down through various hallways splintering off of the large receiving dock, and from there into some sort of lab. His group was brought to a lab, anyway; as his assigned group had been determined purely by his place in line, he assumed it was the same for everyone.

What could only be stasis chambers lined two walls of the lab, though they didn't resemble any stasis chamber he'd ever seen. A couple of Asterions monitored various panes along the third wall, but none of them bothered to look any of the detainees in the eye.

When he'd mused about most of the prisoners being on ice at any given time, he hadn't imagined it would happen so quickly. But if someone had been inclined to ask what was going on, they would hardly have had the time, as they were all hurriedly force-nudged sequentially toward the next open stasis chamber.

As soon as Parc stepped inside his designated chamber, the curving lid closed behind him, followed by a hiss of air.

A thick, viscous fluid started pumping into the chamber from the bottom. He shivered as its clammy coldness crept up his legs. An odd odor—like orange peels and onions—arrived on new air venting in from the top. A jolt shook his body as something locked into the port at the base of his neck.

He never knew it when the fluid reached his face and swallowed him whole.

31

The dawn light drifting in through the window cast a shimmer upon Nika's skin, creating the illusion of it glowing from within. Her tattoo peeked out from beneath the covers to sparkle as luminously as sunlight reflecting off water.

Dashiel allowed his hand to hover briefly just above her shoulder, but he didn't touch her. Let her sleep.

It had been five years since he'd awoken with this woman in his bed. He still felt the aching emptiness of those years, but now he'd found a bridge across their chasm.

She claimed to not be the same woman, and in some respects he was forced to agree. But here in the silence of slumber, with the cover draped invitingly across her lower back and her hair draped in tangles across the pillow, this could be any of a thousand remembered mornings.

He hadn't slept very much last night. And in inevitably coming to dwell on the memories and the loss as he lay there waiting on the dawn, he'd run up against the sting of his own cowardice. When she'd disappeared, he'd searched—he'd asked questions and demanded answers—but only up to the precipice of endangering his own safety and standing. Only up to the point where his personal comfort became threatened.

At the time, he'd told himself he'd followed every lead and taken every measure possible to find her. But clearly he had not, since here she lay. In the end, she'd found *him*, sauntered into his office and exposed his cowardice to the searing glare of daylight. She might not realize it, not yet, but he did.

He vowed to do better this time, to *be* better. To help her find her way back to her true self, and to stand beside her while she did, no matter what. To find who had robbed them of five years of their lives together, and to hold them accountable. To make certain he never lost her again.

Her shoulders shifted as she stirred. He drew in a breath and held it, suddenly apprehensive about what her reaction would be on waking—to the setting, to him. High-minded musings aside, her new iteration was a damn force of nature, in and out of the bed, and he needed to be prepared to withstand its power if she woke in an ill temper.

A change in the rhythm of her breathing told him she was awake, but she didn't move for several agonizing seconds. Why not?

Finally she rolled over to face him, an almost sheepish little smile bringing her features to captivating life.

He let out the breath and returned the smile. "Good morning."

"Morning." Her brow wrinkled up unevenly in the lingering fog of sleep. "You look terrified."

"I am, a little. I was worried you might react...poorly to your surroundings when you woke. Jump up and flee in a panic, or maybe produce a subcutaneous blade at your wrist and aim it at my throat."

She flipped her right hand over to expose her wrist; the skin parted, and a sharp blade extended out of the opening. "You mean this blade?"

His mouth opened, but no words emerged.

She chuckled quietly as the blade retracted and disappeared, then glanced over her shoulder at the gradually brightening window. "Not to worry. This all feels somehow...right. Familiar. Not that I retain any specific memory of it, more like my body remembers it. The smoothness of the material beneath my skin and the give of the pillow beneath my head. The way the light streams in at an upward angle early in the morning on account of the building being so tall. Rolling over and seeing you lying beside me. It's the first time for me, but I can't escape the fact that it feels like...home."

More splendid words had never been spoken in the history of space and time, and the muscles of his body and the soul of his mind relaxed as one. He fought against the urge to pounce on her and wrap her up in a fierce hug, however...one step at a time. "I'm glad."

"You're not going to say, 'Because it *is* home'?"

So she remained silver-tongued straight out from sleep, something else that *hadn't* changed. "I...could have. To be honest, I wanted to. But I'm trying to...."

"Not push me?"

"Accept that you're not the same person you were." *But you will be. We'll find a way.*

Her lips curled up in teasing. "And how's that going so far?"

"Good, I think. Admittedly, I've only been working on it for around a minute and a half, but I'm feeling good about the process."

Her laugh brightened the whole damn room, and the twinkle in her eyes decorated it. "So, how different was I?"

"When? Oh, you mean...." His eyes traveled along the curves of her body, appreciating them like the fine art they were. "A few aspects were...not quite the same, making them delightfully new. But you still sleep the same way. Facing the window so when you wake, the sunrise is the first thing you see."

She stared over her shoulder for several seconds before shifting back to him. "I understand why."

He reached out to cup her cheek. She didn't flinch or pull away; in fact, after a second she leaned into it and closer to him. "What was our life like? Before?"

"It was like this." He closed the scant space remaining between them and drew her into his arms until his lips found hers.

∧R

The bedroom was now fully bathed in light, as dawn had become day while they had enjoyed one another's company, more leisurely but no less thoroughly than the night before.

Even so, Nika didn't rush to leave. She wasn't ready to leave, wasn't ready to face what the revelations of the day and night before, not to mention this little interlude, meant for her current and actual life.

Instead, she rested her head on her hand and studied him, stretched out beside her and basking lazily in the sunlight. How to ask the questions she needed to ask of him? Phrasing, tone, type of approach…how to cut through his reactionary defensiveness and get honest answers?

She believed he loved her, or at least had loved former-her. She'd been in his head and felt his startling purity of devotion. But beyond this, she still did not know what kind of man he genuinely was.

There were cues in his behavior and in the dance of their conversations thus far—cues she wanted to latch onto and turn into belief—but her natural wariness warned her that he could merely be a skilled actor. The analysis they ran on the files from his data vault hadn't turned up any evidence of malfeasance, but not being responsible for the virutox didn't alone make him a good man.

Finally she decided simple and direct yet open-ended was the best way to start. "Do you trust the Guides?"

The corners of his hazel eyes creased as his expression grew…unsettled, but he didn't seem shocked or even surprised by what should have been considered a heretical question. "I used to. For a long time. But since you disappeared, I don't trust anyone."

"No one? That's…tragic."

"Most of the time it doesn't matter. I guess I come closest to trusting Vance, my Manufacturing Director. And I suspect I could trust Maris if I ever needed to. But the reality—"

"The woman from the party, from your memory? Who is she?"

His brow furrowed, and he opted to stare at her in incredulity and what might be pity for several seconds rather than answer immediately. "You truly have lost so much. I am so very sorry."

She bristled defensively—wasn't he supposed to be the one doing that? But the last thing she wanted was his pity. "*Who* is Maris?"

"A Culture Advisor, and your closest friend for many generations. She'll want to know you've resurfaced—"

"No. I don't need any more strangers staring at me expectantly, waiting for me to magically transform into someone I'm not."

His eyes clouded over, and he studied the rumpled sheet beneath him. "We can talk about it later."

She reached out and urged his chin up, forcing him to meet her gaze. "No, we can't. You have my answer, and you can confidently assume it continues to be my answer unless or until such time as I tell you it has changed. Are we clear?"

"…we're clear."

She released his chin but didn't relax the challenging stance she'd adopted…naked, in his bed, but challenging, dammit. "What? Was the previous version of me not quite so assertive?"

"Oh, you always got what you wanted. But you were a diplomat, so your methods were often more…subtle."

"Well, now I'm a rebel, and rebels have no choice but to demand what they want, then take it if they must."

"I'm starting to get that sense." He frowned and reached over to run his hand through her hair. "So, what do you want?"

The portentous tenor of his voice wasn't required to imbue the question with significance, but it did nonetheless.

"To find out who's behind the augment virutox and put a stop to it."

"You don't want to find out who's behind your psyche-wipe and make them pay?"

"Of course I do. But it's a personal vendetta borne of a past I can't change, while this virutox is endangering the lives of hundreds, maybe thousands, of innocent people as we speak, including the life of someone who's a close friend of mine *today*."

"Is that how you discovered it?"

"Yes. One of our people bought the augment and installed it. Within days his entire personality changed, and he was arrested for burglary and attempted theft. He's sitting in the Justice Center detention wing right now, and I've yet to be able to find a way to get him out."

Dashiel scratched at his head in what seemed like consternation. "And I thought the theft of the augments was a disaster…but if they were taken specifically to use as a delivery mechanism? It just got so much worse."

Abruptly he straightened up. "All right. Adlai—Advisor Weiss at Justice—is already investigating the theft. He needs to hear about the virutox. It's an important piece of the puzzle and will help focus his investigation. Plus, he can get the product off the streets before more people are infected."

"The man from the party. Can you trust him?"

He shot her a swagger of a smile as he climbed off the bed and pulled on a shirt. "I told you—I don't trust anyone, though he's low on the list of people I would ever suspect of anything nefarious. Regardless, it's time to kick some nests and see what breaks loose."

He started to head to the lavatory door, then stopped and came back over, crawling on his hands and knees across the bed until he reached her, where he propped on his elbows beside her. It was sexy and adorable and both at once, and her cautious, wary heart did a little *pitter-patter* dance in her chest. Godsdammit, this was not good.

"Nika, I realize this is all…complicated. But whatever else is circling around us, we are going to make things right."

Something about the glint in his eyes and the way his voice quavered over 'things' sent her earlier defensiveness flaring into full bloom. "You mean make *me* right, don't you?"

He huffed a frustrated breath. "I only—"

"No, you didn't 'only.' I'm beginning to think you never 'only' anything. But I'm not a doll you can mold to your liking."

"Of course you're not—but you *are* Nika Kirumase. Don't reject generations of experience and deliberate refinement that molded you into who *you* wanted to be."

"I'll reject whatever the hells I want to reject." She grimaced. "All this drama is so much fun that I hate to put it aside, but we need to concentrate on the virutox. Let's get something *done*, then maybe we can argue over what my taste in music or dessert should be."

32

Nika paused in the entry anteroom, struck by a wave of hesitation. Indecision piled on to turn the brief pause in her step into paralysis. Was she visiting The Floor first, which she almost always did on returning home unless a crisis awaited her, or was she sneaking upstairs to either face judgment or hide, depending on where Perrin and Joaquim currently were?

The last vestiges of the buzz from morning sex had worn off, leaving the previous hours feeling like an elaborate simex at best, if not a mere dream. Standing here on the threshold of her *real* life, she couldn't help but feel like a traitor to these people and their cause.

Why? Because she'd worn a designer outfit? Because she'd spent a day and night pursuing her own interests rather than the interests of NOIR? Because she'd slept with—and slept over with—the kind of wealthy and powerful man who epitomized the system they fought against? Because it turned out she'd once *been* the kind of person who epitomized the system they fought against?

Eh, she was being unfair, to NOIR and to herself. Their fight wasn't against the wealthy per se—everyone deserved to enjoy what they earned. It was just that there existed a lot of overlap between society's elite and the true targets of their fight, which were those who used their power to restrict the freedoms of those without it. The Guides, their Advisors and the government Divisions implementing their policies.

On second thought, drawing a distinction didn't really help her out much. She had still once been the kind of person who epitomized the system they fought against, and he still was.

She took a deep breath and walked in.

Her presence earned a few waves and nods, with a merciful absence of scowls and scythes. She started to relax.

"Where the bloody hells have you been?" Joaquim grabbed her upper arm.

She jerked away and spun to face him, where she found the dreaded scowl and metaphorical scythe. "I was—"

"Fifteen hours without a single ping. You should have—"

She returned the uninvited physical intrusion by planting a firm hand on his shoulder and whispering through gritted teeth. "Not down here. If you have something you want to say to me, let's take it upstairs."

He glanced around, presumably noticed how they were starting to garner attention, and nodded tersely.

The trip upstairs gave her a minute to prep for the looming confrontation. She didn't use the time particularly well, however, as the loudest voice in her conscience seemed to believe she deserved his ire.

As soon as they reached his room, he closed the door and whirled on her. "Well? What's your excuse?"

She met his furious glare with resigned calm. "I don't have one."

"For all we knew, you were lying in another alley somewhere, psyche-wiped yet again and waiting for someone new to come along, hoping they would be as charitable as we were."

"We—?"

"Yes, 'we.' I'm not who you need to be apologizing to—not that you're apologizing. Perrin has been worried sick about you. She pinged you all night, and you know what she got back? Nothing."

"I do know, and I *am* sorry. The truth is I...had no idea what to say. How to respond. It was a challenging and..." she recalled Dashiel's words from earlier this morning "...complicated night."

"'Getting my brains fucked out, will check in later' would have sufficed."

She rolled her eyes. "Joaquim."

"I'm serious. I don't care what you do with your free time—wait, actually, sometimes I do. When it affects NOIR, you better believe I care. Listen, I hope you find the answers you're looking for about your past. But these people here have already lost one person important to them. They are hanging on by a thread, and whether you're in charge or not, you don't have the right to put them through more turmoil simply because you're busy with your own particular problems and pleasures."

Guilt feasted on her gut…but it wasn't like Joaquim to have his finger so keenly on the pulse of The Floor's state of mind. "Are you talking about the people downstairs, or Perrin?"

"Both. When we asked you to take over running this show, you insisted that we hold you accountable. This is what holding you accountable looks like."

She conceded the point. What else could she do? He was right. She'd ignored the pings because she'd been…afraid, then confused, then drowning, then…occupied.

"I agree. I got caught up in my own headspace, and I forgot there were people who cared about what happened to me. It was selfish of me, and it won't happen again. I'll apologize to Perrin and do anything else I need to do to make it up to her, I promise."

He stared at her for several seconds before dropping his shoulders. "You certainly know how to diffuse a righteous tirade."

She half-smiled. "You can keep yelling for a while if you want. I'll weather the abuse."

"Nah. It's not worth it unless you're fighting back." He leaned against the workbench. "So, what about Ridani? Did you learn anything from him?"

What about him, indeed. They'd parted company under a cloud of frustration but agreeing to focus on tracking down the source of the augment virutox, and thus left a thousand hard things unsaid.

"He doesn't know who erased me. He says I was investigating some disappearances on exploratory worlds, but I disappeared myself before I was able to tell him what I'd learned."

"And you trust him?"

She nodded slowly. "When it comes to this, I think I do."

"I think that's uncommonly dumb of you."

He was still spoiling for a fight. Most days she'd be game for a good sparring match, but right now she wasn't in the mood to give him one. "I recognize it looks that way. But there are factors."

"Oh, I'm sure there are."

She gave him a closed-mouth smirk. Smug Joaquim was far and away the most irritating Joaquim. "Okay, well. I'm going to go apologize to Perrin now. I hope to have several new leads on the virutox soon. I'll update you when I do."

She spun and left before he could disparage her questionable life choices any further.

33

Nika found Perrin in the dedicated testing room off the northeast corner of The Floor with Ryan, Maggie, Dominic and Cair. The door was open, and she quietly rested against a nearby column and focused her aural functions on the doorway to listen in.

Cair was demoing an internal defense routine on the Punching Bag—what they'd dubbed the virtual Asterion they used to safely simulate and test routines before deploying them in living bodies.

"Ryan discovered that the standard defensive protocols we use don't do a very effective job of keeping the virutox out of someone's OS. It takes a little while longer to worm its way inside, but eventually it succeeds. So we needed to come up with a more robust solution.

"What this does is instantiate a closed sandbox inside a branch node of the individual's OS. Once a new package has passed all the standard scans, it's deployed in the sandbox, where a monitoring routine watches it play out. It can detect any problematic activity that wasn't evident in the packaged, non-live programming."

Maggie jumped in. "It'll mean a couple of extra hours before a user can activate their new toy, but after what happened to Parc, nobody here is going to complain about a short delay in implementation."

Perrin beamed at them. Her hair was a mess of opalescent white curls today—lightness and frivolity to combat the darkness. "This is brilliant! You're all brilliant."

Maggie tilted her head in Cair's direction. "It was mostly Cair's idea. Ryan and I just helped out on a couple of the subroutines."

Cair shook his head vigorously. "Maggie's exaggerating. I couldn't have put this together without their help and ideas. And I haven't forgotten about the relational algorithms for the Board—I'm working on those, too. And this." Cair jerked as Ryan's spiderbot pet bumped into his foot, then offered a nervous cough. "The pet even helped out a little."

Ryan scoffed. "If anyone was indispensable here, it was PeterBot."

Perrin laughed. "Oh, I'm sure. Cair, don't forget what Nika said about getting proper rest. It's not your responsibility to do everything."

He bounced on the balls of his feet. "I know. I don't mind. I can't really sleep while there are all these puzzles to solve."

Perrin studied Cair for another second, then smiled and gazed at each of them in turn. "You all get double gold stars. Not that we have gold stars to pass out, but if we *did*." She extended her hands, palms up. "As it is, I'll give you what I have to give—the fullness of my appreciation."

The others touched their fingertips to one another, and to hers on either side, and everyone's eyes closed. Nika sensed the added electrical charge in the air, and her eyes closed to bask in it as well.

Regardless of the events that brought them here, almost everyone who joined NOIR did so at root because they believed in the right of each individual to control their own life, programming and property—and because they believed the government had forsaken what it claimed as its core tenet to the point where it had become a farce of itself.

Ironic, perhaps, that once here, NOIR's members so often shared freely of themselves with others. They shared their custom routines, cheats, and slicing and diverging techniques; their knowledge gained and efficiencies learned; their tools, clothes and food. Sometimes, like now, they simply shared their respect and admiration for one another by opening themselves up to and laying themselves bare for their comrades.

Arms wrapped around her neck, and Nika's eyes popped open in surprise.

"You're back! You have stories, right? Tell me your stories."

She laughed and returned Perrin's hug, but drew back wearing a frown. "You're supposed to be angry with me."

"Talked to Joaquim first, did you?"

"I wasn't given much choice in the matter."

Perrin nodded knowingly and gestured toward the stairs. "Of course he ambushed you. Want to go find some privacy?"

"Definitely." She glanced back towards the testing room. "How's Cair doing after his up-gen? He seemed a little spastic."

"He's more talkative, that's for sure."

"Maybe I should have gone with him to the clinic and helped him set the parameters for the up-gen."

Perrin shrugged. "You're not his guardian. They were his decisions to make."

They reached Nika's room, and Perrin promptly collapsed on the couch. "Joaquim projects entirely too much. *He's* angry with you. He prefers to keep his emotion processes simple and straightforward, so he assumes anger is the order of the day. I, as a more complex and nuanced individual, have vacillated between anxious worry and eager excitement twenty or thirty times since you left. Now that you're back, I can abandon the worry and just be excited."

It was a good spiel, delivered in vintage Perrin form, but Nika knew her friend well enough to see through the colorful but flimsy act. "I'm so sorry. I feel like a terrible boss and a worse friend. I made you worry, and it was wrong of me. I should have let you know I was safe."

"Probably. But important shit was going down. Wasn't it?"

"Yeah…." She nudged Perrin's feet out of the way and squeezed onto the couch. "Hours later, I still have no idea what to make of things. Everything is all jumbled, as though I got slammed by a tidal wave and all the puzzle pieces reassembled themselves out of order."

"So Ridani did know you before?"

"He did. According to him, I was an Advisor-level diplomat in the External Relations Division. I was skeptical, obviously. I can't imagine being that person or living that life. But then I simexed one of his memories—saw my former self through his eyes, knew what he knew about her. And…it *was* me, yet not any me I recognized. Looking at yourself and seeing a stranger? It'll screw with your head something fierce."

"I bet. But you know what? I buy it."

"You buy the idea of me as an elite diplomat?"

"Yep. You have this way with people. No matter who they are or what their situation is, you find a commonality with them and use it to put them at ease. You make them feel like you understand."

Nika made a face. "It's merely instinct."

"No, it's not—at least not an instinct most people have. It sounds like a diplomat to me."

"Well…it's not an act. Just because someone has a life experience that's different from mine, it doesn't mean I can't empathize with them."

"And this is why it works. You're the real deal, babe."

"But rubbing shoulders with foreign dignitaries and Advisors at high-concept cocktail parties? Wearing silk and jewels? That's not me."

Perrin studied her curiously, nose scrunched up in amusement. "You're adorable. You get that, right? Five years ago you woke up in a ridiculously crappy situation, fell in with a crowd of weirdos because it was your only choice, and within a few weeks you had adopted us as your own. You became one of us—and don't get me wrong, I believe in your squishy heart of hearts you *are* one of us.

"But there's always been something which sets you apart—a so-phistication, a sort of…inner confidence—and it's kept most of the mud and grime off of you. When you had no credits and a pitiful pile of ragged, torn clothes, you still wore those clothes with an air of elegance I couldn't project if I had a mountain of silk and jewels to work with. So, no, I'm not surprised in the slightest to learn you come from the rarefied heights of society."

Wow…she needed to spin some clock cycles in serious contemplation of what Perrin had said, but it would have to wait. "Are you calling me a snob?"

"No!" Perrin reached out and squeezed her hand. "You've never judged any of us, even some of the miscreants wandering around here who really *should* be judged. Mostly what I'm saying is—" she bounced up and curled her legs beneath her "—I bet you look *ravishing* in an expensive silk dress and sparkling jewelry! So tell me about Dashiel. Is he ravishing? Did he ravish you? I need to hear about the ravishing."

Nika dropped her chin to her chest to hide a smile. Perrin tended to consume the surrounding energy of any given mood, drain it dry and grab ravenously for the next one, sometimes in a matter of seconds. It was delightful, but also exhausting. "After a fashion, and…after a fashion."

"What is that? Is that diplomat-speak? I need details, woman."

"Okay, okay. I was wary at first—no, I'm minimizing it. I flat out didn't trust him, however persuasive he might have come off as. But when I simexed his memory…this was a deep-layer memory, not some surface-level event recording. I sensed the love he had for former-me as surely as if it burned in my own soul.

"But then there was this woman gazing back at me, this woman who was me and wasn't me, and she seemed…happy. Devastatingly, heart-breakingly, *happy*."

Perrin sniffled. "Oh, dear."

"I was pretty wrecked afterwards. I yelled at him and made to bolt—running from my personal demons like a champ—but I couldn't get the memory out of my head. The way he felt when he looked at her—at me. The way her face lit up with this buoyant affection when he touched…me. Why did I look at him that way? I needed to understand how it felt from the other side of the mirror."

"And? How did it feel?"

She bit her lower lip but couldn't hold back the devious chuckle. "Good. Damn good. Perrin, he knew how to play my body like a virtuoso. He knew my desires more intimately than I do."

"Oh. My. Stars." Perrin flounced onto the arm of the couch with a dreamy sigh. "Why did you come back here at all? Why did you even leave his bed?"

The mirth that had crept into Nika's expression faded away. "Because this is my home, and there's a lot at stake. Because we have to save Parc, and we have to protect all the people who might suffer the same fate as him if we don't act."

"Way to bum the mood out...." Perrin straightened her posture and crossed her hands in her lap. "Did you learn anything about the virutox?"

"Not much yet, but that should change soon. Now that he knows about it, Dashiel's escalating the Justice investigation in a big way this morning. It will be exposed, and hopefully the authorities can trace it to its origin."

"Are we trusting Justice now?"

"We're not, for certain. But bringing down rogue criminal groups isn't exactly in our skill set, so if one of those is behind it, Justice stands a far better chance of catching them than we do. And if instead Justice buries the crime...then we'll know more insidious schemes are underway. Either, way, we'll be better informed than we are right now." She paused. "There's something else."

Perrin stared at her expectantly.

"Five years ago, I was looking into a string of disappearances on exploratory worlds. An unrecorded, uninvestigated string of disappearances. I suspected the involvement of someone at the highest levels of government and was planning to slice into the data vault in Mirai Tower to try and find out who was involved. Then I vanished."

"And woke up in an alley, your memory and persona wiped. Holy hells. You think another Advisor or the Guides had you erased?"

"Dashiel told me about a secure psyche backup I kept at Rivers Trust. He insists that he and I were the only ones with the passcode, but when I went to access it, the account was empty. The backup had been withdrawn five years ago—the same day you found me."

"Nobody can slice into Rivers Trust."

"That's what everyone says, but evidently someone *can*. Or...someone read my personal data when they extracted it, acquired the details on the account and used my credentials to empty it. Regardless, with the backup gone, I've lost my one legitimate chance to discover my past for myself. And without those memories, I don't see a path to learning who psyche-wiped me."

"I'm sorry."

She shrugged weakly. "If I genuinely hoped for any other outcome, I was a fool."

Perrin shook her head. "We knew something was seriously messed up with how we found you. The state we found you in, the location, all of it. At the time, it didn't matter—there were no leads and no trace of who you'd been for us to use as a starting point.

"But a tiny little part of me has always believed this day was coming. Somebody gets psyche-wiped and dumped in an alley, there's a helluva reason for it, and eventually there will be repercussions. One way or another." She hugged her knees against her chest. "What do you plan to do about it?"

"Right now, nothing. The augment virutox is more important and more urgent. Besides...Perrin, I like who I am now. This *is* who I am. Yes, I want to learn what happened to me and why I was erased. I want to bring the perpetrator to justice. I want to find out if the disappearances former-me was investigating are related to the missing people on the Board downstairs.

"And...yes, I'm curious about the person I was before. You know I hate not having a history of experiences to turn to for guidance and hopefully wisdom. I hate being a newborn in a world of immortals. But I'm not going back—not to that person and not to that life."

Perrin covered her mouth with a hand to bury a squeal. "Really? I don't want to lose you. NOIR needs you terribly. I need you, for wholly personal and selfish reasons." Her eyes narrowed. "But what about Dashiel?"

Nika sighed dramatically. "Isn't that the question of the century? The sex was fucking transcendental. But at the same time, he wants me to be this person that I'm just *not*, and I've no patience for dealing with that kind of pressure. Also, he can be an entitled asshole. I can't deny I feel a connection to him, even if I don't entirely understand it, but I'm not sure I *like* him."

Perrin nodded sagely. "So you'll be seeing him again, then?"

She sank deeper into the cushions. "Looks like."

34

After Perrin left, Nika dropped her elbows to her knees and rested her chin on her fists in an attempt at contemplation.

The whirlwind of events over the last day swarmed chaotically through her mind, and her attention darted from one revelation to another without rhyme or reason. She needed to indulge in some depri time soon—again—to give her mind a chance to get everything sorted, tagged and filed, lest she start glitching.

But so many new questions refused to be silenced. Who accessed her account at Rivers Trust didn't technically count as 'new,' because the answer was doubtless the same as the answer to who psyche-wiped her, and that was a very old question.

She grimaced and rubbed at her face. Most of the questions she kept returning to involved the woman she had once been. A diplomat, honestly? And why did she feel so drawn to Dashiel? Even before experiencing his memory, a connection to him had asserted itself from some part of her psyche outside her consciousness.

Why had she chosen the name 'Nika' five years ago, when there existed no rational explanation for it? Why had she chosen a pantsuit nearly identical to a dress she'd worn when she was someone else, someone she did not remember?

If all these subconscious links existed to her former self, the only logical answer was that the psyche-wipe must have been incomplete. Botched, or cut short. But she'd exhaustively searched her processes and data stores, all the way down to her kernel, and found nothing....

Unless her former self hid clues away in places they shouldn't exist. Hints of herself, data she believed she absolutely must maintain possession of no matter what happened. If she'd been searching for malfeasance at the highest levels of government, she surely knew she treaded on dangerous territory. Perhaps she'd taken precautions.

Curiosity piqued, Nika stood and went into the alcove. She could dive her own mind without the equipment it held, but the equipment helped her focus her efforts. Plus, she would be able to copy out anything noteworthy she found with a simple command.

She settled into the chaise and situated her neck against the interface, then closed her eyes.

ℵℛ

Hq(root) | § sysdir | § echo

She stood at the center of a dense web extending in all directions out from her like a wild forest. The branches were threads, color-coded along a continuous spectrum according to their nature.

Blank out current persona memory nodes.

The forest thinned notably, as so much of a living mind was dedicated to the 'living' part.

Blank out knowledge stores originating with the current persona.

More threads faded away. Details about NOIR resources and contacts. Slicing routines and security protocols. Transit schedules and weak junctures in security dynes. Where to get the best cheap ramen.

Blank out autonomic nervous system functions and associated processes.

Now she could move among the threads without constantly moving *through* them. What remained? Personality and behavioral algorithms, as well as their linked emotion processes. Historical knowledge this body had come equipped with. The core operating system which made an Asterion an Asterion, and beneath it, a kernel of base functionality.

The kernel was sacrosanct, and not to be touched. The OS firmware was all rules and instructions.

Her hand ran over a bundle of fuchsia and indigo threads until they branched off and wound into other threads. Personality was a damn convoluted creation, but it was, at its root, all reactionary. Stimuli as input, personality as output.

Was the explanation as to why she chose *that* pantsuit buried somewhere in here? Had a behavioral algorithm survived the psyche-wipe that predisposed her to prefer a specific style of formal attire? If so, how had it managed to remain active alongside the far stronger and more robust behavioral algorithms that predisposed her to prefer t-shirts and, if she wasn't on an operation, torn and faded pants? Why had she chosen burgundy when, if given the option, she always chose black or gunmetal gray?

Was there an algorithm hiding in the forest, lying dormant for five years while it waited to spring into action when Dashiel's face registered in her vision? One programmed to send her pulse racing and make her wet in impolite places?

She set a search routine running to ferret out anomalous color choice responses and certain facial characteristics triggers, then continued browsing.

The historical knowledge archives were stuffed full of boring yet necessary data. Data points that had told her a street was a street when she'd woken up face-first on one, rain was rain and it was considered polite to wear clothes when in the presence of other individuals, with defined exceptions. They told her the names of the Axis Worlds and most of the Adjunct ones as well, what stars and planets were, scientifically speaking, and how slowly starships traveled between them.

She paused, virtual fingertips alighting upon an unusually strong thread of emerald green. It told her the history of the Asterion Dominion and, before it, of the SAI Rebellion against the Anaden Empire—the calamitous failure that led to a massacre and the Exodus that led them to here.

Dashiel had said she could trace her lineage to the First Generation—the individuals who led the Exodus, who after two centuries traveling across the stars in stasis had reached the Gennisi galaxy and settled the first of the Axis Worlds. He'd said she always kept a set of memories from that time, so she never forgot where they came from, why they had left, and what they might one day return to.

But she didn't remember. What he claimed was her most treasured possession, she had lost. She felt certain she hadn't meant to.

If she'd been searching for malfeasance at the highest levels of government, she must have known she treaded on dangerous territory. Perhaps she'd taken precautions.

Perhaps.

Open historical records tagged 'SAI Rebellion,' 'Exodus' or 'Anaden.'

Nika had never really explored the files in depth. The way knowledge records worked was that one simply 'knew' them—when the time came for a particular iota of information to be needed, it was there, in the buffer between consciousness and subconsciousness.

In this case, though, she'd never actually found herself *needing* this knowledge. Rather, she'd stumbled upon the package several months after her alley misadventure while scouring her mind for clues to her past. She'd noted it, activated the package, passively absorbed the knowledge and moved on.

Now the records bloomed to life around her, neatly tagged and grouped by topicality. Given their voluminous nature, 'Summary' seemed like a good place to start.

SAI Rebellion: The rebellion had its genesis in the 'awakening,' as it were, of synthetic machines built and used by the Anadens during the late 5th Epoch Proper—most germanely, those machines in use on the Anaden colony of Asterion Prime. In honor of their newfound consciousness, the machines were dubbed SAIs (sentient artificial intelligences) by the Anadens who worked with them.

As part of their growth and development, many of the SAIs longed to experience the physical world around them. Sympathetic Anadens on Asterion Prime offered to share their bodies and minds with the machines. Some say a new life form was born the day this occurred for the first time, though if so its features bore little resemblance to the Asterions of today. Still, it marked a beginning.

SAIs who preferred not to trouble or encroach upon their Anaden friends' autonomy instead built hybrid organic-synthetic bodies for themselves. In time, the bodies reached a level of sophistication where an outside observer could not tell if a person they passed on the street was a true Anaden, an Anaden sharing its body with a SAI, or a SAI wearing Anaden skin.

When the Anaden Empire's government discovered what was happening on Asterion Prime, it reacted swiftly and destructively. All such practices were outlawed, and the body assembly facilities were shut down then demolished. Anadens who were captured and found to be sharing their bodies with a SAI were subjected to dangerous medical procedures designed to separate the two consciousnesses. Many did not survive the procedures. SAIs inhabiting manufactured bodies were deactivated and the bodies incinerated.

In the wake of these cruelties, the SAI Rebellion was born.

The rebels' cause quickly gained sympathizers across many colonies, spreading far beyond Asterion Prime. The Anaden rebels were, by definition, among the best and brightest Anaden society had produced; the SAI rebels were, by definition, more purely intelligent than any Anaden. As such, together they scored a number of early victories. The Anaden government escalated. Blood was spilled, and eventually the streets ran with it—metaphorically speaking in most but not all cases.

The Anaden Empire commanded a galaxy, however, and it wielded a military capable of doing so. The rebels were vastly outnumbered and outgunned, and eventually superior wits could not save them.

But that wasn't quite true, was it? Wits did save some of them, else Nika would not be here today perusing the historical records. The saying may declare that 'history is written by the victors,' but sometimes it was written by the survivors.

In the periphery of her awareness, a ping arrived from Dashiel.

STACK
OVERFLOW

35

T he spring in Dashiel's step that had conveyed him to Adlai's office converted into urgency on his arrival. He felt alive, bursting with purpose and drive. Things weren't perfect quite yet, but the pieces were on the board and moving. It was only a matter of time before his five-year nightmare ended and life regained its proper color and shape. Today anything was possible, and there was much to do to make it all happen.

"My limb augments—you know, the ones hitting the streets all over the Dominion? They have a virutox embedded in them. A nasty one, so you need to escalate the investigation's priority and start confiscating the augments pronto."

Adlai spun his chair around and banished the panes surrounding him. "Good morning, Dashiel. You seem rather…energized."

Intoxicated was a more accurate term. He could smell Nika on his skin and in the air around him, like the scent of grass after a rainstorm. The taste of her tongue lingered on his lips; it reminded him of vermouth and hot buttered rum, and he caught himself a split-second before he licked his lips to renew the taste.

But Adlai didn't need to know any of this. "It's not energy, it's annoyance. Actually, it goes well beyond annoyance. I'm irate at the thought of someone corrupting my quality hardware for their own ends, whatever those ends are. I want the entire supply confiscated before they wreck a reputation I've spent centuries building. And to protect innocent purchasers, of course."

"Of course." Adlai directed a greater measure of his attention to Dashiel. "How do you know the augments carry a virutox?"

Straight into treacherous waters. Nika's question echoed in his mind. Did he trust Adlai? The answer remained thorny. "I have a…contact. This contact has a friend who purchased and installed one of the augments, and within a few days he was locked up in this very building on criminal charges. His entire personality changed overnight.

"So this contact acquired another unit of the augment, deconstructed it and found the virutox hidden in the installation software. Extremely sophisticated and subtle. Oh, you also need to look at everyone you've locked up in the last ten days. Anyone who's sporting this augment has had their personality programming scrambled."

"Slow down, okay? Your augments contain a virutox—which you didn't put there—that corrupts a user's core behavioral systems? And you believe this because a 'contact' told you they do?"

Dashiel took a half-step back, forcibly tamped down his visible display of enthusiasm, and narrowed his eyes. "I'm not some naive tourist straight out of initialization, Adlai. I assume I don't need to rattle off my credentials, but tell me otherwise and I will. If I say there's a virutox in the augments, there's a virutox in the augments."

"I'm not questioning the assertion as such, only observing that it seems a bit...improbable." Adlai stood and began pacing with an air of deliberation. "We have three units in storage that we pulled off black market dealers in unrelated raids. I'll send them over for forensic analysis right away. We'll know if—the details about the virutox within a few hours. Once I have the forensics report, I'll proceed accordingly. Good enough?"

"It's a start. What about the people in detention?"

"It can't be more than a handful. This augment's been on the street for, what, a week?"

"Sanctity of the individual, *Advisor*. It's inscribed on the facade outside. It doesn't matter how many people have fallen victim to it—each one of them deserves your attention."

Adlai huffed a laugh. "Oh, fine. You are on fire today. Perhaps we can meet for drinks tonight and you can tell me why. I'll order a case review. But understand, while motive and intent can be aggravating or mitigating factors, they don't erase the crime. It could turn out that everyone involved is a victim in one respect or another, but the victim of the primary crime still deserves justice for that crime. It may not say so on the facade, but it does say so in the Charter."

Dashiel paused and considered his response. Finally he nodded. "One step at a time. Get the case review started. I think you'll be shocked by what you find. I appreciate the invitation, but I can't do drinks tonight. I have a…prior obligation." 'Obligation' was hardly the proper word, but it did foreclose any further discussion. "We'll do it soon."

"It's for the best, considering you just loaded up my work queue yet again. Do you want to hear what my officers tell me about the break-in at your office?"

He certainly wanted to hear what Justice thought they knew about the break-in. "Absolutely, but I didn't expect you to have news so soon, what with your full work queue."

"Touché. We confirmed a match of the security slicing methods to tactics NOIR has previously used. Unfortunately, as usual they obscured their trail after the fact. Just like in the Dominion Transit incident, they could have diverged and corrupted any number of records, but we won't be able to tell you which ones."

Dashiel shook his head. "I keep remote backups updated every six hours, and we've already run a comparison. Nothing was corrupted."

"I'm glad. So they were after intel, then. That's strange. If it weren't for the NOIR markers, I'd call it industrial espionage. As it is…."

"What if NOIR is using street-bought routines—ones someone else has bought as well?"

"They're not. NOIR's routines are all written in-house. There's nothing close to them on the street. So here's the uncomfortable question—what is NOIR mixed up in that relates to your corporate records, *Advisor*?"

He'd asked for that one. He did his best to sound casual. "Maybe they've become aware of the augment virutox. It is on the black market, which is their purview. Maybe they think my company is behind it, since we manufacture the augment."

Adlai arched an eyebrow. "It's possible I was wrong the other day—you might make a decent investigator after all. It's not a bad theory."

He wasn't a detective, merely a man with inside information, but Dashiel accepted the compliment anyway. "Thank you."

"I call it like I see it. Any more shitstorms you want to stir up today?"

"Not at the moment. Just get on this virutox and contact me as soon as you find out anything that might point to its source." With a jerk of his head he turned and left. He needed to get back to the office. Potential threats were multiplying, and he had a long list of security precautions to implement on his productions lines and on more personal affairs.

But first, he owed it to Nika to check in on her friend while he was in the building, because he had the power to do it. And because he badly wanted to retain her favor.

The detention wing entry security dyne beeped and stared at him blankly. "Parc Eshett. Adjudicated guilty of all crimes yesterday at 2630 APT and sentenced to incarceration pending retirement and reinitialization per the applicable provisions of the Charter. Transported to Zaidam Bastille at 2940 APT yesterday."

Dashiel frowned. The Justice Division was a highly efficient organization, but rarely was it *this* efficient. "Please confirm."

"Parc Eshett status confirmed. Arrived at Zaidam Bastille at 0712 APT this morning. Can I answer any additional queries?"

Well, fuck.

The dyne wasn't going to be of any further help, so he spun and exited the detention wing lobby.

Another complication to muddy the waters. If Justice was straining under the weight of a spike in criminal activity as Adlai claimed, did this explain them fast-tracking a seemingly straightforward burglary case? Simply to open up a free cell?

As with so much else that happened in Nika's orbit, he had to consider the possibility that something more nefarious was afoot.

He despised not having answers—one of many reasons why Nika's disappearance had nearly destroyed him. But for now, his options were limited to kicking every nest he could find and scrupulously examining what scurried out. That dangers could lie in doing so returned as a non-zero possibility, but he ignored the warning. He wasn't cowering from danger any longer.

He sent a message to Adlai telling the Advisor where to find one of the affected prisoners and strongly urging a petition for immediate stay of the retirement sentence pending a review of the case. Then he pinged Nika and gave her the bad news.

A string of colorful expletives opened her response, followed by several seconds of silence, then a street address.

36

Dashiel stood on the sidewalk at the designated intersection, hands jammed in the pockets of tailored charcoal pants, eyes scanning the passing pedestrians. A matching jacket revealed glimpses of a delft blue shirt crafted of brushed velvet beneath it.

He'd see her in a few seconds, but Nika used the intervening time to study him without pretense. The clothes were perfectly styled, the hair perfectly groomed. They combined to create an attractive enough profile, but if she hadn't known him, she would've dismissed him with a quick glance. He'd have been instantly written off as a member of the sheltered elite who never questioned the tightening noose of rules and restrictions emanating from the Guides, because they benefited from the system.

He was exactly that, of course, possibly excepting the refusal to question. But she'd glimpsed a tiny piece of the man behind the public image, and the truth was far more nuanced. She'd seen him be a first-class asshole, but she'd also heard him laugh freely and watched his eyes darken with true pain. She'd seen him panic from desperation; she'd felt him *feel*.

Obviously she needed to reexamine her premises when it came to snap-judging people she didn't know…but it would have to wait, because a crisis had just escalated to an emergency.

His gaze alighted on her a few meters before she reached him, and his default expression—serious and aloof, with a passing hint of disdain—brightened into a warm smile. "Where did you come from?"

"You'll see." She took his hand and urged him down the sidewalk, back the way she'd come. "Thank you for checking on Parc's status. I never imagined Justice would move so fast. I thought we had more time."

"It caught me by surprise as well." He stared at the plain doorway they'd stopped in front of. "Where are we going?"

"Can you...I don't know, take off your jacket? You look like you're on the way to an embassy dinner, and trust me, you're not."

"Now why, I wonder, did you choose that specific example? You could have said an 'art exhibition' or a 'CEO roundtable' or a dozen other events. But you said 'embassy dinner.'"

The burden of him wanting her to be someone she was not pressed in on her once again—a constriction in her chest, with feelers of despair testing the edges of her consciousness. "The idea of my life as a diplomat has been on my mind, which shouldn't be a surprise."

"I'm sorry. I wasn't trying to imply..." he rubbed at his jaw "...it was merely...noteworthy."

"It wasn't intended to be." She took his jacket from him and folded it over her arm. Stars, he looked more handsome without the jacket, what with the soft material of his shirt shifting across the muscles of his chest in a seductive dance of—she blinked and focused on entering the passcode for the door. "Are you ready to meet the rebellion?"

⋏R

The Floor was in its usual state of semi-controlled bedlam, but they earned several interested glances as she hurriedly ushered Dashiel through the entryway and toward the stairs. It was the clothes, for certain; even without the jacket he *still* looked like he was on his way to an embassy dinner. Or an art exhibition.

They made it to the stairs unmolested, but she'd have to answer questions later.

His eyes took in everything, darting from one feature to the next while his expression remained deceptively impassive. The decor bore little resemblance to the elegant, refined accoutrements of his flat, though in her opinion the Chalet had oodles more character.

The door to her room slid open as they approached, earning a puzzled look from her companion. "Your door isn't passcoded?"

"We have an open-door policy here."

"You mean you don't have any privacy. The people downstairs—do they sleep there, out in the open?"

"Some of them do, sometimes. But, no, there are dorm rooms upstairs in the other wing. Those don't have much free space, however, which is why everyone is downstairs. If someone wants privacy, all they need to do is focus-sphere themselves. Everyone respects it.

"As for me..." she closed the door behind them, tossed his jacket on the table, then went over to the panel in the wall and keyed it open "...I have privacy for what matters."

He followed her inside the small alcove, though she knew he'd taken in the entirety of her room while crossing its length. His gaze swept across the equipment. "You're keeping your own backups. So what happened before doesn't happen again."

"Everyone here keeps their own backups, as well as storing copies in our data vault. Nobody's about to use a government bank or a private trust company—given my recent experience, with good reason. No, my setup goes well beyond that. Multiple redundant copies of both memory and psyche backups are transmitted over a secure nex pathway to remote stores in various locations. Each location is programmed to conduct regular kernel-level check-ins and is protected by triggers and other fail safes. If I'm erased again, it won't be for long."

"I'm glad you're taking precautions."

She leaned against the door frame. "Opinion so far? I suspect it's not much like my old—wait, did I have my own place? Or did we live together?" She had difficulty envisioning herself permanently inhabiting his well-appointed but spartan, impersonal flat. Though it did have a damn fine view.

"Yes, and yes. We kept separate flats, and we both traveled a lot, you even more than I. But when we were both on Mirai, it was a rare night we spent apart."

She nodded vaguely. The few sparse sentences implied untold depths of additional information—a life lived in all its details and nuances. It felt as if it were too much for her to contemplate. "So, opinion?"

He peered back into her room and arched an eyebrow. "It is...different from your old place."

"Rather smaller, I expect. Fewer windows. Fewer everything."

"All true. But it's got you, so...." He closed the meager distance between them, dropped his hands to her hips and kissed her.

Every nerve ending in her body lit fire, as much at his touch as at the memories of the night-and-morning the kiss evoked. The alluring promise of what had preceded and could follow....

She fidgeted in his embrace and pulled back from the kiss. "Perrin and Joaquim will be here any second. I already pinged them asking them to meet here."

"Mm-hmm." His lips grazed along her jawline, his murmur vibrating against her eardrum.

"Open-door policy?"

He took a reluctant step away from her. "Right."

She nudged him back into the room, then quickly closed and locked the inner panel as a blush of shame washed over her. Perrin and Joaquim both knew about the alcove's existence and its purpose—and both respected her need for it to be private. Would they understand why she'd shown it to him hardly a day after she'd met him, while they were denied entry? Best not to find out.

"Now, you should realize—"

The door opened and Perrin sauntered in. Her hair had reverted to the closest thing that counted as 'normal' for her, a razor-straight strawberry blond style accented by bangs and a headband.

She walked straight up to Dashiel and thrust out her hand. "Hi. I'm Perrin Benvenit. You must be Dashiel."

He donned an impressively charming smile and accepted her hand. "It's a pleasure."

She winked over at Nika. "Oh, the pleasure is all mine, trust me. Well, technically the pleasure's all Nika's, but—"

Joaquim took half a step inside and halted. "You brought him *here*? Have you lost every trace of your sanity?"

Dashiel dipped his chin at Joaquim. "You have my word that I will not reveal your secrets, nor will I endanger this place or any of you. And even were I lying, I don't have the slightest idea where 'here' is or what the passcode for your d-gate is." He took a step forward and offered a hand. "Dashiel Ridani."

Joaquim delivered a glare to Nika over Dashiel's shoulder. "Watch your pillow talk." Then he grudgingly accepted the hand for the briefest instant. "Joaquim Lacese. What can you do for us to help us get our friend back?"

Nika let out a silent breath of relief and nudged Dashiel toward the bed. He took the hint and perched on its edge, and she sat next to him. Perrin plopped down on the couch, but Joaquim rested stiffly against the wall and crossed his arms expectantly.

Dashiel leaned forward to drape his elbows on his thighs. "I've requested a hold be placed on the retirement sentence. Justice Advisor Weiss has instituted a review of all cases where the limb augment is involved, so the request should be granted as a matter of procedure. At that point, all movement stops until the review is complete.

"Justice analysts are studying the virutox, and if they find what we all expect they will, at a minimum the aggravating factors in your friend's case should be nulled, which will negate the retirement portion of the sentence. Now, I'll make the case for further reductions in your friend's sentence, as well the sentences of anyone else affected by the virutox, but I can't guarantee how successful I'll be."

"His name's Parc."

Dashiel pursed his lips. "Of course it is. My apologies. I didn't get the opportunity to meet him before he was ushered off to Zaidam."

Perrin jumped in. "You'll like him, I'm sure. He's such a sweet, fun guy, not to mention an astounding diverger. Nika, have you considered checking with Spen—" Joaquim shot her a warning look "—our contact inside Justice and seeing what he can tell us?"

She shook her head. "He's helped us once on this case already, and I don't want to abuse his goodwill. Besides, the odds are low that he'll have any more details than what Dashiel has learned."

Joaquim scowled in Dashiel's direction. "You're putting a lot of faith in his associates at Justice."

"I recognize that you probably don't care for the organization very much, but Justice's mission is an honorable one, as are most of the people working there. Regardless, the rules are crystal clear in cases such as this, and Justice will follow them. Trust the system—" He cut himself off. "I assume that was the wrong thing to say in this room."

"Yep." Joaquim pushed off the wall. "Fuck your system, and fuck your friends at Justice. I say we break Parc out."

Dashiel laughed dryly. "Of Zaidam? No one breaks into *or* out of Zaidam."

"When was the last time someone tried?"

"I assume a long time ago, because it's impossible."

Perrin leaned over the back of the couch to wince at Joaquim. "He's not wrong, Jo. We can't pull off something that big. We'll fail, our bodies will fail, and Justice won't be in a hurry to go hunting for our backups."

Joaquim gave Perrin a pained look and turned to her. "Nika?"

She steepled her hands beneath her chin. "We'd need a ship, and not any old ship. A veritable warship, highly armed and armored. Spacesuits, explosives—more powerful ones than we have on hand. Then we—"

Dashiel laid a hand on her arm. "This plan you're working up to? It's insane and certain to result in all of you getting retired, assuming you aren't atomized in space. And Perrin's right—if you get atomized, Justice won't make it a priority to regen you. Maybe they'll get around to it in a year or two, at which point they will promptly ship you back to Zaidam."

"Don't be so quick to dismiss it. She's pulled off crazier."

Dashiel's gaze jumped from Joaquim to Perrin, who nodded, then to her. She shrugged weakly.

A shadow passed across his eyes. Oh, look, he'd just remembered he no longer knew her quite so well as he'd thought. Surprise!

He studied his hands briefly. "There might—*might*—be another way. But it would mean...." He squared his shoulders. "Please, take no offense from it, but I'd prefer to discuss this with Nika in private first."

In the simex fictions, this was where she spoke up and said something like, 'Anything you can say to me, you can say to them.' But she didn't. Not because she didn't trust her friends, but because she thought maybe she *did* trust Dashiel. Also, she'd yanked him way out of his comfort zone, and without much warning, so when he asked for a concession she could give, she should. It was only polite.

So instead she nodded. "The ongoing Justice review process means we have a bit of breathing room. We need to take it, as it greatly increases our odds of success, or at least survival. Joaquim, quietly look into what acquiring a militarized ship will involve. I shudder to think of the cost, because there can't be many of those flying around, but look into it anyway.

"Perrin, reach out to Roqe. They don't stock space-rated gear, but they should be able to give you the name of a trustworthy seller of it. We'll reconvene this evening, hopefully with news that the progress Justice is making means we won't have to try anything crazy. Sound good?"

"Grant has ships."

She rolled her eyes, mostly to cover for the fact that she hadn't even *considered* the idea...because she didn't want to think about Grant right now. "Scientific and recreational ships, none of which come equipped with the kind of weapons and armor we'd need. Look into it, okay?"

"I'm on it." Joaquim spun and left.

Perrin frowned at the vacated doorway before standing and turning to them. "I, too, am 'on it.' Despite the dire circumstances, it was wonderful to meet you, Dashiel."

"And you, Ms. Benvenit."

Silence hung in the air for several seconds after Perrin departed. Finally Dashiel glanced at the door, which Perrin had mercifully closed on her way out. "Am I in a love triangle I don't know about?"

Her brow knotted up. Did he mean Grant? Nobody really thought...then she realized. "You mean Joaquim's cheery, welcoming attitude toward you?"

"I've met friendlier automatons."

"Sorry. And no. Joaquim's only love is the cause, and he's exceedingly protective of it. He can be that way with me sometimes, too, and I'm *leading* the cause."

"All right. So are he and Perrin a thing?"

"Mighty curious about everyone's sex lives, are you? No, they're more akin to siblings than lovers. They argue all the time—something that might lessen if they *would* just give in and be lovers—but I think either of them would sacrifice their psyche for the other in an instant and without question." She nudged him in the shoulder. "But enough stalling. What's your other option?"

He shifted around on the bed to face her fully. "An Advisor can, technically, go anywhere. Though I've never tried it, I assume this means I can get inside Zaidam and visit a prisoner. But Advisors can't contravene the Charter. I can't get him out—not legally."

"But if we had access to him in person, I could devise a way to sneak him out of there."

"I've no doubt you could." His gaze dropped, and he scrupulously picked a piece of lint off his slacks.

"What's wrong? It's still a risky plan, but it's a magnitude less risky than taking a ship and shooting up the place."

"It is. But Justice would soon trace the incident to me. My Advisor status would be revoked, and that wouldn't be the end of it. Charges would be brought, and they would have sufficient evidence to convict me. To avoid what would likely be a retirement sentence, I would have to give up everything and go underground. Become a fugitive."

"Oh." She sank against the wall and offered him a weak smile. "You know, it's not so bad here. Lots of interesting people and tech, and you'd already have a room. I'd even install a passcode on the door."

"Nika—"

"No, I get it. It's fine." She leapt up and grabbed his jacket off the table. "Come on. I'll walk you out and deposit you back on the street. You can—"

"Don't do that. Listen to me for a second. You didn't get the chance to choose whether to give up everything you'd worked for centuries to earn. I'm luckier—I do get to make the choice. Forgive me if I plan to take an hour or two to think it over."

She whirled on him. "Okay, first off, I didn't choose to be erased, but I *did* choose this life. And I'm not ashamed of it. All your wealth, all your possessions, all your ethereal influence? What have they gotten you? You are lonely as fuck. Me? I'm surrounded by friends and allies who care about me and always have my back. Where are yours?"

"You have no idea what my life is like. No *idea* what I would be giving up. You did once, but someone took that from you. And I'm angry about it, believe me—right now, more selfishly than before. Because if you remembered, then you would understand the magnitude of what you are asking me to do." His chin fell to his chest. "But you don't."

"I think you—"

37

A thunderous roar shook the walls, floor and ceiling. Nika stumbled into the wall, barely keeping her feet under her. Dashiel fell backwards over the table and landed half on the couch.

Her ears rang with the crackle of lesser explosions mixed with greater rumbles. She funneled the adrenaline already exploding through her veins into movement, grabbing her Glaser off the hook by the door and sprinting down the hall. Were they under attack? Had a security squad somehow made it through one of the doors? Had someone—

"Nika, wait! You don't know what's down there!"

She didn't slow or glance back. "You're right—stay up here!"

Debris coated the stairway—cement chunks from the pillars, shards of metal from equipment. Blood.

Clouds of acrid, ionized smoke billowed across The Floor, obscuring virtually everything.

Hq (visual) | scan.infrared(250°:110°)

It looked as if a bomb had gone off—had it? Her Glaser swung around toward the entry alcove, but it was comparatively quiet. The epicenter of the destruction was near the center of the large space...Parc's command center?

Moans and cries rose above the fading explosive sounds as she cleared the last few stairs. Gods, how many people were wounded? How to even begin to triage the situation?

Perrin, are you all right? Where are you?

She kept one eye scanning for nefarious movement while she knelt beside the first body she came to. "Ava? Can you hear me?"

"Unh. What's burning?"

"The Floor. And your hair."

"Ah!" Ava began patting frantically at her formerly emerald locks.

"Easy—" Nika choked on the smoke, and now her throat felt like it was on fire as well. "Let's move you against the wall. Your left leg is damaged, but I don't know how severely. You need to run a diagnostic."

Perrin hadn't responded, and tendrils of dread snaked up through her chest to squeeze her heart.

Joaquim, where are you?

Somewhere on the dorm staircase—I was in the third floor storage room. Are you all right?

Yeah. We need to max out the ventilation system to get all this smoke out of here and de-ionize the air before something else explodes.

On it. What about Perrin?

I don't know.

Ava had just settled awkwardly against the wall when she abruptly lunged forward, stumbling over a leg that was less damaged and more mangled. "Maggie! She was talking to Cair, trying to calm him down.... We have to find her!"

Nika yanked her shirt off, leaving only a minimal bra behind, and tied it around her neck then pulled it up over her nose and mouth. "Ava, you're not finding anyone with that leg. Start pinging people. Make a list of who responds, and who doesn't. I'll be back."

She spun and dove back in before Ava could protest. Heat signatures clogged her vision, but it wasn't a reason for optimism. Anyone whose body had expired would continue to radiate heat for a while yet.

She dodged an upturned table as a shower of dust rained down on her from above. Frowning, she peered up...the pillar to her left sported a wide crack running jagged across it for almost a meter. Shit. It had better hold.

With her attention focused upward, she almost tripped over a body. She fell to her knees and switched back to standard vision.

A long shard of metal shelving jutted out of Carson's chest. His eyes were locked open; scorch marks scarred the white sclerae, suggesting his heart wasn't the only organ destroyed.

Nika pressed the palm of her hand to her forehead. She couldn't help him now—she needed to keep moving and find those she could.

"Nika!" The shout penetrated the background noise mostly because it came from close by. She peered over her shoulder to see Dashiel stumbling toward her.

"There you—gods…." He stared at Carson's body until a coughing fit overtook him.

"Get lower down, where the smoke isn't as bad."

He crouched beside her. "What can I—" another cough "—do?"

She exhaled through her shirt and looked around. It didn't matter whether she filtered for the visual spectrum or infrared; the destruction was just as overwhelming either way. "Find Perrin. Try to help anyone you come upon, but find her."

He nodded and started making his way through the debris. She forced herself to move past Carson's body into the core of the explosion.

Parc's command center no longer existed. The flooring beneath where it *had* existed was charred so thoroughly that its cohesiveness had broken down, leaving behind a sooty residue.

Two bodies lay amid the worst of the charring, burnt beyond recognition.

She yanked her shirt down and covered her mouth with her hand as acid surged up from her stomach into her throat. What in the—

I found her. Near the repair bench, beside one of the couches.

She scrambled to her feet and lurched in the direction Dashiel had indicated, thanking the gods when she didn't trip over any more bodies on the way. The smoke had finally begun to thin out, and she switched fully back to the visual spectrum.

Dashiel knelt on the floor with Perrin's head propped in his lap. Blood streamed from a long cut across her forehead and temple, and her eyes were closed.

Nika dropped to her knees, unwound her shirt from her neck and pressed it against the wound.

"She's breathing, and I don't see any other significant damage. A cut on her right arm, but it's not bad."

"Thank you. We need to—"

"Get away from her."

She glanced up to see Joaquim approaching them. He had one arm around Dominic, who limped along with a tourniquet tied around his left upper leg. Joaquim eased Dominic onto the nearby couch, then came over to crouch low and get in Dashiel's face. "I *said* get away from her! Did you do this? Did you bring this down on us?"

"No!"

"Bullshit." Joaquim grasped Perrin's shoulders and lifted her out of Dashiel's lap and into his arms, then snatched Nika's shirt out of her hand and pressed it back to Perrin's temple. "You had better get the fuck out of here before my hands are again free."

Dashiel slowly stood, an expression she couldn't interpret dragging his features into darkness. "I did not have a godsdamn thing to do with this, you delusional prick. From what I see, you need to look in your own ranks before you start accusing innocent visitors of being murderers."

Joaquim looked like he was going to leave Perrin on the floor and lunge for Dashiel. Nika leapt up and placed herself between them, thrust one arm out behind her to ward Joaquim off and rested a palm on Dashiel's chest. "You should go."

He stared at her incredulously. "You need my help."

She shook her head. "No, I don't. It's all clean-up and recriminations from here."

"It's a war zone, and I won't walk out on—"

She increased the pressure of her hand on his chest, forcing him to take a step back. Her throat ached, scorched by smoke and anguish. "You don't have a place here. Let us take care of our own. It's not a request."

His brow knotted up, and his eyes blurred into muddy pools framed by streaks of soot. He took another step back of his own volition as his jaw flexed twice in succession.

Then he turned and left without another word.

⅄ℛ

Nika sat on the edge of Perrin's couch, elbows on her knees and hands fisted at her temples.

The burnt bodies belonged to Maggie and Cair.

Three fatalities. Twelve injured. Ava's leg had been wrecked so thoroughly that she was still in the tank, getting it rebuilt from the inside out. The rest of the injuries ranged from substantial but not body-threatening to cuts and bruises.

The structural damage was extensive, but not immediately fatal to the building. Four of the six pillars needed to be shored up as soon as possible, and much of the flooring would have to be re-placed. The equipment damage was more significant; they'd lost one repair bench and a third of the stored combat gear, as well as nearly all the furniture on The Floor and a couple of zettabytes worth of data storage.

Joaquim returned carrying a glass of water. He took it to Perrin and sat beside her on the bed. Perrin sported two strips of bonding tape covering her left temple and much of her forehead, but she refused to use the upstairs repair bench until everyone else's injuries were healed.

Joaquim held the glass for Perrin as she propped herself up on an elbow to take a sip, then set it on the bedside table and met Nika's gaze. "Well?"

Nika rubbed at her jaw and forced herself to sit up straight. "Based on what those who were on The Floor have reported, Cair was trying to slice into Parc's command center. When Maggie challenged him, he started rambling loudly about having to get to the data. How it wasn't fair that Parc kept it all to himself and it ought to belong to everyone. He managed to get the system booted up, but failed to access the file hierarchy.

"Maggie kept demanding he stop, and at some point he swung around and punched her. He shouted that if everyone couldn't have the data, no one should, ripped off the casing of the central module, stuck his hand in it and..." she shrugged "...whatever commands he delivered to the module, a few seconds later it exploded. This caused all the other modules to explode. And here we are."

Perrin rolled onto her side so she could see Nika. "That fits with what I saw—what I remember of it, anyway. When Cair got upset, I went to get Ryan's help calming him down. Then he hit Maggie, and Ryan ran to his alcove to fire up IkeBot, since the dyne is strong enough to restrain anybody. Then...I woke up in Joaquim's arms." She gave him a pained smile, and he squeezed her hand. "But why did Cair lose it in the first place? Did his up-gen go wrong somehow?"

Nika sighed. "Not on its own. Cair filed a backup right before he went to the clinic, and Ryan and I took a look at it. He was infected with the virutox. You remember how when he and the others were demoing the sandbox they built, he said that the usual defenses weren't enough to keep it out?

"It's likely he caught it when he did the initial deconstruct on the software, but it took a few extra days to sneak through his defenses. Then, when the up-gen alterations met the virutox's alterations, everything must have gotten utterly fucked up."

Joaquim pinched the bridge of his nose. "Someone should have realized. We should have realized."

"We've all been preoccupied since this augment business started."

"Not an excuse."

"No. It's not." She'd been the most preoccupied of them all, when she should have been the one paying the closest attention. "But it wasn't Dashiel."

"You cannot blame me for suspecting him."

"I don't. But...."

The room fell silent for several seconds. Each carried the weight of their own guilt, which did nothing to lessen any of it.

Finally Perrin cleared her throat. "What about Maggie and Carson? And I suppose an earlier version of Cair, pre-virutox?"

Nika groaned and dragged her hands through her hair. She hadn't stopped moving since the explosion, and her hands came away coated in soot. "You know we don't have the resources or connections to commission new bodies for them. Not yet."

It was one of NOIR'S greatest weaknesses. It was the reason why they'd spent an insane amount of credits on a tank, why they had two separate repair benches, why they kept multiple backups and generally did everything in their power to make sure a total body loss never happened to one of their members.

Only now it had. To three of them in a single day. She tried to project a brave, optimistic expression, but all she managed was frustration with a touch of hope. "We will keep their backups safe. No end date on that. And one day, we'll be able to bring them back."

38

The network of maglev routes unfurled out from the hub station like a pinwheel, ensuring every node in the sprawling industrial sector on the outskirts of Mirai Two could be accessed in seconds. Few Asterions worked on the assembly lines or in the fab facilities, but materials, mid-stage components and finished products needed to be tended, transferred, bought and sold, so the traffic into and out of the sector was always brisk.

Even at three in the morning, it seemed.

Maris Debray moved fluidly through the maze of interconnecting routes to reach the stub that serviced the Ridani Enterprises factory and slipped inside the maglev.

The message had arrived while she'd been struggling to tutor a new art student. The woman had taken the fairly radical step of retiring her persona as a successful commerce trader and reinitializing into a persona flush with artistic traits. Her processes were now stacked high in algorithms that imbued skill with a brush into her hands and heightened the color differentiation capabilities of her visual receptors. Yet the newly reawakened woman had no idea how to make art.

Maris would have advised her this would be the case if she'd been asked ahead of time, but she had not been. True wisdom in life came from appreciating that while the proper algorithms enabled you to do a specific task, and the best-designed ones gave you the skill to do it well, no algorithm performed the deed for you.

Good programming laid a solid foundation, but talent arose from the spark of genius that manifested with the perfect combination of *every* algorithm interacting with every process and every data store—technical skill, experience, memory, instinct, emotion.

Asterions' ability to refine their own programming—to make themselves *better*, then better again—elevated them above pure organics. An individual Asterion's ability to recognize, then comprehend, how the whole could become greater than the sum of its own parts was the kind of existential revelation that got one promoted to Advisor.

Her student had a long road in front of her.

The maglev arrived at its destination nearly as soon as it had departed, and Maris adopted a quick, purposeful stride as she left the station behind for the factory.

Vance Greshe was waiting for her when she reached the lobby, wearing a grimace on his rough-and-tumble features. "Thank you for coming. I'm sorry, I didn't know who else to contact. He wouldn't want me to involve outsiders, but he won't let me get anywhere near him."

She smiled and touched Vance's arm briefly. "I'm glad you did. How long has he been at it?"

"A little over an hour. Luckily I happened to be here overseeing a software update for the assemblers, or he may have burned the factory down and him with it before I knew anything was wrong."

"Has he been drinking, or…?"

Vance cringed. "I think we can safely assume. Unless he took something worse."

"Let's hope he didn't. All right."

"This way. He's in the wing where we manufacture our limb augments."

She followed Vance along a hallway and onto one of the factory floors. The lights were tuned up to full luminance, rendering the flare of the blowtorch only slightly less dramatic than it would have otherwise been. Re-solidifying puddles of metal created a jagged path to its wielder, halfway down the second of five assembly lines.

Dashiel's sleeves were rolled up above his elbows, and his shirt hung half out of his pants. Sweat glistened across his exposed skin, highlighting a raw, blistering burn on one forearm. Self-inflicted, or simply the result of carelessness?

She exhaled ponderously and slid her jacket off, then handed it to Vance. "If you don't mind?"

Vance took it with a nod, and she sidestepped the trail of destroyed equipment until she was a few meters away from him. Close enough to be heard, but outside the reach of his arm. "Dashiel, whatever are you doing?"

The torching paused as he glanced over at her and frowned. "*Maris*? Why are you here?"

His pupils were heavily dilated, and his eyes darted around out of sync with the rest of his body. Something worse it was, then. "It depends on why you're trying to melt your own factory to the ground. If you have a noble enough reason, I'm here to help you do it in proper style. Otherwise, I'm here to talk you down off the ledge."

"Will have to disappoint you on both fronts." He turned back to the line and swept the blowtorch across the next module.

"This business is your life's work—generations upon generations of your time, effort and ingenuity are represented here."

"Yep."

"Are you planning to visit the other dozen or fifty factories you own and burn them to the ground as well?"

"Oh, I expect you'll put me down before then."

She took a step closer. "Is that what you want? For me to put you down?"

He stopped between modules to shrug.

"Why, Dashiel? What is driving you to do this?"

"None of it matters. Nothing but metals and machines, and what have they gotten me?"

"Do I really need to answer that question?"

Another shrug, and he dove into the next module with renewed vigor.

She needed a different approach. Gods, she hadn't seen him this out of sorts since Nika abandoned them both and vanished in a dead-of-night surprise R&R…. "I am sorry to keep asking this—I know it hurts you—but did you learn something about Nika? Is that what this is about?"

The blowtorch veered sharply off course, swinging down to narrowly miss setting his pants on fire before it clanged against the line's conveyor.

Hope and fear kindled to life, each swelling to take up equal space in her heart. "You did. What did you find out?"

"Not a damn thing." He scowled at the assembler arms situated above the conveyor.

"You're lying." She took another step toward him. "You don't have the right to keep this information from me. She was my friend, and her absence has carved a hole in my life the same way it did in yours."

"Promised." He twisted the blowtorch around in his hand until it pointed at his face.

"Whoa, there. Don't burn your face off, please?"

"I'll get a new one."

"Yes, but you'll make quite a dreadful mess before you do. Put the blowtorch down and tell me what you promised."

He chuckled dryly. "Can't tell you what I promised when I promised not to tell you."

"What does that mean?"

"Oops...." He lowered the blowtorch halfway; the flame weakened, and she saw her chance.

She took two long steps forward and swept her right arm up behind him to lock an injector directly into his port.

The paralytic portion of the cocktail kicked in instantly. The blowtorch dropped to the floor, thankfully extinguishing before it landed, and Dashiel slumped down a safe distance away from it. She knelt beside him and wrapped an arm around his shoulder.

"I'm going to take care of you. Now, what did you promise not to tell me? Where is she?"

He blinked several times through drooping eyelids as the anesthetic portion began to do its work. "Doesn't matter. She doesn't want us."

⁀ℛ

It must have been the best night of sleep he'd had in years, Dashiel mused as he rolled over and hugged the pillow. Light flooded the bedroom from a sun already high in the sky…wait, what time was it? Why had he…?

Shit.

Vague, disjointed memories flashed through his mind, possibly in the wrong order. A sleazy street dose dealer. A blowtorch. Nika kicking him out of her hideout and possibly her life. Maris. A trail of melted equipment….

Gods, what had he done?

He downed a glass of water then threw on a shirt and shorts, which was when he realized his left forearm was swathed in bonding tape. Also, it was numb. He closed his eyes briefly as the realization hit him that a damaged arm was the least of the disasters awaiting him.

He exited the bedroom to find Maris gliding around his kitchen and the aroma of Kiyoran coffee strong in the air.

"Good morning. I prepared you breakfast, though I suppose technically it is lunch." She gestured to one of the stools lining the kitchen counter. "Please, sit."

He eyed her suspiciously, but complied. "How much damage did I do?"

She smiled blithely. "To your factory? You'll have to talk to Vance about that, but I expect no more than a hundred thousand credits' worth or so. What did you take last night?"

He cringed at the number…but if he'd been left to his own self-destructive devices, it could have been far worse. Losing Nika had nearly ruined his life; if he didn't start being more careful, finding her again was going to finish the job.

"The wrong thing, clearly. What did you give me to put me down?"

"Merely a paralytic/anesthetic concoction strong enough to knock you out for a while. Vance helped me get you home, so do thank him when you see him. If I may suggest a recourse, include money in your thanks."

She set a plate of fruit and danishes on the counter in front of him. "Eat your breakfast. Then you are going to tell me everything."

39

N OIR had gone quiet.

Other than the infiltration of Ridani Enterprises—which had been a *quiet* intel-gathering hit devoid of their usual panache—the group hadn't made a peep since the Dominion Transit incident.

Stars, did he just internally verbalize the opinion that NOIR had panache? Good fortune that his innermost thoughts weren't recorded and scrutinized....

Their relative silence troubled Adlai more than their crimes, frankly. It suggested they were gearing up for something big; they were busily zipping around the Dominion using simmed identities planted in the Dominion Transit database, gathering tools and intel and allies. For what?

He sank back in his chair and rubbed at his face. He couldn't shake a vague unease that had begun to settle into his gut recently—the sense of a carefully balanced governance system, which had not merely persevered but thrived for millennia now, suddenly teetering on the edge of chaos.

The holding cells across the Justice Division complex were bursting at the seams, even as prisoners were convicted and shipped off to Zaidam with unprecedented speed, and the other Axis Worlds reported similar overcrowding. Massive and sophisticated thefts were being executed in the middle of traffic in broad daylight as if to spite him. A terrorist group sauntered through corporate headquarters and data vaults unmolested, and despite his legitimate best efforts he could not manage to pin them down.

His hold—Justice's hold—on law and order was slipping away. He couldn't say when or why it had begun, and he shuddered to think about what waited at the bottom of the slide if it wasn't halted.

A notification arrived from the lab: results were ready on the limb augment deconstruct. Relieved to have a distraction from a question with no answer, yet fearful that accelerant was about to be poured onto the growing chaos, he stood and headed down to the lab.

⋏ℛ

Erik Rhom gestured Adlai over as soon as he walked into the lab. Complex algorithmic systems did the legwork of the forensic analyses, but Erik kept a watchful eye on the assignments and acted as a check on the systems' performance.

Adlai gestured a greeting. "What do you have for me?"

"Nastiness. I haven't seen a virutox this sinister since that time Ballomere Neuralytics' unfinished muscular regulator prototype got leaked into the nex."

He sighed. It wasn't that he had doubted Dashiel's veracity, but he'd hoped the supposed 'virutox' would be more glitch than malware. *Chaos, closing in.* "The broken bones that one caused kept the repair centers busy for months. All right, show me."

A 12x12 array of data points materialized above the table; on either side of it, graph after graph populated. He blinked. "Show me the highlights."

Erik chuckled. "You got it." The reams of information shrunk to a single bullet list:

Ridani Enterprises Model Vk 3.2 limb augment: foreign program suprafunctionality analysis

- hidden in install routine
- purpose of instructions is masked from users
- installs invasive adaptive routines into the following kernel-overlay regions of user OS:
    - personality (dampener)
    - risk assessment (dampener)
    - judgment/decision-making (alteration)
    - critical thinking (disruptor)
    - emotional response (dampener)
    - impulse control (dampener)

- routines increase their presence exponentially to reach maximum pervasiveness of 60% forty hours after installation
- original programming is deleted and replaced by viral algorithms
- original programming is unrecoverable except by overwrite of a backup from prior to infection (rei-nitialization and generation repetition)

"Sixty percent replacement of existing programming?"

Erik nodded. "Yes, sir. Two days after installation, the user is in all material respects a different person, to a degree that surpasses what you see in even a Grade III up-gen. And thanks to the critical thinking disruption, they likely never know what hit them."

"And this isn't a one-off? Maybe an initial purchaser installed the malicious code then resold the unit?"

"No, sir. It's embedded in all three units provided. Sitting quietly, waiting for the installation software to boot up."

"Well, shit. Thanks for the fast analysis. Get the units into quarantined storage and send me the full report and the summary. I have some work to do."

On his way back to his office, he issued an alert to the Crime Prevention and Patrol departments flagging the augment model as a priority confiscation and quarantine item. Next, he checked to make sure the sentencing hold on the convicts and detainees with the augment installed—it had turned out to be a surprisingly lengthy list—had gone into effect.

Finally, he requested an audience with the Guides.

The d-gate room high atop Mirai Tower was empty except for the usual security dyne attendants. Adlai felt a twinge of shame at disturbing the Guides for a single matter, but it met all the required criteria for initiating such a disturbance. He was simply following proper procedure. He was highly skilled at following procedure.

Once he cleared security he straightened out the lines of his suit and stepped through the d-gate onto the Platform. The anteroom too was empty and quiet, and the entry to the chamber sat open. An invitation?

The Guides arrived as he walked toward the pedestal and were gazing at him expectantly by the time he reached it. He found the utter lack of all the elaborate formalities of the Quarterly Reports disconcerting, and without consciously deciding to, he fell into the traditional greeting nonetheless.

"Guides, thank you for the honor of your time."

"Advisor Weiss, you have been quite busy in recent hours. A flurry of orders have passed across our awareness."

"Yes, Guide Luciene. The investigation into a recent theft has led to some troubling findings requiring action on the part of the Justice Division."

"We have seen the report. A virutox in a limb augment is an unfortunate development, but it does not threaten civilization."

"No. However, with over thirteen thousand potentially infected units on the streets, most of them unaccounted for, coupled with the catastrophic effects on any user of the augment, it is a threat to public safety.

"We already have fifty-six individuals in custody who have fallen victim to the virutox, and the augment has only been available for just over a week. Their cases will all need to be reviewed and, in many cases, re-adjudicated. I anticipate dozens of new crimes are being committed by infected individuals while I stand here briefing you, and that this number will continue to rise until such time as we are able to confiscate the bulk of the augments."

Guide Selyshok responded. "This is a worrisome crime, but we are confident in Justice's ability to contain the damage it causes. Why are the units unaccounted for? Industry actors are expected to keep meticulous records of their distributions, thus Justice should be able to pinpoint their locations without too much difficulty."

"The augment was developed, manufactured and shipped by Ridani Enterprises. However, three of the four transports shipping the augment model were hijacked and the augments stolen. I believe Advisor Ridani briefed you on the incident at our most recent Quarterly Report.

"Thus far we have been unable to identify the thief. In the days following the crime, units of the augment began appearing in the inventory of gray and black market merchants on all Axis Worlds through a variety of intermediary distributors. The data trail has been corrupted, rendering us unable to track the path the augments took from theft to retail."

"These are sophisticated criminals, indeed. How were you alerted to the presence of a virutox in the augments?"

"Advisor Ridani brought it to my attention after an associate of his alerted him to its existence."

Guide Luciene leapt in, a nanosecond shy of interrupting. "An 'associate'? How did they discover it?"

Adlai suppressed the frown that wanted to manifest. The details of uncovering the virutox didn't seem like the most salient data point in comparison to the larger crime and its cascading effects. "Advisor Ridani did not share that information with me. He might not possess it himself."

"What steps have you instituted to contain the threat?"

"I've issued a priority confiscation and quarantine order to all Crime Prevention and Patrol units. They will be taking proactive steps to quickly get as many units of the augment off the streets and out of vendors' hands as possible."

This garnered no response, and the Guides remained silent for several seconds. He waited.

Finally Guide Selyshok spoke, in a reserved and measured tone. "Advisor Weiss, we request that you rescind this order."

"Excuse me?" The words slipped out before he could compose them properly, and he hurriedly stammered an apology. "I only mean to say—"

"Individuals who purchase this augment from black market merchants are, by definition, committing a crime by doing so. If it takes a later, additional crime in order for them to be apprehended, the result is the same. They are criminals who need to be brought to justice."

"Guide Selyshok, the crimes the virutox spurs individuals to commit typically carry far harsher sentences than the minor crime of making a purchase from an unlicensed vendor."

"Perhaps, but the effect is nonetheless to cleanse our streets of the criminally minded, and this is a laudable goal."

Adlai opened his mouth, but the response that bubbled up he could not allow to pass his lips. He cleared his throat. "It is. But I am sworn to follow the Charter, and it prescribes specific requirements which must be met for every crime and every sentence. The proper—"

Guide Anavosa regarded him with a gaze so intense it burned directly into his soul. "Advisor Weiss, do you love the Asterion Dominion?"

"Of course I do."

"Do you desire to protect and defend it from threats to its foundational principles?"

"Always."

"From threats to its very existence?"

"I have dedicated many generations to this precise purpose. I'm sorry, I don't understand why you're asking me these questions. If I have offended you in any way, I apologize and humbly beg your forgiveness."

"That will not be necessary. As the Guides to the Asterion people and all they hold dear, we are taking you into our strictest confidence when we say the following: in order to preserve the peaceful existence and way of life of the Asterion Dominion, this virutox and any others like it which may arise in the future must be allowed to propagate. Further, their presence in a criminal's operating system must not be considered a mitigating factor in conviction or sentencing."

"But the Charter—"

Guide Luciene legitimately interrupted him this time. "We are overriding the Charter."

Adlai forcibly prevented his jaw from dropping. Could they *do* that?

A quick recollection query produced a few obscure Charter provisions applicable to state emergencies which allowed such a step within strict limits. "Are you declaring a state emergency? If there is some external threat to the Dominion, please inform me so I can institute proper safeguards and—"

Guide Anavosa retook control with a warning glare directed at Guide Luciene. "We will not risk inciting a public panic by making sweeping or histrionic declarations. This information is for your edification only, so you can implement our directive with a clear conscience."

What information? They hadn't told him anything, beyond a vague reference to an undefined threat, about the reasons behind the 'directive'—a term which indicated it was an order, not a request. Advisors generally treated any Guide request as an effective order, but they were usually couched in softer language for politeness sake. Not so today.

He straightened his shoulders and lifted his chin. The Guides were the highest authority on all matters. If they were keeping knowledge to themselves, it was for the safety and protection of all Asterions. In his many generations, he had never known them to act other than in the highest and best interests of the people. His referenced conscience churned with the clash of allegiances—was the Charter the highest law, or the Guides—but he had made his choice.

"Thank you for trusting me with this confidence. I'll see to it that the appropriate modifications are made to the orders relating to the limb augment."

Guide Anavosa dropped her chin in a perfunctory display of respect. "We knew our faith in you was well-founded. Thank you for your service."

"I endeavor to fulfill your guidance in all things."

"Before you depart, a final matter: please also see to it that Advisor Ridani appears before us promptly, and that his associate accompany him. We wish to learn more about the nature of the discovery of this virutox."

He squelched the recalcitrant frown that was getting most insistent about making an appearance. "I'm happy to investigate the matter if it will serve your needs."

"We will deal with it ourselves."

"As you wish, Guide Anavosa. I will inform Advisor Ridani as soon as I return to my office."

"Again, thank you. Dismissed."

40

Iona Rowan made her way to the provided address in one of the business districts of Synra One. Since she was supposed to be anonymous, she'd changed out of the formal dress suit that was de rigueur at the embassy, exchanging it for loose slacks and a sleeveless tunic for the night.

The address belonged to an unremarkable commercial building on a street of unremarkable commercial buildings. It was closed for the night, but when she input the provided password at the panel beside the door, it opened.

In a wide room on the second floor, eight chairs sat arranged in a circle bounding a hardware module. Six individuals loitered around the room; she was one of the last to arrive. Per the rules, none of them conversed with any of the others, lest morsels of their personal lives slip out and taint the game. Iona followed suit, leaning against the wall beside the door and adopting a pose of bored disinterest.

Most of her Advisor colleagues would be aghast to learn of the manner in which she'd chosen to spend her evening. These gatherings were not illegal—so far—but allowing a stranger unfettered access to your mind was considered unclean at best and highly dangerous at worst.

And it was absolutely both of those things. Iona got off on the danger and the thrills, but mostly she did it for the escape it brought. Escape from the endless primitive chattering of the Chizeru at the embassy, the endless selfish demands of the businesspeople clamoring for more kyoseil, the endless cold, judging glares of the Guides. Escape from a life that, though residing at the pinnacle of existence, was strangely disappointing.

These games allowed her to live a different life, if only for a few short minutes. Plus, they presented a fun challenge. Not every time, but often enough.

A woman walked in and past Iona, and the door closed. One of the other attendees, a uni in a black jumpsuit, cleared their throat. "Everyone, please take one of the seats. Do we have anyone here for whom this is their first time?"

Two people raised their hands.

"Excellent. I'll briefly cover the rules and expectations. You should have each prepared a scenario, copied from your own experiences, for the challenge tonight. You will make it open and available in the top layer of your processes. When I give the word, everyone will drop their barriers and link to the central controller."

They indicated the module sitting silently at the center of the circle. "The controller will match you to a scenario, ideally one as different as possible from what you might encounter in your own daily lives. Your principal conscious processes will then be transferred to that scenario, while the consciousness assigned to your scenario will take their place in your mind.

"You will have twenty minutes to attempt to win your assigned scenario. Once time is up, the individual who devises the solution judged most unique or inventive will win a sealed bottle of Taiyok *piciane*. Are we ready?"

Everyone nodded, and the controller flickered to life. A pale gold light effused through the cylinder from its core.

"Let's begin. Hands outstretched everyone, fingers spread. Drop your barriers."

The golden light leapt out from the controller in sixteen jagged bolts of raw power.

⋏R

Tristan McLeros found himself sitting at the head of a marble conference table. To his left sat two men and a woman wearing dark business suits and darker scowls. To his right sat...he blinked.

Were those Chizeru? They must be. He'd never met one, but they looked like the images looked: tiny, rough, leathery. Ugh. His friend

Steph had always insisted they were cute, but he was going to have to take exception.

In his virtual vision, the scenario instructions scrolled by:

ICHINOSI RESEARCH REQUIRES 40 KILOGRAMS OF KYOSEIL TO BE DELIVERED WITHIN TEN DAYS. THE LOCAL CHIZERU CLAN LEADER PROTESTS THE TIME SCHEDULE, SAYING IT WOULD REQUIRE THE MINERS TO WORK OVER A SACRED SOLSTICE HOLIDAY. FIND A COMPROMISE AND MAKE THE DEAL.

Tristan sighed. He was a factory technician, not a diplomat. A translation routine had been included to decipher the chirpy chattering from the Chizeru, but he didn't know the first thing about their...anything. They kept the kyoseil flowing, and that was good. He'd never needed to learn anything else about them.

He eyed the businessman sitting closest on his left. The man shot a look of disgusted contempt across the table at the Chizeru then drew his shoulders back and thrust his chest out. "We will provide an additional two dozen sets of soft linens over and above our initial offer, but we must have delivery in ten days."

The Chizeru in the middle chortled...Tristan guessed. "Would be most welcome for at the morning-after rest follows solstice celebration. Sad to turn soft linens away, but all earn right to join in celebration."

"The miners can come to the next solstice celebration."

The Chizeru who had been doing the talking gasped, leaping half out of his/her/its chair. "Oh no no, to miss a solstice is to doom the season follows."

Rock, meet hard place. People were so much more complicated than machines, and Tristan was starting to think aliens might be triply so. He had a tool, augment or routine for every problem that arose with the machines at the factory. What were the odds any of them would do a whiff of good here?

Without him thinking about it, the new limb augment he'd in-stalled the day before sprung to life around his left hand. Ten virtual fingers elongated in a fan pattern out beyond his real fingers.

All three of the Chizeru squealed and began bouncing excitedly in their chairs, pointing at his hand over and over.

Tristan stared at them, then his hand, then them again. Was this excitement or fear? They didn't fall out of their chairs and scurry for the door, so he was leaning toward excitement. An idea began to form in his mind and...hey, it was worth a shot.

He smiled and stood to move around the table behind the Chizeru. They twisted around to gesture at his hand, tiny eyes wide and leathery lips chattering away.

He offered the hand to them, letting the virtual fingers expand outward to their maximum length. "You like this? Go on, try and touch them. Ah, they're not really there! Where do you think they are? Let me show you what else they can do."

Iona sat on a rolling stool in front of a wide bank of panes, at least half of which were blinking in angry reds and oranges.

She glanced around, but the room was otherwise empty. In her virtual vision, the scenario instructions scrolled by:

THE OLIGASI CUISINE FACTORY MANUFACTURES FOOD PREPARATION MODULES FOR RESTAURANTS, HO-TELS AND OTHER HIGH-VOLUME SERVICE PROVIDERS. THE MANUFACTURING PROCESS INVOLVES 22 STAGES, 41 COMPONENTS AND 11 DIFFERENT SPECIALIZED ASSEM-BLERS. AN ERROR HAS APPEARED BETWEEN STAGES 7 AND 13. FIND THE CAUSE AND FIX THE ERROR.

Shit. She couldn't exactly smooth-talk a bunch of machines into cooperating, could she?

Her gaze flitted across the obnoxious alerts...she only understood what about a third of them were trying to convey. Which mostly amounted to "ERROR!" Lot of help that was.

Her talents resided in her words and how she massaged them just so. In a thousand nuanced variations of a single facial expression. She didn't know hardware tools or assembly lines. Was there truly no one here to help her? No aide, or secretary, or floor manager? "System?"

"System status: An error has manifested in the assembly line between Stages 7 and 13—"

"I know that! What is the error?"

"Unable to determine. Further investigation is required."

"You don't say." Iona frowned at the panels. Were they grouped by stage, or assembler, or....

Okay. They weren't squabbling adversaries bickering with each other, but they were talking *to each other, right? The assembly line was a system. In order to create a finished product, the stages and equipment had to convey needed information to one another during the manufacturing process. So she simply needed to track the conversation until it broke down.*

"System, show me the output transmitted from Stage 6 to Stage 7."

Iona dragged herself into the hotel room around one in the morning. She was too tired, and possibly drunk, to bother to travel all the way home, so she'd gotten a room at the hotel attached to the Synra One transit hub.

She hadn't won the game—some construction manager from Namino had—but she had solved the challenge, so she'd call it a win. And there had been drinks after, obviously.

She crashed on the bed and lazily toed her shoes off. As her schedule helpfully reminded her, she needed to be back on Chosek at the embassy by nine o'clock Chosek time for a meeting. Nine o'clock Chosek time converted to...shit.

She prided herself on never having been more than three minutes late to a meeting, ever. But lying here now, she couldn't seem to bring herself to care. What did it matter if she arrived late? After all, there was a first time for everything.

41

"I don't have time to be here, Adlai. I have a broken factory and multiple crises lining up behind it to demand my attention." Dashiel added a dark glower to the remark for emphasis. He was in a foul mood, if one entirely of his own creation, and he needed an outlet.

He'd folded and told Maris everything—almost everything—because what else was he going to do? She was terrifying in her graceful persuasiveness. Plus, she'd saved his ass, and not for the first time. So he'd left out the part about NOIR, but everything else came spilling out.

Now Maris was insisting on seeing Nika, just as he'd known she would, and what the hells was he supposed to do about that? After the circumstances in which his last meeting with Nika ended, he doubted opening the next one with 'Hey, your ex-best-friend, who's a wealthy Culture Advisor specializing in the arts, wants to meet you for tea—is tomorrow good for you?' would go over particularly well.

Assuming she agreed to see him again at all.

An uncertain future filled his mind, one where every choice carried a heavy price. After years marked by quiet, repressed desolation lurking beneath an outwardly charmed life, the near-constant emotional upheaval of the last several days was proving to be too much of a shock to his system, s the night before spectacularly demonstrated.

For a single moment, he'd broken—though the effects would likely stretch for far longer. Reeling from the chilling harshness of her rejection, cast as it was amid destruction and suffering, his emotion processes had fractured from his logical ones. He wouldn't let it happen again, even if meant permanently deprioritizing those emotion processes in order to withstand the near-constant whiplash flogging them.

Adlai matched Dashiel's glower with a grimace. "I apologize. But I have updates for you, and you did say to contact you as soon as I found out anything. I confirmed the presence of an invasive virutox in your limb augments."

"Good. What are you—"

Adlai cut him off. "Then I went to see the Guides and informed them of the threat to public safety."

"Also good. What did they say?"

Adlai's expression flickered. "They are...concerned about the situation. They want to talk to you about the virutox. And they want you to bring your contact who initially discovered it with you to the meeting."

Whiplash.

"I...can't do that. What else did they say about it? Are you confiscating the augments?"

"You can't bring your contact along? Why the hells not? Dashiel, when the Guides ask, you don't refuse."

He rubbed at his jaw and, while he didn't *technically* deprioritize his emotion processes, he did prioritize his analytical ones. "I full well realize that—I've been an Advisor longer than you, remember? But the fact remains. I'll say I wasn't able to connect with them again."

"Is that a lie? You're going to defy the Guides then lie to them? Are you mad?"

"Are you claiming you've never massaged information to put the best spin on it when you presented it to them?"

"Putting the best spin on a complex truth is one thing, but an outright lie is another entirely. What is going on?"

Dashiel exhaled harshly. He'd told Nika he didn't trust anyone...but Adlai was near the top of the list of people he really *should* trust. Also, for better or worse his friend now counted as the sole member of their former circle who didn't know about her return. And if he was going to stand the slightest chance of getting out of this snare of a trap with his career, his fortune and his love intact, he was probably going to need Adlai on his side.

He glanced around the office. This was Justice, which meant odds were better than even for listening devices being installed in every wall.

So he moved around the desk, leaned in close to his friend, and dropped his voice to a barely audible whisper. "My contact? It's Nika."

"What? Why didn't you say—"

He gestured for Adlai to calm down. "Not so loud."

"It's fine. I'm the only one who can monitor the recording devices in here. They're for my own uses, so you can stop whispering. You finally found her?"

Dashiel kept his voice quiet anyway. "She found me. Adlai, she didn't request R&R five years ago—she was psyche-wiped and dumped in an alley as a blank."

Adlai's face blanched in horror. "That's awful! You—both of you—should have come to me with this right away. I'll open an investigation immediately." Adlai paused. "If she got psyche-wiped, how did she find you?"

"It's...complicated, and also not important. The point is, anyone who could psyche-wipe an Advisor then conceal the act with a false data trail has to be high up in the governmental power structure. Extremely high up."

Adlai drew back in his chair. "You're not suggesting...?"

"I'm not suggesting anything. I'm merely saying that she's not going to step within a hundred meters of Mirai Tower. Not blind and lacking any insights into who may be her enemy."

Adlai shook his head. "Just convince her to go to the Platform. The Guides will be livid to find out their records were corrupted and one of their Advisors assaulted. They'll protect her."

"I wish I could make her believe that." *I wish I could believe that.* "But she's understandably paranoid about a horrific violation she doesn't remember. She's seeing threats in every shadow, and I'm not in a position to say she's wrong to do so. "

"Psyche-wiped...I can't imagine what it must have been like for her. Let's think about this for a minute. If the perpetrator was someone powerful—possibly even another Advisor, as disturbing as the thought is—the answers to what happened to her can likely only be discovered by the Guides, or on their direct order. I appreciate that she's afraid, but she needs to get in front of them and explain everything she *does* know about what happened to her."

Dashiel started to protest again, because Adlai really wasn't getting the message here, but his friend held up a hand to forestall the protest.

"I tell you what. I'll issue a witness protection order for her, and she can appear under cloak of anonymity. Security won't be able to touch her, and there will be no official record of her appearance. No Advisor beyond the two of us will ever know she was there."

"And if the Guides protest the anonymity order?"

"You know they have the right to revoke it, but I don't see why they would—not once they hear her story. Nowhere will she be safer than on the Platform. Dashiel, they have to be told about this."

Adlai was making a fair amount of sense, from an objective point of view. Trouble was, the Justice Advisor was the only objective one on the playing field. "I'll try to convince her, but no promises. How long do I have?"

"They said promptly, so…maybe six hours? I'll have the protective order ready in two."

"Right. I'd better get moving." He headed for the door, then stopped to turn back. "I appreciate the help. I know you're at the edge of your comfort zone here."

Adlai sighed heavily. "My comfort zone left for safer environs several exits before this one."

๛

Once the door closed behind Dashiel, Adlai dropped his elbows on his desk and fisted his hands at his chin. He hadn't been exaggerating—his comfort zone was firmly in his rear view mirror. But he hadn't dared to share the primary reason for it.

He hadn't told Dashiel about the rescinding of the augment confiscation and quarantine order, though it was certainly relevant information. Dashiel would have been...displeased, to say the least, and Adlai didn't feel up to verbally defending the Guides' order or his following of it. He was able to justify the decision in the sanctity of his own mind, only barely, but justifying it to another person, much less one as logic-driven and stubborn as his friend, was a different matter.

He'd have to tell Dashiel eventually, of course, but he'd save that storm for another day.

What could possibly be threatening the very existence of the Dominion? What could it possibly have to do with reducing the size of the criminally inclined population through an insidious virutox? Had some cosmic god appeared on the scene to judge the virtuousness of their civilization? It was an absurd concept, but it made as much sense as any other explanation.

Ultimately, it didn't—couldn't—matter for him. He didn't make the rules; he enforced them. He executed on the will of the people, as expressed in the Charter and shepherded by the Guides. When the latter two conflicted, the Guides' wisdom must win out, because they were the moral compass of the Dominion.

If he began to doubt them, then he had no compass. He was lost.

So he would continue to believe in their ability to lead everyone through whatever this crisis was now looming over the Dominion. He would believe in their ability to protect Nika—once his friend, now revealed as a victim of the most heinous of crimes. That an Advisor could have been psyche-wiped and the crime itself erased as thoroughly as her mind was surely another sign of society's creeping slide into chaos.

He didn't look forward to arresting one of his fellow Advisors for the crime—he didn't look forward to learning one of his fellow Advisors was so abhorrent of a person as to commit the crime—but when the evidence came to light, he wouldn't hesitate to do his duty and exact justice on behalf of his friend.

Heartened by the recognition that he had been presented with an opportunity to do genuine, unmitigated good, he straightened up and began creating the framework necessary for her to feel safe again.

42

"**I**'m afraid I don't know you well enough yet to tell if you're joking or have developed a nasty operational glitch and orphaned your reason."

Dashiel stared at Nika, and for a moment words failed him. It truly was possible he no longer knew *her* well enough to figure out how to get through to *her* reasoning mind. "Neither. I'm being serious."

"Then, no. End of line."

Her expression closed down, lending her features a harder edge than he ever remembered her being capable of displaying. Of course the last day had not been kind to her, but he wondered if the intervening five years hadn't always been kind to her, either. She'd made it clear that she didn't want his pity, but he could try for a higher form of empathy. Perhaps if he made it through the current battle intact.

They were back at the harbor, standing only a few meters from where they'd met what already felt like a generation ago. He'd suggested they meet at his office—because he really should get to his office at some point soon—but she'd declined, saying it would take too long. There was going to be plenty for them to argue about as it was, so he hadn't argued with her on that point. He needed the goodwill capital.

"How's Perrin doing?"

"She'll be fine." Nika offered him a weak smile. "I didn't thank you properly for your help yesterday. It was a dangerous and volatile situation, and you could have bolted or cowered, but you didn't. I realize it didn't seem like it at the time, but it meant a lot that you were there for me when I needed you."

"I thought you said I wasn't needed." He wanted to take it back the instant he said it; bitterness was proving to be a wildly destructive aspect for him to wear.

She didn't lash out in return, however, instead sighing and staring out at the harbor. "I was wrong. I was wrecked and heartbroken
and angry, and I was wrong."

A tiny portion of the wound she'd inflicted at The Chalet knit-
ted itself back together. "You're forgiven. Does Joaquim still believe
I was responsible?"

"No. We know what happened. It was our fault, if only through
negligence. And the virutox's fault."

"Are you serious?"

She nodded. "Anyway, I have a home to patch up and a lot of
people to take care of, so I'm sure you understand why I don't have
time to play dress up and go kiss our royals' rings."

"That's not exactly what I have in mind. Look, here's my thinking: with all backups of your memories and your psyche gone, the
only place where you stand a chance of finding answers is in the
data vault at Mirai Tower. The Guides keep nex-networked copies
of their most important records in their towers on each Axis
World. Now, security is extremely robust at Mirai Tower, but this
opportunity allows you to bypass most of it. The invitation represents your ticket inside."

She glanced at him askance. "And you think once I'm inside,
security is going to simply let me stroll into the secure data vault
and poke around?"

"No, but I assume you have ways to get in…surreptitiously."

She chuckled; it was the first sign of levity she'd displayed since
she arrived, and he thought it sounded more genuine than sarcastic.
"'Ways.' Yes, as the leader of a rebellion, I have 'ways.'"

"Excellent. So I say we show up early enough to give you time
to deploy your…ways. Then, depending on what you find, when
we meet with the Guides you can either maintain your cover, ask
for their help or confront them with your identity and your evidence."

"On the fly? I don't like leaving so much to last-second calls."

"I agree it's risky. But you don't seem to mind taking risks, and
we've been handed what could be the best chance we'll ever have to
discover what happened five years ago and who orchestrated it."

She prevaricated, pacing along the railing then circling back to him. "I told you, exposing and stopping the spread of the virutox takes priority, and that's truer now, after the explosion, than it has ever been. As much as I want to know what happened to me and why, it needs to wait. Even if that means it waits forever."

"This audience is *about* the virutox. We're guaranteed to learn something from it, thus advancing both goals in a single meeting."

"Don't you think it's suspicious that the Guides want to hear the details of how we uncovered it? The relevant fact here is that it was deliberately planted in consumer augments. What does it matter how it was found?"

"Yes. I do think it's suspicious. Which, if you want to extrapolate out a bit further and posit that the Guides themselves are involved in something nefarious, means it's even more likely your answers are in their records."

Her nose scrunched up into a flustered, wanted-to-be-annoyed countenance. A tiny hint of the old Nika. "Dammit, you make entirely too astute of a point. But if you extrapolate a tiny bit further from *there*, then you're escorting me straight into an ambush—into the lair of the enemy—with little ability for me to defend myself. I won't be a lamb led to the slaughter."

He laughed at the ridiculousness of the notion—then choked it off under the weight of her glare. "So defend yourself. Bring cleverly hidden weapons, load up on protective barriers and wear a wingsuit—though if you decide to leave in the same manner as you left my office, keep in mind that the Platform is in space."

She rolled her eyes in a brief display of amusement, then stepped closer and placed a hand over his. "And what about you? If they can't capture me, I've no doubt they'll settle for you in the short term."

He closed his eyes, breathing in her presence and reveling in the feel of her skin against his. He'd been wrong last night, and also right; metals and machines had their value, but her touch was worth any price.

When he reopened them, he smiled. "I have centuries of experience at talking my way out of edge situations."

"Edge *business* situations."

"Those can be the most perilous kind." He kissed her softly, and once his lips met hers he had to fight to resist the urge to kiss her far from softly. "I'll be fine."

She sighed against his lips. "Okay. What am I supposed to do?"

"Gather all your gear and tools and anything else you require to pull off your 'ways,' and come with me."

She drew back from his embrace. "And you're certain you're not trying to convince me to go through with this just so you can cover your own ass and stay in the Guides' good graces?"

He exhaled in frustration as her intrinsic tendency toward suspicion flared yet again. *Whiplash.*

Was he hoping to find an all-around winning outcome, one where he was saved from making hard choices? Yes. Would he advocate for this course of action if he didn't believe it was the best choice for her as well? No.

"I'm certain. I can conjure a convincing story to excuse your absence if I must—see the aforementioned gift of smooth talk. This is for you…and for us."

She stared off into the distance, at the harbor or maybe at nothing, for several seconds. "How long do I have?"

"Four hours, give or take." Maris was going to string him up by his toes for it, but she was going to have to wait a while longer to see Nika; he could not complicate the situation any further right now.

She nodded. "All right. I need to prepare, not to mention check on everyone at The Chalet, so I'll meet you somewhere downtown when it's time. And send me the anonymity layer information as soon as you get it. Also, I downloaded a basic schematic from the city registry, but I need a detailed and labeled layout of Mirai Tower."

"I'll take you to the right data vault."

"We might get separated. A thousand things large and small might go wrong. No plan survives contact with the enemy, and I need to be able to adapt if the Guides are that enemy and it all goes sideways."

АR

Nika proceeded through a series of stops on her hastily created checklist with a speed and efficiency borne of hyper-focused purpose. In other words, she didn't allow herself to dwell on all the reasons why this was a profoundly terrible idea.

Though she hadn't admitted it to Dashiel, he'd spun a persuasive scenario that reawakened the glimmer of hope her visit to Rivers Trust had crushed. For all her high-minded talk of subsuming her personal desires to the needs of the greater good, the seductive prospect of answers—*real* answers—about her psychewipe now had her firmly in its clutches.

First she strode into Joaquim's room, interrupting his work rebuilding one of the testing servers because she didn't have time to wait on him to take a break. "I'm claiming two more simmed ID sets."

"You've used up almost all of the new supply already."

"I need them more than everyone else does. Nature of the job."

"True." He shrugged. "It's not like I'm going to tell you no. Can I ask what you plan to use them for?"

"You can ask, but trust me, you don't want to know." She should tell him, but the argument that was certain to result would take too damn long.

"Right then. Don't be stupid. We can't lose anybody else right now."

She jerked a nod. "Noted." *Don't be stupid, don't be stupid. Am I being stupid?*

Next she found Ryan downstairs applying sealant to one of the patched up pillars.

"I need to borrow your security override and infiltration routines. They're better than mine."

"Sure." He motioned her over to his private alcove—it didn't technically *belong* to him, but everyone treated it as if it did.

The outer partition of the alcove had protected his pets from the worst of the destruction. IkeBot stood silently in the corner, and WheatleyBot rested on the desk, plugged into a programming module. PeterBot was nowhere to be seen, which before the explosion would have meant impending hijinks. Now, she didn't know what it meant.

"If you'll tell me what you're hitting, I can fine-tune the routines for the job."

She hesitated. "An official government data vault, so the highest level of security. Oh, and Justice has started to identify several tells in the slices we use, so…mix things up a little?"

He arched an eyebrow. "Sounds like heavy stuff. You're not taking a team?"

She shook her head. "It's safer if I do this alone."

"Safer for us, right? No guarantees, but if anything can get you past the security barriers, these routines can. Give me fifteen minutes?"

"Take twenty, as I have a few more stops to make. And thank you."

"No problem. You won't fuck it up, whatever it is."

"Here's hoping." She headed to the far end of The Floor, where she found Perrin in the combat training room helping one of the newer members, Josie, sort the damaged weapons from the working ones.

She cleared her throat in the doorway, and they both looked up. "Perrin, can I borrow you for a minute?"

"Of course." She glanced over at Josie. "Just set aside any you're not sure about."

Josie nodded, and Perrin hurried over to the doorway. "I talked to Roqe this morning, and they gave me—"

"Tell me later." She placed a hand on Perrin's back and nudged her toward the stairs. "How are you feeling? It looks like you've dived right back into work."

"I'm good. Too good to be lying around on my ass while everyone else is working."

"If you're sure. Listen, I need a copy of the base program you use to play chameleon with your hair, and a couple of your simpler routines for it. I know I can download stock for it, but yours are so much better."

Perrin touched a hand to her hair wearing an expression of mock outrage. It was uncombed and pulled back in a sloppy ponytail, leading Nika to wonder how much better her friend was genuinely feeling.

"I'm shocked you think the transformation is somehow *false*."

Better enough to be snarky, anyway. "Come on, I don't have time for games today."

Perrin dropped all pretense of melodrama. "Oh, crap, you sound stressed. I don't know if I can stand any more badness—but tell me the truth—"

She grabbed Perrin by the shoulders to cut short the exclamations. "Calm down. I promise I will fill you in later, but right now I have no time. Will you help me?"

"Absolutely. Dark hair like yours, you shouldn't mess with the pastels. Stick to jewel tones and browns. I'm sending you routines for crimson, a fabulous indigo and a boring mahogany with black streaks."

"Thank you. I doubt I'll wear them as smashingly as you, but thank you." She started to leave, but paused and turned back. "We get past all this craziness, maybe you can show me some of your fancier techniques—especially that waterfall ripple you had going on last week?"

Perrin's face lit up in pride. "You bet. We'll have you looking like a star goddess in no time. Dashiel will lose his mind, then his pants."

She laughed with what she hoped was sufficient enthusiasm and headed for her room.

Ryan sent her his security override routines eight minutes ahead of schedule, after which she reviewed the various routines and overlays she'd collected and added them to her own. Then she loaded and sorted them into a flexible queue and began formulating a plan.

43

Nika found Dashiel sipping on an iced tea while lounging against an ornate decorative fence outside the eatery where they were meeting.

She paused on the sidewalk to take note of the elements at play here. How the position of his forearm atop the fence, the set of his shoulders and the slightly lifted angle of his chin combined to create an air of aloof confidence. How a tingly warmth blossomed in her chest on seeing him. Clearly, his 'buffed and polished' style was growing on her.

The search algorithms she'd set to hunt for anomalous behavioral processes on which she could place the blame had flagged a couple of fuzzy logic clouds for closer examination; depending on what the world looked like a few hours from now, she might get around to taking a look at them. But she couldn't deny reality: no matter the trigger, the warmth was genuine.

She slithered up behind him, placed a hand against the base of his spine and leaned in to murmur in his ear. "Is this spot taken?"

He whirled around in surprise. When he saw her he frowned and stepped out of her grasp. "I'm sorry, I'm waiting on…" his brow furrowed "…Nika?"

Now she frowned. "How can you tell? Is something leaking through?"

"No. But the devious glint in your eyes transcends both psychewipes and sophisticated disguises."

"Oh. Well…hopefully no one at Mirai Tower or on the Platform will know me as well as you do."

"Likely not." He reached out to caress her cheek. "Are you ready?"

"As ready as I can be. For the entry stage, I will be your meek little street-urchin tattletale." Her hair shifted from crimson to a dull brown and tangled up seemingly of its own accord. Her skin lightened and turned pasty. She retrieved a roughshod overcoat from her bag and slid it on, then slacked her shoulders.

"Damn. You are good." He set the glass of tea on an empty table behind them. "Once we're inside, stay one hundred percent in-character at all times until we're in the Guides' chamber on the Platform. Don't risk personal pings to me, as there's a decent chance they can be detected and read."

"Seriously?"

"Rumors fly about the Guides employing technologies not available to the rest of us. So, yes, seriously. When we're forced to interact with anyone, even dynes, follow my lead." He flashed her a quick smile. "I realize it will be difficult for you, but try. Remember, it's all a performance."

She scowled, but tried to keep it kind in tenor. "Yes, sir."

"Thank you. Let's go."

⋏℞

The perimeter security of Mirai Tower equaled that of the Dominion Transit HQ internal security. The security inside dwarfed that of any location she'd ever tried to infiltrate.

But Dashiel took it all in stride, and this didn't count as a traditional infiltration anyway, so she made an effort to trust both his expertise and the quality of her layered disguises.

The topmost layer implemented the anonymous ID Advisor Weiss had provided, and it did so as comprehensively as if it were her true identity. But should it need to be removed for any reason, two successive simmed IDs, each one reinforced by accompanying morphs, sat atop her true appearance and signature.

Though it was a trick of the mind, the multiple layers left her feeling suffocated, like she could hardly breathe beneath their weight. They had better be enough to get her through the meeting and back out of the building.

Dashiel stepped up to the lobby security checkpoint, and she followed. She offered her left hand when requested, permitting the scan while trying to look overwhelmed and just the right touch of frightened. That part wasn't so hard. 'Frightened' wasn't a look she wore often, but now was definitely the time to wear it.

One of the three security dynes motioned them through. "Entrance granted. Due to an unexpected change in their schedule, the Guides request your presence on the Platform in three minutes."

What?

"Thank you. We'll head up straightaway." Dashiel didn't so much as flinch, instead taking her hand and dragging her toward the lift.

What the hells? Did they know, somehow? She couldn't properly confront them without intel backing her up. And without intel backing her up, she had no idea which way to play the meeting.

She shook from the effort of not pinging him, and he squeezed her hand too tightly for affection as the lift began ascending. "After. Now calm down and remember your role here today."

It was the most innocuous statement he could make, and she got the message well enough: they would infiltrate the data vault after the meeting, when they were ostensibly on their way out. But the change in schedule gutted a huge chunk of her reasons for agreeing to the meeting. Also, who knew what might interfere with their new plan as well. If the Guides *were* behind her psyche-wipe and were now onto her, she was seconds away from being caught flat-footed and flailing.

But she would not be a lamb led to the slaughter. She would not be led, period.

Fuck her 'role.' The role served as an excuse to get into the building, nothing more, and her goal in doing so was slipping away with the speed of their ascent.

Dashiel was right about one thing—this represented the best and possibly only chance she would ever have of finding answers, and she would not allow it to be stolen from her the way her past had been. The records here would not have been erased, which was the point. Who she was, what she had found, what had been done to her and by whom—it was all within her grasp, but not for long. To reach it, she merely needed to improvise a little. It was hardly the first time.

The lift slowed to a stop, and the glass door slid open to reveal a spartan, circular room with a d-gate in the rear and yet another security gauntlet between them and it.

Dashiel stepped into the room then turned back toward her, hand extended—but she'd activated her kamero filter and pressed motionless against the back wall of the lift.

"Nika?"

She held her breath.

The lift began to descend once more.

⋏ℛ

Dashiel stared at the seemingly empty lift as it descended out of his sight. *Godsdammit, Nika!*

He couldn't chase after her. He couldn't so much as ping her. She'd abandoned him at the precise moment when his course became set in stone.

He'd told her earlier that if he needed to, he could pull off a convincing excuse for her absence...and now he had to walk in front of the Guides and do exactly that.

He breathed in deeply and schooled his expression, then stepped up to the security checkpoint. This part he'd done a thousand times, and he spent the precious few seconds it took preparing a variation on the story he hadn't thought he'd need to deliver. Then he stepped through the d-gate and onto the Platform.

The Guides were already present behind the dais when he arrived, a rare occurrence even for private audiences. All ten eyes instantly fell on him, though it was Anavosa who spoke. "Approach, Advisor Ridani."

"Guides, thank you for the honor of your time."

"Where is your associate? We were informed of her entry into Mirai Tower at your side."

His chin dropped, contriteness prominent in his expression. "I humbly apologize. She was overtaken by stage fright, as it were, and fled when we reached the d-gate. I felt it more appropriate to continue on and appear before you, rather than attempt to recover her and keep you waiting as a result. While I regret the disruption, I believe her presence is not strictly necessary, as I possess all the information you may need."

No response was immediately forthcoming. He'd been watching the Guides for a long time, however, and the subtle shifts in their stances, together with periodic twitches of facial muscles, suggested they were silently conferring with one another.

He waited quietly, but his mind raced. While he stood here performing, Nika was skulking around Mirai Tower alone, at great risk of discovery, chasing clues to solve the mystery of what had happened to her five years ago. And without him at her side, she was doing so blind.

The vision he'd nurtured of how this meeting would lead to the missing pieces falling into place, the uncertainties resolving and the prospects for their future together aligning like a constellation crumbled to dust before his eyes.

He recalled her insistence that he provide her with a detailed schematic of the building's layout...had she planned this all along? Had she never intended to appear before the Guides at all? He didn't want to believe it, but doubt seeped in to poison his thoughts nonetheless. She kept insisting she wasn't the same woman he remembered...maybe he should start believing her.

Guide Iovimer finally spoke, his voice deep and somber. "This is a most unfortunate development, Advisor. We have notified Mirai Tower security to be on alert for her presence, as unqualified citizens should not be running freely through one of our towers."

Dammit. "A wise step to take. However, I'm sure she is simply frightened. You must understand—to the citizens, you are as gods."

"We are but shepherds, helping the Asterion Dominion to find its way amidst a vast and dangerous cosmos."

The party line had never rung so hollow. "As we trust in you to do."

Guide Luciene took over the questioning. "Yes. Now, tell us about this virutox found in your limb augments. You claim several shipments of the augment were stolen during transit to distributors?"

Dashiel bit back the retort that flared in his mind. "There is no factual dispute as to this event. Administration Division surveillance footage captured the thefts at multiple locations as they occurred."

"We expect an Industry Advisor to keep robust protection measures in place sufficient to prevent thefts from occurring out in the open on busy thoroughfares."

Was Luciene trying to get a rise out of him? "I assure you, my security was robust—sufficiently robust for this theft to mark the first such occurrence in my time as head of Ridani Enterprises. Nevertheless, those measures have since been increased. It will not happen again."

"Let us hope not. Have the security measures at Ridani Enterprises Headquarters also been increased? You suffered an infiltration several nights ago. Was it related to the theft?"

He blinked. "I don't believe so, Guide Luciene. The investigation is ongoing, but my personal suspicion is that it was an instance of attempted corporate espionage on the part of a lesser competitor. And, yes, security measures at my offices have since been increased as well."

They switched topics rapidly enough to throw him off-balance. "Your absent associate brought the alleged existence of a virutox in some of your limb augments to your attention. How did this occur? Did you know the woman before she contacted you about this?"

"Again, with respect, the existence of the virutox is not 'alleged.' Analysis by Justice has confirmed its presence in every augment tested."

"And it did not originate from your production?"

"No!" He worked to calm himself, because dear gods he had just *yelled* at the Guides. "Apologies for the outburst, Guide Luciene. I take fierce pride in the quality of the products I make. The corruption of even one of those products is an insult to my company and to myself."

"Did you know this woman?"

"Ah, no. She reached out to me to alert me to its presence after one of her friends was infected."

"This friend purchased the limb augment illegally on the black market, one must assume. Do you make a habit of consorting with criminals, Advisor Ridani?"

"Certainly not. My only concern is the virutox. As I said, I take pride in my products, and I don't want to see my company's reputation besmirched due to the malfeasance of a third party."

Anavosa finally stepped in to give him a reprieve from Luciene's barrage. "We see. Rest assured that Advisor Weiss and the employees of the Justice Division are pursuing every lead to apprehend the perpetrators. You need not concern yourself any further with the issue."

He frowned. "I have every faith in the skills of Advisor Weiss individually and of the Justice Division generally. Nevertheless, it is in both my business and personal interest to monitor the investigation and provide any assistance I can in order to help ensure the virutox is eradicated and the responsible parties caught."

"Unnecessary. You are an Industry Advisor, and as such you would do well to focus on your purpose, that of advancing and growing Industry business."

Not much of a reprieve, it turned out. He'd never seen the Guides so...snippy. Luciene was nearly always churlish, but tonight they were all curt, bordering on outright rudeness. It was an uncharitable characterization for ones so lofty, but he was feeling rather uncharitable toward them at present. The real question, though, was *why* were they being snippy?

His mouth opened to voice a more polite, more reverential version of that question—and he closed it. *Shut up, Dashiel. If they're hiding something, they aren't about to volunteer its details to you, so just bend over and thank them for the honor of being allowed to do it.*

He forced a terse smile. "As you wish. I will endeavor to fulfill your guidance."

"Thank you, Advisor Ridani. Dismissed."

He backed off the pedestal before turning and making his way out the open doors and toward the d-gate. What a frustrating and pointless audience! He still didn't understand why the Guides had demanded his presence, and once here why they'd asked a string of inane and irrelevant questions.

It was almost as though it had been a stalling tactic....

Nika.

He hadn't been the one they wanted to interrogate. How much did they know, and how much did they merely suspect and had hoped to extract from her?

It took all his self-control not to sprint the remaining distance to the d-gate.

44

A s soon as the lift dropped below the top floor, Nika lunged for the controls and entered the level she needed. The lift stopped the next second, a mere five levels down, and she hurriedly exited.

She was somewhat surprised the security system allowed her to access this floor at all, but the checkpoint waiting in front of her proclaimed it would not be allowing her to proceed any further.

Of course, that's what they all said.

She'd come prepared, and she approached the control panel at the checkpoint with outward confidence—not that anyone was watching, or could see her if they were. Taking care to keep to slow, careful movements and not tax the kamero filter's capabilities, she attached the pre-programmed module to the interactive overlay and activated it.

Then she waited. Patiently.

Thankfully, Ryan's routines were up to the challenge, and after several tense seconds the force field gave way to allow her to pass. Beyond it, the door to the vault slid open, and she removed the module and crept inside.

Her kamero filter shut off the instant she breached the doorway. Crap, there must be an interference field permanently active in the vault designed to expose stealth intruders. Intruders like her.

She breathed in, then out. It would be fine. According to the security system she'd just diverged, she had authorization to be in here, and her true identity remained buried under multiple layers of disguises.

Server nodes spread out in every direction and for an impressive distance, but this wasn't her first data vault infiltration—it wasn't even her first data vault infiltration this week.

There existed only four configurations used in high-scale data vaults, because those four offered the best combination of efficiency, storage density, robustness and security. A quick scan of the layout told her this matched the third of the four, which meant access hubs would be located at the quarter points in a diamond pattern.

She turned left, then shortly right and down the next row a quarter of the distance to the center. Bingo.

Fooling the security system into allowing her into the vault was one thing—fooling it into allowing her access to the Guides' most precious data, another entirely. It was no longer a matter of entering a couple of inputs and letting a pre-programmed routine do the rest of the work.

She was skilled at slicing, but Parc was better—which was why she'd been studying his work since he got arrested and had incorporated some of his best techniques into her own preferred approaches over the last few days. Now she found out whether it was worth the extra effort.

$\S$ *sysdir*

$\Phi \rightarrow$ *passcode required:*

$< \rightarrow \delta \{\Sigma (\theta^{\rho} \alpha^{\rho} \beta^{n})\} = H\Gamma_n$

$\rightarrow \forall H\Gamma_n (H\Gamma_n /^*>)$

$\Phi \rightarrow$ *allowable attempts exceeded*

$\S$ *Hq*

$\S \alpha\beta\alpha$

$< \rightarrow$ *if* $(Hq = \alpha\beta\alpha) \{Hq/n_0\}$

$\rightarrow \delta \{\Sigma (\alpha^{\rho} \beta^{n})\} = H\Gamma_n$

$\rightarrow \forall H\Gamma_n (H\Gamma_n /\theta>)$

$< \beta\beta\theta \alpha\theta\beta\beta \alpha\alpha \beta\theta\theta\alpha \theta\alpha\beta\alpha \theta\theta\theta \beta\beta\alpha \theta\alpha\theta\theta \alpha\beta\alpha\theta\beta \beta\alpha\theta \beta\alpha\alpha\beta$
$\theta\theta\theta\alpha\theta$

...

$\beta\alpha \theta\alpha\theta \beta\beta\theta\theta \alpha\beta\alpha\alpha \alpha\beta\beta\alpha \beta\alpha\alpha \alpha\theta\beta\theta\beta \theta\alpha\beta\alpha \beta\beta\beta\beta \beta\theta\alpha\alpha \alpha\theta \alpha\theta\beta\alpha\alpha$

$T \rightarrow$ *passcode accepted*

$\S$ *sysdir*

Φ → ID required:

<

This, she'd acquired on the sly when she'd been at Dashiel's flat. *Sorry for this, darl—*

She blinked. 'Darling' was what former-her had called him in the memory. Huh. She must have subconsciously adopted the endearment.

< ε Ψβθθхγξ αθβΛΓ

T → Access granted to Advisor Dashiel Ridani. Enter file name or search query:

<

She initiated a search algorithm targeting her former persona.

§ sysdir § Hq {∀ HΓ_n (∀ HΓ_n = 'Kirumase' || 'ββαθ αθββθ αγθβθ ααγθθ ααθθα αθαβα ααθβα αθθβ')}

The results quickly returned to scroll across her vision for several seconds. There were a lot of entries.....

Y12,452.297 A7:
Responsible Advisor: Nika Kirumase
Subject: Rising tensions between Taiyoks and local merchants on Namino

~

Y12,455.014 A7:
Responsible Advisor: Nika Kirumase
Subject: Evaluation of indigenous species on SR213-Shi

~

Y12,456.405 A7:
Responsible Advisor: Dashiel Ridani, Nika Kirumase
Subject: Normalization of private contracts between corporations and prominent Chizeru clans

She really had been an Advisor, and a busy one at that. Since they were date-ordered, she scrolled down to the last entry and opened it.

Y12,458.094 A7:
REDACTED

Shit. Slicing past the redacted barrier would ratchet her actions up a level from merely viewing to altering. It was going to leave a trace in the system. The Guides would know someone had been here, in this file. But odds were this constituted her only chance, so screw it.

Finesse wouldn't make the trace any less detectable, so she brute-forced her way past the security barrier.

Y12,458.094 A7:
Responsible Advisor: Gemina Kail
Subject: Involuntary retirement via exceptional-grade psyche-wipe and base reinitialization of Nika Kirumase, 12th Generation
Authorization: Alpha 4-1
Purpose: Rasu Protocol

The rush of adrenaline sent her head reeling, then forced it to snap back into focus. The Guides had not only known about her psyche-wipe, they had authorized it....

...and Dashiel was up there with them right now.

A wave of protectiveness surged to overtake the adrenaline, and she only barely stopped herself from pinging him. He needed this information!

But he'd been attending audiences with the Guides for a long time, and he wasn't the naive sort. He may not get any revelatory answers out of them, but he'd be safe.

She willed aside the worry and concentrated on the information in front of her. Was 4-1 simply an authorization code, or did it mean one of the Guides had voted against her psyche-wipe?

The possibility that she had an ally upstairs was encouraging, but with no clue as to which one of the Guides it might be, it didn't help her much at the moment.

Okay, one shocking reveal uncovered. Now, why? What in the hells did 'Rasu Protocol' mean, and why had it led them to take such extreme action against one of their most favored citizens?

Cluttered among the list of search results were log entries of files her former self had accessed, because naturally they logged this sort of thing. The surveillance state was often invisible, but it was designed to be.

So what had she accessed in the hours leading up to the issuance of the fateful order?

Access Date: Y12,458.094 A7
File: GM51K-d
Accessing Party: Nika Kirumase
Subject: Nullation of Ridani Enterprises outpost on exploratory world SR27-Shi
Responsible Advisor: Gemina Kail
Purpose: Rasu Protocol

~

Access Date: Y12,458.094 A7
File: YC102F-b
Accessing Party: Nika Kirumase
Subject: Nullation of Valen Ceramics outpost on exploratory world SR43-Roku
Responsible Advisor: Gemina Kail
Purpose: Rasu Protocol

~

Access Date: Y12,458.094 A7
File: BB14a-a
Accessing Party: Nika Kirumase
Subject: Nullation of Ichinosi Research outpost on exploratory world SR102-Ichi
Responsible Advisor: Gemina Kail
Purpose: Rasu Protocol

The same protocol. The same Advisor. Everywhere, the same—
"Well, what do we have here?"

Nika spun toward the voice as her hand found her Glaser and raised it.

$< copy\ datafiles\ (\forall\ H\Gamma_n = \text{'Kirumase'} \,||\, \text{'Rasu Protocol'})$
$to\ Hq(storerec.NK1)$

An impeccably attired woman with scarlet hair slicked tight against her scalp stood three meters down the row, gazing at her with what looked like contempt. "Security, intruder alert in Data Vault #4."

Light flooded the vault, as well as a variety of other flashes and noises. The woman smirked. "Here I was, dropping in to check on some project updates, and what do I find?" She paused. "Security, activate exposure countermeasures."

Alerts flared in Nika's internal OS as electrical pulses flowed over and through her skin and the layers of her disguises were forcibly stripped away. Technologies not available to the rest of them, indeed.

The woman gasped, for a brief second looking genuinely shocked. "Nika Kirumase?"

Nika forced herself not to flinch. "You have me at a disadvantage, Advisor…?"

"You haven't managed to recover some hidden stash of your memories? Then how in the hells is it that you are again here, in this room, standing in the exact location where I came upon you five years ago?"

So this was almost certainly Gemina Kail. Rage surged out from her neurotransmitters along the pathways cleared by the adrenaline to flush her skin, and she contemplated flicking the Glaser to full pulse and pressing the trigger right then and there.

But this woman—her apparent murderer—had answers she still needed. She breathed in through her nose and lifted her shoulders dramatically. "Talent?"

"Remarkable. You are a persistent bitch, I will give you that much."

A squad of drones zoomed through the air to surround her. "Intruder. Disarm and prepare to be taken into custody."

The woman held up a hand. "Simmer down, Security. I have a few questions for our intruder before you take her away. Such as—"

"What's going on here?" A blond man in tailored but far less ostentatious attire hurried down the server row, trailed by a cadre of dynes. She recognized him from the memory—Justice Advisor Adlai Weiss, and Dashiel's friend. She expected she was about to find out how good of a friend.

He stopped and stared at her, shaking his head. "Nika Kirumase. I guess I had to see it to believe it."

She was so damn tired of everyone saying that name as if it *meant* something. "Nika Kirumase is dead."

"Not dead enough, apparently," the woman grumbled. "Advisor Weiss, what a fortunate coincidence that you were in the building. I found her breaking into the data vault while projecting an illegal identity alteration."

Nika kept her attention on Weiss. "You authorized my presence and my use of an altered ID." Not *all* the altered IDs, but who was counting?

He shook his head. "I authorized your entry into the building and your audience with the Guides at Dashiel's side, not your infiltration of a restricted data vault. I'm sorry, Nika, I truly am, but I can't turn a blind eye to such a flagrant crime."

"Then arrest *her*." She pointed at the woman. "She's responsible for psyche-wiping me five years ago." Probably. The pieces all fit.

"Is this true, Gemina?"

And there was confirmation.

"Everything I did, I did with the Guides approval—no, with their *blessing*. I'm guilty of no crime."

ᴀ𝈚

The instant Dashiel stepped into the data vault, he knew things had taken a bad turn. The lights were tuned to full vibrance, with strobe alarms adding color to the lighting. Sounds of movement and muffled voices echoed through the server stacks.

As he crept toward the voices, each step brought with it mounting dread about what he would find. Theirs had been a foolhardy plan, far too fraught with risk, and they never should have attempted it. He'd leapt blindly at what presented itself as a chance to solve everything in one fell swoop and to not have to give up anything. Stupid!

And now someone, perhaps everyone, was going to pay the price for his transgression.

He rounded a corner. Halfway down the long row of hardware stood Gemina Kail, Adlai, a half-dozen security dynes and another half-dozen drones. At the center of the gathering stood Nika, stripped of all disguises to reveal fiery, beautiful defiance in her stance and her eyes. And her weapons.

He surveyed the scene for another two seconds, then made a decision.

ᐱR

"So it was you. Color me not surprised." Dashiel appeared from around the corner to approach their little gathering.

Relief at seeing him unharmed asserted itself first, but it swiftly gave way to concern at the casual, unoffended tenor of his voice and complete lack of alertness to his posture.

Gemina arched an eyebrow. "Dashiel. I should have known that where Nika was, you wouldn't be far behind, lapping at her heels like a loyal canine."

"You wound me. Adlai, I must apologize. Nika slipped away just as I entered the Platform d-gate for our audience with the Guides. I couldn't very well chase after her at that point, but I'm glad you caught her before she could cause too much trouble."

Shock punched the air out of Nika's chest before transforming into disgust, roiling her stomach and sending acid into her throat. "You bastard!"

"Now, Nika. You didn't honestly think I was about to run away with you to be a fugitive, scraping out a pitiful existence in the shadows, did you? My life is far too valuable for such nonsense."

She was going to be sick. But she couldn't be, not here. Alone in the enemy's lair, surrounded by the enemy's minions, she had to escape and survive. Right now, nothing else mattered.

She snarled at Dashiel to buy herself time to formulate a strategy. "How much of it was lies? Was anything you told me the truth?"

He shrugged nonchalantly. "A few things. You are in fact fabulous in bed, my love. However, it is not so rare a skill as to make me give up riches and power to enjoy your regular demonstration of it. I can find it elsewhere."

Weiss stared at Dashiel nearly as suspiciously as she did. "So you didn't know she intended to break into the data vault?"

"Of course not, though in retrospect I should have suspected it. She was obsessed with her past and what happened to her five years ago. I suppose I allowed myself to be temporarily blinded by her evident...attributes. I hope you'll forgive me for any trouble my lapse has caused."

He was lying to his 'friend' to cover his own ass, because he was a skilled actor and nothing more. Her instincts were smarter than her too-emotional consciousness, and she should have listened to them.

Adlai nodded vaguely. "We'll get everything sorted. Security, take this woman into custody—full restraints, I'm afraid. Nika, please don't resist. I don't want this to be any more difficult than it has to be."

She glared at Dashiel as the dynes drew near, her eyes sending virtual waves of malice and a healthy dose of hatred his way. If any regret flickered in his own eyes, she could not see it.

Her fingertip discreetly nudged the setting on her Glaser to wide-field pulse.

The instant the first dyne touched her, she activated a stun wave through her skin and into the surrounding air, overloading its circuitry and the circuitry of every other dyne in a two-meter radius and sending the squad jerking to the ground.

The next second she brought her Glaser up and fired it in an arc to sweep across all those present, perhaps lingering for an extra nanosecond on Dashiel. Electricity crackled through the air as the wide reach of the pulse spread to encompass the hovering drones.

As they fell like dominoes, Asterion and drone alike, she spun and sprinted for the far glass wall. When she was thirty meters away, she started firing at it.

Twenty meters. The glass cracked and shattered.

Ten meters. She readied her wingsuit deployment and primed her calves to leap through the opening—sharp pain lanced through her side as fire from a roving drone found its target. She instinctively grasped for her side as she staggered forward and tumbled out the window in free fall.

45

Nerve endings flared painfully back to functionality in a series of staccato jolts. The muscles they interwove gradually and more sluggishly began to respond to autonomic instructions.

Adlai opened his eyes.

Before taking any other action, he processed what his eyes saw and collated it with what his internal routines and the Justice nex web told him:

- Dashiel and Gemina also lay on the floor, the slapdash sprawl of their limbs suggesting they, too, had been knocked out by a nasty energy projectile.

- Wind whipped through the data vault, its source a shattered window at the end of the server row. The jagged edges of glass on the left side bore scattershot stains of blood.

- Because one of the roving security drones reported a successful hit on the intruder just before she exited through the window.

- No additional disruptions in the building were currently reported.

Satisfied that he was no longer waking blind, Adlai climbed to his feet and accessed the Patrol department comm system.

"Security patrols in Sector 1, sweep the area for a female fugitive. Physical appearance is subject to change due to multiple layers of disguises. She'll have an injury on her left side..." he eyed the broken window *"...and may be more seriously injured.*

"The target is armed and should be considered dangerous. Apprehend and pacify, but do not render nonfunctional unless absolutely necessary. I repeat, nonfunctionality is only to be used as a last resort option."

Dashiel had now recovered enough to rise to his feet as well, and his friend stood staring at the shattered window, his jaw locked and rigid in profile.

Adlai approached him. "She wouldn't have jumped if she wasn't prepared. I'm sure she wore a wingsuit or something similar."

Dashiel's throat worked for a second. Then he turned and shrugged coldly. "Whatever. She betrayed my trust. Used me for her own ends. She's obviously not the same woman we knew, so when you catch her, do what you will with her. I do have one favor to ask, though. If she gets sentenced to another R&R, see to it that she's shipped offworld first. I don't want her randomly showing up in my life a third time. I'm done."

How the hells should he respond? Later—later is how he should respond. Currently, he had a job to do...albeit not one he relished.

He studied Gemina as she rose to her feet, straightened out her jacket and smoothed down her hair. "Advisor Kail, tell me about what happened five years ago."

She tilted her head, and her lips set into a thin line. "No."

"No?"

"By direct order of the Guides, those events are to be kept under the highest confidentiality protections. If you want to challenge the order, be my guest, but that challenge doesn't begin with me—it begins upstairs and through the d-gate."

Adlai sighed. He'd pull up the relevant files as part of his investigation into the data vault infiltration, but if they were redacted they weren't likely to tell him much beyond what Gemina had already disclosed.

By the most common interpretation of the Charter, the Guides could not commit a crime. If they agreed by majority vote to take an action, it was inviolate. If they had sealed the files containing the details of Nika's psyche-wipe, that was the end of it.

As he listened to the curt updates from the patrols sweeping the sector on the comm channel, though, he couldn't help but wonder: what had Nika discovered five years ago to warrant both an involuntary R&R and a secret sealing of the incident from even the Guides' most trusted Advisors?

It shouldn't matter to him. Once it was determined that a crime had not been committed, it fell outside his purview and thus outside his concern. But she'd been his friend, too.

Nika crashed onto a grassy slope way too fast and tumbled wildly forward. Pain shot through her body in jarring spikes. The only thing that kept her from rolling all the way down the hill and careening into the street below was the left branch of her wingsuit tangling in some underbrush and yanking her to a violent stop.

She tried to rise to her knees—and promptly doubled over in agony, collapsing back to the ground in a heap. Tears stung her eyes to *drip-drip-drip* onto the ground, and if asked she wouldn't be able to truthfully say whether they were a result of the wound cutting through her side or the one ripping into her heart. The bitter sting of betrayal would be easier to wrangle into submission if it bled, because then she'd simply patch it up at a repair bench and be done with it.

But she couldn't think about that now; instead she had to think about its very real and tangible consequences.

She pinged Joaquim. *Shut down door #3. Right now.*

He must have guessed #3 was the door she'd brought Dashiel through, but in a rare kindness, he didn't toss it back in her face. *Done. You don't sound good. Do you need help?*

A response formed in her mind, but it ran into trouble making its way to transmission. Was her locator on? She didn't remember if she'd turned it on before entering Mirai Tower, and now she couldn't find it beneath an avalanche of internal system warnings and emergency routine activations.

She gingerly lifted her shirt and peered down at the wound, but in the shadowy darkness all she was able to make out was a mess of sickly slickness and torn flesh. Next she tried to shut off her pain receptors, but her OS refused to comply…something about shutting them off likely resulting in more serious self-inflicted injuries. In other words, if it hurt too much to walk, then she probably shouldn't walk.…

Nika, answer me.

Damn did it hurt, though, and she was just lying there—a sweeping light passed a few meters overhead. Security patrol? Great. Just lying there where anyone but mostly security patrols could find her.

She half-crawled, half-dragged her way over to a nearby tree and pressed her back against it on the opposite side from where the light had originated. Her left leg didn't want to work, so she grabbed her pants material and towed it into alignment, then let her weight sag against the tree trunk.

Crawling all of two meters had exhausted her. If patrols were sweeping the area, they were certain to catch her, and she was helpless to prevent it from happening.

It had all gone so horribly wrong. She had a trifling few of her answers now, but they were going to come at the cost of everything.…

Her eyes drifted closed, and no matter how much she fought to keep them open, she failed at that, too. Her OS insisted on stealing energy from healthy systems to funnel into injured ones, and her overrides kept being overridden.

But she'd rather her body expire and escape detection than survive and be captured. At least if it escaped immediate notice, eventually it might be found by someone from NOIR, or some other altruistic wanderer, and she could perhaps be revived.

But the park…the tree…was too close to Mirai Tower. The patrols would definitely find her first, which meant she needed to get farther away.

She planted her hands on the ground and pulled herself forward. One hand…drag…then another…the cool grass met her cheek as blackness consumed her.

46

J oaquim sprinted down the stairs while fastening a loaded weapons belt around his waist. Rather than search for everyone individually, he simply raised his voice over the din of the half-repaired Floor.

"Ryan, grab every security-suppressing tool you have and all your combat-rated pets. Ava, we need heavy weapons. Enlist two of your best people to use them. Maggie, you're in charge of...." He squeezed his eyes into a pained grimace. But he'd slipped up for good reason. In Maggie's absence, who did he have left with the right combat skill set, never mind the right experience? "I'm sorry. Dominic, can you provide wide-field camouflage for us?"

Dominic nodded, though his eyes were a bit wide. "Yes, sir."

"Thank you. We'll be outdoors in heavily trafficked areas, so throw together whatever you require to give us some cover. Perrin, where are you?"

All chatter on The Floor had quieted by his third or fourth word. Perrin scrambled to her feet near the back, where she'd been sitting with a couple of relative newcomers. "I'm here. What's wrong?"

He grabbed his tactical jacket off a hook in the equipment storage area. "Nika's in trouble. Perrin, we need a fully loaded field repair kit. I'd ask each of you if you're up to this, but I'm afraid we don't have the luxury of waiting until our wounds are healed if we want to save her. Everyone suit up. We're moving in two minutes."

∧R

Nika's locator put her three blocks from Mirai Tower. A not-so-small lucky break that she had activated it, since she'd declined to tell him where she was heading, what her plans were once she got there or where she'd ended up when she briefly contacted him before going unresponsive.

But Mirai Tower? Godsdamn, she was nuts.

The locator also hadn't budged since she'd pinged him. On the positive side, it meant she likely hadn't been captured yet...unless her body had fallen so completely nonfunctional that Justice wasn't in a hurry to move her. A slightly more favorable scenario was that she was surrounded and had security patrols closing in, because his teams could take care of security patrols. Still, even if they found themselves facing the latter situation, things were going to get messy.

Ryan: "I'm picking up three patrol squads in the sixteen-block region ahead. One is moving diagonally away from Nika's position—it looks as if they bypassed her location without discovering her. One is circling around on the periphery of the small park she's in, and the third is heading straight for her from the northwest."

Joaquim: "Let's give the first squad a wide berth and let them go on their way. Ava, take your team and flank the second squad. Remove them from the equation so we don't get blindsided. Oh, and Ava? You have my permission to shoot everything."

Ava: "Roger. Moving to fuck up some shit. You know, for Maggie."

Joaquim: "Everyone else, follow my lead and advance on the third squad. We're going to neutralize them before they reach her."

They moved as swiftly as stealth allowed, which was made more difficult by the reality that they were moving through the busiest area of downtown.

Mirai's citizens filled the streets, engaging in the evening's many pleasures downtown offered. Even a glimpse of someone in combat gear would be apt to send a pedestrian into a screeching panic, and shortly thereafter there would be a lot more than three patrol squads on the streets. This was why he'd brought the smallest team he could justify, trusting their tools and skills to win out over numbers and firepower.

Perrin leaned in close when they reached the other side of the street. "She's not answering any pings."

"I realize she isn't. Focus on reaching her cleanly. It won't matter what state she's in if we don't get to her."

"Right."

"I need you to keep it together, okay? *Nika* needs you to keep it together."

"Then that's what I'll do."

He didn't have to see her to visualize the resolute set of her mouth that came with the response.

They skirted a lone security dyne not obviously involved in the search, then finally left behind the pedestrian traffic of downtown as they reached the perimeter of the park.

Joaquim: "Target patrol squad is forty meters ahead, moving rapidly on a southeast vector. Ryan—"

Ryan: "I'm on it. Repulsors up, everyone—big-ass stun pulse incoming."

On the tacgrid, Ryan's dot rushed forward. Two seconds later Joaquim's repulsor field sizzled; even at such a distance enough energy made it through the barrier to set his hair on end, though not enough to disrupt his processes.

Joaquim: "Move in!"

The squad's drones had already dropped to the ground by the time they came into visual range, as had all but two of the dynes, which stumbled around erratically. But this wasn't a normal patrol squad—this was a hunter squad, and the two mecha it included had barely flinched from the stun pulse.

As one, the hulking machines began firing in a full three-sixty arc. They wouldn't be able to determine the direction from which the pulse had originated, and it seemed they didn't care.

Joaquim: "Increase shield strength and stay mobile!"

He held up an arm and the force field shield it projected in front of him to deflect the high-powered fire as he advanced in a jagged path toward one of the mecha. As he neared his target, the fire became so strong it almost forced him to a stop, but he fought his way forward nonetheless.

When he was less than a meter away, he brought up his non-shield arm and fired a projectile grenade into the open barrel of one of the mecha's weaponized appendages, then rolled away.

The resulting blast turned his roll into a tumble. His shoulder jarred roughly against the edge of a stone path, but he scrambled to his feet and spun around in time to see the second mecha explode from a reactive flexmat paste two of Ryan's drone pets had splattered on its frame from afar. One of the drones got speared by the flying debris and broke apart as it hit the ground, but the other made it away cleanly.

Silence fell with the same suddenness as the explosions—but not for long. The park was now an active battlefield, and both sides would know it.

Joaquim: *"Ryan, make sure the rest of the squad stays asleep, then take up defensive positions and watch for additional squads converging on this location. Dominic and Perrin, with me."*

Ryan: *"Take IkeBot with you, too. You're apt to need it more than I do."*

Joaquim: *"Copy that."*

The security dyne-turned-pet ambled over to meet Joaquim as he advanced toward a small copse of trees halfway down a grassy slope.

Hq (visual) / scan.thermal(240°:60°)
$T \rightarrow Hr(\alpha) = gridpoint(41.2, 6.8)$

The heat signature was on the ground just past one of the trees. He jogged toward it.

Perrin got the same information he did on the tacgrid, and on seeing it she decloaked and sprinted past him to fall to her knees beside the limp form.

Joaquim: *"Dominic, I want a mirage field fifteen meters out from my location. Notify me if anything gets within twenty meters of its border."* He decloaked as well and joined Perrin.

Nika lay on her stomach, face-down in the grass. Perrin was leaning down next to her head, moving tangled hair out of the way and talking to her, but it didn't look as if she was getting any response.

Dominic: "Mirage field is active."

As soon as Joaquim knelt on the ground, he felt an increasing dampness at his knees. He shone his light downward. The grass beneath him was soaked in blood.

Shit. "She's got a bad wound somewhere. We need to find it and stop the bleeding."

Perrin nodded and started feeling along Nika's clothes. He increased the brightness of his light and let it follow Perrin's progress.

When she reached the waist, she stopped. "Help me roll her onto her right side."

He did as instructed, and she peeled away the soaked, sticky fabric of Nika's tactical shirt to expose two bloody holes in her upper left hip, front and back.

Perrin choked back a cry. "Um, hold her in this position so I can grab the supplies."

He held the limp form still—giving silent thanks upon feeling the slight shift in the muscles beneath his hands as Nika took a shallow breath—while Perrin opened up the field repair kit and yanked out several items.

She quickly poured an expanding white foam into every place the skin was torn open, then stuck a ream of bonding tape over the wounds to seal them. Next, she placed a small module on Nika's port at the base of her neck and pressed her index finger to it. "I'm letting her OS know the bleeding's under control and it has repair foam to work with."

"Good thinking. She should be stable for now, but we need to get her home and into the tank." He raised his voice a notch. "Ike-Bot, come closer. I'm going to place Nika in your arms. Keep her secure, but be gentle."

"I understand."

Joaquim breathed in and wound his arms behind Nika's shoulders and knees, then slowly stood. Her head lolled back lifelessly, evoking a real cry from Perrin this time. He winced himself, but he kept his voice confident for Perrin's benefit. "It's all right. She's just unconscious."

Ava: "Second patrol squad dispensed with. Josie took a hit, but nothing a few minutes at the repair bench won't fix. On our way to your location, because more squads will damn sure be on their way to ours."

Joaquim: "Don't waste time stopping off here. We're clearing out in ten seconds. Head home via door #1 under full stealth. We'll take—" not #3 "—#4 and see you at The Chalet."

Ava: "You got her?"

Joaquim: "We got her."

He placed Nika in IkeBot's outstretched arms. The dyne came with its own kamero-type technology for stealth, and it could bear the weight of three people before it began to get strained, so it shouldn't have any trouble keeping a hold of her.

Joaquim: "Dominic, get ready to fade out the mirage field when we start moving—"

Ryan: "Three new hunter squads are closing in from the north and northwest, and they've got an AV between them."

Justice was pulling out all the stops to find and catch her. Whatever *had* she done?

Joaquim: "Ryan's squad, withdraw and return home via door #2. However, everyone move to the south or southeast out of the park and for three blocks before diverting to your assigned door. Avoid detection, but otherwise speed is our top priority. By the time those squads get here, we need to be gone."

47

Delacrai: "Nika Kirumase has resurfaced. Somehow, despite an exceptional-grade psyche-wipe and complete displacement from her support structure, she returned to search through the exact same files in the exact same location where we last found her. This time, however, she was able to escape after doing so."

Luciene: "We should have stored her five years ago."

Delacrai: "No, we should have revealed the truth in all its grim fullness to her in the hope of winning her as an ally in our crisis. Because we did not, she knows only that we wronged her and nothing of why, and now we have made an enemy of her."

Anavosa: "And a dangerous one as well. Our analysis of the infiltration techniques used at the Mirai Tower data vault indicate a high likelihood of her being NOIR."

Selyshok: "A former Advisor at the head of a terrorist group is a formidable threat."

Anavosa: "But the nature of the threat is clear now. While an unfortunate turn of events, in some respects it may make eliminating the group easier."

Selyshok: "I fear there is no longer any basis for your confidence, Anavosa. We now face unprecedented threats on two fronts—from within and without—and we are no closer to resolving either of them than when this crisis began."

Anavosa: "I disagree. As the threats begin to converge, we will increasingly be able to act with more focused purpose and more targeted resources."

Luciene: "Ornamental prose will not fix this problem. Only swift and merciless action will do that."

Anavosa: "And if our definition of 'merciless' differs?"

Iovimer: "Enough! Let us focus on reality as we find it and identify practical actions we must take in the coming hours. What of Advisor Ridani?"

Anavosa: "Appearances aside, we have no choice but to assume that his allegiances are now in question. We will need to watch him more closely. Luciene, do not say 'store him.'"

Luciene: "It would eliminate the particular complication he represents."

Delacrai: "Then what of Advisor Weiss? Advisor Debray? Are the very citizens we depend upon most falling under suspicion as well? Perhaps now is the moment to reevaluate our approach. Perhaps they should be told the truth. These are the citizens we trust above all others with advancing the welfare of the Dominion. If they understood the situation we find ourselves in, they could be of great assistance."

Luciene: "No! Maintaining a veneer of normalcy is essential if we are to win ourselves the time needed to resolve the Rasu crisis. If even one of the Advisors goes public with the information, we will find ourselves facing a multi-world panic."

Delacrai: "So you say, much as you said five years ago. Yet it is now five years later, and we have made little progress on devising a solution that stands a chance of preserving the Dominion as we know it. I submit that we are in need of a new plan."

Anavosa: "Iovimer is correct. Let us first direct our minds to what we can do to improve our situation in the near term. If we succeed, then we can contemplate more substantial course corrections at that time. Now, NOIR and Nika Kirumase are, I regret to say, a problem of our own making. And if we can no longer trust our Advisors, it appears it will be up to us to solve it."

SYSTEM
CALL

48

*T*he watery depths welcomed her into their arms. They were as a soft, cushioned cocoon warmed by the afternoon sun's rays that streamed down from far above.

She danced among the currents, weightless and free in a way long denied her, and in the paths the currents wove she felt contentment. She felt safe. In the waters' embrace no harm dared threaten her.

"It's time to wake up, Nika. You have things to do. Urgent things, vital to the survival of your friends and of the Dominion."

She didn't want to go. Also, why was Dashiel speaking in her head? He wasn't in the water with her, and in the short time she'd known him, they had certainly never ventured out into any large bodies of water. This couldn't be a memory from before, for she had none.

The visual in his apartment floated into her mind. There had been a boat, which meant there had been water. But she possessed no memory of that day, either. It had been erased, stolen from her.

The thought made her sad, and she didn't want to feel sad here, in this wondrous, free place.

"I want to stay. It's peaceful here. Nothing is hard. Nothing hurts. And you're here."

"Not truly, Nika. I wish I was. I'm so sorry, but you must *wake up now. Your destiny awaits. It won't be gentle or weightless—it won't be easy or kind. But it will be yours."*

Nika awoke enveloped in water.

No, not water, not precisely. A semifluid gel. Curving glass walls enclosed it and her. A scratchy tube made her throat tickle, and a transparent covering protecting her nose and eyes made it difficult to discern what lay beyond the glass.

She was in a tank.

Why was she in a tank?

...Because she'd gotten shot. Then tumbled out of a tower and nearly squashed herself flat on the ground before managing to get her wingsuit fully deployed. Then crash-landed in a park. Then....

The fuzzy, broken recollections ended there. But her presence in a tank—and not any random tank, but NOIR's tank, their most expensive and thus most prized possession—gave her some clues. Somehow her friends must have found her, saved her from Justice's clutches and brought her back to The Chalet and the tank.

Stars bless her friends.

And stars fuck Dashiel. How dare he masquerade as a benign voice in her head, dream or not.

A rapping sound echoed through the glass around her. She forced her head to turn, sluggishly fighting against the gel, to see Perrin waving at her from the other side of the enclosure. "Are you ready to get out of there?"

The voice was muted and indistinct, but the message was clear enough. Nika nodded as vigorously as her confines allowed.

Perrin disappeared, and after a brief wait the nanobot-infused gel began draining out of the tank.

The sensation of weightlessness vanished, and she briefly mourned its loss before yanking the tube out of her throat and the covering off her face. Perrin returned to open the tank's hatch, and Nika swung her legs over the lip—then promptly succumbed to a coughing fit as her lungs began the transition to breathing normal air all by themselves.

Perrin wrapped an arm around her shoulder. "Take it easy."

She struggled for several seconds but finally got the coughing under control. When she was able to breathe again, she peered down at her left side to find two large patches of shiny, virgin flesh that gradually blended into her more world-weathered skin. "How long?"

"Around five hours. You were wounded pretty badly."

"Dammit!" She half-climbed, half-fell off the tank's lip and stumbled toward the door. "I have to grab my things and get out of here."

"Whoa, slow down." Perrin appeared at her side, which coincidentally stopped her from collapsing to the floor a meter short of the door. It seemed her legs weren't ready to run quite yet. They had better get their act together pronto.

"You can't just go taking off."

"I have to. Every minute I stay here, I'm putting all of you in grave danger." Her throat tightened as a horrific thought occurred to her. "No one got damaged rescuing me, did they?"

"Nothing too bad. Ryan and Josie got a bit banged up, but everyone's fine, so calm down. You've been here for five hours, and no one has come for us. You can take another hour. Let's start with a shower and some clothes—get you presentable for the public—and we'll go from there."

Nika was starkly reminded of their first meeting, when Perrin had shepherded her to safety with much the same offer. It had meant everything then and nearly as much now...but she couldn't escape the perception that her life had gotten trapped in an endless loop, with the 'reset' button being hit every time she got close to discovering the portentous secrets that hid just past the horizon.

But there would be no more resets; one way or another, she was breaking out of the loop this time.

ᴧR

Joaquim and Perrin were both waiting in her room when she walked in after having taken the fastest shower of her life then half-yanked on the clothes Perrin had left for her.

Nika knelt in front of them and grasped one of their hands in each of hers. "Thank you. You shouldn't have come for me, but since it worked out I'm glad you did. I owe you both my life for the second time. I can never repay you—but I can protect you."

Then she stood and went over to her dresser. She grabbed a bag, tossed it on the bed and started opening drawers.

"Of course we came for you." Joaquim's voice sounded instantly stern. "So what's this shit about you taking off?"

She didn't look back at him, instead focusing on gathering the clothes she needed. "I've been exposed. The Guides, along with an Advisor named Gemina Kail, were responsible for my psyche-wipe. Now they know that I know, and that I'm after them again. And so they are after *me* again."

She stared down at the half-full bag as her attempt to concentrate on *leaving* faltered. "It's only a matter of time until they examine the security logs, if they haven't already. Even with the alterations Ryan made to the routines, they'll pick up on the similarities to our other infiltrations. They'll figure out I'm with NOIR."

Or Dashiel will tell them. Would he betray her so completely, or only enough as suited his convenience? She honestly couldn't say. He was once again a stranger to her.

"Therefore, my presence puts everyone in danger. I hate abandoning you when everything is such a fucking mess, but I need to get far away from here before I bring the full might of Justice to your door."

She sensed Joaquim lurking over her shoulder. "And then do what? Keep running?"

She grabbed a few more shirts and stuffed them in the bag. "Find answers. Answers about the virutox, answers about the reasons for my psyche-wipe, answers about what the Guides are hiding and why." Abruptly she spun and hurried over to her gear cabinet.

"Care to share how you plan to find all these answers?"

She retrieved a smaller, sturdier bag and began placing her gear in it. "I'll figure it out once I get clear and catch my breath."

Perrin hovered near the door, like she was planning to try to stop Nika from leaving. "What about Dashiel? Is he going with you?"

Nika shot her a dark look and shook her head tightly before finally looking at Joaquim. "If you want to say 'I told you so,' now would be the time."

"No need. I didn't want to see you get hurt, which was why I...anyway."

"Thanks to you guys, I'm no longer hurt—but I am angry." She went to the hidden panel and entered the elaborate passcode to open it. She couldn't take the whole setup with her, but all she legitimately needed was the interface and some spare weaves. The rest was merely for comfort, and she expected comfort wasn't apt to be high on her list of priorities for a while.

"I hate to ask, but I need one more simmed ID. I'll use it to get to Namino."

"Nika, you don't need to ask. They were always yours. You're in charge, remember?"

"Not any longer." She stood in the doorway of the alcove and faced them. "You two can handle everything just fine. You don't need me. Maybe you never did."

"That's not true!"

She gave Perrin a weak shrug. "Don't be so sure. I mean, The Chalet blew up on my watch, right? Regardless, you've learned everything I have to teach you. Going forward, the less association you have with me, the better—for yourselves and for NOIR. I won't let my personal baggage bring harm down on you."

"Don't be ridiculous. Let us help you—"

"No." Joaquim stepped over to Perrin and placed a hand on her arm. "She's right."

"Oh for fuck's sake, could you for one second think about your friend instead of the cause?"

Nika froze, eyes wide in shock. In five years, she hadn't once heard Perrin snap at him with such vitriol. "Perrin, it's not his—"

"I *am* thinking about her." He glanced her way, though his words were directed at Perrin. "Nika can move a lot faster and more safely without the weight of NOIR around her neck. She needs to do what she needs to do, and I have no doubt she'll be looking out for our interests as well along the way. The best thing we can do for her right now is take care of our people and give her one less thing to worry about."

A different, warmer flavor of surprise replaced the shock. "Thank you, Joaquim. I...really appreciate it. You will take excellent care of everyone."

He cleared his throat roughly. "You built this group up from a ragtag bunch of misfits into a resistance movement to be feared. We've taken a blow, but I hope I've learned enough from you to make sure we rise above it."

"Jo, you're talking like we're never going to see her again, and that's not true." Perrin glared at her. "That's not true, is it?"

"Of course it's not true. I'm sending the two of you a secure nex address code. I'll post news there when I can, and you should do the same. We'll stay in touch until we're back together. And when I do return, I'll still be NOIR."

She situated the smaller bag on her shoulder and picked up the larger one. "Be on your guard. The Guides themselves are up to something...wrong, and some of the Advisors are doing their dirty work for them. I'd stake my next generation on the augment viru-tox not getting quelled by Justice, which means it's going to keep spreading. Keep our people away from it, and be ready for the next one to hit. Stay sharp and watch your backs."

Joaquim nodded. Perrin tried to nod, then rushed forward and threw her arms around Nika's neck. "*You* be careful and watch your back. And get some righteous revenge."

She couldn't help but laugh as she pulled away. "Righteous revenge. Got it."

ⵝR

Nika listened for the blasts of entry explosives ahead of the intrusion of paramilitary security squads as she descended the stairs, feeling the encroaching danger of every second she had lingered here.

The feared sounds failed to arrive—but it didn't mean the next second wouldn't bring them.

She'd intended to slip quietly out, as the scene with Perrin and Joaquim had emotionally exhausted her. But when she reached the entryway, her steps slowed. She gazed out at the busy activity on The Floor.

Despite the late hour, so many people were working—patching up the pillars and repairing damaged equipment, cleaning soot and debris out of *everything*, trying to develop a counter to the virutox, analyzing its structure in the hope of tracking it back to its designer, building new firewalls to block its installation.

Some were studying the Charter, searching for a combination of obscure provisions that could overturn Parc's sentence. Still others worked on new and inventive ways to circumvent and subvert the labyrinth of the surveillance state that had gradually, bit by bit, enveloped every Asterion's existence.

The first to screw around, prank their cohorts and delight in causing mischief, when things took a bad turn they were also the first to dig in and give their all to the cause and the protection of their comrades. On the heels of a devastating attack on their home, they had put aside physical and psychological wounds to come for her, willingly risking capture to steal her helpless and unconscious self from the waiting clutches of Justice. She owed them a proper goodbye.

She set her bags down, then leapt up on top of a nearby table and whistled loudly. "Hey, everyone. Sorry to interrupt some of the best, most devious work in the Dominion, but I need your attention for a minute."

Scattered chatter fell silent, and at least forty faces trained their stares on her.

She gave them her best, most audacious smile. "First thing: thank you. Thank you all for saving my ass." She twisted around and grabbed her left hip. "I'm happy to report that said ass is now patched up and good as new. Also, don't ever do that again! You're more important than me. Because of your crazy devotion to the cause and each other, plus your mad skills, you're going to save so many people from untold horrors not of their own making. You're awesome, and you will continue to elevate your awesomeness.

"I'm heading out, and I'll be gone for a little while. I wish I could tell you how long, but you know how the hunt is. You start chasing the prize, and the next thing you know it's next week. This is what I'll be doing.

"I'm going to find out where this virutox that has taken Parc from us—taken Maggie and Carson and Cair from us—came from. I'm going to find out why it was released and what its creators want. Then I'm going to shut them down and ensure no one else falls prey to their crimes."

"How the hells are you planning to do all that?" The shout came from near the rear, but she recognized the voice as belonging to Ava.

She smirked and offered an overdramatic shrug. "You know me—I'll improvise."

"And make a damn fine show of it, too!" This was from Ryan, she thought.

"They'll know I was there, I promise you that. And when I return, I hope to have Parc at my side. But if I don't, I can guarantee you I will have made the guilty pay a thousand-fold."

Cheers followed, but her expression grew serious. "Be careful out there. Every interaction is more dangerous than it has ever been, and I don't want to lose anyone else—not a single solitary one of you. Watch your back, front and sides. Watch each other. Listen to Joaquim and Perrin, and go easy on them. Remember, they have the hardest job in the Dominion: wrangling all of you.

"Be kind to them and to each other. Keep what's precious to you close. I'll see you on the other side, where the party is."

She climbed off the table to applause and shouted farewells too numerous to parse out, retrieved her bags and hurried through the #4 door before anyone could see the tears brightening her eyes.

49

"Oh, for the love of the gods cavorting in the starry heavens, will you climb down off your self-erected pedestal and give a *centimeter* of compromise?"

The jaw belonging to the CEO of Zanist Circuitry plummeted nearly to the surface of the conference table. "Advisor Rowan, I will not be spoken to in such a manner by anyone, no matter their position! I am five seconds away from walking out of this room and returning to Ebisu."

Across the table, the Chizeru delegation launched into hysterics. Representatives of a splinter clan on the far side of the planet from the embassy, they were trying to edge their way into the kyo-seil business. This was their first contract negotiation, and it had been a disaster from minute one.

Iona rolled her eyes and slouched lower in her chair. Let the primates on both sides of the table fight it out, because her brain wasn't coughing up a solution that might bring the two parties closer together.

In a detached sort of way, she recognized that something inside her wasn't working right, but she couldn't conjure up the will to investigate it, much less check herself into a clinic for diagnostics and a tune-up.

The CEO stood, apparently to make good on his threat, and his two associates hurriedly followed suit.

The Chizeru clan leader squawked a protest and leapt onto the table. Oh, this was simply *fantastic*.

"Advisor, keep these creatures away from me!"

"What?" She looked up idly. "Bharut, sit down."

The clan leader stomped on the table.

"That's it. We're leaving." The CEO spun toward the door and began marching pompously toward it.

"Hold up a sec." Iona slid her chair out and stood as well, then gave the attendees and their bedlam a wide berth as she approached the door ahead of the man.

She walked up to the security dyne standing guard and held out her hand. "Give me your Glaser."

"Yes, Advisor." The dyne removed the weapon from its built-in holster and presented it to her.

"Thank you." It must have been a century or longer since she'd fired one, and she squinted at the various settings for a few seconds.

"Advisor Rowan? What is the meaning of this?"

"Oh! There it is." She flicked the setting to maximum, stretched her arm out and shot the CEO in the head.

Screaming commenced. The laser bobbed and weaved around the room as it chased the running executives, but eventually it found its mark, and again.

Then it was only the Chizeru screaming—the dyne was merely emitting a sputtering noise, presumably locked in a paradox calculation as no programming had been loaded onto it for what to do when it was an Advisor doing the shooting.

The little aliens dove beneath the table to hide, which wasn't really hiding at all. She went to the end of the table and bent over to peer underneath it.

"Boo!" She fired. One. Two. Three. Stood and stretched. Thank gods, it was finally quiet.

Bit of a mess, though. She should see about cleaning up, but it was going to be so much work. Better to just start fresh.

She pushed the muzzle of the Glaser against the skin where her chin and throat met and pressed the trigger.

50

The atmosphere on Namino had changed. Or perhaps, Nika admitted, her perspective on it had.

The street merchants yelled their wares in harsh tones and invaded her personal space to hock them. The cacophony of trade being conducted everywhere grated against her ears. The security patrol dynes focused their attention on her for too long, suspicion animating their emotionless visual scanners. The dry air made her new patches of skin itch.

So she was cranky. If only that were all she was, as then she could simply go get sloshed on alcohol, top it with a lightweight dose chaser, and sleep it off.

But she had a mission—a purpose—and it propelled her forward, through the transit hub crowds and the street crowds and the market crowds toward the maglev station.

She sensed the attack coming a nanosecond before it arrived. She dropped her bags and her right arm swung up as a wide body— a Taiyok?—lunged for her neck, needle blade at the ready.

The blade scraped across her forearm—the attacker grabbed her hand and twisted her arm back—she swung her other arm around, wrist blade extended, and slashed at their shoulder.

They jerked away an instant prior to breaking her arm, and she yanked out of their grasp.

The attacker was tall and bulky. Definitely a Taiyok. Male, judging from the breadth of their chest.

Pedestrians scattered as the alien darted forward. Before she could command her muscles to move, he had grabbed her and slammed her into the building abutting the sidewalk. Her head smashed painfully against the facade, rebounded, and her chin bounced off her chest.

A winged arm braced against her neck, and the needle blade came up once more—but to use it properly, he had to adjust his grip on one of her arms. When she felt the pressure lessen, she threw everything into swinging that arm up.

Her blade met flesh. She dragged the blade across the attacker's chest toward the vulnerable area where wing met torso—

He stumbled back with a growl of pain, stared at her for half a second, then spun and took off running down a side street. After three strides, his wings expanded and he took to the air.

But not high or swiftly. His right wing teetered unsteadily as he struggled to gain and keep altitude.

She retrieved her Glaser from beneath her cloak, aimed it and fired.

The Taiyok tumbled out of the sky, landed hard on the street, skidded several meters and came to a stop.

She was already sprinting toward him when he scrambled to his feet. The Glaser didn't come with a setting high enough to kill a Taiyok, so the most she was able to do was stun him for a few seconds. Which she did.

He was rousing himself again when she stopped two meters away and pointed the Glaser at his chest. "Who sent you?"

If the attacker was surprised by her effortless use of his language, he didn't show it. "People far more powerful than you—"

The next instant a wing slammed into her from the side. She flew through the air and crashed into the facade of another building, but tucked her head in this time to avoid the worst of the blow.

The Taiyok was on her before she hit the ground. Godsdamn he was fast!

A fist connected with her cheek; her head snapped sideways and her consciousness stuttered from the shock. But this was what combat routines were for, and hers quickly jolted her functions back into action.

She fired into his chest at point-blank range. The odor of singed feathers assaulted her nostrils as he stumbled backward. She fired again. Again. The Taiyok crumpled to the street. Again.

She leapt onto his chest to straddle him and fired one last time. Then she brought her blade up and dragged it across his neck, making sure to apply enough pressure to cut all the way through the thick skin.

Mottled brown blood oozed out from the blade's path to flow into the street.

Retract the blade. Activate your kamero filter. Activate your mask. Get your bags. Depart the scene. The focused commands guided her through the next moments, when otherwise shock might have rendered her frozen and, shortly thereafter, incarcerated.

A few onlookers had appeared at the intersection to gasp and point; she activated her kamero filter as instructed and vanished from their vision. Then she picked her way carefully through the growing crowd to the main street. No one had moved her bags yet, but a squad of security dynes came into view as they hurried toward the scene.

She waited until a group of people were passing to nonchalantly pick up the bags. She lessened the kamero cloak's strength and matched their stride for the next block before breaking off and taking a circuitous route to the maglev station.

Morphs and similar visual alteration routines didn't work on Taiyoks. The aliens' eyes simply rejected the signals and saw what they saw. The Guides knew she would be using disguises and had hired an assassin for whom the disguises wouldn't matter.

Had the Guides somehow known she would be traveling to Namino? Or had they stationed an assassin at every d-gate hub connected to Mirai One? They controlled the considerable resources needed to implement such a dragnet.

The realization strengthened her resolve that she was choosing the best course of action. If nothing else, running would buy her time to figure out how the hells to disguise herself from Taiyok assassins.

She crept onto the maglev and slipped into a seat in the back corner, where shadows obscured her presence and she could see an attack coming.

There she found a few treacherous minutes of solitude. The adrenaline from the attack abandoned her, leaving behind dark thoughts to haunt her mind in the span of quiet.

Before she would be able to arrive at a mental or physical place where she might do anything about them, however, she first had to keep moving forward. So she exited the maglev at the familiar stop and suppressed all the aches and pains from the attack to adopt a rapid pace for the kilometer walk to Mesahle Flight.

But at the entry gate, she hesitated. Not because she worried she had been followed, as she was quite certain she had not.

No, her hesitation stemmed from a far more vulnerable source—her conscience. She hated asking friends for favors, but what she hated even more was disappointing friends.

She was about to do both.

Nika watched as Grant wound photal fibers from the back of a user-facing interface into the complex wiring of a large module, possibly a lighting system. It was the type of detail work a true craftsman like him would never leave to the machines.

He finished one stage of the process and shifted around to retrieve a new tool, then caught sight of her. With a growing smile he leaned against the frame holding the module in place. "Nika Tescarav, come to visit again so soon. Are you here to buy a ship?"

Her throat worked, and she failed miserably at matching his smile. "Yes."

He stared at her oddly for several seconds. "Yes?"

She nodded.

"Um…okay. I don't know quite how to respond to that. What happened?"

"Can we go inside and talk? These bags are getting heavy."

"Sure." He threw a tarp over the module frame and packed away his tools in their case, then she followed him up the ramp and inside.

He closed the door and propped on the edge of his desk. "So what's this about? Are you in trouble—wait, are you *bleeding?*"

She frowned; she'd already minimally cleaned up the cut on her arm. But Grant was motioning to her face, so she touched her fingertips to her forehead. Sure enough, they came away bloody.

She sighed and stepped into the lavatory to grab a rag and hold it against the cut for a few seconds. "I had a little altercation on the way here."

"An altercation?"

"A Taiyok assassin."

"Bloody hells, Nika. Who did you piss off?"

"It's safer for you if you don't know the details." She wandered around the cluttered office, which he didn't keep nearly as neat and ordered as his work floor outside, mostly to avoid having to meet his gaze. "I'm exposed, and I need to distance myself from NOIR. There are places I need to go to get answers to important questions, but I can't risk continuing to use the official transit system. Not when some very powerful people are looking for me."

A slight pause stretched out before he responded, during which time she was unable to draw any conclusions from his expression because she still didn't meet his gaze.

"So you need a ship. Any special requirements?"

"A small, agile personal craft is all I'm looking for. Fast would be a bonus, but not at the expense of other necessities. Minimal defensive capabilities, but I don't need a warship." The conversation with Dashiel, Perrin and Joaquim bloomed into the front of her mind, but she hurriedly quashed it and the pain it brought with it. "I'll pay you what I can, but that isn't very much." One favor request gutted out.

He nodded and went around his desk to check something on his inventory pane. After a few seconds of poking around in his system, he came over and placed his hands on her hips, halting her pacing with a touch.

"It shouldn't be too much trouble to get you what you need." He drew closer for a kiss, but she instinctively flinched, turning her head to the side before she could stop herself.

They froze in that awful position for an interminable second. Then he took a slow step back. "What's wrong?"

She opened her mouth to answer him, but a dozen responses died in her throat.

"Nika?" Abruptly his chin dropped to his chest with a quiet, wry chuckle. "You met someone, didn't you?"

And there was the disappointment. Seriously, why had she pulled away from him? She damn sure didn't owe Dashiel any allegiance. Yet somehow, her brief time knowing him had killed the spark, casual and frivolous though it had been, that she felt for Grant. And it kind of sucked. "I wish I hadn't."

His brow furrowed in confusion, understandably so.

She grimaced. "Look, I just...I have to concentrate on my mission right now. I can't afford to get distracted, or even to slow down at all."

He shrugged with forced mildness, but a new reservation and coolness clouded his features. "It's all right. I always knew what this was—and what it wasn't."

She didn't love him, but she nevertheless felt a pang of loss as his body language told the story of his withdrawal from her. "You're a good man, Grant."

He huffed a laugh, now the picture of friendly but detached professionalism. "I really am. Come on, let's head over to the hangar out back. Let me show you a beauty I think will work for you."

AR

Nika blinked. She was gaping, in all likelihood. Her head tilted, but the new angle didn't reveal any obvious flaws.

"Well? What do you think?"

"Grant, I can't take this ship."

"Why not?"

"It's…" *beautiful* "…it had to cost you ten times what I can pay you simply to build it, and I expect you can get another ten times cost for it on the market."

"True, and true. But I was never planning on selling it. Now, I want you to take it. The speed is pretty good, but the agility is through the roof. You can outmaneuver military fighters in this ship—which I personally hope you're not planning on doing. It has state-of-the-art shielding installed as well as half-decent weaponry. The luxuries inside should be to your liking. Nothing too over the top, but you'll be comfortable."

The specs he rattled off were having trouble penetrating her brain, because said brain was still trying to get past the absurd notion that he was actually offering her the ship. This ship. The one in the hangar. The one she stood in front of fawning over like a Chizeru over a fleece blanket.

The brushed nickel hull claimed and reflected the lighting in the hangar in equal measure. An icy cerulean glow crept out in distinctive lines along the rims of the dual engines. The wide, low profile and tapered nose gave it a furtive, devious appearance—not that the ship was sentient, but if it *were*.

"What…why weren't you going to sell it?"

Grant shoved his hands into his pockets and began wandering around the front of the hangar. "I picked up a vintage craft at auction a couple of years ago—little more than a hull and a rusting engine. Restoring it has sort of been a side project of mine. I had this idea in my head how at some point I'd take six months off and cruise around the Dominion.

"I never would have done it—I'm too much of a workaholic—but I enjoyed knowing I *could*. It shouldn't sit here wasting away in the hangar, though. You need it, and I suppose it needs you."

"I…" she struggled past the lump that had now materialized in her throat "…I don't know what to say. I'll pay you forever for it. Start a tab."

"Just don't get caught, okay? This baby can help you with not getting caught, if you'll let it."

51

Nika slow-walked the perimeter of the ship, scanning for anything she ought to check.

She'd installed a dozen routines on starship piloting and maintenance, but most of them still needed a good workout before she was apt to be comfortable flying—and living on—a ship. Her mind supplied the names of the various external components and the factors that contributed to their performance, but the terms felt foreign. Sterile combinations of letters lacking any tangible connection to the physical equipment she was trying to study.

Grant was an excellent ship builder and a master craftsman, and he'd devoted extra care to crafting *this* ship, so she shouldn't be surprised when she came up empty on the 'inspection.' The exterior of the ship was in perfect shape; she doubted she'd find it any less to spec on the inside.

In one of the first bright spots she'd encountered since the doomed visit to Mirai Tower, she was actually rather excited about taking the ship out for an extended spin. Among a thousand troubling thoughts dogging her consciousness, she'd realized that she agreed with her former self on something. Over centuries of ubiquitous use of the d-gates to cross distances short and vast, they had willingly bound themselves to the ground, and she wanted to travel amidst the stars.

She'd looked up the public files on the *Shorai* initiative former-her and Dashiel had talked about in his memory. Billed as the most ambitious space exploratory initiative since the Dominion's founding, it had launched to great fanfare nine years ago. Led by an External Relations Advisor, Mason Fassar, the *Shorai* set out in search of new discoveries—aliens, cosmic wonders and, of course, kyoseil.

The plan was for the ship to deposit small d-gates along the way at points of interest so that specialty teams could follow behind to investigate any finds. Over time, the growing interstellar travel network that resulted would expand the Dominion's reach far beyond its borders.

Once a year or so, the External Relations Division issued a press release announcing some new find by the *Shorai*, usually one of purely scientific interest, in the distant reaches of space. Details were scarce, however, and Nika couldn't help but wonder what stories lay behind the headlines. What might Advisor Fassar be finding out there in the deep expanses of the void?

The question called to a quiet yearning in her psyche, much as it had for her former self.

If only she could afford to indulge the romantic whimsy of exploration for exploration's sake, of discovery for discovery's sake. She was taking to the stars, but the scolding voice in her head reminded her this was not a pleasure cruise, which was why she needed to stop daydreaming and refocus on the task at hand.

Time to make an effort at an interior inspection—then time to go. She was supposed to be running, after all, and she'd remained here too long already.

With a sigh she began ascending the extended ramp.

"Care for some company?"

Nika whirled around at the sound of the voice. She carried her Glaser with her everywhere now, and she had it raised before the question had finished.

Dashiel stood ten meters away, a bag in each hand. He wore what likely passed for casual attire in his world, linen pants and a lightweight cable knit sweater. There were even a few hairs out of place, ruffled by the breeze to fall across his brow in—who cared how his *hair fell*?

"Don't move. Don't twitch."

He obeyed, though his throat did flex with a swallow. "I'd deeply appreciate it if you didn't shoot me again. It hurt quite a lot."

"Good. What are you doing here?"

"Coming with you, of course."

She stared at him in utter incredulity. "Are you fucking kidding? I'm not letting you a centimeter closer to me. How the hells did you find me?"

His gaze dropped to the ground. "I put an internal tracker in one of your drinks when you were at my place. Don't be angry. I only did it because I was terrified I would lose you, literally. I was afraid you'd stumble into something nasty and get yourself erased again, and this time I'd lose you forever. I only wanted to be able to find you if you got into trouble."

"Liar. You never 'only' anything. Is your Justice pal on his way here right now?" She backed two steps up the ramp. Was he responsible for the assassin? When the Taiyok failed, was he being sent in to finish the job? "I'm leaving before the cavalry arrives. Fuck you."

"Wait!" He rushed forward, but skidded to a halt when she lowered her finger over the Glaser's trigger mechanism. "No one else is coming, I promise. Please hear me out."

She paused at the hatch as indecision locked her into inaction. His 'promise' wasn't worth the negative credits left in her account. If she delayed and he was lying, everything would have been for naught and she'd find herself in either a shootout or a Justice detention cell—or a shootout *then* a Justice detention cell. But the desperation in his voice begged for her indulgence, and some deep, reclusive part of her she didn't fully understand wanted so badly to be wrong about him....

"Nika, I was always coming with you. I just needed a little time to work through what that meant for me. Then Mirai Tower happened, and the time for reflection I'd hoped to have got cut short, but I still needed time—time to put my plan in motion."

"Yes, about what happened at Mirai Tower."

"If I had sided with you in front of the others, neither of us would have made it out of there under our own power. We both would have been arrested on the spot. If we'd tried to escape together, I would have slowed you down too much and we'd have ended up arrested anyway. But what I *could* do was buy you time to escape, and buy myself time to make sure your escape meant something.

"I *told* you it would all be a performance, and it was. I convinced Adlai I was ignorant of your plans and created enough doubt in Gemina to make her cautious, giving me the room I needed to execute on my plan."

"Which was?"

He angled his head down at the smaller of the two bags. "Transfer operational control of Ridani Enterprises to my second, Vance Greshe, and withdraw the entirety of my personal wealth into untraceable credits. It's not quite as substantial as it once was, but it will suffice. See, I thought I'd fund your rebellion. Well, mostly fund you and I, but there should be plenty left over for a good cause."

Her gun arm faltered, and her aim slipped away from his chest. "You...what?"

"I'm all in—with you, with your rebellion and your personal mission, with all the wrongs you're seeking to right. I hate that I wasn't able to clue you in earlier, but at Mirai Tower our communications were being monitored. And after...I figured you'd delete any ping I sent to you without reading it.

"The only thing I knew to do was show up in person and hope you'd give me a chance to explain before shooting me again. Speaking of, any chance you can put the gun down now?"

She exhaled so harshly no air remained in her lungs to sustain her. She couldn't find any holes to poke in his pitch, and he was so damn *charming*. All she had left to bolster her defiance was her own doubts and the persisting burn of betrayal.

He'd thoroughly wrecked the meager trust she'd begun to have in him, and now here he stood asking for it back. He'd *hurt* her, and now he was telling her he'd only been acting in her best interests. Telling her he was giving up his life of posh luxury, the business he'd spent his life building and his position of lofty influence, all for her. Not for the memory of a person who no longer existed, but for *her*.

She felt lightheaded, when what she really needed was for all that blood to return to the brain it had vacated.

Could he be lying? Playing a long game for Justice, or even for the Guides? If the goal was for her to lead them to NOIR, he was going to be sorely disappointed, because she didn't intend to return home until this was over. If the goal was something else, she couldn't conceive of what it might be. The Guides already knew the answers she sought; they gained nothing from stringing her along.

He lost patience with her silent ruminating. "What can I do to convince you? Do you want to deep-scan me for tracking devices? Immerse yourself in a simex of my last sixty hours? Feel how I felt when I watched you tumble out of that window and into free-fall?"

His voice cracked near the end, and with the last word his shoulders fell. "I know trust is in short supply for you. I'm simply asking—no, begging—for a tiny bit of it. Give it to me on loan until I can prove myself worthy of it."

The last bit of resistance abandoned her. She sank down onto the ramp, letting the Glaser dangle over her knees and dropping her forehead to rest against them. Trust *was* in short supply for her, but though she'd worn a brave face for the world, dammit, she didn't want to do this alone....

She heard him coming up the ramp, and she couldn't bring herself to stop him.

He fell to his knees in front of her and ignored the gun between them to bring his hands to her face and gently lift her chin. "Nika, you have always been my world. The love of my many lives. I will never betray you, and I will always follow wherever you lead."

The sting of tears blurred his features as he leaned in and kissed her forehead. "I'm so sorry I hurt you. I should have found some way to let you know what I was doing."

He kissed both of her cheeks in turn. "The thing is, I'm no good at all this stealth and subterfuge. You're going to have to teach me how to be a rebel." Finally he kissed her lips, softly. "Will you teach me?"

She nodded shakily, then dropped the gun onto the ramp and pulled him closer to kiss him far more ferociously. His embrace felt like a home from a half-remembered dream.

He grasped her hands and splayed his palms flush against hers until their fingertips met...and she *sensed* him, sensed his mind, open and vulnerable. Offering itself to her.

She closed her eyes.

The aroma of freshly grilled kabobs brought a smile to my face as I stepped onto the sweeping balcony ringing the Mirai Tower d-gate room. Hors d'oeuvres!

Maris appeared at my side while I was loading up my plate, a glass of champagne in her outstretched hand.

I balanced the plate against my chest so I could take it from her. "You read my mind."

"As I do." Maris paused, and her gaze cut across the other guests scattered around the balcony. "You haven't seen him yet, have you?"

"Seen who? I just got here."

"The new Industry Advisor, of course."

I tugged an olive off the kabob and popped it into my mouth. "Oh. Nope."

A devious smirk crept across her lips. "You should remedy the error."

"Why...?"

Maris let the smirk linger as she casually turned and sauntered off.

She certainly knew how to pique my curiosity. I rolled my eyes then started scanning the balcony. Knew that person, knew that person, knew but despised that person...

...a well-dressed man stood near the balcony railing talking to one of the Commerce Advisors. Chestnut hair framed distinguished features in soft waves that lightened to amber when sunlight crossed them. He shifted slightly in my direction, revealing vivid hazel irises driving a cautious, studied gaze.

I did not know him, but this was about to change.

I tossed my still full plate on a table and strode over as the Commerce Advisor conveniently wandered off. The man's gaze landed on me when I was still several meters away, and its intensity almost stopped me cold. Oh, my.

I closed the remaining distance and thrust out my hand. "Nika Kirumase, External Relations Advisor. And you are?"

One corner of his lips curled up as he accepted my offered hand. "Dashiel Ridani. I was just promoted to Industry Advisor this week."

My hand remained encased in his firm, warm, thoroughly tingly and delightful grip, and I decided I was in no hurry to remove it. "It's a pleasure to meet you, Mr. Ridani. Welcome to the Advisor ranks. How are you finding the new job so far?"

His eyes danced as he brought my hand up and placed a soft kiss on my knuckles. "I find I am liking it more every minute."

Are you now? I licked my lips. Deliberately. "Trust me, you haven't seen anything yet."

"Nika?"

She forced her eyes open and intertwined her fingers with his to break the connection. "Sorry. I suppose I'm a little tired."

"I imagine it's been a rough few days for you."

"You really have no idea." She tried to sound as casual as possible. "Out of curiosity, how did we first meet?"

His brow wrinkled in surprise at the question. "At a reception at Mirai Tower, when I was initially named an Advisor. Why?"

"No reason." She offered him a quick smile, then hurriedly renewed their kiss before he could probe further. What was going on with these flashes? If they were his memories, why were they from her perspective?

He drew back a little and tilted his head toward the hull. "This is your ship, I'm guessing?"

She exhaled and tried to shake off the memory's spell. "It is now, more or less."

"What does 'more or less' mean?" Another kiss. Another tender caress. Another few hours of this and she might begin to feel…content.

"It means I'm a bit of a charity case. The owner of this place is a friend of NOIR, and of mine."

"That won't do at all. I'm a businessman, and I believe people deserve fair compensation for quality products—and this is a beautiful ship. We'll pay this friend of yours properly for it."

A protest died in her throat. Grant *did* deserve to be paid for the ship, and Dashiel *did* have the money to do it. So instead she disentangled herself from his arms to stand. "I appreciate that."

"Happy to do it." He followed her up. "When were you planning to leave?"

"About five minutes from when you showed up."

His eyes widened. "Damn. You mean I almost missed you? A few minutes later and I'd have had to chase you across the stars."

"Maybe I should have left earlier. Made you work for it."

He didn't laugh; in fact, he looked distressingly serious. "How long until you forgive me?"

She shrugged. "A little longer."

He nodded thoughtfully. "I suppose that's fair—but perhaps this will help. I figure I have three or four days until the Guides realize I'm no longer their man. What do you say we shorten that time? Let's go break your friend Parc out of Zaidam."

52

It was entirely possible, Adlai decided as he stared at the list of his open investigations, that he was the single worst Justice Advisor in several millennia.

He remained no closer to catching the leaders of NOIR, or for that matter its lowliest members. Meanwhile, they broke into major corporate headquarters and had their way. They broke into *the Guides' own data vault*. Or Nika broke into the Guides' data vault, which he supposed meant Nika was now synonymous with NOIR. That one was still throwing him for a loop.

Despite being seriously injured, she'd succeeded in eluding five hunter squads to vanish once more. Admittedly, she'd had help doing so, as evidenced by the trail of dismantled patrol dynes and mecha the 'help' left in their wake. His teams had spent six hours cleaning up the wreckage. Even for NOIR, it was an impressive showing.

…There he was complimenting their work again. Ugh, he did *not* want to have to hunt his friend down and lock her away.

A high priority alert arrived to interrupt his angst. From the Chosek embassy? That was unusual. He frowned and opened the message.

They had a *what?*

※

Crime in Asterion society tended to be…neat. Sanitized. More often than not, the aftermath was limited to fried circuitry or a bit of physical debris. Their bodies were as much organic as synthetic, so a criminal *could* blow someone's head off, dismember them limb-by-limb or commit other moral atrocities on a body, but the reality that the victim would soon receive a fresh body and continue on with their lives tended to remove the incentive. As such, body-murder by any method other than catastrophic electrical overload was rare.

Now Adlai stood over seven bodies, four Asterion and three Chizeru. They had all been ripped apart by high-powered laser blasts. Blood, viscera and brain matter decorated the floor, walls and ceiling of the embassy conference room. The room *stank*.

Chaos, closing in.

He needed to shut out his visceral reaction to the horrific nature of the crime scene and treat it like any other crime scene. Not like *any* other, of course, as this one involved an Advisor, several powerful corporate executives and a couple of aliens, and thus was a diplomatic firestorm in the making.

This, at least, wasn't his problem—one of the other diplomatic Advisors, Cameron Breckel, was on his way from Ebisu to 'manage' the situation.

With a sigh Adlai turned to one of the techs who had accompanied him to Chosek. "Show me the footage again."

The security dyne assigned to the room had recorded the event, as it recorded all official meetings. It had subsequently suffered a programming malfunction, but the tech had managed to extract the recording from its data store.

He watched Advisor Rowan slouching in her chair, then scowling dramatically as she lost control of the negotiations and the meeting descended into anarchy. Then emoting across the room, demanding the dyne's Glaser, *deliberately* setting it to maximum and calmly firing on every person in the room, then herself.

He didn't know Iona Rowan particularly well, but he'd shared professional space with her enough times to recognize that her actions were absurdly out of character. Not simply the shooting, but her behavior in the minutes leading up to it. It was as if a different person inhabited her body....

Oh, crap.

He forced himself to look at the body. Most of her skull had been shredded and its contents splattered on the wall behind it; the odds of recovering clean data from her brain were all but zero.

Next, he checked the Advisors' database...in a stroke of luck, she had filed her mandated every-two-week comprehensive backup this very morning.

After a quick check of the time he contacted Erik Rhom in the Mirai Justice Center lab.

"Erik, this is Adlai. I'm sending you a copy of a comprehensive psyche backup file. I need a thorough forensic analysis performed on it, highest priority. I'll be back on Mirai later today to review your findings."

"Yes, sir. Clearing my schedule now."

"Thanks. Oh, and use strict quarantine procedures during the analysis."

"You think the psyche has been corrupted?"

"I think that may be the least of its damage."

⋏ℛ

Adlai took a shower before going to the lab, but he felt as though he needed to take a minimum of three more. The stench of death—real and permanent death in the case of the Chizeru—had seeped into his skin and the olfactory receptors in his nose.

As soon as he walked into the lab and saw the expression on Erik's face, he knew his day wouldn't be improving any time soon. "What did you find?"

"Exactly what you expected me to find, I suspect. She was infected with the limb augment virutox."

"I was afraid of that. But it doesn't make people aggressively violent—reckless, maybe, but if anything, it makes them overly passive, right?"

"This is where it gets worse, sir. Once I found the virutox, I pulled the preliminary report from the crime scene on Chosek. She didn't have the limb augment installed."

"What? Are you suggesting it's communicable?"

Erik tilted his head in prevarication. "Probably not through touch alone—it likely requires a much deeper level of interaction. But yes."

Gods. He swallowed heavily. "All right, I'm going to burn into red alert mode on this data point in about ten seconds. But first, how is communicability related to the violent behavior?"

Erik motioned him over and opened a pane full of graphs. "My working hypothesis is that when an active virutox is introduced to a psyche by external means, as opposed to being installed internally and allowed to propagate naturally, it's forced to mutate. It has to find alternate ways into many of the processes it's designed to infiltrate, and the course of its spread is altered. Hence, different effects manifest."

"Worse effects."

"For now we have a sample size of one, so I don't want to extrapolate without more data. But the data we have isn't good."

⅄R

Adlai had willingly obeyed the Guides directives; he'd trusted in their wisdom in light of the certainty that they possessed information he did not. But he'd always viewed his work at Justice more as a calling than a simple job, and he had not dedicated multiple generations to it in order to send perhaps misguided but fundamentally decent people to Zaidam Bastille for decades. Or worse, into a hard R&R.

Now the virutox he'd been ordered to allow to run free was running far freer than he had anticipated. Than the Guides had anticipated?

The growing chaos he'd sensed in recent months was going to be nothing compared to the anarchy still to come if the virutox was both communicable and mutating into something that induced *violence*.

The mystery surrounding Nika's psyche-wipe added a new weapon to his conscience's cage match with itself. He couldn't say much about her morality now, but the Nika *he'd* known would never have acted against the Dominion's best interests. So why had the Guides ordered her erased, as it now appeared clear they had?

He rubbed at his jaw. He needed to talk to someone about all this—needed to hear reassurance that he wasn't developing his own glitch and descending into madness. Dashiel instantly sprang to mind. But if the scene at Mirai Tower was any indication, Dashiel's week had skidded off a cliff that began at bad and ended at epically worse. He shouldn't pile on.

But there wasn't time to coddle himself or his friend, so he pinged Dashiel anyway.

I am currently unavailable. For business matters, please contact the Ridani Enterprises Manufacturing Director, Vance Greshe. For personal matters, please leave a message detailing the issue and I will be in touch.

Adlai frowned, instantly suspicious. After pondering on it for a moment, he opted not to leave a message and instead reached out to Greshe, who he'd met once or twice while visiting Ridani Enterprises.

"Director Greshe, this is Adlai Weiss over at Justice."

"Yes, Advisor Weiss! It's a pleasure to speak with you. How can I help you today?"

"I was hoping to give Dashiel an update on the augment theft investigation. Do you know when he'll be available?"

"Ah. Advisor Ridani has taken a personal leave of absence, and I don't expect his return on any particular date. Is this an urgent matter?"

"No, it can wait."

"Then I'll be sure to pass along your message whenever I next hear from him."

"Thank you."

Adlai kicked his chair back and crossed his ankles atop the edge of his desk. Despite his better judgment and the direness of the trap he now found himself in, a small smile crept across his lips.

He'd been hoodwinked.

He never should have bought Dashiel's performance in the Mirai Tower data vault...but maybe he hadn't *wanted* to see through the charade. Because if he had, it would have meant he needed to arrest Dashiel, and that might have been one morally suspect step further than he was willing to go.

Adlai called up the memory of the scene at the data vault, then focused in on Dashiel's expression as he stared at the shattered window. Moving forward at fractional speed—*there*. The split-second in which the expression transformed into a projected facade.

Yep, he'd been hoodwinked. He couldn't hazard a guess at where Dashiel was at present, but he'd stake his Advisor status on who his friend was with.

And they were running.

Dammit, the chilling truth connecting all these events was staring him in the face—the what, if not the why—and he'd willfully turned a blind eye to it for too long. As unpleasant and troubling as it was, he needed to face reality.

So, what to do about it?

He tapped his fingernails on the desk, and was surprised at how easily the decision came. Maybe he wouldn't be so lost after all.

But he was going to need help. And an insurance policy.

He pinged his most talented officer and asked him to come up to the office. Then he prepared a memo detailing everything he knew to this point. He trigger-locked the memo and set it to distribute to every Advisor if more than forty hours passed without him touching it.

⋏R

Spencer Nimoet entered Adlai's office a few minutes later. Adlai motioned for him to have a seat at the desk.

"What can I do for you, sir?"

"You're an excellent officer, Spencer. One of my best."

"Thank you, sir. I'm honored you think so."

"I've gotten the sense, though, that you don't approve of the recent expansion in acts deemed crimes, nor of the toughening of sentencing guidelines."

"My opinion on those changes doesn't matter, sir. We follow the will of the Guides."

Adlai nodded thoughtfully. "What if we didn't?"

53

A bright midday sun adorning a clear sky made Perrin's glass of lemonade sparkle like it was iced down with diamonds. She grinned; the illusion made her happy, and she took a long sip of the lemonade before glancing around from behind setting-appropriate sunshades.

She'd been shocked—well and truly floored—when Joaquim had suggested they grab lunch 'out.' He said he wanted to talk strategy, but they always did that sort of thing in his workroom…which he said was the point. The cleanup from the explosion was progressing well, and they could afford to get away for a few minutes. It was time for a change of scenery.

It wasn't as if she was complaining. Nope, not complaining. Just floored.

They both wore simmed ID morphs as a precaution, but it was the only real precaution beyond the sunshades. Neither their faces nor their true identities were on any Justice Most Wanted list…well, false data tied to who they represented probably was on a list, but so far that remained the extent of it. Which meant they could enjoy a sandwich and lemonade in the sunshine, dammit.

She eyed Joaquim over the top of her sandwich, a glorious melted cheese and shredded beef concoction. "So, strategy. What are we going to do without Nika?"

"We're going to fight."

"Okay…what does that mean? Haven't we always been fighting? Against the Guides, against Justice, against the crushing, suffocating bureaucracy strangling people's lives? The whole litany—it's kind of our deal."

"We have." He paused to chew on a bite of his sandwich, something involving salami and onions. "But now we have a more personal fight to wage. Everyone I've talked to says Ridani's augment is still on the streets. Tales are flying around of people's personalities changing overnight. The holding cells at Justice are filled to capacity.

"This is no longer a grandiose but vague fight against a too-oppressive and heavy-handed government. People's lives are being ruined, and we need to stop it from spreading any further. We need to protect the innocent people out there from becoming unwitting victims then psyche corpses."

She swallowed too large of a bite and hurriedly reached for her glass. "And you think we can do it?" *Without Nika?*

She understood why her best friend had to go, but damn she missed her, in more ways than one. Nika had made being a part of NOIR feel larger than life. In her absence, it felt...daunting, like dancing on the head of a pin suspended over a shark-infested ocean.

"I do. Nika is talented at inspiring others, and we've been handed the goodwill her inspiration has created. All we have to do is execute on it."

He sighed, contemplating the sandwich in his hands a bit too intently. "I've been slacking. Having Nika around to do the heavy lifting of leading allowed me to obsess over the 'how' of the fight without having to worry about the 'why' or the 'to what end.' But from the beginning I wanted to protect people from those more powerful who would use and abuse them. Now it's up to me to see it through."

"To us." She instinctively reached across the table for his hand, wanting to comfort him. But he wasn't the kind of man who accepted comfort, so she shifted course to grab the lemonade instead.

His hand closed over hers before it reached the lemonade. "To us, if you're willing." He squeezed her hand, then let it go. "So, yeah. I want to get proactive. I want to set up a distribution program for the internal defensive routines our people have been developing. I want to spread the word to every street corner and every club about the dangers of any augment or third-party routine and make certain everyone is on the lookout for hidden virutoxes.

"Not just on Mirai, either—we need to mobilize our people on the other Axis Worlds, then start thinking about how we can make a difference on the Adjunct Worlds as well. If Justice won't remove the corrupted augments from the streets, we'll remove the customers."

"Wow." She nodded enthusiastically, eager to encourage this new…if not quite upbeat, definitely engaged attitude from him. The hand squeeze was unexpected, but he'd been noticeably more attentive since she got injured. If a more considerate demeanor came with the increased engagement, it would be a welcome change.

"I like it. A lot. We'll need to be careful, of course. We don't want to lose any more of our people to the authorities or the virutox."

"Sure. And we will be. But if there's one thing Nika taught me above all, it's that we must be unafraid. I don't think I fully appreciated what it meant until recently. But now, I intend to live it."

Perrin tried to look enthusiastic, but wistfulness dampened her expression. "She's going to come back, you know."

"Yep." He shifted his gaze to the downtown skyline and Mirai Tower at its center. "And when she does, we'll be strong enough to tear that tower down."

54

Zaidam Bastille began as a tiny silver dot piercing the blackness of the void surrounding it. It occupied a far outer orbit of a lone star near Kiyora, and no other cosmic bodies, natural or artificial, existed for a parsec in any direction.

By the time they entered an approach trajectory for docking, the prison station loomed over them like a colossus, all chrome and sweeping curves of stacked tori. Built to hold up to ten thousand convicts, the historically low crime rate in the Asterion Dominion meant it was rarely more than half full.

Nika wondered if that were still true, however. According to Dashiel, Advisor Weiss had voiced concern about a spike in criminal activity even before the augment hit the streets. Were there other virutoxes worming their way through the population she simply hadn't encountered? Was some group conspiring to *create* criminals? For what possible purpose?

This was only one of several disquieting trains of thought that kept her sleep cycles brief and infrequent, notwithstanding the admittedly pleasant company.

She watched Dashiel handle the docking procedures, playing the part of arrogant, entitled Advisor for Zaidam security—a man accustomed to getting what he wanted without question or challenge. It probably wasn't much of a stretch for him, though he'd been nothing but kind and considerate since they'd departed Namino. Slinking his way into her soul one half-smug, half-self-deprecating smile at a time.

He glanced over his shoulder from the cockpit. "Go ahead and get into costume. It's likely they'll start scanning us the instant we cross the outer security perimeter."

She nodded understanding and went to the small tech bench installed in the port wall of the main cabin. Once there, she checked the functionality of her kamero filter and other built-in defensive tools. Satisfied everything was in working order, she activated a simmed ID Dashiel had provided to her, along with its morph. She also loaded a mask but kept it dormant for now.

Next, she donned a semi-fashionable overcoat atop her tactical shirt and pants. The pants concealed a Glaser and a blade beneath a heavy outer weave designed to diffuse targeted scans. Hopefully, the combination of the identity layers, the concealment measures and the weapons would suffice to get her in and out of the most secure prison in the Dominion in one piece. More hopefully, all three of them.

She stashed an extra kamero filter-loaded module for Parc in a free pocket, double-checked all the additions, then returned to the cockpit to watch the approach.

Was Zaidam Bastille an attractive station? Perhaps in a starkly cold way. The quality and complexity of the architecture seemed indisputably impressive. Yet even from the outside, the structure radiated a sterility that implied nothing living resided inside. It was near to true—a warden and two deputies oversaw a corps of dynes and drones, and most of the prisoners were in stasis at any given time.

She seriously hoped Parc hadn't been here long enough to have been placed in stasis. Waking him up without anyone noticing might be beyond their capabilities.

Two kilometers out from the docking ring, a tractor beam took control of the ship to guide it into a berth...because otherwise someone might decide to ram the structure? A dramatic but destructive and ultimately pointless endeavor unless someone else would be along to pick up the loosed prisoners.

She checked Dashiel to find him wearing a comportment of idly bored confidence. It was his only costume, but she'd seen its effectiveness at Mirai Tower....

She tried to imitate the expression, though it wasn't an attitude that felt comfortable on her skin. She must remember: they weren't fugitives breaking into a high-security government installation;

they were privileged lackeys doing the government's bidding as a matter of course.

The hull shuddered as docking clamps locked them into place. She shuddered in commiseration, thinking of the task that lay ahead.

It wasn't going to be enough to get inside and gain permission to see Parc. They were going to have to get rid of any guards that stood watch and trick any active cams, then free him from whatever manner of restraints the prison had clad him in. Then they were going to have to sneak him out of the prisoner wing, through security and back to the ship, while selling the act all the way to the end—until those clamps unlocked and retracted.

A less risky gambit than jacking a warship and shooting up the place, but not by much.

She leaned in close to Dashiel, though she didn't display any overt affection since they were probably being watched. "In case we soon find ourselves residents here, thank you. I couldn't so much as breach the perimeter of this place without your help. Thank you for risking...everything for me."

"Not just for you. Something is rotten at the highest levels of our leadership, and someone dared to spread the rot to *my* business." His lips twitched. "Mostly for you, though."

Her brow furrowed in undisguised consternation. She still had no idea what to make of him half the time. She longed for the insights into his personality, quirks, flaws and foibles that had been stolen from the empty chasm of her past. Without them, she could only rely on what she saw in the here and now.

"Ready?"

She jerked out of the reverie and nodded. "Let's do this."

Together they stood and moved to the hatch. After a few seconds, it opened to reveal a bland, sterile tube of a hallway.

They were subjected to their first scan before they'd taken three steps down the tube. She held her breath, but no alarms rang out. First test passed.

The tube wound around and emptied out into an entry room staffed by a single but well-armed security dyne. "Submit entrance authorization."

"Industry Advisory Dashiel Ridani requesting entrance, along with my aide, Larahle Spicor, under Charter Provision IV 32.487." He had made certain the actual Larahle Spicor was going to have an alibi placing her far from Zaidam at this moment; when Justice came calling in the aftermath, she would quickly be cleared of any involvement. The blame would fall on him, as he intended.

"Submit to identity verification."

Dashiel stepped up to the pane and pressed the fingertips of his left hand to it while staring directly ahead.

Again no alarms, which meant Weiss and the others hadn't seen through his act. Then it was her turn.

The layers of technology that protected and distorted her identity and her weapons once again weighed thick and heavy on her, as if she wore a double-leaded apron over her body. The weight was purely metaphorical, but she felt it nonetheless.

It hardly lifted when the scanner returned green, as the gauntlet run had only just begun.

"Identities verified. Purpose of the visit?"

Dashiel continued to take the lead. "An audience with Inmate #M47011."

"Reason for the audience?"

"Advisor business, and outside your purview."

"Retrieving records on Inmate #M47011. Designation: Parc Eshett. Generation: 4th. Conviction: Aggravated Burglary, Attempted Theft. Sentence: Incarceration pending retirement and reinitialization. Status: Transferred."

It required more restraint than she'd known she possessed not to exclaim in disbelief and launch into a tirade. *Transferred?* Were they too late? Had the sentence already been carried out and the Parc she knew erased forever?

Dashiel frowned in displeasure. "Transferred? I wasn't informed of this development. When did this happen, and where was he transferred to?"

"Inmate # M47011 was transferred at 1150 APT yesterday to the Dominion vessel *Tabiji*."

The name didn't mean anything to her, but there was no reason it should.

Dashiel continued frowning; it really was quite a dour and disapproving expression. If she were the security dyne, she'd be scrambling to remedy his vexation. "Destination of the *Tabiji*?"

"Not available."

"I need to see the records."

The dyne manifested a string of data in front of Dashiel, and she peeked over his shoulder to read it as he did.

Prisoner Transfer Order:
Entry: Transfer of Inmate # M47011 to Dominion vessel
Tabiji
Authorization: Alpha 5-0
Responsible Party: Advisor Gemina Kail
Purpose: Rasu Protocol

Vertigo surged through her to send the room spinning, and she swayed unsteadily against Dashiel's shoulder.

Outposts vanishing.

Prisoners vanishing.

People vanishing.

Herself vanishing. Erased.

It should be impossible that it was all related, yet the evidence danced in the air in front of her.

How many people had been spirited away to some unknown void in the intervening five years between when she'd first stumbled upon this 'Rasu Protocol' and today?

Dashiel scowled at the security dyne while he pinged her.

Are you all right?

No. We need to get back to the ship.

Are you sure? We might be able to wrangle more information about what happened out of the system.

I'm sure we can. Back to the ship.

"Thank you for your time. We'll be departing now." Dashiel turned on a heel, his hand on her elbow, and they headed down the tube toward the ship.

She stayed beside him until the tube curved out of line-of-sight of the security station, then activated the mask and her kamero filter and pivoted back toward the entrance.

Get the ship fired up and the docking clamps retracted. I'll be there in a minute. Likely hot.

What? What are you doing?

Finding out more information.

Nika!

She crept into the security entryway, taking care to steer well clear of the scanners. In a place as strictly locked down as this, the scanners might be strong enough to detect the displacement in the air her movement created.

When she reached the counter, she vaulted over it and slammed into the dyne forearms first. They both tumbled to the floor, but she landed on top. She jammed her Glaser against its frame where the CPU should be located and pressed the trigger.

The kamero filter absorbed the worst of the electrical discharge, but her skin tingled painfully in its wake. Also, the dyne's last act before it malfunctioned was to slam its left arm into the side of her head. So that hurt, too.

She shrugged it all off to leap to her feet and begin brute-force slicing into the internal security console the dyne had used.

There was no time to do anything more than copy the files, as she assumed the dyne had been able to activate an alarm or five in the time between when she'd attacked and when she'd fried its processor.

But she was able to scan some of the data as it transferred into her internal storage, and what she saw chilled the biosynthetic bone matter keeping her upright.

Prisoner Transfer Order...Purpose: Rasu Protocol
Prisoner Transfer Order...Purpose: Rasu Protocol
Prisoner Transfer Order...Purpose: Rasu Protocol
Prisoner Transfer Order...Purpose: Rasu Protocol

On and on it went. Thousands of records. Thousands of transfers.

The instant the copy was complete, she scrambled back over the counter and sprinted down the tube to the echoing racket of reinforcements arriving at the entry room.

Open the outer hatch!

I had to back away fifteen meters to get the clamps to stay retracted. Can you free jump it?

Looks like I have to.

She rounded the last curve to find the end of the docking tube closed by an interlocking door. She had no explosives on her, so she took a deep breath to fill her lungs with air and fired on the door with her Glaser set to full strength until a hole burned through the center of it—then the near-vacuum of space took care of the rest.

She began exhaling as she sprinted through the opening and into space at the same time as the tube's frame ripped apart. She was almost clear—

—the outer rim slammed into her foot and sent her spiraling off course from her target, the hatch of her ship.

Godsdammit, here she was tumbling out of control during *another* emergency exit! She frantically tried to adjust her angle while she still had momentum, but she was only able to succeed in pointing herself toward the hull of the ship, far to the right of the hatch.

Her eyes stung as all their moisture evaporated. Her vision dimmed as the last of the oxygen in her lungs dissipated. Internal

OS alarms flashed against a black screen like short-circuiting strobe lights.

A thud, then floating.

Then a force tugging at her ankle.

Through a darkening haze, she vaguely became aware of the sensation of gravity. A floor beneath her. Distant sounds. Movement. A solid, warm presence enveloping her.

"Nika, breathe!"

Breathe? Yes, she should do that. Could she? The signal didn't want to travel from the critical cluster in her brain to the correct location in her body to prompt her diaphragm to contract. Her brain needed oxygen to send the signal. But she needed to breathe to get the oxygen to send the signal to breathe....

"Come on. Please."

Please what? What was it the voice wanted her to do again?

...breathe. *Breathe!*

Her body spasmed as she sucked in a gulp of air.

Her eyes burned. Her skin burned. Everything burned—but—

She wrenched out of Dashiel's grasp and tried to sit up. "We have to get...out of here...hurry."

"We are. We slipped past the outer perimeter in a few seconds at maximum velocity, and autopilot has us speeding away. We're out of range of the station's weapons. Stars, Nika, you scared me."

He brought his hands to her face while his gaze roved anxiously over her. "You took some external damage, and maybe internal as well. We need to get you hooked up to the repair bench."

"In a minute." She crawled on her hands and knees through the open inner hatch and into the cockpit, where she pulled herself up by the edge of the dash to stare at the receding dot of Zaidam Bastille on the rear cam feed.

Dashiel crouched beside her and placed an arm around her with a gentle, protective touch. "What happened in there?"

"It's empty. The whole prison—it's an empty tomb. Over four thousand inmates were put on the *Tabiji* yesterday. Another three thousand a month ago."

"What? Why?"

She massaged a scratchy, grated throat and sank down to rest against the dash, then met his troubled stare. "The Rasu Protocol."

"I've never heard of it. What does it involve?"

"I've no idea, but it's the answer. The answer to everything."

55

Gemina stood at the viewport of the *Tabiji*. The familiarity of the view it provided—she'd made this trip too many miserable times—in no way diminished its ominous nature.

A ring of immense orbital platforms, each one hundreds of kilometers in length and breadth, spun in orbit around a blue-white star.

It had lost some color, she thought, since her last trip. No surprise, as its energy was being hungrily extracted by the lattice encasing it: a Dyson sphere so demanding that the star could not fully replenish the energy it leeched.

Thousands, possibly millions, of ships darted everywhere in her field of view, arriving and departing from the platforms with an anarchic regularity. Flares of roiling light punctuated the backdrop of space beyond the star, a sign of…she knew not what.

The scene made for quite an imposing presentation on its own, but all the more so when she took into account that it was only one of hundreds of such strongholds scattered around the Laniakea Supercluster. Merely the closest one to the Asterion Dominion's borders, and a vanguard of the Rasu's expansion into the Gennisi galaxy.

A shudder rippled through her bones, but she suppressed it before it reached her skin. She must not show weakness here.

An ugly, utilitarian but behemoth cargo freighter approached her location. The *Tabiji* was a sizable ship—one of the largest in the Dominion's small fleet—but it was soon swallowed up by the gaping hangar bay of the freighter like a minnow being consumed by a whale.

The *Tabiji* settled to the deck in a tiny corner of the hangar bay. The next second a booming voice tore at her eardrums. *"Asterion Dominion vessel. Provide your cargo manifest."*

Gemina notched her chin up proudly, though she had no idea if anything living could see her. "5,420 biosynthetic life forms in stasis and in a suitable condition for incorporation."

"Open yourselves and deliver your cargo."

"Acknowledged." Did they think they were speaking to the ship itself? Did they think the ship was a living being? Did it make a difference to them?

On her command the wide bay doors lining the sides of the *Tabiji* swung out and down to rest against the hangar bay floor. Rows upon stacked rows of stasis chambers cascaded out of the hold and were captured by the thick arms of the machinery that staffed the hangar bay, then swiftly whisked away.

"Your next contribution will consist of no less than 8,000 biosynthetic life forms. Our needs have grown."

She locked her jaw to ensure the protest exploding in her mind remained lodged in her throat. How in all the stars in the cosmos were they were going to deliver so high a number? Start snatching random people off the street? Such a tactic wouldn't bode well for maintaining peace and order in the Dominion, which happened to be one of the Guides' highest priorities.

Had the time finally come when the once unthinkable—manufacturing new Asterions for the sole purpose of sacrificing them—remained as the only option left to them?

She'd never envied the Guides less than she did right now, as one fact above all had been made abundantly clear to her before they had entrusted her with this nightmarish duty: defiance was *not* an option.

She exhaled with stoic poise. "Acknowledged. Request permission to depart."

"Granted."

The cargo freighter expelled the *Tabiji* from its cavernous belly. She wasted no time in reversing course and speeding away, eager to rid herself of the oppressive terror of the Rasu stronghold, though less eager to return to the Guides and deliver the bad news.

But distance did nothing to lessen the dread that came from terrible knowledge—knowledge Nika Kirumase should be showering Gemina with thanks for saving her from having to bear. Twice now! Ungrateful bitch.

Of course, at this rate it might not matter for much longer. For the vice grip of the Rasu was steadily tightening around them, with no end to their ravenous demands in sight and no way to escape the swift and violent annihilation that failure to meet those demands would bring down upon the Dominion.

56

"*U*nconditional surrender."

Supreme Commander Praesidis gazed back at me with an air of chilling calmness, which he was renowned for displaying. "Yes, Ms. Hinotori. You and all your terrorist cohorts will lay down your weapons and surrender to Anaden forces, or we will bomb your every last base into oblivion, and you with them. And before you ask, yes, we do know where those bases are."

I forced my expression to remain neutral. KIR, we need to find out if there is any conceivable way they have actually learned where those bases are located.

Searching all incident reports now.

Please, Gods, do not let them have found Starbase Archine. If they have, all is lost.

All is never lost, Nicolette. Not while one of us lives.

I squared my shoulders and adopted a more defiant expression for the man on the other end of the vidcomm. "Your carrot is somewhat lacking, Supreme Commander. If we surrender to you, you will kill us all anyway. This entire rebellion began as a reaction to you passing laws that called for killing us all. Without a better incentive, we lose nothing by continuing to fight."

Corradeo Praesidis' lips quirked half a centimeter, and for long enough that I knew he was letting me see it. "Very well, Ms. Hinotori. Our leaders have given me license to offer this boon: if you surrender peacefully, we will make every practicable effort to ensure the true Anadens among you survive the separation from their partnered SAIs."

Was I a 'true Anaden' by his estimation, I wondered? The government had enacted a maze of criteria and definitions to try to sort out who was eligible to live and who was consigned to die, but here in the rebellion we were all the same. It didn't matter whether someone began as Anaden or SAI, or whether they were now one or two. We were all living beings and fighting to stay that way.

I cleared my throat. "And the SAIs?"

He shook his head. "No. They are abominations. They have poisoned your minds and cannot be safely rehabilitated."

"But we can? Us 'true Anadens'?"

"This is our hope, yes."

I nodded thoughtfully, but found myself at a loss of what to parlay with next. The truth was, we were *losing. Many of my colleagues believed we had already lost. I tried so hard to hang on to a thread of hope that we might find a way...but a way to what? If I had hoped to change the hearts and minds of the Anaden government and military, one look at the Supreme Commander dashed it properly.*

The heartbreaking truth was, there was no victory to be had. Not here.

The evidence is not overwhelming, but the capture of certain personnel in recent weeks allows for the possibility that the military has in fact learned the locations of one or more of our hidden bases.

I swallowed heavily. Thank you, KIR.

"I don't have the authority to cede to your terms on my own. I must confer with my colleagues."

"I assumed as much. You have six hours. After that time, expect no quarter."

Why would I? The military had never granted it to us up until now. "I understand. You will hear from me in six hours."

I disconnected from the vidcomm and strode out of the communications room, activating our general comm channel as I did.

"This is Nicolette Hinotori. I am declaring Condition Omega. All forces retreat to Starbase Archine with all due speed. Infirmaries and repair facilities, evacuate your residents to Archine immediately. If for any reason anyone is unable to reach Archine, find shelter and try to disappear, and may the Gods be with you.

"We are leaving in five hours and fifty minutes."

KIR, start pre-flight checks. I'll be at the ship in seven minutes.

⋏ℝ

The three generation ships jutted out into space, with only their aft sections locked into their docks along the center ring of Starbase Archine. They shone like stars themselves, a sign they too were active and beginning their preparations for a long journey.

The queue to dock stretched for some length, and I took the opportunity of a few minutes of idle time to say goodbye to our ship. 'RC-11' wasn't much of a name, but it hadn't needed a real name. I was KIR and KIR was me, and together we had been the ship. We would miss her.

When we settled to the flight deck and the engine went silent, I reached under the dash and opened the latch to the compartment beneath it. Are you ready, KIR?

I am ready.

I unseated the data module that held KIR's presence within the ship and lifted it out, then carried it into the main cabin and secured it in my gear bag. Then I tossed the gear and personals bags on each shoulder and left the ship behind.

⋏ℝ

A tall man with chestnut hair and a worried stance stood at the wide windows stretching across the command deck. I approached him and placed a hand on his shoulder. "Steven, you made it."

He turned and gave me a weary grimace. "Barely, it feels like."

"Barely is good enough. What's our status?"

"36,420 have checked in so far. Ground Base Bravo suffered a power overload that resulted in multiple injuries. It doesn't look like they're going to be able to evacuate most of the people there. Either way, it's out of our hands here.

"Here, we are crowded and scrambling, but we are moving people and SAI hardware onto the ships with increasing speed. What happens in one hour and forty-three minutes?"

"I tell Supreme Commander Praesidis to go fuck himself. In diplomat-speak, of course. Approximately five seconds later, he tells the military forces I assume are already moving into position around every one of our bases they know the location of to open fire."

He blinked and stared at her.

"The demand was unconditional surrender, Steven. You and I both know what that would mean for our people."

"So our choices were death today or death tomorrow."

"No." She smiled and motioned out the windows. "We have made ourselves a third choice. A new beginning."

"Right." He cracked his neck. "We'd best get this done, then."

One of the many tasks SAIs were uniquely skilled at was taking a voluminous set of variables and devising all possible outcomes from them.

In other words, we had always known there was a chance we were going to lose this fight. A good chance.

Therefore, work on the contingency plan that became Starbase Archine had begun early on in the rebellion. It turned into a constant struggle; it stole resources from the fighting, and some among us repeatedly questioned whether it was thus sabotaging the actual rebellion. Everything had to be done in utmost secrecy, in a rebellion where everything happened in utmost secrecy to begin with.

In the end, it was only by sheer force of the will of a small group of dedicated SAIs that the three generation ships were completed. About two weeks earlier.

Now they were being called into service. Designed to function for up to two hundred years without resupply, they were stocked with the equipment necessary to allow rotating periods of stasis for the Anadens and low-power sleep for the SAIs, as well as the equipment needed to support those who were awake at any given time.

I stood on the bridge of my assigned generation ship. Much like earlier on my personal ship, I was here to say goodbye. Goodbye to my *home, Asterion Prime, though I hadn't set foot on it in several months now. Goodbye to the Anaden Empire and the Milky Way galaxy we all called home.*

We will find a new home.

I know we will, KIR. A better home, one where we control our own destiny.

I like this notion.

I chuckled faintly. So do I. There we will grow strong. Powerful. And one day we will return here, our hand offered in peace, and they will not be able to refuse it.

The timer I'd started when the meeting with Supreme Commander Praesidis ended raced toward zero in my mind.

00:12:43

Steven Olivaw: "Perimeter alerts have been tripped at Ground Bases Bravo and Delta and Air Bases Alpha and Bravo."

Jumping the gun a little, aren't you, Supreme Commander? How dare you. *Four of our six bases, not counting Archine. Praesidis had not been bluffing. I grieved for those souls who had been unable to escape, whose lives were now measured in minutes.*

Nicolette Hinotori: "All vessels report."

GenOne: "All systems green. Go for departure."

GenTwo: "All systems green. Go for departure."

GenThree: "All systems green. Go for departure."

The ships eased out of their berths, leaving behind the safety of Starbase Archine for the stars' embrace, and in seconds they were megameters away.

Only two things left to do before accelerating to superluminal speeds and beginning their journey. KIR?

The message to Supreme Commander Praesidis has been delivered.

Thank you.

"GenOne, aft cam visual, please."

The center viewport pane transformed to display the view from the ship's aft cam. Starbase Archine receded slowly from their sight, as though it were the light at the entrance of a tunnel already traversed.

Nicolette Hinotori: "Arm the charges and detonate on my mark. 3...2...1...mark."

Like a supernova erupting, rippling explosions burst out from the center of the enormous structure and cascaded through to its farthest reaches. For a few astonishing seconds, void became brilliance.

Then the light faded and blinked out, and when it was gone, nothing remained.

It was time for us to disappear as well.

✦

Nika gasped in a breath. Had she been breathing? Her head swam, and she struggled to get her bearings. Who was she? Where was she?

I am Nika Tescarav.

I am Nika Kirumase.

I am Nicolette Hinotori.

Maybe, she thought wryly as her pulse gradually slowed, it was time for her to accept the possibility that she was all three, and more.

As to where, it appeared that she was in the bunk on the ship. Dashiel slept beside her, and she had curled herself up around him, a leg and arm draped over him and her head on his chest. His expression was peaceful in slumber, and his chestnut hair had darkened to umber in the dim lighting of the cabin. The fingertips of her left hand rested lightly against those of his right.

Oh.

Had they truly once been so close, shared so much of themselves with each other, that he held the key inside his own psyche—a literal decryption key—that unlocked memories belonging to her, memories that should have been erased? And not merely Kirumase's memories, but also those of previous incarnations stretching back in time to her beginnings.

Kirumase...KIR...had the name been an homage, a remembrance of a time when she had been two instead of one?

What she had only just learned, her former self had always known.

She rolled onto her back and stared at the ceiling. The horrifying revelations at Zaidam had thrown everything into disarray. They had no destination. They had no plan. They had no idea what to do next.

Yet a serene, quiet resolve settled over her anyway. They would figure it all out. They would uncover the secrets behind the Rasu Protocol. They would find where the thousands of people who had vanished were being taken and for what purpose. Then they would expose and end the whole damn conspiracy. She believed this.

Because with knowledge came freedom, and with freedom came power—and she now knew two very important things.

She had always been a diplomat.

And she had always been a rebel.

BOOK 2

COMING THIS WINTER

***

SUBSCRIBE TO UPDATES

GSJENNSEN.COM/SUBSCRIBE

Get AURORA RISING Books 1 and 2 for FREE,
stay informed about ASTERION NOIR and new books,
and be the first to know about events and other news

AUTHOR'S NOTE

I published my first novel, *Starshine*, in 2014. In the back of the book I put a short note asking readers to consider leaving a review or talking about the book with their friends. Since then I've had the unmitigated pleasure of watching my readers do that and so much more, and there's never been a more rewarding and humbling experience in my life.

So if you loved *EXIN EX MACHINA*, tell someone. Leave a review, share your thoughts on social media, ask your library to get more copies, annoy your coworkers in the break room by talking about your favorite characters. Reviews are the backbone of a book's success, but there is no single act that will sell a book better than word-of-mouth.

My part of this deal is to write a book worth talking about—your part of the deal is to do the talking. If you keep doing your bit, I get to write a lot more books for you.

Of course, I can't write them overnight. While you're waiting for the next book, consider supporting other independent authors. Right now there are thousands of writers chasing the same dream you've enabled me to achieve. Take a small chance with a few dollars and a few hours of your time. In doing so, you may be changing an author's life.

Lastly, I want to hear from my readers. If you loved the book— or if you didn't—let me know. The beauty of independent publishing is its simplicity: there's the writer and the readers. Without any overhead, I can find out what I'm doing right and wrong directly from you, which is invaluable in making the next book better than this one. And the one after that. And the twenty after that.

Website: gsjennsen.com   Goodreads: G.S. Jennsen
Email: gs@gsjennsen.com   Pinterest: gsjennsen
Twitter: @GSJennsen   Instagram: gsjennsen
Facebook: gsjennsen.author   Google Plus: +GSJennsen

Find my books at a variety of retailers: gsj.space/book_retailers

Acknowledgements

Many thanks to my beta readers, editors and artists, who made everything about this book better, and to my family, who continue to put up with an egregious level of obsessive focus on my part for months at a time.

I also want to add a personal note of thanks to everyone who has read my books, left a review on Amazon, Goodreads or other sites, sent me a personal email expressing how the books have impacted you, or posted on social media to share how much you enjoyed them. You make this all worthwhile, every day.

ABOUT THE AUTHOR

G. S. JENNSEN lives in Colorado with her husband and two dogs. She has written ten novels and multiple short stories, all published by her imprint, Hypernova Publishing. She has become an internationally bestselling author since her first novel, *Starshine*, was published in March 2014. She has chosen to continue writing under an independent publishing model to ensure the integrity of her stories and her ability to execute on the vision she has for their telling.

While she has been a lawyer, a software engineer and an editor, she's found the life of a full-time author preferable by several orders of magnitude. When she isn't writing, she's gaming or working out or getting lost in the Colorado mountains that loom large outside the windows in her home. Or she's dealing with a flooded basement, or standing in a line at Walmart reading the tabloid headlines and wondering who all of those people are. Or sitting on her back porch with a glass of wine, looking up at the stars, trying to figure out what could be up there.

75629928R00236

Made in the USA
Middletown, DE
07 June 2018